STICK AND BALL

Kiki Astor

Table of Contents

CHAPTER 1

CHAPTER 2

CHAPTER 3

CHAPTER 4

CHAPTER 5

CHAPTER 6

CHAPTER 7

CHAPTER 8

CHAPTER 9

CHAPTER 10

CHAPTER 11

CHAPTER 12

CHAPTER 13

CHAPTER 14

CHAPTER 15

CHAPTER 16

CHAPTER 17

CHAPTER 18

CHAPTER 19

CHAPTER 20

CHAPTER 21

CHAPTER 22

CHAPTER 23

CHAPTER 24

CHAPTER 25

CHAPTER 26

CHAPTER 27

CHAPTER 28

CHAPTER 29

CHAPTER 30

CHAPTER 31

CHAPTER 32

CHAPTER 33

CHAPTER 34

CHAPTER 35

CHAPTER 36

CHAPTER 37

Chapter 1

All was peaceful in the stables. That was because he wasn't home yet. The whole atmosphere on the farm would change when he arrived. Whenever Robert came home, especially if he was in one of his moods, which was all the time these days, the very air around them would become electrically charged. Ashley would feel it. The horses would feel it. Even the birds would suspend their chirping. Ashley picked up the pace as she went about completing her chores. Ever since Sissy had left, there had been too much work for just one person, but still, Ashley made sure to get it all done, even if if meant pushing herself to the limit. The horses neighed gently at her. She paused and patted her favorite one on the nose. Mystic. A beautiful bay colored mare with a long, dark mane that she liked to braid. In the too-short spring and summer season, she loved to stick flowers in it and make Mystic look like a truly magical creature.

Ashley checked her watch again. A nervous habit. Just a few more hours left, and she still had to muck a few stalls and get Midnight exercised and cleaned up. The others had been out all day and could wait til tomorrow, but Midnight was full of energy. The exercise part, at least, was fun. When she was on horseback, galloping in the field, she could fantasize that she could just keep on going, until she got out of here. Forever. But she knew she wouldn't leave. There was Momma and Sissy, and even if they were an hour and a half away, and at least an hour and a half from each other, she couldn't leave them.

Before heading to Midnight's stall to bring him out and get him tacked up, she took one last look up and down the stables' aisle. Hopefully this time she had done a good enough job, at least according to whichever standards were convenient for Robert today.

As she tacked up Midnight, clucking to him to keep him calm, Ashley ventured a look out of the big sliding barn door. As she'd thought. There were gathering clouds, steel-gray and engorged, scuttling across the low sky. A storm was coming. Midnight always got nervous right before a big storm, and now, so did she. She used to love storms, but storms meant rain, and they needed to get a new roof onto the barn before winter. Any big weather event meant possible long-term damage to the underlayment. Robert had been putting the work off, saying he was too busy with his project in town, in the abandoned general store by the post office. Once Ashley was done in the stables, she would go back to the house and make sure it was impeccably clean.

Ashley galloped Midnight across the field, making sure to keep the reins short in case he got spooked by a peal of thunder. She spoke to him soothingly under her breath. It was tempting to give the horse his head, to let him run out of control, as he wanted to. She could handle it. Riding was as natural for her as walking, in fact maybe even more so, as her sister used to tease. It was true that she was prone to clumsiness. Momma had always pointed that out, too. But not on horseback. She loosened Midnight's reins just a bit, and he broke into a gallop, tossing his head. Ashley laughed and took hold of his mane, just in case. She momentarily felt like herself. Strong. Competent.

But then, as soon as the horse slowed and they returned to the stables, the elated feeling evaporated. She couldn't believe she'd become this kind of person. A woman afraid of her own shadow. A woman whose whole life centered on keeping everything perfect to keep the peace with a man she barely recognized anymore. When she'd first met Robert, she had thought he was prince Charming. He'd come in from out of town with his shiny red truck, his bright smile, and tales of the huge property his family owned in Idaho. He'd been hard working, and had wanted to give her everything in those early days. But then, he'd started to change, and she'd realized that there was no family property in Idaho. In fact, Robert didn't seem to have a family. He'd decided to start terrorizing hers instead. And he'd only been getting worse, just like his drinking had. If he came home today and she hadn't done everything perfectly, it would be devastating for her. Emotionally. Physically.

The warm smell of the straw in the horses' boxes reassured her for a moment and made her feel more at home. But those warm and fuzzy memories of good times with Papa and Sissy on the farm they grew up on could only take her so far. Ashley took one last look at the barn. Noted the dust motes floating in a ray of strangely colored light. Took another worried glance at the gathering clouds. And headed towards the farmhouse.

When they'd first taken the place, Ashley had thought she could make it into a heaven on earth, despite Momma telling her it was beyond repair. The farmhouse was old, but pretty and well maintained, with gleaming pine floors and ample windows set with wavy glass that was original to the hundred-year-old property. The smell of cedar permeated the closets. There were two working fireplaces to sit in front of in the winter. And the stables had allowed them to build her horse training and boarding business. But now, the whole place felt like a prison.

Each morning, Robert took the red truck, which was the same one he had ridden into town in, now much less shiny. Ever since he had sold off Ashley's beloved little car, the truck had become their only mode of transportation. Ashley hadn't had a cell phone in years, ever since Robert had thrown the old flip phone her Momma had given her against the wall in a fit of undeserved jealousy. For a while, they'd at least still had a landline. And then Robert had ripped the cord out of the wall one day, and that had been that.

For a while, Robert had let her call Momma from his cell phone. Her mother insisted on pretending that everything was rosy, and that anything less than ideal was no doubt due to Ashley's shortcomings, and Robert liked having her on his side.

Ashley remembered her last call with her mother like it was yesterday. Her mother had sounded off, and Ashley had been worried. Momma and Sissy were, after all, the only family she had left.

"Everything all right?" Ashley had asked. "Is it Sissy?"

Her mother and Sissy were barely on speaking terms, but Ashley worried so much about Sissy, felt so guilty about Sissy, that she was always in the forefront of her mind.

"Her. She never bothers to check on me. No, I'm stressed out because I kind of need a little loan this month, honey."

Ashley had squeezed her eyes shut. In what world did her mother think she had any money at all, let alone for a loan to cover rent that should have been paid before her Momma gave in to her QVC shopping addiction?

When Papa was still alive, he used to force Momma to return some of the dolls that crowded the guest room, and Momma would yell and carry on and threaten divorce, but she never really did anything. If her father had still been alive, he probably would have driven over to the farm himself to force Robert to treat his daughter better. Or maybe he would still be running the farm, and Robert would never had hitched his wagon to Ashley. But right now, the only person who could save her was herself, and she didn't feel capable.

Coming in from the stables, Ashley opened the front door of the house and immediately felt uncomfortable. It had felt better outside, despite the storm brewing and the electricity in the air. Inside, the atmosphere was emotionally charged, as if something horrible was about to happen. Ashley looked around. She had done a good job cleaning this morning already. As far as she could tell, everything was perfect, but Robert would find something to complain about. She peeked into the living room. It was bathed in a sickly purplish light, the approaching storm warping what was left of the daylight.

When they had first moved here, Ashley had loved the cozy chintz sofa, a relic from Grandmama, and the moss green color she'd chosen for the walls. In fact, the whole effect reminded her of her grandparents' house. She had buffed the antique furniture she'd collected and inherited over the years to a shine, and she and Robert had spent Sundays here as newlyweds watching football games and giving each other foot massages. But now, they hadn't watched anything together in years.

When they'd first moved, friends had wondered out loud to Ashley how she could live so far out in the country without being bored. In those early days, she'd told them that she was too busy to be bored, and she and Robert had been far too wrapped up in each other. Now, if anyone had asked, which they didn't, because she had lost contact, if she'd felt like being truthful, she would have told them that she spent her time being terrified, listening to make sure Robert's car wasn't coming down the drive. The sound of the pickup truck's tires crunching on the gravel was always enough to make sweat run between her shoulder blades and stiffen her back.

What was she going to make for dinner tonight? She had some frozen corn and some pork chops. She'd noticed that the lettuce in the vegetable drawer was wilted. Not really her fault, since she couldn't even go to the supermarket. They would have to make do. She couldn't even really remember when the last time was that she'd been out and about. All she remembered was that she'd been line in the supermarket and had heard something on the news about some prince who was marrying an American movie star. It sounded romantic, but she didn't know what had happened since then. They were probably living a charmed life with a couple of adorable kids, in a beautiful English country house like the ones she'd seen on TV, long ago. Ashley started working on the food, washing and cutting up the wilted lettuce, putting some water on the boil for the corn. Robert was probably going to complain that the corn had freezer burn. Too bad, that's what they had.

Then she heard it. The wheels crunching up the driveway. The farmhouse was far enough away from everything, sitting on the Montana plains, with no one but the sky to witness their cataclysmic fights. She thought of the movie trailer she'd seen once. *Out here, no one can hear you scream.* She stiffened and forced herself to keep working in the kitchen, as if nothing in the world was wrong. She heard the mud room door slam. Work boots hitting the floor, one at a time. Robert was going to be in the kitchen in a matter of seconds. She pasted a smile onto her face.

"There you are," he said.

She couldn't tell which version of him she would get today, yet.

"Yes," she smiled. "Here I am."

Her voice sounded falsely cheerful to her own ears, but it was the best she could do.

"Did you get the chores done?" he asked.

"Everything you told me to do, yes. The horses are fed, the stalls are clean. I gave them fresh water. I even managed to clean the floor in the dining room where the dog had an accident."

"Where the dog had an accident because you didn't take it out," Robert said.

They both knew this wasn't true. The dog was old and incontinent, and she didn't even know why it was still allowed inside. Maybe just to catch her out, to create more work for her. Come to think of it, she hadn't seen the old dog in a few hours. But she didn't have time to think about that.

"Dinner will be ready soon," she said. "Why don't you freshen up?"

Sometimes, the suggestion would offend him, but today, she watched Robert's retreating form as he headed towards the main bedroom of the farmhouse. He always called it master suite, which he probably thought made it sound fancier, but it set Ashley's teeth on edge.

She hurried up and put the corn kernels in the boiling water and got the pork chops breaded. She heard the shower turn on and breathed a sigh of relief. A few minutes of respite. That's all she needed. That's all she was asking for. His time in the shower was all too brief, though. Soon, she heard the shower turning off. The towel coming off the hook. She froze. Had she remembered to change the towels, or was he going to complain about his towel being damp or dirty? She couldn't remember.

When he came into the kitchen, though, he had his poker face on. She couldn't tell if he was happy or angry. This was happening all too often of late, and it was disconcerting, to say the least.

"Here, have a seat," she said. "I'll pour you a drink. Dinner will be ready soon."

"I'll have a beer," he said.

"Coming right up," she responded, false cheerfully.

She deposited the can on the table, but before she could go back to the stove, he grabbed her wrist.

"This can is dirty. Disgusting. Why did you give this to me like this?"

"I'm so sorry- I didn't notice," she stammered. "I thought I'd cleaned off all the cans when I put them away."

"Are you trying to kill me? Make me sick? You'd like that, wouldn't you?"

"No, never," she cried.

She wondered if he would hit her in the face again. Last time, her mother had seen her, and had asked her if she'd smudged her makeup. Again, she had wondered if her mother was being wilfully ignorant. But it was better that way. She couldn't risk her mother fake-innocently asking Robert why he was being such a meanie to her daughter. Ashley watched her husband. His jaw clenched as he chewed the pork chops. She herself didn't have an appetite, but she forced herself to take a few bites, the food feeling like sawdust in her mouth.

"Did you remember to iron my shirts?" Robert asked.

"Yes, they're in the closet."

Robert worked as a contractor in town. Nothing that necessitated a freshly ironed shirt.

"I polished your shoes too," she said.

"Good."

They had the rest of the meal in silence. Which was better than a fight, Ashley supposed. Finally, Robert got up from the table without so much as a thanks and went off towards the bedroom, presumably to watch the game in bed. She knew he didn't expect her to join him, so she started cleaning up. His voice came from the bedroom.

"Hey, Ashley?"

"Yeah?" she responded quickly, fearfully.

"You put my pillow on the wrong side."

"No, I didn't," she said.

She cringed. Why had she contradicted him?

"Are you trying to say I don't know the difference between your pillow and my pillow?" he asked.

She didn't respond. She was sure that the pillow on his side was his, but she wasn't about to contradict him. Robert barrelled into the kitchen. Ashley recognized the look on his face, and she didn't like it. Last time she'd seen it, she'd found herself on the receiving end of a punch.

"Did you do it on purpose?" he asked. "Did you want me to get a sore neck? Did you want me to be uncomfortable?"

"No," she cried. "I would never do that."

He grabbed her wrists. She made the mistake of fighting back for a moment, and he squeezed harder. Wrenching her arm. Making her scared that he would break it, just snap it in half. She'd seen him get into a bar fight once, when some guy had harassed her at the beginning of their relationship, and she'd thought he was so strong and brave, but now she hated that she hadn't taken heed of very violent impulse she'd noticed in him. She was glad she was now the only one taking care of the horses. He had been cruel to them. He had kicked them and beat them when they hadn't done his bidding.

"I'm so sorry, just switch the pillows. I promise I'll never do it again," she said.

But the pressure on her wrist grew stronger. What was he going to do to her this time? She saw the glint in his eye. It was murderous. He'd never been this bad before- yes, he'd been building up to this, but this was something different. She was running out of time, needed to get out. She felt bad about what would happen to Sissy, and to her mother, but she needed to take care of herself now. She squeezed her eyes shut and prayed for the mood to pass. Outside, she could hear the thunder, imagine the lightning flashing, and she almost laughed at how cliché it all was.

Finally, it was over. Robert gave Ashley's wrist a final shake and she stood there, stock-still, until he went into the bedroom. He would punish her if she didn't sleep in his bed, but she would wait until she heard him snoring. She finished doing the dishes and then sat on the sofa for a long time, thinking, listening to the clock ticking.

She needed to make a decision. She couldn't just sit around waiting for the day that this would all escalate into something like what had happened to Sissy. But how would she get away? He took the truck to work every day. If she dared drive away while he slept, he would have an APB out immediately. He had some buddies in the police, he'd told her, and apparently, they had some kind of twisted bro code. But she was running out of options. Dread in her heart, she tiptoed into the room and silently, slowly slipped under the bedcovers.

Chapter 2

When Ashley woke up in the morning, Robert was already gone. It was such a relief. She slowly got up, rubbing her wrist. It was still sore and bruised. She padded into the kitchen, discreetly making sure that Robert wasn't lurking in some corner of the house. He'd left her a to-do list on the counter. It was as if he challenged her each day with more, and like he was just waiting for her to not be able to do something, just once, so that he'd have another excuse to punish her. She poured herself a cup of black coffee from the machine that she had programmed the night before. At least that was one thing she would never fail him on. Always a nice coffee, right on time, unless the power went off. She looked in the fridge. There were some eggs left, thank goodness, and she would hopefully find some more today. The hens had been laying a little bit less lately, as if the stress from the house was impacting them as well. That was another thing Robert had gotten mad about. He'd thought she was lying- that she'd given the dog some of the eggs, or maybe sold some to the neighbors. He'd started realizing, maybe, that she'd been skimming off a few dollars here and there, back when he still let her go do the groceries. That was probably why he had made her stop.

She thought about the money under the floorboard. Almost $500.00. It had taken her ages to accumulate but was really not enough for anything at all. She had stolen a few bills from her mother's wallet, too, last time they had visited, but there wasn't much. And she'd risked taking a dollar or two from Robert's wallet each week, but the stress of it was nearly killing her.

"I'll go to the mailbox today," she said to the dog, who had decided to show up again, and was watching her, probably hoping for some of the eggs that yes, as a matter of fact, she did give him when she could.

"I'll pick up the mail early. And maybe I can talk to the mailman."

The dog didn't react one way or another. She thought he might be deaf by now. She thought of the mailman. Ashley wasn't sure it was the same one as last time she had seen him, but the one she remembered was kind of sweet. But who knew? She couldn't be sure of who was friends with her husband. Robert had initially won everyone in town over by claiming that Ashley's dad had designated him as his successor at the farm, when in fact Papa had been dead by the time Robert had arrived and was probably spinning in his grave now seeing how things had gone down. Momma had never condescended to living on the family farm, forcing them all to live a few towns over, which according to Robert made people see her a foreigner, and him as a local.

At least she had the horses. She could love them, whisper her secrets to them. She had to be her best self around the horses, so that they wouldn't feel the stress and get upset. Horses were such delicate creatures, so strong but so sensitive. Ashley threw on her work clothes and headed over to the barn, doing all her chores in double time. She enjoyed the feeling of fatigue in her arms that told her that she was working those muscles, that maybe she was getting stronger. She was glad her wrist wasn't hurting her too much. Last time Robert had really roughed her up, she had been out of commission for almost two weeks. She'd felt everything getting weaker and weaker, and she didn't like the feeling of not being able to defend herself and not being able to run away. Not that she'd risked doing either one of those things. But the moment was getting closer and closer. It had to.

She checked her watch, her father's old Timex, the only thing she had to remember him by. Momma had been holding onto or selling everything else. She always acted destitute even though Papa had left a significant family trust, which he intended to be passed down for generations. Her dad had died when she was a teenager. He and her mom had had a decent relationship, mostly his doing, and it was something that she'd really looked up to. She'd always thought she would marry someone like Papa. And then look at what she'd done.

Before she knew it, she had exercised the horses and cleaned everything up, and it was almost 3:00 o'clock. This was around the time that the mail would usually come in this season. Did she dare go to the mailbox? It was a risk. Sometimes Robert came home early, and if he saw her lurking by the mailbox, he would get suspicious. The mailbox was in the middle of open ground. You could see it from maybe a mile away, the long roads weaving like ribbons to the horizon, barely a hill to break it all up.

There were gathering storm clouds again, Ashley noticed. It had been a strange summer, and then the fall had quickly gotten cold, with these stormy afternoons, and then frosts in the morning. She felt chilled to the bone, even though she was sweating from the exertion of her chores. Did she dare go to the mailbox? She could meet the mailman. Ask him if maybe she could borrow his phone to text someone. She had memorized the numbers of only three people. Her mother's. Her sister's. Robert's.

Her sister didn't always pick up the phone. Robert's fault, of course, but hers, as well. When would she stop being so weak?

Finally, Ashley made up her mind. She would go to the mailbox. She dusted herself off and threw on her old wool coat. She raked her fingers through her hair, which she wore long and wavy. Her hair was still her crowning glory, despite the fact that Robert didn't let her buy any of her favorite shampoo anymore. She'd taken to using the Mane n' Tail she used on the horses and felt that it might have worked even better. She was afraid to look in the mirror most days, because more often than not, she was sporting some kind of bruise or some kind of scared look in her eye that made her not even want to look at herself anymore. At least her outfit made her look like all the other farm girls in the area. Jeans, paddock boots. A no nonsense plaid shirt and a wool sweater. She was a little bit on the skinny side, skinnier than she would have liked. But she was just so nervous all the time.

She started trekking down the driveway. The wind picked up as she walked, whistling in her ears, not doing her any favors, by blocking out the possible tell-tale sound of Robert's truck's engine. It was further to the mailbox than it looked, a trick of the eye caused by the long, straight driveway. Every step strengthened her resolve. If the mailman came, and if she could speak to him, she would borrow his phone. But what if he was friends with Robert? It was a gamble she would have to take. It was her only option. A few weeks ago, she had thought that maybe she would flag down some stranger on the road to drive her to town, to the library, where she could log online and look up women's shelters she could escape to. But she had lost her nerve. No, the mailman was a better choice. If he was the one she remembered, he had a friendly, open face. He would understand. And if it turned out he was friends with Robert and let him know, maybe then Robert would finally beat her enough to put her out of her misery. Anything was better than this hell for the rest of her life.

The sky grew darker, and Ashley wondered if she'd missed the arrival of the mail van. She'd been in the stables all afternoon, doing her chores. What if he had come early today? Today, of all days. She scanned the horizon, looking for Robert's red truck or for the mail van, whichever came first. She trembled. Did she dare? There was still time. She could just turn around and go back home as if nothing had happened and try to get a decent meal on the table from the scarce scraps and cans that were remaining. Robert had told her they would go grocery shopping tomorrow. She knew that what that meant was that he'd be keeping an eye on her and using any glance in the wrong direction from her as an excuse to chastise her, or worse.

She finally came within ten paces of the mailbox. Then, on the horizon, she saw something moving. She shuddered. Was it Robert, or was it the mail? She squinted. It was hard to tell at this distance. What would she tell Robert if he found her out here? She didn't have any kind of dust mop or any other cleaning implement that she could use to tell him that she'd thought that there might be spiders in the mailbox this time of year. Her mother had always taught her that black widows or brown recluses could hide in there. That was a thought. She could plant a spider in the mailbox. But where would she even get a spider? She was really getting crazy desperate. She squinted again. If it was Robert, it was already too late for her. He would have seen her already. He hadn't told her to pick up the mail as one of her chores. She could always try to say that she wanted to surprise him by doing an extra chore for him, because that was his love language, as he'd told her several times. Chores done right. So there she was, taking initiative. How could he be mad at that?

She squinted again. Now she was sure of it. It wasn't Robert. It was the mail van. Her heart leapt now. All she could hope for was that Robert's truck didn't appear behind it, following it down the road. She needed at least a few minutes to talk to the mailman. Wayne, she thought his name was. She would pretend everything was normal, tell him that her phone was out of juice and that she just needed to wish her mother a happy birthday or something. She tried to remember. How did those new-fangled phones everyone had now work? How did the messages work? Could she send a message and then delete it so that the mailman didn't get suspicious? Maybe it was safer to make a phone call. Would he let her make a phone call?

She debated. Who would she call? The mother who didn't want to face the truth and would make her think she was acting crazy, or the sister who wouldn't talk to her? Her mother, she decided. That was the best thing to do. The mail van got closer, with thankfully no sighting of Robert on the horizon. The mail truck came to a halt.

"Hey!" said the mailman, looking pleased and surprised to see her.

"Wayne, right?" she asked.

He nodded and beamed, pleased that she remembered his name.

"Nice to see you- Ashley, right?"

Ashley nodded.

"I haven't seen you or your husband in ages," said Wayne.

Ashley wrinkled her brow, perplexed. Robert had told her that he was working on the general store in town, just a few doors down from the post office. But she didn't have time to worry about that.

"Hey Wayne, I really need a favor from you," she said quickly, her voice shaking. "I'm worried about my mom, and my phone died, and I was wondering- is there any way that I can just use your phone to call my mom? Just to check on her, you know?"

She was rambling. She bit her tongue to make herself stop explaining.

"Sure," said Wayne. "But I don't know if you have a reception over here."

He handed over his phone. As she'd feared, it was one of those modern things, with a rectangular screen and no buttons.

"I'm sorry- I know this is weird, but could you show me how to dial?" she asked.

"Just give me her number and I'll input it for you."

She handed the phone back and gave Wayne the number. He tapped at the screen and handed it back to her. She glued her ear to the glass and metal contraption, but there was no dial tone.

"I don't think it's working," she said.

"Yeah, you don't have very good reception at your farm. You don't have a land line? Or a car?"

Ashley shook her head. Wayne gave her a pitying glance.

"You must get real bored out here. Is Robert keeping you all cooped up?"

He smiled; his tone jovial. If only he knew.

"Well, sorry I couldn't help," he said, lightly, as if it was no big deal.

Ashley's heart started beating. She had come this far. She couldn't give up now.

"Listen, you've got my mom's number now. Is there any way that you can send her a message or give her a call for me? Tell her that Ashley says hi and maybe she wants to come visit or something."

Wayne gave her a strange look.

"Doesn't Robert have a phone?"

"Never mind. You're right," said Ashley. "I'm being silly. I'll call her when Robert gets home. I was just kind of impatient to have her have some news of me."

Wayne looked at her strangely.

"You sure you're OK, Ashley? "

"Yeah, I'm fine, thank you so much," she said.

"Well, here's the mail in any case," he said, handing her a stack of envelopes.

"Thanks so much, Wayne," she said, snatching up the stack.

She waved at him as he pulled away. She had put so much hope in this moment, and she'd been thwarted. What would she do now? Once Wayne had driven down the street, she gave one last worried glance at the horizon. Still nothing. She stuffed the envelopes into the mailbox without even looking at them. There was nothing that could save her now. She hurried back to the house.

She was furiously dusting when Robert came in, clutching the envelopes in his hand.

"Hey," he said. "You have a good day?"

Ashley almost laughed at how normal the question sounded, as if he didn't know that she'd had a dreadful day, a lonely day, a day of doing nothing but his bidding. A day of having her great plan fail pathetically.

"Yeah, it was fine. The chickens still aren't laying," she said. "I'm glad we're going to the supermarket tomorrow. There's a lot of stuff we need."

She had taken to looking forward to her supermarket trips. Maybe she could find someone else whose phone she could use while Robert was distracted in the beer section.

"I went just now. Why don't you go to the truck and get the groceries? I'm gonna take a shower,"

"Sure," Ashley said.

A pit formed in her stomach. She'd been hoping that maybe the grocery store would be the expedition that would get her out of there for a minute. That would enable her to seize a precious minute of time, during which she could get someone's attention- or maybe even run. But that was ridiculous. She'd been shopping with him before, and she hadn't done anything like that. And if she ran, where the hell would she go? She was as good as jailed away for the rest of her life at this point. She thought back to that made for TV movie she had watched once with her mom, long ago, the one about an abused woman in some country in the Middle East, who didn't want to leave without her daughter. Ashley had thought to herself how lucky she was to live in America. And funnily enough, here she was in America, and she wasn't any better off, except that thankfully, she didn't have a kid to worry about.

As she turned away, Robert called her back.

"Hey Ash?"

"Yes?"

Her heart started beating triple time. Maybe he had forgotten something at the market and was going to offer that they go.

"You've gotta tell that bitch mother of yours to stop harassing me about her water heater. I'll get to it when I get to it. If she bothers me again, she's gonna regret it."

"OK."

As she turned away, Ashley almost laughed out loud. How the hell was she supposed to tell Momma anything when she didn't even have a phone? And also, her mother never listened to anything she said, not really. Robert could tell her his damn self.

She shuffled over to the truck that sat in the driveway. When Robert had first come into town, it had been all shiny. She had called him her knight in shining armor because of it. Now, the truck was all dented and dusty. It was strange what Wayne had said about not seeing Robert in town, even though his work site was supposedly right there, near the post office.

Did she dare ask Robert where he was actually working? Or maybe his bad mood was because he *wasn't* working. Would it make such a difference in her life if he wasn't? Probably not. There was a single bag of groceries in the bed of the truck. She heaved it out and brought it into the house. Unpacking everything onto the counters, she thought back to when they had first met, when they used to go grocery shopping together on a Thursday or Friday night, and it would be like a date for them. They would linger in the aisles, exchanging kisses and taking their time picking out something nice as a special treat at the end of the week. Nothing extravagant- they had spent all the money they had getting the farm back in order, because Momma hadn't deemed it worthy of using the money from the trust- but something like a pack of Twinkies to share, maybe a cherry pie or a box of doughnuts. Some silly thing that they would both enjoy simply because they were having it together.

There was nothing like that now. Just basic items. Robert's 6-pack of beer. Potatoes. A cheap piece of meat. Some sliced bread. Butter. A pale tomato. A box of canned green beans. A small carton of milk for Robert's coffee. Ashley took hers black. And no eggs because, well, he would blame her for the chickens not laying, and she would have to make those eggs come out of nowhere. Her stomach rumbled. She was hungry. She stared at the food, trying to figure out if there was some way of making something appetizing out of this pitiful assemblage of foodstuffs that looked like the dregs from a normal person's pantry. Taking a deep breath, she put everything away.

Robert came back into the room.

"Is that a scowl? Are you scowling? Do you not like what I bought for us?"

"No, it's great," she said. "I was just thinking I was going to make maybe some mashed potatoes or something. Does that sound good?"

He could complain that she used his milk for the potatoes, but oh well.

"I was thinking more a baked potato," Robert said. "You know I hate mashed potatoes. They're greasy."

"Oh, sorry, yeah, you're right," Ashley said. "Why don't you go relax? Watch some TV. I'll get dinner going."

Robert had had the TV channels restricted to the sheer minimum. It seemed that all the TV played was sports, not that she had had time to investigate further. She used to love watching soap operas when she was growing up. But not anymore. There were a few paperbacks in the house that her mom had gifted her, romance novels that were so laughably far from her current existence that she could barely bring herself to read them. What wouldn't she have given for a library membership? Except, even if Robert had condescended to drive her to a library, they had closed down the one in town, and the one the next town over wasn't winning any awards. They used to have internet at the house, long ago. But no longer. Was it because Robert wanted to cut her off from everyone and everything even further? It was hard to tell. Not that it mattered. Thinking about it too much would make it even worse. Ashley tried to quiet her racing thoughts.

She sliced the mealy tomato. Put the potatoes in the oven and went about tenderizing the scrap of meat Robert had brought back. She was going to have to make some chicken fried steaks out of it.

When they sat down to dinner, Robert glared at her.

"You complain I don't talk to you, but you don't even try to make conversation with me. Wives are supposed to be charming and attentive, and you do nothing but pout. What the hell's wrong with you?"

"Sorry," she said.

She wracked her brain to come up with a plausible reason for pouting other than the truth, which was that she was married to an abusive bastard.

"One of the horses is not well, I'm just a little bit worried."

Robert sat up straight and glared at her. *Shit.* Wrong thing to say.

"What do you mean one of the horses is not well? Which one? If one of those horses goes lame, it's on you. Have you even been taking care of them?"

"Of course I have," said Ashley.

She yearned for the time when they'd had people coming from miles around for riding lessons, or for the dude ranch lifestyle. Back then, her sister was there to help them out. The business had been thriving- between the lessons and the boarding, they were flush. But then, Robert had started scaring away some of the clients, and word had gotten around. Sissy had had her accident. Robert liked to blame the business falling apart on Ashley's laziness, but this was squarely on him. Even if he hadn't made it abundantly clear he didn't want people around, he had started to refuse to put in the minimum investment to keep thing running, even though the horse business was way more lucrative than the odd jobs he did as a so-called contractor. Ashley really missed those days. Just being able to feel there was a purpose to her life and being around other people. Seeing the light in kids' eyes when they got on a horse for the first time. When the business had started drying up, Ashley had thought of getting government funds to start a program for handicapped children to ride as therapy, and it had started going somewhere. But then of course, Robert had put his foot down and said he didn't want any of those "retards" around the farm. That it was a liability.

Ashley brushed away a tear.

Robert scoffed at her.

"Wow. Are you crying, now? What are you crying about? What do you have to cry about? Your life is easy. You have no worries. I bring home the bacon while you sit around the house all day. And now you're crying."

"I'm not crying," she said. "I must have just splashed some water in my face from the sink while I was getting dinner ready."

She tensed up, waiting for a blow, but none came, and little by little she started to relax. As Robert started to make to leave the room, she knew that, as there was no game on, he would get ready for bed. Brush his teeth. And then, with a little luck, she could count on him to be asleep within 20 minutes. As long as she could avoid him for that amount of time, she'd be fine. Of course, about once a week he would insist on her going to bed at the same time as him, and she hated those moments. But she always had to give in, because if she didn't, it meant more punishment.

Ashley got ready to pick up her needlepoint from the kit her mother had gifted her, the one thing she had to occupy herself. What did her mother think this was? Little House on the Prairie? It was laughable. But it was something. She was finishing it as slowly as possible to make it last. Next time, she would see if her mother would give her another romance novel or two. If Robert ever condescended to let them visit. Funnily enough, if she had been able to get the mailman's phone to work, her big plan was to tell her mom to call Robert and tell him something in the house wasn't working, to give them an excuse to come. And now she realized, her mom had been calling, about her water heater, and Robert had no intention of going.

"Ashley, aren't you coming to bed?" came the voice from the bedroom.

Ashley's shoulders went right back up to by her ears. *Dammit.* She made her way towards the room, a bundle of lead weighing down her gut. There was Robert, on the bed, waiting for her under the covers. She could guess that he was naked, save for his socks. He still looked OK, she supposed. But her heart hadn't been in it for a long time. She tried not to sigh too audibly as she took off her work clothes and folded them on the chair in the corner. She got into bed, shivering.

"You cold?" Robert asked.

She closed her eyes and nodded and then tried to think of something else, anything else, as he went through the motions of foreplay. This was nothing that would actually be considered play, it was more a rotes et of actions that served to get Robert excited. It was nothing that would prepare her for the assault that was about to come. At first, Ashley used to try to remember the times back when they used to have fun at this. Back when Robert was kind, and handsome, with washboard abs and a twinkle in his eye, and was gentle and loving with her. Thinking about those moments used to be enough to make her pretend that she was enjoying it, so that there would be no repercussions. But lately, that didn't work. She had to make up scenarios in her head, featuring handsome men as unlike Robert as possible, in environments far removed from the farm. A beach, maybe. A tropical garden. She fantasized about these men caring about her pleasure.

Chapter 3

After, she fell into a deep sleep. When the gray light of morning woke her up, she kept her eyes screwed shut, wondering why she could still feel the weight of him in bed next to her. *Shit.* Sometimes, Robert woke up with a bee in his bonnet, with some fight in him over something that he must have dreamt up during the night. Or maybe he was just going over his day in his head, which wasn't much better. That sometimes pissed him off, too. Ashley really hadn't spoken to him about his work lately. She was half tempted to ask whether the rumor was true that he hadn't been seen in town. But what did it matter to her? It wasn't like she cared whether he was faithful anymore, or whether he was working, as long as she had a roof over her head. Actually, even no roof would be better than this constant oppression that she lived with. What would happen if he told her that they had no more money? Would they have to leave the house her great-grandfather had built with his own two hands? Would she go back to her mother's house? Or Sissy's house, if only Sissy could forgive her? Would Robert actually let her go, or would he try to find some new situation even worse than this one? It was too frightening to consider.

Her leg was numb from the weight of his knee against it, and she risked shifting just a little bit.

"Are you awake?" Robert asked.

Ashley froze again. She thought of feigning sleep for a moment but knew that Robert didn't care if she was asleep or not if he had something to tell her. He had shaken her awake on multiple occasions. Why would this one be any different?

"Just waking up," she said pleasantly. "Everything good? Did you sleep well?"

The sweet words almost got stuck in her throat, but she forced them out. Better to be polite and friendly.

"I was thinking," Robert said. "I saw Wayne driving down the road as I was coming home. And it seemed like he was a little bit later than he usually is. You didn't see him or talk to him, did you?"

Ashley froze and held her breath. She had spoken to the mailman all of two minutes, maximum. No way did that make a measurable difference in his route. And anyway, his route varied sometimes. How could Robert think she'd had anything to do with it. Unless he was watching her. Did he have a camera installed somewhere? She started to tremble and clenched every muscle to keep it under control.

"What do you mean, Wayne? Who is Wayne?"

"Wayne, the mail guy. Did you go out to the mailbox yesterday?"

"Why would I go out to the mailbox?" Ashley asked. "I had all my chores to do, and I know you like to pick up the mail. Why would I go all the way out there?"

"Just checking," Robert said. "If you try to talk to some other guy, you know what will happen, right?"

Ashley nodded. She didn't know exactly what would happen, but she knew that whatever it was, it wouldn't be good.

"I have no interest in talking to anyone," she said, trying to summon an indignant tone.

"Well, good," Robert responded. "Just make one exception, will you? I have a package that's going to be delivered today. You need to sign for it. Don't let the guy show up and not find you."

"What is it?" Ashley asked.

There was something odd and ominous about Robert receiving an important package suddenly.

"It's a gun. I think we need to protect ourselves. I've heard about some crimes in the area."

"You bought a gun?"

She knew they had- or used to have- Daddy's rifle, which Robert used to use for hunting. She didn't even know where it was anymore, hadn't seen it in a while. That was probably a good thing.

"I thought you had the rifle already," she said.

"That piece of shit? Sold it. So I picked this one up at a gun show. The guy said they shipped it to me special, so it has no serial number. Can't be traced."

Ashley shuddered. Why was Robert telling her this? It sounded menacing. He had threatened her brother-in-law before. He'd said horrible things to her mother. Was he going to use this gun on one of them, or on her?

"Anyway, it's none of your concern what it's for. They're going to deliver the gun, and you need to sign for it. I can't be there. But don't talk to him. Don't say anything to him, you hear?"

"What would I say to him?" Ashley asked. "You're acting like I want to have conversations with strangers."

She clamped her mouth shut. She was coming dangerously close to angering Robert again, she knew. She wondered what kind of person was going to come to deliver the gun. Was it some normal delivery man, a UPS driver or something? Or was it going to be a criminal, someone who dealt in stolen guns? Would she be able to use this person's phone? There was no reception at the house, and she didn't know the WiFi password Robert used, so she knew that wouldn't work. Maybe she could hitch a ride into town. Her heart raced.

"I would have been able to call you on the house phone with any updates about what time they're coming, but since you were being unreasonable the other day, I can't do that, can I?" said Robert.

In her mind's eye, Ashley saw Robert yanking the cord out of the wall. She couldn't even remember what had set him off that time.

"Just be on the lookout," he said.

Being on the lookout for this person was a problem. Because she was damned if she didn't finish her chores, but damned if she missed signing for the package that Robert was waiting for. How would she do both? She decided she would leave the stable doors open and step out every few minutes. It was going to waste a lot of time, but what else could she do?

As soon as Robert left the house and she heard his truck rolling down the driveway, Ashley threw on her most comfortable, warm outfit, and her most sturdy boots. She had a crazy thought. Just in case, she packed a purse, containing her wallet, which contained her old, almost expired driver's license, a few old packs of gum, and the bills she had managed to skim from Robert and her mother at various points over the past couple years. She counted out the cash. $479. Pathetic, but at least it was something. How far it would get her? She knew she should focus on getting far away. But then what would she do? She didn't want to waste the money on something like a stay in a motel. She could stay in a women's shelter, maybe. But where could she get a job where she could actually start paying some rent without anyone asking for any references? She hadn't had a real job in years. Not since she'd met Robert. He'd made her quit. At first, she'd been happy to quit. She thought they would have a family, and she knew she could make Papa's farm into a paradise for them. Now, she realized it had all been about control. And she didn't have any skills that she could monetize, other than taking care of horses.

She was really in a terrible situation, wasn't she? She put the purse on the kitchen counter, where she could grab it quickly if she needed to. It was crazy, she thought. The delivery guy was probably some criminal, and she would only end up hiding the purse away again, praying for another opportunity. But just in case, she brushed her hair. Dug out the old cherry flavored lip balm that had at least a little bit of color in it. Robert didn't like for her to wear makeup.

As she took care of the horses, only a cup of black coffee in her stomach to ease the hunger pangs, she made sure to be especially kind to each of the horses. She even patted the old dog, even though he was technically Robert's and didn't seem to care too much about her. What would the horses do if she ever managed to get out? Would Robert treat them properly? Would he find some other stupid girl to take care of them the way she had? If only Sissy hadn't had her accident. If only things hadn't gone to shit.

Chapter 4

She was shoveling hay when she heard wheels crunching on gravel. She stiffened- her usual reaction. And then, she remembered. It wasn't Robert. It was probably the delivery guy- the mysterious guy bringing the gun. She was going to have to make a snap decision. If the man looked even remotely kind or remotely trustable, she was going to ask for a ride to town or to anywhere with a bus terminal. She couldn't go to Momma's or Sissy's, she knew. Robert would find her and take her right back here, if he didn't kill her.

As the truck came into view, she noticed brown color and the letters. UPS. Her heart jumped into her throat. This guy was probably a reputable professional. Hopefully somebody she could trust. She hustled towards the van and the delivery man came out holding a box.

"Hi, are you the lady of the house? I need a signature for this thing," he said.

"I am, yeah. Do you have a pen?" She asked.

"Oh, it's a digital signature," he said.

The man looked kind enough. Slim, tall. Shaggy, sandy farm-boy hair and nice brown eyes. He handed her a clipboard.

"Oh, great. Thanks," she said, scribbling her name on the screen. The man started handing her the box. She could tell by his body language that he was ready to spin on his heel, planning his next delivery. He really did have kind eyes, she decided. She needed to decide- *shit or get off the pot*. The world started spinning around her and she took a deep breath to steady herself. The man was heading back to his truck. It was now or never. She watched him get behind the wheel, about to turn the key in the ignition.

"Hey," she said.

He turned the key, the engine revving to life.

"Hey," she said louder now, panicked, waving her arms and rushing towards the truck. He noticed her and paused, waiting for her to approach the open door.

"Listen, I know this is crazy," Ashley said. "But do you know my husband, Robert?"

The man looked at her, puzzled.

"Sorry. I'm not really from around here. I'm from a few towns over."

Now he started to look a bit concerned, like he had come across a crazy lady and needed to get out of there.

"OK, listen, wait- don't go… this is a weird question, but how many deliveries do you have left today?"

"I'm actually nearing the end of my shift," he said cautiously.

"Is there a bus station in your town or nearby?"

"Yeah. Greyhound… Are you OK, lady?" he asked, narrowing his eyes.

"Listen, I need to get away from my husband. I don't have any money. I have nothing. I'm so sorry, but this is the only chance I've had in a long time. Is there any way you can drop me off?"

The delivery man looked at her.

"Ma'am, your husband's not going to come after me if he finds out I picked you up, is he?"

"He won't know. He's suspicious of the mailman right now," said Ashley. She hoped she wasn't lying. That Robert didn't in fact have some kind of camera on her. But she didn't have a choice.

"Lord," said the delivery man, rolling his eyes. "I hope I don't regret this. OK, get in the truck."

"I'm Ashley, by the way. Can I hide in the back? You know- in case he's driving down the road."

The UPS guy took in her face. He must have sensed that she was truly afraid. He took a deep breath.

"Elijah. Yeah, you hide," he said. "It's going to be a while, I'm going to make a couple more stops, and then we're going to go to my town. Maybe when I get to reception there's someone you can call. Maybe you have a family member or something?"

"Thank you. I just need to go to the bus station."

Momma would have only told her she was being crazy, she realized.

"OK," Elijah said. "You get comfortable back there. Let's get out of here."

Ashley climbed up the steps and headed to the back of the truck as it pulled away. She found a little bench to sit on and tried to keep her balance, boxes shaking all around her, soon feeling nauseous from the movement. Despite the cold outside, it was warm in the truck, and she started to sweat through her coat. After a few stops, she felt the truck pulling over and Elijah's head poked into the back of the truck.

"OK, I have reception. Do you want to try to make a phone call? We're about half an hour away from the depot. From there, we'll take my car to the station, if you still wanna do that."

"Thanks," she said.

She'd changed her mind during her time in the back of the truck. Maybe momma would be supportive, and she owed her an update, in case she worried. She picked up the phone- now she was a bit more familiar with these contraptions- and tried to dial her mother. No response. Where was momma? She was usually at home at this time.

"Do you mind if I try my sister?" Ashley asked.

Elijah motioned for her to go ahead.

She tried her sister, knowing it was more normal for Sissy not to pick up if her husband was working. Her sister was often tired and in bed, immobilized after the accident. Pangs of guilt hit her again, but she didn't have time for that. She thought of leaving a message for her mother, but then she thought to herself, *What if Robert is there? What if Robert went to Momma's house to fix the water heater, and did something to her? What if he's listening to her messages, too?*

Why was she thinking these crazy thoughts? Despite what Wayne the mail carrier had said, Robert was working in on a project in town. Still, she didn't leave a message. She hung up. She looked at the delivery man.

"Sorry- there's no answer. I don't want to take you out of your way, but you're still OK taking me to the greyhound terminal?"

"Sure," he said. "We'll get my vehicle and go."

"Thank you so much," Ashley said, pathetically grateful. She needed to get out of here, just get away somewhere far away.

Chapter 5

The greyhound terminal shone like a beacon, lit from within. But it looked empty, and there were no cars in front of it. *Shit.* Ashley got out of the truck. She had no other choice. Elijah hesitated.

"Do you want me to wait here and make sure that there's a bus coming or something for you?"

Ashley was about to nod when she noticed that there was someone inside. A woman behind the counter.

"No, it's OK. Thank you so much. You've done enough for me already."

"Good luck," said Elijah. "Now get far away from here."

Ashley clenched her purse more tightly and walked into the terminal, towards the woman at the desk. She was short and heavyset, with curly auburn hair and kind eyes that you could tell had seen a lot of things. The woman looked Ashley up and down.

"Hey sweetheart. Which bus are you trying to get? Cause there's not another bus tonight, and I'm closin' in an hour."

Ashley's heart sank.

"Oh wait- actually there is that one bus in a few hours, going over to Ontario Mills."

"Oh yeah, that's the one I was going to take," Ashley lied. She hadn't heard of Ontario Mills and hoped it wouldn't take her back closer to home. "You mean I can't wait inside for it?"

"Honey, that bus is just a few regulars," said the woman. She looked at Ashley with suspicion. "I don't think you're going to Ontario Mills."

"Why not?" Ashley asked, her heart beating.

Did this woman somehow know Robert?

"You'll freeze to death waiting for that bus."

"It's fine," said Ashley. "I'm used to being outside."

Her shivering probably said otherwise. She looked around the bus terminal for a map, as the woman stared at her with growing impatience. Finally, she just asked the woman.

"I'm sorry, do you have a map? Where can I go from Ontario Mills?"

The woman sighed.

"I don't know what you're trying to pull honey, but Ontario Mills is the prison. And you clearly didn't know that so why are you saying you're going there?"

Ashley tried to prevent the flow of tears that was gathering as if behind a dam, but it was no use. She had come this far, and now she was fucked. She would freeze to death in front of a Greyhound station. As tears and snot ran down her face, understanding started to dawn in the woman's eyes.

"Wait a second. You're just trying to get away, aren't you, honey?"

Ashley just nodded, sniffling. The woman stared into her eyes. Ashley tried to look away.

"Listen, girlie, I've been there. You're not going to take that damn bus. You're going to come home with me and we're going to figure this out, OK?"

Ashley just nodded, trying to repress a relieved sob.

"Do you have a husband who's bad to you? Is that what it is?"

Ashley nodded again, trying to smile through the tears. The kindness strangers had shown her today was heartbreaking, compared to how Robert had treated her. But then, she started to panic. Was this the nearest greyhound station to home? Would Robert figure out that she was trying to get out this way? The bus was the cheapest mode of transport. There was no train station, no taxi, no other options. Unless she hitchhiked. Robert might go check at Momma's house and Sissy's house, but as soon as he'd eliminated those options, he would be here.

"What time did you say you get off?" Ashley asked. "I'm just scared that if he figures out that I wanted to take the bus to get away, he'll come by, and I don't want to get you in trouble."

The woman checked her watch.

"You know what, honey? If there was ever an excuse to quit early, I think I just found the best one. Come on, let's go."

The woman got up from behind the counter, grabbed her purse and turned off the lights, escorted Ashley out, and locked the door.

Ashley's head was as if on a pivot, as she looked all around, fearful she'd see Robert's pickup truck. She held her breath at each car that drove by on the county Road., but soon, they were rounding the corner of the building, and getting into the woman's car, a red Toyota sedan. Ashley wished it was a more discreet color, but she reasoned with herself, Robert wouldn't be looking for any specific car, would he? They drove for about fifteen minutes and pulled into an apartment complex. Ashley could have cried from relief as they made their way into the apartment. Framed pictures of chubby children were the only art on the walls.

"My grandkids," the woman said proudly.

Ashley opened her eyes wide. The woman didn't look old enough to be a grandmother.

"I know, I know," the woman laughed. "I was a teenage mom. It's OK. I grew up with my kids and now my grandkids are my life. I get to babysit them a lot. My daughter is kind of a bitch, but it's OK. She'll make it through."

"They're adorable. Thank you so much for doing this for me," said Ashley. "You don't even know me. I don't even know your name. I'm Ashley, by the way."

"I can tell good people when I see them," said the woman. "I'm Kim."

"Thank you so much, Kim. I'm so sorry I saddled you with my troubles, but I just didn't have any other options."

"No need for apology," Kim said. "And I'm not gonna ask you what's going on if you don't want to tell me. But let's make a plan for you, honey. Do you have any family, anyone you can go to?"

Ashley shook her head.

"He'll know to look there first. And even so, he might hurt them. My mom lives about an hour and a half away, but she's not answering the phone and I'm afraid to leave a message because you never know."

Kim shook her head, a hard expression in her eyes.

"That's right, you never know. Never leave a message and don't call from the same number multiple times."

Ashley opened her eyes wide.

"Do you think he would be able to trace it?"

"Listen to me," said Kim. "I was in a situation like you once. And believe me, it was not easy to get away. Honey, never underestimate what they can do, and will do. Do you have anyone else you could go to?"

"I have sister, but she's handicapped," said Ashley. "I've been trying to call her too, but sometimes when her husband's away at work, she can't pick up the phone."

"What time does he get off?" asked Kim. "Do you want to try again from my phone?"

"I guess so," said Ashley.

She didn't know how that would help, but at least she could tell Sissy she had gotten away, ask for advice. Kim handed her the phone. To Ashley's relief, the phone picked up.

"Hello?"

It was Craig, her sister's husband. His voice sounded strained, a little hostile. Ashley was taken aback, but not surprised. He was a good man, but his life was stressful, and he probably thought it was a robo-caller.

"Craig, it's Ashley. Is Sissy there? I mean, I know she's there, but is she able to talk to me?"

"Oh. Sorry, I didn't recognize the number. Everything OK?"

"Yeah. I'm fine. Long story. I just need to talk to Sissy."

"I don't know, Ashley," said Craig. "She's not been doing great, but we can try. She's been down lately."

Ashley cringed. It was all her fault. No surprise if her sister didn't want to talk to her.

"Has mom called?"

"Not recently. OK, I'm heading down the hall," said Craig. "SO where are you calling from? It's not like you to be not at home," he said. "I'm surprised Robert let you out, haha."

His laugh was artificial. He knew damn well Robert would never have let her out.

"Yeah, speaking of that, can you do me a favor after you hang up with me? Can you lose this number?"

Craig was silent for a moment.

"Are you in trouble, Ashley?"

"Probably. But don't worry about me."

"OK, here's Sissy."

"Hello," said a weak voice.

Ashley bit her lip so as not to start crying again at the sound of the familiar voice.

"Ashley, are you OK? What's going on? I can tell you've just done something crazy," said Sissy.

"Kinda crazy. And I can't reach Mom," said Ashley.

"She'll turn up," said her sister. "You know how she is."

"Listen," said Ashley. "I need to go somewhere. Somewhere really, really far away. Any ideas?"

"You left him?" asked Sissy, her voice rising an octave. For a moment, the surprise almost made her sound like the old Sissy. The one from before the accident.

"I'm trying," said Ashley, her resolve weakening each second. This truly was an idiotic idea. She would never get away with it. "I mean, it's fine if you can't think of anything," she said, after a moment. "I feel like I should just go as far as possible, keep running, until I hit the edge of the continent, you know what I mean?"

"What did you say?" asked Sissy.

"You know, I've always dreamed of going to the coast- California. I know it's crazy…" Ashley's voice trailed off.

"Wait. I think I can help you with that." said her sister. "You know I have that college friend, Kari. She lives over in Santa Barbara. Or Montecito. Something like that. Some town that's really fancy. She works with horses there, at a Polo Club."

"Sounds dreamy," said Ashley.

But what she was thinking was, how would she ever fit in somewhere like that?

"I spoke to her last week. She called me totally out of the blue. She was saying she needed help. Maybe you could go over there."

Was it a sign? Ashley didn't dare get her hopes up.

"Could you talk to her? I don't want her friend's little sis to make her feel pressured."

"Yeah, sit tight. Let me try to call her and see what the deal is. Should I call you back on this number?"

"No," said Ashley. "I want you to lose this number. I'll just call you back in an hour. How's that?"

"OK, said her sister. "I'm glad you're getting away."

Ashley hung up, feeling guilty as hell. There was no subtext to what her sister had told her, but she felt terrible that she might actually get away, while it was too late for Sissy. If Sissy hadn't stuck by her side at the farm, she wouldn't be in this state.

Ashley and Kim sat and enjoyed a simple Mac and cheese dinner in front of something Kim called *Reality TV*. Ashley hadn't ever seen anything like it before. Maybe she hadn't been missing anything after all after Robert cut off all those extra channels. Still, it would have been nice to have the choice.

"Listen, I know this question might sound crazy," she said to Kim, "But what's happening in the world?"

Kim laughed.

"What do you mean?"

"I don't watch the news. We don't get the paper. I haven't been talking to anyone except for Momma, and, well, she's in her own world…and Sissy has other things to worry about. I've just been taking care of my horses all day long."

"Well, honey," said Kim. "That's probably a good thing. There's not much good stuff happening in this world. Just lots of wars and trouble and shootings."

Ashley shuddered, thinking of the gun that had been delivered to the house. She could never go back, could she?

"So how did you leave it with your sister?" asked Kim. "Are you going to call her back for something?"

"Yeah," said Ashley.

The less Kim knew, the better. Then again, she was going to need her help.

"She has a friend somewhere that I might be able to go work with. Robert doesn't know anything about her. So it should be safe. She's just going to let me know whether I can go. You're not going to tell anyone that you saw me, right?"

"Of course not, honey. Your secret's safe with me," said Kim. "I just think that, back when I was in your situation, I would have loved it if somebody had helped. So here we are. Just make sure that you don't squander your second chance, OK? You live life for you from now on."

"Thank you so much," said Ashley, tears rolling down her face.

It was time to call Sissy back. She dialed the number again. This time, her sister responded on the first ring.

"I'm so sorry, I realized I never asked you how you are," said Ashley, maybe to delay hearing any disappointing news.

"Feeling like hammered shit," said her sister. "It sucks every day, but at least Craig's here for me. I just need to resign myself to the fact that this is my life… in any case, your situation's much crappier than mine right now, sis."

"Thanks," said Ashley. "That makes me feel better. So did you talk to Kari?"

"I did," said Sissy. "And yeah, she could probably use another person to help her, but there'll be some kind of trial period. Apparently, it's a crazy situation. She couldn't tell me a lot because she said she had something called an NDA."

"What's that?"

"I'm sure she'll explain it. In any case, she can put you up for a little bit in her apartment at the stables. I'm going to give you the address. You just go straight over to Santa Barbara. Don't stop anywhere. And if Robert calls us, I never talked to you."

Ashley breathed a sigh of relief.

Her sister gave her the address and phone number, and Ashley carefully wrote them down, and committed them to memory. This tiny scrap of paper held her whole future. What if she lost it? She burned the information into her retinas. 1384 Avocado Lane, Carpinteria, CA. That town sure didn't sound that fancy- more like there were carpenters there. And Avocado Lane? She wondered if avocados grew there all year. Whoopee. Weren't avocados those fruits that seemed more like a vegetable that were rock hard one minute, rotten the next?

She looked up at her benefactor, Kim.

"OK," Ashley said. "I have to figure out how to get to California. I don't want to give you any other details, but which bus do I need to take?"

"Well, honey, you're going to need to switch buses a few times before you get to any bus that's going to anywhere as exciting as California. I envy you. First thing in the morning, we're going to get you on a bus that gets you the furthest away from here, to the biggest town, and then we can have you switch. Sound good?"

Ashley nodded.

"Wait. Do you have any money?"

"I have $479."

"I'm guessing that's all you have to your name. OK, I'll try to apply some discounts so that you don't end up with nothing. We're going to figure it out."

Kim grabbed a calculator and a booklet out of the junk drawer in her cramped kitchen and started plugging away at it.

"OK honey, here it goes. You're going to take the bus tomorrow morning at 6:45 AM to Buffalo Town. From there, there's a bus to Billings. And from Billings, you head to Idaho, to Washington state, and into California, all the way down to Anaheim. From there you take the Surfliner train to Santa Barbara."

Ashley nodded. The leg from there to Billings would be the most dangerous. Billings was a given for anyone going anywhere. After that, Robert had no way of knowing which direction she might go in.

"OK, let's get you to bed- well, to the sofa. You've got a long day ahead of you tomorrow, and an early start," said Kim.

Chapter 6

Ashley woke up the next morning early, without the alarm, as usual. Out of habit, she stayed rigid, immobile, and then she realized that she was on a sofa. Robert wasn't in bed next to her. It was the first time in years that she'd not had to worry that her husband was going to punch her out the minute she opened her eyes. She carefully folded her blanket and got herself ready, being careful to leave the bathroom the way she'd found it. She'd brushed her teeth with a finger and hoped she might find a toothbrush somewhere soon. She sat quietly in the living room, waiting for Kim to get ready.

"You're up. Perfect," said Kim. "I've made you a little goodie bag for your trips. I'm sure you don't have things like a toothbrush, and dry shampoo. And I got you some beef jerky, a few pretzels. Couple of the grandkids' juice boxes. I know it's nothing fancy, but this should tide you over. I wish I had a phone for you. My son left me his old flip phone, but I can't find a charger for it."

Ashley was mortified.

"No, you've done so much for me already. I just hope you don't get into trouble for helping me."

Kim said, "Listen, I would have done it no matter what. We women have to help each other out. Let's go."

This was it. They left the apartment. As they drove down the street, Ashley kept hallucinating that she saw Robert's red pickup truck pulling up or driving past. She yanked the hood of her sweatshirt right up to her eyes and tucked her neck into her jacket. Not only because she was cold, but also because maybe she could hide herself that much more. There was no way Robert would know she was going to that particular Greyhound station at that specific time, she reasoned with herself. But was there really no way he could know? She was glad she hadn't managed to reach her mother. It would be just like her to tattle on her, for her own good. Still, she was worried. where was her mother? Why hadn't she heard from her? And what if Robert had terrorized Craig and Sissy after she'd talked to them last, and they had said something? There were so many possible disasters that could happen, and Ashley had no control over any of them.

They pulled up to the bus station, which was dark, with no one in the parking lot. Kim pulled up behind the station, so it looked like nobody was there, but once she got in, it would be lit up like a Christmas tree. No hiding there.

"What time did you say the bus comes?"

"15 minutes from now, darling, don't worry. Once you're past Billings, there's no way he's going to find you."

Ashley clenched her jaw. Kim didn't know how determined Robert could be. Even before he'd started acting truly scary, when Ashley was still able to go places on her own, he'd had ways of tracking her down. And now? He had managed to take away everything. Her means of communication, her connection to the outside world... Hell, a bomb could have gone off, and she would have had no idea.

Ashley sat tight while Kim turned on the lights in the bus terminal and started to fire up her computer. A few trucks started pulling up to the station, dropping off passengers, mostly. Scrawny younger people wearing jeans and dark jackets, their hands stuffed in their pockets. A few guys who looked like ex-cons, if you asked Ashley. But who was she to judge? She was running away, too. She just kept to her corner and tried not to draw any attention to herself.

Finally, Kim came up to Ashley and handed her a few tickets.

"Most people have these on their phone," she said. "But I know you don't have one of those. So I printed them out. Don't lose them."

"OK, thank you so much," said Ashley. "Wait- I didn't pay you."

"It's OK," said Kim, "you're going to need every dollar you have. I managed to find a bunch of promotions, and this is on me. Part of those sweet, sweet Greyhound employee benefits. Don't worry, girl. You know what? One day, maybe you'll pay me back, once you get to California. I always wanted to live there."

Ashley bit her lip to keep from tearing up. She got into the middle of the line of people slowly shuffling onto the bus, which had just pulled up like a dark behemoth with glowing eyes. She flipped through the papers that Kim had handed her and selected the correct ticket, the one taking her to Buffalo City. She didn't have any entertainment to keep her going during the trip, but that didn't matter. Maybe she would be able to sleep again on the bus. It felt like she hadn't slept in years. She started to put her head against the window and close her eyes, when the seat shifted next to her. Her eyes flew open, but it turned out her seatmate was a matronly kind looking woman with a huge handbag.

"Hey, honey," said the woman. "What are you doing in Buffalo City? I'm going to go see my son. He's got these grandbabies. I can't wait to see them."

"Oh, nice," said Ashley politely. "Just going for a job interview," she lied.

"Well, looks like you didn't make too much of an effort to get dressed for your interview," said the woman.

Not so kind after all.

"Yeah, it's for a farm position," said Ashley.

She channeled her grandmama, Papa's mother, who had supposedly come from a fancy background, and kept her tone just polite enough, but just dismissive enough to stop any further questions.

The bus pulled away, and Ashley breathed a sigh of relief. It was one more step separating her from her husband. One more layer of challenge for him to find her. But she couldn't make any mistakes, no missteps that would lead him back to her. No feeling guilty and calling him in the middle of the night and apologizing. She knew that he had a way of making her feel like she was the crazy one. *Gaslighting,* they called it. Sometimes, it felt like Momma did that to her, too. She needed to be strong. Because if not, she would end up like her sister. Robert still denied that he'd had anything to do with her sister's accident, that it was all her fault. But she could still remember that terrible day, the horse rearing up, Robert smirking, whip in hand. Her sister falling. The cracking sound that changed Sissy's life forever. If Ashley hadn't been so weak, she would have been on that horse instead of Sissy.

Ashley squeezed her eyes shut. Then before she knew it, she felt a lurch, and the bus was stopping.

"Where are we?" she asked the woman.

"Buffalo City, silly. You better wake up. You're going to look all bleary eyed for your interview."

"Yeah, thank you," Ashley said.

She made her way into the station, feeling the woman's eyes still on her back. She went up to the counter.

"How long until the bus to Billings?" she asked.

"About 45 minutes, ma'am."

"OK, thanks."

Ashley went and used the restroom, which was filthy. She brushed her teeth, splashed water into her face, tried to straighten up her hair a little bit, and braided it, thinking that maybe having it away from her face would make her look a little different. Should she dye her hair in the bathroom like they did in those movies where a woman on the run would suddenly chop off her hair in a gas station bathroom and be rendered unrecognizable? No, it was ridiculous, she thought. Her hair was dishwater blonde anyway. Nothing remarkable, but wavy and nicely thick. She smoothed down her eyebrows with a wet finger. Robert had never allowed her to pluck them or groom them in any way. Not since the wedding. She washed under her arms. Tucked in her shirt a little bit better. And gathered her purse and the goodie bag that Kim had packed for her to her chest. She made her way back into the main room of the station and watched everyone there.

Chapter 7

She hadn't been to Billings since she was a kid, when her mom used to take her shopping there before school started. It had always made her feel like they were going to the big city, even though there wasn't really that much there. Still, she would have loved to go there once in a while to go on a date, back when she and Robert were starting out. Her mother had told her she didn't work hard enough to make things romantic with Robert. Would it have changed anything if she had? Probably not. The first time Robert had hit her it was after a date. Their last date, if she remembered correctly. And how could she forget?

Ashley remembered it so clearly. Sitting in the restaurant. Her hair done the way he said he liked. This was before he'd stopped giving her any money to buy makeup. She'd been wearing the pendant he'd given her that Christmas. The one with a heart with red garnets in it. She'd never really liked garnets. They made her think of dried blood, but they were his favorite stone, apparently. So that's what she got.

And so they sat there, in the uncomfortably tight dress that she had found at that boutique in town that was barely a boutique, more like a consignment store. He was looking into her eyes in that way, the way that said, *just you wait til we get home. You're gonna get some.* Back then, getting some was a good thing.

She still remembered some of those night long sessions. Tangled in the sheets. Their bodies sweaty. His hands on her in that way she liked. He liked to tease her. With his fingers. With his tongue. With his kisses. He had been a good kisser, at first. He was always particular about the exact reaction he wanted from her. He still liked to tease a reaction from her, but now, it was in a different way. Now, she wondered if he was getting those other urges met elsewhere. There was no way that their weekly session was filling his needs. Earlier in their relationship, he'd been so demanding. At the beginning, he would come home every day, horny as hell, and she would be waiting for him. He would drag her into the laundry room, or she would meet him at the door of the truck, and he would take her right there, standing up, her hands against the red metal. Once, he'd found her in the stables, and they'd had an actual roll in the hay. And she'd loved that. It had made her feel wanted and needed. But then, sex with Robert had become just a perfunctory, necessary thing, like personal hygiene.

And then, on that last date, he'd been looking at her in a weird way. And then she'd said something- she couldn't even remember what it was. Maybe something about something her mother had said. Her mother had a way of infuriating Robert through her very presence. Her sister too, come to think of it. She must have said something about her family, or maybe have compared Robert to her father. He didn't measure up to her father in any way, she knew now. Papa had been an upstanding man. She wished that he would have lived until she was an adult, because maybe then she would have had a better role model for the kind of man she would marry.

In an instant, Robert's eyes had changed. Ashley had seen a sort of silent fury in them. At first, she'd thought he was kidding. She'd seen he had a potential for violence. But not against her, she'd thought. At first. Once, he'd gotten into fights with a guy in a bar. As she'd been trying to hold Robert back, he'd lashed out at her. She hadn't really thought he meant it. Otherwise, he'd been an angel, mostly. But now, his attention was fixed on her, and she was so uncomfortable, she almost wanted to push it to see where it would go.

It had always been there in the background- this unhealthy urge of hers to hit rock bottom. The same urge that had seen her almost failing high school and getting told off for insubordination more than once.

"Are you serious?" she'd asked. "You're pissed off because I compared you to my dad?"

"You're being disrespectful," he said. "You're trying to say something negative about me. You shouldn't compare any other man to your husband."

"He's not just any other man. He's my father," she said.

Robert's hands gripped the table. Ashley could see how white his knuckles were.

"Seriously, you're actually freaking out over my dad. I can't believe this."

"You're gonna see what happens if you don't stop talking, Missy. Stop talking."

"Or what?" she'd asked, secure in the knowledge that they were in a public space and that anyway, nothing had ever happened like this. He loved her. He had always been taking care of her ever since they first met, except for that one time, or maybe two. But Momma had pointed out that she'd been in the wrong. Anyway, this time, they were in a public place. This fight would simmer down.

"Have you drunk too much? I'll drive home," she said.

"No, I'll drive. You don't touch my truck," he said.

She couldn't believe her ears.

"Are you like, playing a role or something?" she asked.

Had he hit his head at work? They paid the bill, finishing the rest of the meal and getting up in silence. For the first time, she started to wonder what would happen once they got out of the public space. Was he really going to carry out his threats? They started walking down the street towards the truck, and Robert's hand gripped her arm more and more forcefully.

"Ow- you're hurting me," she said.

"You hurt me," he said.

"I didn't mean it. I swear I didn't mean it. I never would have said anything if I'd thought you'd get so upset. I just… I wasn't saying…"

"Yes, you were. You don't even know what you said. And then you hurt me."

His fingers were like a metal vise on her arm. The pain was excruciating.

"You're really, really hurting me," she cried.

"Shut up."

He opened the door on the passenger side of the truck. That was one of the things she'd always liked about him, that he was a gentleman. But this time, he shoved her in and almost slammed the door on her leg before she got a chance to get completely inside the vehicle. By this point, she was terrified.

Maybe he would calm down while he drove. He always liked to drive, so she sat there in silence. But Robert was ranting at her the whole time. Lecturing. At some point, she stopped listening.

Because what was the use? Had she really said something so offensive?

Her sister had told her once that Robert had a tendency to gaslight her. And she had told Sissy she was ridiculous, and her sister had looked at her like she was brainwashed or something. Now, she had started to realize, was she?

"Robert, if I hurt you, I'm so sorry. I didn't mean to, and I'll never do it again," she said.

Without warning, Robert's hand came out and smacked her right in the mouth. She could feel the blood on her lips. She tested her teeth with her tongue, hoping none of them were loose. They just hurt. She hoped it would be OK. She was going to have a bruise. She couldn't believe she was just taking stock of the injuries, rather than examining how absolutely wrong the fact that her own husband had hit her was.

That had just been the first time of many. Once the dam had been breached, the floodgates had been opened. Anything became an excuse for him to shake her, to slap her, punch her, kick her. At this point she could no longer count how many times it had happened. Some days, she could barely get up. Things hurt so much- her ribs, for example. She was sure one or two had been cracked. She took a deep breath. Trying to shake the memories away.

Chapter 8

Her eyes flew open.

"Sorry, what?"

A young man stood before her. He was skinny. He looked like what Robert called a meth addict, but with kind eyes.

"Miss, I think I heard you're going to Billings. Your bus is coming soon, and I saw that maybe you were asleep. I just wanted to help you out."

Ashley's heart melted.

"Thank you. Thank you so much for letting me know," she said.

"Ma'am, do you have any money for me? Anything you could give me?"

She had nothing, or almost nothing,

"Yeah, sure," she said.

She took out some bills. She'd been smart enough to peel off just a few to put in her pocket for necessities, so that no one at the bus station would notice that she had all of $497.00 to her name. Maybe some people were even worse off than she was.

"Here you go."

She gave the young man a five-dollar bill.

"You don't have anything more?" the boy asked, his kind eyes suddenly turning violent and angry.

Something in Ashley snapped.

"No, I don't have anything else. Get out of my face."

The kid held up his hands, as if she'd physically assaulted her.

"Woah, woah, lady…calm down."

The bus pulled up. Ashley double checked that the panel on the front said Billings. The idea of Santa Barbara shimmered in her imagination like a golden mirage. The things she had surmised about Santa Barbara all came from a soap opera that had been on TV when she was a kid. She never much liked the show- it didn't seem like it had any relation to her life, but she remembered the opening credits with sailboats and beautiful green hillsides dotted with white mansions. Was that what it was going to be like? Would she make any friends? Would she make a life? Would she able to live there? She'd never been alone. She thought of avocados and pomegranates, lemons, and olives, all those foods that she'd read about in their history lessons about the missions, she remembered now. Maybe she'd find herself one of those white houses on the hillside, too. Maybe she'd be stuffing herself full of free fruit. It really sounded like heaven.

Her sister had literally offered her a ticket to paradise. She was beyond grateful, especially since she was sure that Sissy still blamed her for her accident. If Ashley hadn't been so passive, if she hadn't let Robert get away with his behavior, if she'd stood up to him, and done her own work, Sissy never would have had the accident. And if Sissy blamed her, she couldn't blame her for it. In fact, in the past year, Ashley had purposely taken a step back from Sissy, to spare her sister her presence, but Sissy had probably resented that, too.

Ashley sat in her bus seat, thankful that there was no one sitting next to her, and rested her head against the plexiglass of the window. Somewhere in the back of the bus, a girl started singing a soft gospel song. It was beautiful. Ashley thought she had heard the girl talking to her neighbor.

"I'm going to LA. I'm gonna become a superstar," she said.

She did have the voice of an angel, but Ashley knew what could happen to dreams. They could so easily go to shit. She hoped that the girl wouldn't grow disillusioned after landing in LA and finding a job as a cleaner instead of as a singer. Or that she wouldn't end up in some strip club like so many of the girls she'd gone to high school with. It was funny that Ashley had been the one who was always in trouble in school, had almost flunked out, and some of the girls who did the best, those who focused on people pleasing, they'd ended up on some ranch with a bunch of prostitutes and a meth habit.

Ashley looked out the window at the rays of winter light. It was only October, but it was already feeling like February. Well, it wouldn't be that way in Santa Barbara. Santa Barbara was summer year-round, she decided. She looked down at her denim clad legs and her feet, in their old paddock boots. Registered her coat, her flannel shirt, and her sweatshirt around her. She would have to figure out what she would wear in Santa Barbara once she got there. She wondered if Sissy's friend Kari might direct her to the Salvation Army or something.

An older lady piped up.

"I'm going to California too- to Pasadena. I'm gonna have an artist studio there. My daughter lives there and I'm gonna babysit her kids sometimes, and I'm gonna paint and I'm gonna eat oranges."

Ashley smiled. The oranges. She had thought about oranges, too. Why was it that everyone thought of citrus when they thought of the West Coast? Citrus and golden sunlight. Was that all she needed to heal? Just a little sweetness, and a little light? She checked the schedule that Kim had printed out for her. She had a few hours hours on this bus, enough time to take a nap, especially now that she felt like maybe there was enough distance between her and Robert.

She started closing her eyes, when a shrill shriek started coming from all over the bus. *What the hell?* She thought. It sounded like an alarm or something horrible. She heard whispers. *Amber Alert,* said someone. *What's that?* asked a child on a bus. *Oh, it's for a missing person or somebody who's been kidnapped. Funny, it says it's an adult woman. An adult woman was kidnapped?* The child asked.

Ashley shuddered. Was the alert for her?

They stopped briefly in a tiny armpit of a town. Ashley didn't even know where, but it didn't matter, because she was heading towards her new life, and she wouldn't look back. She knew implicitly that she needed to heal from this whole situation. Not just physically. If she let what Robert had done to her color her behavior, she was letting him win, wasn't she? For a moment, Ashley worried about her mother. Why hadn't she heard from her? When she got to Santa Barbara, she would find a phone that she could use to try to call her mom. Maybe she would ask Craig to go check on her. Even though Craig and Sissy lived a good hour and a half away, and Sissy seemed to have soured on Momma. Her mom was probably just busy, off shopping or getting her nails done with whatever was left of Grandmama's and Papa's trust, however much she could get out of it. Ashley had normally been able to reach her when she needed to. She noticed the kindness that Kim had done her in planning the bus schedule. There weren't any long waits that would force Ashley to find a place to sleep in some dangerous spot.

What was the first thing she would eat when she got to Santa Barbara? She wondered. She bit into the beef jerky Kim had kindly included in her care package. Maybe she would give an avocado the benefit of the doubt. Maybe she'd have an orange, too. She heard they were making wine in California. She thought that maybe one of these days, she'd have a glass of wine. Robert didn't really let her drink. Or rather, he just didn't stock anything other than his cheap beer in the fridge. And she wasn't about to condescend to having some of that.

When they got to Billings, she hustled off the bus and went to the bathroom in the bus station. It was filthy as expected. Again, she wondered if she should change her appearance. No, once she was away from Billings, the chances of Robert finding her organically were slim. She considered herself in the mirror. Maybe the California sunlight would give her some free highlights. Maybe she would get a little tan. Maybe she would look a little bit more alive. She'd really felt like she'd been dead these past years. How many years had it been now with Robert? 6 maybe? She was 32 years old and had nothing to show for it. She had thought she would have a baby by now. Or in a job and a career. And a loving husband. And, well, she'd just failed at everything, hadn't she? At least she'd had the horses, and now those were lost too, because she would never go back, no matter what happened. She worried about the horses. *Shit.* She'd been so selfish. She hadn't given it a serious enough thought. What would happen to them, with her gone?

Somebody hammered at the door, and she jumped.

"Hey lady, you're taking forever. There are other people on this earth, you know?"

Yes, she knew there were other people on this earth, probably people with sadder stories than hers.

"I'm getting out. I'm getting out," she said.

She stepped out of the bathroom. An irate woman with platinum hair and black roots gave her a pointed look and marched into the bathroom. Ashley stood in a corner of the bus station, trying to be as unremarkable as possible, in case another one of those Amber Alerts came through, this one with a picture of her. Could Robert really circulate a picture of her? It wasn't like she was wanted or anything. It wasn't like she was a child. Wasn't she allowed to go somewhere without the authorities looking for her? She must have made a mistake. That Amber Alert wasn't for her. It must have been some poor child who'd been kidnapped.

Chapter 9

The bus pulled up.

"Is this the bus to Butte?" she asked the kindly looking older woman who had said she was going to Pasadena.

"Yes, honey, is that your final destination?"

"No, it's funny, like you, I'm trying to get to California," Ashley began.

She froze. She shouldn't tell anyone anything. But then again, California was such a vast state. That was the beauty of it. You could get lost in California. The old woman looked at her kindly and said, "Oh, and don't follow me the whole way- before I go to California, I'll be stopping Arizona to visit my friend and hopefully see some cacti. Do you like cacti, darling?"

"Honestly, I've never really seen a cactus in real life, I think," Ashley laughed. "Maybe in the supermarket? Does a Christmas cactus count?"

"Well, I'm sure you'll have a wonderful time in California, my dear. Do you have a suitor there? Is that why you're going?"

The old woman obviously wanted to make conversation.

"No, but maybe I'll meet someone," said Ashley. "I'm newly single," she said.

The old woman's eyes drifted to Ashley's finger, where she still wore her wedding band. She'd wanted a simple, classic gold one. But Robert had insisted on getting her a tacky diamond encrusted thing that might have been fake, as far as she knew.

Ashley cut the conversation short, and when she got onto the bus, she wrenched the ring off her finger. She looked at the indent it left in the pale flesh and rubbed at it. How long would it take for this mark to go away? This ring had been there for six years of her life. For six years, it had been suffocating her finger without her even realizing it. It was funny how she had never taken it off before, despite her marriage vows feeling so stale, and like such a lie. It felt good to have it off. *Should I just throw it out the window?* she thought. Good thing the windows were plexiglass and didn't open that well. What if the ring was worth something? What if she could sell it and have a little bit more money? She inspected it to see if there was a stamp that would tell her what it was made of.

Then she saw it. The stamp said 925. Well, at least it was sterling silver. But it was worth, at best, twenty dollars. She considered letting the ring roll along the floor of the bus to be found by some teenager who would appreciate it and maybe wear it on a chain around her neck. No, she would keep it, just to remind herself of what not to do. She tucked the ring into her purse and silently counted in her head. How much did motels cost in Santa Barbara? Where would she find a place to stay? How long would Kari be OK with her staying with her? Would she have a long-term job at the stables? What if it didn't work out? Would she find another job? How would she get a car? She hadn't driven in years, but she used to be a good driver, so that would be fine. Or maybe she'd get a bicycle- a beach cruiser, she thought they called them. Where had she heard that?

She looked out the window. The landscape didn't offer anything interesting to the eye, and this was just the beginning of a long journey. She thought of the romance novels her mom had given her that she'd stashed under the mattress, for her entertainment, if she ever wasn't doing chores. She wished she had brought one with her to read on the bus. Then, as if by magic, she happened to look over at the old lady across the aisle, who winked at her.

"Hey, darling," said the old lady, "I've just finished reading this delightfully shocking book. You wouldn't want to read it by any chance, would you?"

"Thank you so much. You must be my fairy godmother," said Ashley.

"A fairy godmother bearing smut," the old lady winked.

Ashley took the book and examined the cover. It featured a shirtless man with a tie around his neck. She guessed he was supposed to be some kind of sexy CEO. A bit ridiculous, and so far removed from her existence to date that it was laughable. She didn't know much more than cowboys and other blue-collar professions. *50 Shades of Grey*, she read on the cover. She would have preferred 50 shades of gold- the gold of the California sunsets. No matter. This was what she had to read. Maybe it would teach her something about people who were not the same types of people as what she'd grown up with. She opened the book to start reading and promptly fell asleep. She woke up as the bus was coming to a halt.

"Butte," chirped the old lady. "I saw you got a good sleep. Well, it starts off slow. Don't worry, it gets good. Keep reading. And it was so lovely meeting you, darling. I wish all the best."

"Thank you," Ashley said, her hand on her heart, trying to keep from crying.

In the past few days, she'd experienced more kindness from strangers than she had experienced in her marriage for the past six years. But of course, she should not be naive. There were other people out there too, greedy people. People who didn't want the best for her.

"Well, enjoy the cacti," said Ashley.

She got off the bus. Made a quick restroom break. She checked the schedule again. The bus to Missoula was coming in about 10 minutes, just enough time to maybe buy something from the vending machine as a treat to herself. She looked at the selection of Hostess cupcakes and other junk food that she remembered from her childhood. Why not, for old times' sake? After making her selection, she noticed that the vending machine only took credit cards and exact change. She went to the counter to make change for one of her $10 bills. The boy at the counter gave her a look.

"You don't have a credit card?" he asked, incredulous. "You can even pay with your phone, you know."

Ashley shook her head.

"Sorry, bad credit," she said.

The boy smiled and nodded.

"Well, join the club," he said. "You know, you can get a debit card that you pre-load, though."

"Yeah, I've gotta get on that," said Ashley.

How would she even do that, she worried. She didn't have any credit at all. How would she build it? She didn't know how these things worked. If only she had attended the Home Economics class in high school and hadn't failed that personal finance exam in community college, maybe she would know about opening an account and things like that. Sissy had taken care of the business details for their operation. She had been the hands-on one. So why had she let Sissy get on a dangerous horse?

"So what are you gonna get from the vending machine?" the boy asked.

"I can't remember- what's less disgusting, Twinkies or Ding Dongs?"

"I'd go for that Twinkie every time," he said. "More disgusting, in a way, but kind of delicious too."

That's what she was looking for. Disgusting, but delicious. It seemed a bit illicit. A little naughty. The boy pointed to the book poking out of her purse.

"I heard that's pretty raunchy. Are you enjoying it?" he winked.

"I haven't really started it yet. It was given to me by an old lady."

She smiled, enjoying the boy's shocked expression.

She had felt like she was ancient at 32, but now she felt like maybe she had a whole other life spread out in front of her. Maybe even when she was a real old lady, she'd have a whole other life too.

After Missoula, she would be out of Montana. And then from there, they would go up through Idaho, into Washington State and Oregon, and then down into California at last. Kim had told her the Surfliner train would take her to downtown Santa Barbara, and then she'd have to figure out how to get to Kari at the stables. She had Kari's number written down on that piece of paper. Hopefully, Kari might pick her up. Or maybe she would walk. She didn't know what the lay of the land was. She realized that people had maps on their phones these days. She would really have to get a phone, but for now, that was the least of her worries. She wondered if she could really get a job working with horses. That, after all, what she was good at. Would it be like the horse world in Montana, where everyone knew each other? Would it make it easier for Robert to find her? She didn't really have a choice, anyway. Where else would she work? The supermarket? She should at least do something she enjoyed after all this time suffering. She deserved it.

Ashley got on the bus. The young girl who'd been singing gospel was on this one, too. Ashley smiled at her. She was glad that someone else had dreams just as crazy as hers. A dream of a happy life. As she leaned back in the bus seat, Ashley smiled to herself, heart filling with hope. Maybe she would meet someone in Santa Barbara and have a beautiful romance. Something to cure her from Robert. She wondered what kind of guys were in Santa Barbara. Were they ridiculously sophisticated, like the guy on the cover of her *50 Shades of Grey* book? She took out the book again and started reading. After a few pages, she was already frustrated. It was the worst writing ever. The female character annoyed the hell out of her. But then again, beggars couldn't be choosers, and if she, Ashley, was in a book, the readers would probably think she was a dumbass. As she read more about the young heroine of the book, she thought, *why doesn't she see the red lights, the red flags? That man's an abuser.* Ashley just couldn't find Christian Grey's behavior sexy. A man who hurt people for fun, and who was excited by that. Now, she wished the old woman hadn't given her the book, because she was both horrified by it, but desperate for entertainment. Soon, thankfully, she started nodding off again. There was something about the hum of the engine, the rush of the landscape going by, and yes, this was the first time she could sleep without fear. She tightened her hood around her and went to sleep.

Chapter 10

After two whole days of travel including stops in rainy Pacific Northwest towns, finishing her infuriating book, and a brief stop in sunny Anaheim, where she wished she could have visited Disneyland, Ashley stepped off the Surfliner train, blinking her eyes.

The sunlight was pure gold, just as she'd dreamed. She'd never had Champagne before, but the balmy air felt like what she imagined Champagne bubbles would feel like, popping on her skin. She looked around. Even though this was a parking lot, she could see pink mountains glistening in the afternoon sun, glimpse some bright pink flowers that looked very exotic against a blinding white wall, and guess at the ocean nearby. That ocean of blue had been a soothing visual balm to Ashley as she made her way from LA to Santa Barbara, She had already seen multiple dolphins and surfers, and now she felt an irrepressible urge to dip her toes into the Pacific. She had never so much as seen it, and now she was on the actual edge of the continent. She wanted to mark this important moment with some sort of ceremonial action. She cast glances around the parking lot. She had called Kari and had left a message mentioning what time her train was coming in. She had Kari's address in case Kari was not there. Last time she'd seen Kari had been almost a decade ago. Why would Kari even come to pick up her college friend's kid sister, especially one who had ruined her friend's life?

Ashley noticed a taxi stand at the far end of the lot. Well, at least she had that option, though it would eat away at her meager cash stores. The other passengers finished getting off the train and scattered, some of them jumping into waiting cars, others plugging away at their phones or setting off on foot.

Ashley sighed and took one last look around. Well, no Kari, as far as she could tell. Suddenly, a shout:

"Ashley!"

She turned towards the sound. A woman stood by a pickup truck in the parking lot, the sun at her back, obscuring her features. But the woman's height, posture, and coiled bronze hair were unmistakable. Kari hadn't changed a bit.

"God, I haven't seen you since Sissy's wedding," said Kari as Ashley approached. "How is she, really?" she asked gravely.

"She's hanging in there," said Ashley, relief at having been picked up making her voice much lighter than the question and answer warranted. "Thank you so much for picking me up. I didn't even know how I would make it if you hadn't. I'm not sure how much Sissy told you but…"

"Girl, I've got you," said Kari, cutting her off. "I've been there, done that. We stick together. But you know I can't keep you for long at my place. I leave myself in two weeks for another job. But we're going to figure something out for you. Don't you worry."

Ashley smiled broadly, blinking back tears of relief.

"So you live near the polo fields, you say?" she asked, trying to focus on the present.

"Yeah," said Kari. "It's kind of ridiculously glamorous, isn't it? Me, a cowgirl from Montana, living at the Polo fields? I'm basically a glorified stable hand. But I take care of these amazing ponies, and I get to see all the games. You're gonna love it. Especially now that you're a single girl."

"What do you mean, now that I'm single?" asked Ashley.

"You're gonna hafta try to not to give in to the advances of all those hot polo players. Just know that they like to play games."

"Oh, I don't think I'm ready for any kind of relationship yet," said Ashley. "I'm just trying to get out of my current one and stay safe and try to build myself up. We'll see about all of that stuff later."

"Believe me, you'll be tempted. They're hard to resist," said Kari. "And I'm married. You'll see. Let's get going. I'll give you a little tour of Santa Barbara on the way if you're not too exhausted."

"I would love that," said Ashley.

"Wait- where's your luggage? Shit- Did you forget it on the train?"

Kari looked panicked for a minute. Ashley blushed.

"I don't have any luggage. So maybe… I don't know… Maybe I can go somewhere cheap, like maybe you have a Goodwill store?"

"We'll figure it out," said Kari. "Don't worry."

So Ashley tried not to worry. Kari did have a natural authority that made Ashley feel like her sister's friend had everything under control. She focused on looking around.

Kari gestured up and down.

"Santa Barbara is unique in that our beaches run East-West instead of North-South like most of the California coast. We have the mountains at our back and then the ocean in front of us, with the Channel Islands protecting us from too much weather and surf. We've got wine country to our north and Los Angeles to our south, and a ton of different universes and microclimates in between. A lot of the people here like to complain about how cold it is here, which just makes me laugh. They've never spent a winter in Montana."

They got into Kari's truck.

"I'm taking you for a celebratory drink," said Kari.

As they drove along, Kari pointed out fancy gates leading to giant estates, the likes of which Ashley had never seen in her life.

"How do the people here get so rich?" she asked.

"Oh, they don't get rich here," said Kari. "They bring their money here. You start elsewhere, and once you've made it you go to live in Santa Barbara, or Montecito, or Hope Ranch."

"But what about these places here?" asked Ashley, gesturing at a residential neighborhood of closely packed modest beach homes. "They can't cost that much."

"Ha!" Kari barked, a bitter expression on her pretty face. "I know they would cost 50k outside of Billings, but they're at least 3 million dollars here."

Ashley blanched.

"How does anyone else afford to live here?"

"We scrape by," said Kari. "It's a struggle. There's a word-of-mouth system for apartments and things like that. There are some deals. You can get maybe somebody's pool house. We'll figure it out, don't you worry."

Ashley looked out the window. They were driving along a road that seemed to be on top of a cliff now, the dark blue Pacific Ocean below them. She'd literally gone as far as she could possibly go without actually leaving the country.

"Kari, I know this is stupid, but can I maybe dip my toes in the ocean? I've never been at a beach."

Kari smiled.

"Yeah, I know what that's like. When I first got here, you should have seen me. I was like a total fool, dancing around in the water, everybody staring at me, wondering what the hell I was doing. They don't understand what it's like to be a country girl who's never been anywhere. And now I barely even really pay attention to it. I'll actually be happy to go to the beach. I haven't set foot in the water in probably a month. Can you believe that?"

"Well, if I lived here, I mean, now that I live here," said Ashley, "I think I'll go every day."

"Yeah, you'll see," said Kari. "Maybe you'll get sick of it too, or maybe you'll take it for granted."

"I don't want to ever take this for granted," said Ashley. "Look at this, look at the light."

"I know," said. Kari, "it's magical. Let me take you to the beach and we'll have a little drink. There's a place around the corner. It's called Hendry's, it's a boathouse and they've got cocktails and dogs."

Ashley didn't mention that she'd left the poor old dog behind.

"Maybe I'll get one once I settle in."

They pulled into a parking lot, queued behind a few cars, and finally found a spot.

"God, I can't believe there are places just right on the ocean where you can get a drink. This is wild."

They walked towards the boathouse and waited in line at the outdoor bar.

"I don't even know what I want," said Ashley.

She hadn't had a drink in years. She should probably start slow.

"We'll get you a glass of local rosé."

"Rosé?"

"Yeah, it's pink wine. It's good. It's kind of light, and they make it locally."

"Oh, local, yeah, I'll have that. Thanks," said Ashley.

They took their to-go cups and stepped onto the beach. Ashley stripped off her sweater, removed her paddock boots, and ran towards the water. She gasped as the cold Pacific Ocean sucked on her toes and crept around her ankles, and, taking a sip of the pink wine, enjoying the bubbles of Champagne light popping on her forearms and face, she laughed, happy for the first time in a long time. Feeling hopeful, for once.

Chapter 11

When the sun had started to drop towards the horizon, they'd gotten back into Kari's truck to head towards the stables. As they drove, they saw a sign with Smokey the Bear on it. *Fire Danger: High*, it said. Ashley grew alarmed.

"What's that about fire danger?"

"Oh, don't worry, it's a fact of life here," said Kari.

Ashley tried not to worry about it but still, the mood had changed along with the light.

"You don't need to talk about this if you don't want to," said Kari. "But was it really bad?"

Ashley just nodded.

"OK, well, I get it. I'll help keep all those guys I talked about away from you. I'll let them know that you're there to work, and not to flirt with hot polo players."

Ashley smiled.

"Are they really that hot?"

She thought back to how Robert used to be, back when he used to make an effort, and used to love her. She'd only ever been with Robert. She wondered what it would be like to maybe be with one of these Latin lovers Kari was describing. "Well, maybe don't keep them too far away," she laughed.

Kari winked at her.

"I think you'll do just fine here. By the way, I don't want to get your hopes up, but I've been talking to the people at the polo fields, and I think that there might a permanent position open for you if you want to work there."

Ashley's heart leapt.

"Thank you so much. I'm so happy that you're doing this for a near stranger."

"Are you kidding me? Your sister and I, we go way back. I would do anything for her family, even if she barely talks to me anymore. In fact, I was pleased and surprised to hear from her when she called about you. I know she had an accident last year, but she won't tell me anything."

Ashley bit her lip. Her heart swelled with love, but shrank with guilt as she thought of what it must have taken for Sissy to call Kari for her, for a job having to do with horses. Sissy had been the better horsewoman of the two of them, if not the more passionate one.

"It's complicated," said Ashley. "It's hard. Sissy doesn't want to talk to me half the time, and I get it. It's like, her life as she knew it is over, but she's still here."

"Is her husband helping out?"

"He is. He's amazing. But it's just not a life, as far as she's concerned."

"I can't imagine," said Kari.

"Neither can I," said Ashley.

"But really," asked Kari. "She never told me- what happened?"

Ashley screwed her eyes shut. Saw Robert, slapping the horses' hindquarters, yelling. Midnight, rearing up. She didn't want to think about it. She couldn't think about it.

"It was all so fast," said Ashley.

She took a gulp of her rosé from the sippy cup she had brought back into the truck and resisted the urge to cough. "This is good," she said, holding up the cup.

"Yeah, I know. Be careful. It goes down easy," said Kari.

They were on a street called Cabrillo Boulevard now, fringed with palm trees bathed in a golden glow, the ocean baby blue and lavender to their right, the mountains pink to their left.

"God, it's the most beautiful thing I've ever seen," said Ashley.

"Oh, you've seen nothing yet. Round every corner is something ridiculously gorgeous here," said Kari. "I'm taking you along the scenic route so that you can see everything along the coast, and then maybe tomorrow, or the day after, I'll show you more. Here's the Montecito Country Mart," she said as they went around a traffic circle.

Kari pointed at some nondescript group of buildings.

"It doesn't look like anything that special," said Ashley.

"Oh, I know, but it's all these super expensive shops where the Montecito ladies who lunch like to go and pick up little overpriced clothing items and gifts for themselves," said Kari.

"Ladies who lunch?" asked Ashley. "What does that mean?"

"It's these women that don't do anything much. They don't have a job or anything, so they play tennis, and they have lunch and that's about it," said Kari.

"Sounds a little boring," said Ashley.

"Yeah, I know, but they don't think it is. Also, they have to primp for dinner. You know, lots of things that keep them terribly busy."

Ashley did not completely understand this whole concept, but was intrigued, nonetheless. They drove down Coast Village Road.

"This is cute," said Ashley. "Maybe I could get a little place above one of these shops."

Kari laughed.

"You wish. This is prime real estate. Those places are completely unaffordable. Anyway, we'll find you a place. Don't worry. But this street is fun. We'll check out a restaurant here sometime. It's called Honor Bar. It's where everybody comes to pick up people."

"It's a singles' spot?" asked Ashley.

"Yeah, kind of. But also, the marrieds looking for someone spot. All the locals come here and sit at the bar. It's quite the scene, and they have good food. Anyway, we've gotta get you settled in. And I'm going to find a few articles of clothing for you. I'm sure you're dying to get out of that outfit that you've been wearing the whole time on the bus."

Ashley blushed.

"Yeah, I feel pretty disgusting."

They drove for a few moments more, and finally, Kari turned into a drive flanked by flags and by two sparkling green fields. In the background, the mountains now loomed purple.

"Wow, what is this place?" asked Ashley.

"This is the Polo Club. I live in a little crappy apartment by the stables. It's not fancy, but it'll do for now, and we'll figure it all out."

"And your husband doesn't mind?" asked Ashley.

"Steve? No, he'll be fine. He's away more than half the time, anyway. He's always traveling around taking care of people's horses, so I'll be glad to have a girlfriend with me. He doesn't come back for a while."

"Great," said Ashley.

They got out of the truck by a modest single-story stucco structure by the stables. The familiar smell of horses almost made tears spring to Ashley's eyes. She missed her horses already. She hoped they would be OK. She wondered what Robert would do with them, once he figured out that she was gone forever. Again, she wondered, was he looking for her? Had he tried to harass her sister or her mom?

Kari opened the door to a ground floor apartment and led Ashley inside.

"Hey, Kari, once I've gotten changed and everything, could I try to call my sister and my mom? I just haven't been able to reach my mom, and I don't have a phone."

"Oh, we're going to need to get you a phone," said Kari. "Everybody does everything with the phone. But smart of you to leave your phone at home, so that your husband couldn't track you."

"Oh, I didn't have a phone."

Kari looked at Ashley, shocked.

"You know Little House on the Prairie?" Ashley asked.

"Yeah?"

"My life was like that, but uglier."

"I think I've got an old iPhone that's like from 3 generations ago. I can give it to you," said Kari. "And then I'll take you to the store and we'll get you a contract."

"I don't know if I can afford it," Ashley admitted.

"Don't worry," said Kari. "Listen, I don't have much, but once you start working, you can pay me back."

Ashley gave her a tight hug and Kari gently disentangled herself.

"You can stay in this room."

Kari gestured towards a small, cluttered office with a daybed in it. It looked like an overflow storage room, but Ashley was just so relieved to have a place to sleep that she almost started crying again.

"Yeah, I know it's a mess," said Kari.

"No, it's great. I'd even be happy if you put me in the chicken coop, frankly."

"Listen, you take a shower, and I'm going to find some clothes for you. And then we'll get dolled up and we'll go to dinner at that place I showed you. The Honor Bar."

Chapter 12

Ashley got in the shower and lathered herself up, wondering about those hot men Kari had talked about. Part of her didn't want to think about being with another man ever again, after all of the things Robert had put her through. But as she soaped herself up, she allowed herself to think what it might be like to be with a man again, to feel his hands on her body. What would it be like to shower with a man after a hot day in the stables? She shuddered, starting to feel feelings she hadn't allowed herself to feel in months, maybe years. She let her hands run over her body, imagining them as a man's hands. Imagining someone kissing her neck. Tugging at her lips with his teeth. Running his hands between her thighs...

She shuddered. She didn't have time to think of this right now. Better to get clean before she started thinking dirty. Funny how just being away from Robert for a few days started to make her feel like herself already.

But she was still scared. She didn't know how badly he wanted to find her. Was it this really going to be this easy to get away? She couldn't believe she'd done it. Couldn't believe she'd taken her courage into her own hands and had done it. It was not possible to come back from this decision. She wondered if she would ever see her mom again. Ever see her sister again. Who knew? Maybe she would end up successful somehow, with a new life. Or maybe she would fail miserably, like Robert had always told her she would, without him. According to Robert, she was incapable of doing anything right. In fact, Momma seemed to have the same opinion, so maybe it was true.

Well. She'd certainly enjoyed the thoughts about the polo players a lot more than this pathetic self-deprecation. She finished rinsing off and shut off the water. She wrapped herself in a towel and came into the room. On the bed was a neat stack of clothes. She popped her head out of the door.

"Kari, are the clothes on the bed for me?"

"Yeah, they are. I think they should fit. I don't know. You and I seem to be about the same size," said Kari.

Right. Maybe they were technically the same dress size, but Kari was about six inches taller and looked like a supermodel.

"Thank you. I don't care. I'll make them fit. Thank you so much."

Ashley considered the pile. There was a pair of stretchy jeans, and a top that looked kind of cute. And maybe she needed a light sweater. It didn't seem to be cold out. Nothing like Montana. She put together something that she hoped would work, paired with her old paddock boots- the only shoes she had to her name. She came out of the room.

"Oh my God, your boots," Kari laughed. "I'm so sorry, I forgot to give you shoes. What size do you wear?"

"8 ½," said Ashley.

"We'll get you something else soon, but in the meantime these should work."

Kari rummaged through a closet and handed Ashley a pair of high heeled sandals.

"High heels?"

"I told you it was a pick-up joint," said Kari, laughing.

"Oh, but I'm wearing jeans."

"Yeah, no, jeans and heels. That's exactly the look here. You got it. You look great."

Ashley looked at her own reflection in the mirror, doubt evident in her expression.

"Did you wanna put on any makeup or anything?" asked Kari.

"I don't have any," Ashley shrugged.

"I have some lip gloss and mascara I bought that I didn't like that could work for you. Lucky for you I never throw anything out," Kari laughed.

"I haven't worn makeup in years. Robert said it was a waste. I wasn't going anywhere, so I never even thought about it."

"Well, you look naturally gorgeous anyway, but…"

Ashley took a deep breath. This was a new life. She was going to be different.

"I would love anything you have that would work for me. Thank you so much."

Kari shuffled Ashley into her bathroom and rummaged through a drawer. She handed Ashley a few lipstick and lip gloss tubes, a mascara, and an eyeliner pencil.

"Thanks, I'll just be a second," said Ashley.

"Take your time."

Kari left the bathroom and Ashley looked at herself in the mirror and applied the mascara and a reddish lip gloss. It was a tiny change, but already she could barely recognize this person in the mirror. She looked, if she dared say it, almost pretty. Her gray eyes shone more than they had in years, even if they were still a little sad.

"Buck up, bitch," she told her reflection.

It was up to her, and her alone, to turn her life around now. Robert was across multiple state lines. If she let his treatment of her keep bothering her, that was on her.

"Go get'em, girl," she whispered to herself, and left the bathroom.

"I'm ready," she told Kari. "Let's go see those hot guys you talked about."

"Whoa, Filly," said Kari. "Slow your roll," she laughed. "I'd love to live vicariously through you- I've been married for so long. But remember, some of these guys are bad news."

They got back into Kari's pickup truck and headed back in the direction Ashley remembered them having come from, back towards Coast Village Road.

Chapter 13

The inside of the Honor bar was dark, both not too fancy, reminiscent of a place Ashley remembered going to in Montana, back when Robert used to take her out, and oddly, impossibly glamorous at the same time. There were booths, and a bar, and dark wood and low lighting, and waitstaff wearing fancy white aprons. The patrons were dressed casually, but there was a certain indescribable gleam about them that told Ashley that they must all be very wealthy.

Kari put in her name with the hostess and found a pair of Adirondack chairs to sit in outside, while they waited for their table to become available. A pretty young waitress took their drinks order. Another rosé for Ashley. An Old Fashioned for Kari. And an order of fries. Just hearing the word, Ashley noticed she was starving.

When the drinks and fries arrived, Ashley tucked in, looking around. The mountains were invisible now, the sky a dark but electric blue. Couples and families strolled down the street. Everyone looked happy. Would she ever be that happy? Maybe this would be the beginning of something beautiful for her. She couldn't imagine ever becoming one of these types of people- so confident and wealthy and polished. But this was it. This was her new life.

Soon, the hostess came to get them and led them to their booth. They enjoyed their meal, Ashley tucking into a fried chicken sandwich so delicious that she was sure she'd never tasted anything so good in her whole entire life. Kari had a salad.

"So, it's true about you California people eating nothing but salads?"

"Oh," Kari laughed. "It's called the Macho Salad because it probably has more calories than your sandwich. But you're right- at least I can pretend I'm being healthy."

"So… what happens tomorrow?" asked Ashley, turning serious. The idea of potentially starting work was intimidating. She had not worked for anybody else in such a long time. She didn't really know how to act in the workplace, or what they would expect of her.

"Oh, yeah. Tomorrow we'll go to the stables, and I'll introduce you to Alex. He's kind of the boss around here. He'll basically lay out what he expects from you, and you're gonna rock it, don't you worry. You know it's not going to be very glamorous stuff, right? Shoveling shit and cleaning the horses and making sure everything is the way it's supposed to be, and that's that."

"That's what I'm good at," Ashley shrugged. "But what about you? Don't you do that?"

"Well, that's the thing," said Kari. "I'm going to go work for a private barn belonging to a celebrity. I kind of needed to find my own replacement, and I guess I found her."

"Wait, so you mean that this would be a permanent position for me if they want me?"

"Yeah, lucky, right?" said Kari.

Ashley almost laughed with relief.

"Yeah, lucky, I guess. I mean, I thought it would be harder than that."

"Oh, there will still be plenty of challenges, don't you worry," said Kari. "But in terms of work, I'm going to officially give them my two weeks' notice tomorrow. I'll be working literally just down the street, but that's the reason that I'm going to be out of the apartment soon, because once I'm not working for them anymore, they're gonna force me to give it up."

Ashley didn't dare ask the question that sprang into her head, which was, *What about me?*

But Kari read her mind.

"Unfortunately, they're going to be fixing my apartment up and then renting it for a fortune to visiting polo players," she said. "It sucks. That's the way with everything around here. My new position comes with a pool house, which is going to be totally awesome. Believe me, Steve was dying for me to leave this job, but he wouldn't have let me if it didn't afford us a place, even though he makes decent money."

"Whose stables are you going to work for?"

Ashley didn't know any current celebrities, but she was still curious.

"I'm not allowed to say yet. I signed an NDA."

"An NDA?" asked Ashley, letting the unfamiliar acronym play on her tongue. Sissy had mentioned this.

"A non-disclosure agreement. You'll have to sign one at the polo club, too. It's something that rich and famous people use to protect their privacy. Alex will explain it to you tomorrow."

"OK," said Ashley. This NDA thing sounded weird, but beggars couldn't be choosers.

"I just can't believe you're doing all of this for me," she told Kari. "I just feel so lucky. A week ago, everything in my life was crappy. But now, I feel like my life is finally turning around."

"I hope so," said Kari, a funny expression on her face.

"What?" asked Ashley, alarm bells going off in her head.

"Nothing. Just… I'm just gonna have to talk you through being careful of some of these people."

"I would appreciate that," said Ashley. "I feel like one of those home schooled kids people used to joke about. No social skills, no street smarts."

Kari laughed.

"You'll be fine."

They finished their meal and headed back to the house.

As soon as her head hit the pillow, Ashley sank into a deep slumber.

Chapter 14

The usual nightmare woke her up. The feeling of Robert's hands squeezing her neck. His rough, calloused palms scraping her skin. Her eyes flew open. Her heart was beating triple time. She looked around, panicked. There was no one in the room. It had just been a dream. She dropped her head back onto the pillow. She was at Kari's place. She was safe. No one knew where she was.

When they had come back from dinner, Ashley had tried to call her mother again. Still no response. Today, she would try to call her sister's house and see if Craig might over and check on Mom, because this was really strange.

There was a light rap on the door. Kari popped her head in.

"Hey, you. Are you awake, sleepyhead? We need to get ready for work. We start early around here."

Ashley took a quick look at what Kari was wearing and selected jeans and a shirt from the pile Kari had left her, with of course her old boots. She took a bird bath and got dressed quickly and guzzled the coffee and scarfed down the piece of buttered toast Kari offered her.

They stepped out of the apartment.

"Well, the good news about this place is that the commute's super easy. You'll be missing that once we're both out," said Kari.

They walked toward the stables. A tall, handsome man with a craggy sun-lined face was standing in the doorway, watching them approach. She could feel his flinty blue-gray eyes on her. It was disconcerting. Ashley hadn't worn jeans as tight as the ones that Kari had lent her in a long time, and she wondered if that what was making him look. But she'd seen a lot of girls dressed like that at the restaurant yesterday, so she didn't know what he was staring at. Kari elbowed her in the ribs.

"Looks like Alex likes what he sees," she hissed. "Just don't let him get you somewhere alone, and you'll be safe."

"Seriously?" Ashley whispered back. "Is he dangerous?"

"No- just a little bit of a letch. I should have warned you."

Ashley gulped. Maybe she wasn't as lucky as she'd thought.

"Hey, Alex, this is Ashley. The girl I was telling you about," said Kari, her voice normal volume and cheerful, but still bearing a trace of tension. "You're gonna be so happy to have her, you won't even miss me," she said. "Ashley worked with horses for years in Montana and had her own horse operation. You'll probably decide that she's so much better than me that you won't even remember my name when I come back to visit."

"I'll remember something else," said Alex, sticking his tongue out.

Kari rolled her eyes.

"You'd better watch yourself, old man."

Alex laughed delightedly, and Ashley reassured herself that Alex might be more harmless than she'd thought.

"Well, anyway, I'm going to show Ashley around, and if there's anything that you want to do in terms of training her and getting her ready to replace me, you can come find us."

"I'm counting on you for the training. But I'm gonna need her to sign some paperwork," said Alex.

"Paperwork?"

The word escaped Ashley's lips in a squeak.

"You know, Social Security number, previous address and employer, banking details for payment, the usual," said Alex. "And the NDA."

"Oh yeah, can we do that tomorrow? Ashley's just getting settled- she's not even had time to breathe, let alone open her bank account, Alex. I'm going to help her with all of that, OK?" Kari said, in a teasing tone.

"Yeah, OK," said Alex. "Just don't go getting hurt before I have proof of insurance. I'd have to bury you out back."

Insurance? Ashley gulped.

"You know damn well she gets insurance working here, Alex. That's one of the benefits. Don't try to be a cheap ass."

Once they were out of earshot, Ashley turned to Kari in a panic.

"I don't have a bank account! I don't have anything. I have my driver's license with me, but what if Robert tracks me down?"

"Girl, we're going to figure it out. We're gonna go to the bank and get you an account as soon as we're off work. And then we're going to go to the DMV and you're just going to get your maiden name back."

"That's a name that Robert can recognize," said Ashley, panicked.

"Seriously, Ashley Johnson? How many Ashley Johnsons do you think there are in this world? A gazillion. You think he's gonna go through every single one of them? I mean, I know he's probably obsessed with your cute ass, but it would take some pretty bad luck for him to put two and two together and decide that Ashley Johnson in Montecito is the Ashley Johnson he's looking for."

Ashley nodded, unsure.

"And then what about the bank account?"

"We'll just open a little checking account for you. You'll put in the cash you have. That should be a good start- we'll get you a prepaid debit card, and then once you start getting some paychecks you can apply for a credit card."

"OK," Ashley gulped.

She had never done any of this stuff. She was starting to realize how Robert had kept her in the dark about how life worked, and how much of the business stuff Sissy had taken on while Ashley was playing with the horses.

"Come on, said Kari. Let me show you around the stables."

"OK," said Ashley. "So… Alex? He seems kind of OK, right? His bark is worse than his bite?"

"Sure," Kari allowed.

"Is there anyone I should look out for around here?"

Kari looked at her. Hesitated.

"You know I signed that NDA. So, some stuff…But basically, all these horse guys- they're generally hot to trot, right? I mean, you'll learn fast. Here's the thing. You need to know that in Montecito, no one really says anything. Even without an NDA. That's why all these celebrities feel safe. If you say too much you can get a bad reputation. Whatever happens, you can tell me. But try not to tell anyone else."

"You're worrying me a little bit," said Ashley.

"Don't be worried," said Kari, a bit brusquely. "Let me walk you through what you're supposed to do every day in the stables."

Kari walked Ashley though the steps, letting Ashley shadow her and help out as she fed the horses, and mucked out each stall and checked on its inhabitant before checking all of the tack and equipment.

Ashley noticed how these horses were high strung and elegant compared to the ones she had back home. Except for Midnight. They were all like Midnight. She briefly squeezed her eyes shut to banish the memory of Midnight rearing up, Sissy coming dislodged from his back, Robert there with his hand raised.

"Am I expected to exercise the horses?" asked Ashley.

"Usually, the guys exercise the horses, but sometimes, they'll want your help. Basically, you're here to assist with anything that needs to be done."

"It doesn't seem that bad," Ashley ventured.

"It's not that bad. In general, I would say that by the end of the morning you should be done with your everyday tasks, and then the afternoons can be kind of up in the air. Sometimes, you'll be running errands or helping Alex with paperwork. Sometimes, if you're lucky, you can even cut out early and go to the beach or something. It just always depends on the day."

It sounded deceptively easy.

"Is Alex a hard boss?" Ashley asked.

"I mean, you saw how he is," Kari said. "He's pretty reasonable when he comes to his expectations. Just do what you're supposed to do, keep your nose down, and you'll be fine. There are some other situations that I am sure you'll become aware of soon enough, but I don't think I'm really allowed to say anything."

"The NDA?" asked Ashley.

"Yep."

"Well, now that I know what's expected, why don't you show me where everything is?"

"Sure thing," said Kari.

She took Ashley to the tack room, which was nicer than anything Ashley had at home, even though Ashley kept her tack room scrupulously clean. This one just had so much shining wood and beautiful equipment. She stared at the stacks of blankets with the logo of the Polo Club on them. She'd never seen anything so chic.

"Wow, I could wear these as a shawl," she exclaimed.

Kari laughed.

"I'll bet. Some of the women of Montecito would probably copy you and say they invented it."

"So… when is polo? Is there a season?" asked Ashley.

"Well, the season's ending now, which is good news for you. It means less urgent stuff and more maintenance. A lot of the guys are going to be traveling to Florida and all over the world, so this is a quieter time. However, more and more of them are going to be staying all year."

"Why?"

"There's, well…you know."

"What do you mean, you know?"

"Ah, never mind," said Kari. "If you don't know what I'm talking about, I guess it's part of the NDA."

"Seriously?" asked Ashley, getting a little annoyed. "What are you talking about?"

"Well, we have a celebrity member. Not just any celebrity. I can't say more, but there is no way you have not heard about this. It's been all over the news."

"I don't watch the news."

"Believe me. You'll figure it out. Anyway," Kari said, switching subjects, "It's going to be a quieter season. There will be some students. And then some of the successful old guys who come in because they're considering starting a team. They like to try out the horses who aren't traveling. You couldn't have come at a better time."

Ashley couldn't have come at any other time. One more day with Robert, and she might have been in even more danger. She thought about how her call to both her mother and sister from Kari's phone the previous evening had not been answered.

"Why don't we wrap up our work, and then we're going to go do our shopping and our banking," Kari suggested, breaking the silence.

As they worked and cleaned, Ashley started to worry more about Sissy and Momma. She would feel so much better if she heard from them. She was starting to get a bad feeling. What if something had happened to her mom and no one knew about it? Who would let her know? Her mother had neighbors, of course, but they weren't on a first name, phone calling kind of basis with Ashley. Not like Ashley had a phone. What if Momma had fallen and hadn't been able to alert anyone? What if she'd had a heart attack? Ashley shuddered. Momma always had accused her of not paying enough attention to her, and if something had happened to her due to Ashley's behavior, she would have proven her point. Ashley hadn't been to visit Momma as much as she should have all these years, mainly because Robert wouldn't let her. But also, the truth was, her mom had annoyed her sometimes, made her angry with her inability to support her own daughter, with her fake positivity, and with her focus on herself. It had been convenient for once to let Robert dictate what Ashley could and could not do, when it came to visiting. She was pathetic. It was one thing to let herself be treated like that, but when it impacted others, it was inexcusable. As soon as she got off work, Ashley decided, she would call. She wondered what Robert was doing right now. Was he raging? Was he breaking things in their house? She hoped he hadn't hurt any of the animals. She wished that she had a close friend nearby that she could call so that she could make sure that the animals were OK. What could she do to save them? She couldn't trust Robert to care for them.

The morning went by in a blur. It felt good to be working without dreading someone coming home and punishing you for a job badly done. Kari came in to survey her work, Alex right behind her.

"Wow, New Girl is good. I guess I won't miss you after all," Alex said, smacking Kari on the butt.

"Alex, I swear to God... Get away from me," said Kari, her hands balling up into fists.

Alex laughed and backed off, putting his hands above his head. Ashley's eyes were wide open. Was this the way she was supposed to talk to Alex, too? She didn't know if she could bring herself to do it. She would just make sure to steer clear of him. But at least she knew he was happy with the work she was doing.

"Alex, we're done here," said Kari. "I'm gonna take Ashley to the bank and do all that stuff so that we can sign her paperwork tomorrow. Sound good?"

"Yeah, I hate to see you leave, but I love to watch you go," he said.

Kari scoffed.

"You did a good job here," Alex told Ashley. "I'll see you here tomorrow. Oh, I almost forgot, there's a cocktail party tonight to celebrate the end of the season. Will you come?"

Kari nodded.

"We'll try to make it. It would be nice for Ashley to meet everyone."

As soon as they got into Kari's car, Ashley said, "I really need to call my sister."

"Yeah, here," said Kari, handing over her phone. "Let me talk to her if you reach her."

Ashley was proud of herself that she managed to figure out how to get into Kari's contacts and find her sister's number. She hit the button and waited. The phone rang and rang, and for a moment, she was afraid that it wouldn't pick up. Finally, she heard Craig's voice on the end of the line.

"Craig, I was worried. I've been trying to reach you guys."

"Yeah, your sister's not doing great."

"The pain?"

"No- it's more her mood. I've been trying to cheer her up with her favorite foods and stuff," said Craig.

He was whispering. Ashley knew he wouldn't want her sister to hear that she was a burden on him in any way.

"Craig, I just want you to know how much I appreciate what you're doing."

"She's my wife. In sickness and in health, right?"

"Do you think I can talk to her?"

"I don't think that's a good idea," said Craig.

Ashley was silent. Sissy was blaming her, wasn't she? Well, it was her fault that she'd let Sissy take the brunt of Robert's moods. And now, here she was living in paradise, and Sissy was still stuck in the same old hell. She wouldn't want to talk to herself, either.

"I understand," Ashley said, the guilt pinching her heart. "Listen Craig, I hate to lay more stuff on you. But have you guys heard from my mom? I've been really worried. I've been trying to call her, and she hasn't responded at all."

Craig paused for a moment.

"Yeah, come to think of it, I don't know. I haven't heard anything about her."

"Is there any way you can go check if Mom is OK?"

"I would," said Craig. "But she's an hour and a half away, and your sister needs me right now. We'll try to call her in the meantime."

"OK, thanks," said Ashley. "I'll try to call you guys back later this week."

She heard Craig take a deep breath on the other end of the line.

"You know, let's try to minimize how much we talk."

Ashley was silent. Did Sissy hate her that much? So much that she shouldn't even call?

"I know what you're thinking," Craig said. "Stop it. It's just that Robert called, and he was raging. He was looking for you."

"He what?" Ashley almost choked. "Why didn't you tell me that right away?"

"I just didn't…whatever. It was stupid. He called. And he was livid. Don't worry, Sissy doesn't know. He thought that we helped you to get away from him or something. He was accusing us of a million different things. He put out some alert for you, claiming that you were kidnapped."

Ashley shuddered. The Amber Alert had been for her after all.

"Did he say anything else? Does he have any idea where I am?"

"I don't think so," said Craig. "I just hope he doesn't decide to pay us a visit. Does he know your sister has a friend in California?"

"Why would he assume that I've gone to see one of her friends? And why that one?"

"Come on, Kari is her closest friend. And if I were him, I would think that you probably tried to get as far away as possible, which is the coast. Did you ever mention California to him?"

"No," said Ashley, indignant.

But then she froze. Maybe she *had* said something about California once, back when they were still going on occasional dates. She could remember it now. Stupidly thinking that a move would make everything better. Telling him that it would be nice if they opened a horse operation somewhere where they could go to the beach and see palm trees. There was no way Robert was listening to her. Absolutely no way he would remember. *Or would he?*

Damn Craig for making her question herself. She'd just gotten to Santa Barbara. She wasn't gonna pick up and run on some assumption that maybe Robert had some inkling that she was there. At some point, she needed to be able to settle down and feel safe. She wracked her brain. Had she said anything about Santa Barbara specifically, or just Southern California in general?

Still, maybe Robert would put two and two together. They'd been to her sister's wedding, and he'd met Kari. Had Kari talked about Santa Barbara or Montecito at the wedding? Ashley couldn't remember.

Craig broke the silence.

"Hey, are you still there?"

"Yeah, I'm still here. I guess I'll let you go- give Sissy a big hug for me?"

"Sure thing," said Craig. "I've got her."

"OK. Bye."

Ashley hung up and handed the phone back to Kari, tears in her eyes.

"That didn't sound great," said Kari.

"Yeah, Sissy is down. You know, it was always so important to her to be athletic. And I think that when winter starts coming around, her mood gets worse."

She didn't mention about Sissy probably rightfully blaming her for what had happened.

"She could come over here," said Kari. "We could show her a good time."

Ashley paused. How little had Sissy told her friend about her condition?

"Let's keep hoping."

"What did I hear you saying about your mom? I'm sorry, I eavesdropped, but that sounds a little worrisome," said Kari.

Ashley was glad she didn't need to explain any more about Sissy's condition.

"Yeah," said Ashley. "I haven't been able to reach my mom. Can I try her again one more time?"

Kari handed her the phone. Ashley dialed the familiar number and sat as the phone rang and rang and rang. The answering machine came on and Kari snatched the phone back.

"Don't leave a message. You never know. What if Robert is at her house and hears you and gets my number? That would be a disaster."

Ashley shuddered. Kari was right. She'd already ruined her sister's life, and now here she was putting another person's life in danger.

"Here, let's go get a sandwich," said Kari, pulling into a parking lot. You've got a ton on your mind, and I personally always feel better with a good sandwich. This place does the best French sandwiches you've ever tasted. They got out of the truck and walked into the Montecito Country Mart. Ashley tried not to stare at the Montecito tennis moms in their short skirts and perfectly flipped blonde ponytails. Kari ordered two simple looking ham sandwiches on long pieces of crusty bread. They sat down at a white picnic table. Ashley looked at her sandwich.

"What in the world? This doesn't even have any cheese or mayo on it. Can I ask for Miracle Whip?"

"It's a French sandwich," said Kari. "Don't knock it 'til you've tried it."

She opened a little plastic container that had come with their order. "Look, these little pickles, they're called *cornichons*. You put them in there." She gestured to her open sandwich.

"Why don't they put them in themselves?" asked Ashley.

"Because they're French. Don't question. Just taste it."

Ashley took a bite and her taste buds started to tingle. Despite her stress and exhaustion, a smile crept onto her face.

"Oh my God, this is delicious. I thought Subway had some good sandwiches. This is beyond."

Once they'd finished, they got up.

"OK, time to go the DMV," said Kari.

They drove up to the DMV, but it was closed.

"What now?" asked Ashley, a bit dejected.

"What's your married name?"

"Miller."

Ashley cringed as she said it. She couldn't wait to be rid of it.

"It isn't much rarer than your maiden name," said Kari. "Why don't you just keep that for now?"

Ashley was silent.

"C'mon. There are probably thousands of Ashley Millers. You can change it later. But the bonus is, he probably would never believe you would keep the name."

Ashley shuddered. She didn't want to keep his name. Not for another second. Just the idea of his name in her mouth made her want to throw up.

"Listen, it's just temporary," said Kari. "We'll get you a bank account, and you can always do a name change and come up with something exotic and sexy once you're settled in, sound good?"

By this time, they were already at the Wells Fargo office in the upper village of Montecito. It was off what looked at first like a normal parking lot, but once you drove in, there were a bunch of elegant shops, including a cute bookstore.

"I told them we were coming," said Kari. "And I got us an appointment with the nicest woman. She's pregnant, she doesn't give a fuck. She'll open the account for you, no problem. You brought your money, right?"

"Yes," said Ashley, patting her pocket, which now contained $182 of the original $497. It was everything she had in the world. They walked into the bank.

"Armelle Lopez, please," Kari told a teller. "We have an appointment."

After a few minutes, the teller came and got them at the seating area where they had been waiting.

"Ms. Lopez will see you now."

They were led to a glass fronted office towards the back of the bank.

"Do you want your privacy?" asked Kari.

"No, come with me. I don't even know what to say. I've never opened a bank account," hissed Ashley.

She felt so stupid. Like a child. She should have known how to do these things by now. They walked into the office.

"Hey, Armelle, how're you doing?" asked Kari. "Wow, you're really coming along. Your bump looks adorable. When are you due?"

Armelle Lopaz looked pleased. She playfully batted her long eyelashes and smiled.

"Just another month and a half. My last day is next week, and then I get to be a lazy pig until the baby comes. I hope it doesn't come early. I'm going to be enjoying my time off," she said.

"Do you have a name picked out already?" asked Kari.

"That's a secret. Everybody always has something to say. So I've learned my lesson."

"Fair enough," laughed Kari. "And how is that cute husband of yours?"

"Oh, he's fine. You know, same old, same old. Construction's crazy these days. He's busy all the time. I know he hopes that we have a boy so that he can help him with the business. Even if it's a girl, she can probably help him with the business."

"A girl would probably be smarter," laughed Kari.

"Yeah, you're right. But you know him, he's a little bit traditional."

"Speaking of traditional, Armelle, we really need your help because poor Ashley here has never had a bank account," Kari said, lowering her voice.

"She's got her driver's license here and some cash that she can put in."

Ashley passed over the bills and the ID, feeling that she had lost everything she owned. Armelle took a look and sighed.

"Yeah, but where's her proof of address? And you need a minimum of $500.00 to open the account."

Ashley's heart sank. Kari spoke up.

"C'mon, Armelle, I'm her proof of address. She's staying with me. Do you need me to add her name to my electricity bill online or something?"

Armelle sighed.

"Yeah. I do."

"On it," said Kari, already pecking at her phone. "As for the money, I'll spot her the rest," she said, as if it was an afterthought.

Ashley gasped.

"No! That's too much!"

Kari silenced her with a gentle hand on her arm.

"Wait," said Armelle.

Ashley froze again.

"Spot her money?" asked Armelle, looking at them suspiciously. "Does she not have any income?"

"Don't be silly. She's got a job at the stables. She needs to have a place to deposit her paychecks."

"OK, cool," said Armelle. "But just so you know, she can have a debit card, but no credit card until she's established her credit. I'm guessing that you have no credit, Ashley?"

"No," said Ashley, embarrassed. Kari put a hand on her knee.

"This is not your fault," she said to Ashley. To Armelle, she added, "She's super responsible. I've known her for a long time. I know her whole family, so I can vouch for her. In fact, if you need a guarantor on her account, I'll do it."

Ashley blinked. Kari was so kind. What would she do without her? She'd be absolutely lost.

"OK, so let me put this account together for you." Armelle tapped at the computer keyboard with her brightly colored fingernails.

Ashley looked towards Kari, but Kari looked to be playing on her phone.

"So, Ashley Miller…"

Ashley tried to avoid wincing when she heard the name.

"Yes, correct."

"So I'm going to give you a debit card. And you've got your bank account. What's your address for the bank statements?"

Panicked, Ashley looked to Kari.

"She'll do paperless," said Kari.

"And she'll update her address with me when she gets a more permanent one, right?"

Armelle looked at Ashley pointedly.

"You know this isn't how it's usually done," said Armelle. "Why do you think I came to you?" asked Kari. "I got you, and you got me, remember?"

"Never forget." Armelle directed a sidelong glance at Ashley.

"OK, so what's the e-mail address for the virtual statements? And don't try to give me yours, Kari. That's going a bit too far."

"Gotcha," said Kari.

"MadameXofMontecito@Gmail.com," she said.

Ashley was about to say something- she didn't have an e-mail address. But Kari nudged her with her foot. Oh well, she probably knew what she was doing.

After a few moments, Armelle said, "OK, all set. Here's your bank card. You can come collect your permanent one in a few days. Welcome to Wells Fargo. We're pleased to have you as a customer."

"Thanks so much," said Ashley, slipping the card into her wallet, which was now devoid of any cash. But at least now she had a debit card. She felt like it was a major step in the right direction. They exited the bank.

"Kari, what was that e-mail address you gave her? Did you just make one up?"

"No. I figured that Alex might want it or the bank might want it. You can always change it later if you're not happy with it, but I figured it's something anonymous but fun, right?"

"Thank you," said Ashley.

"And I know you've got an e-mail address and everything now, but I really don't think you should be opening any social media accounts, OK?" said Kari.

Ashley laughed.

"Right. I haven't even been on e-mail all these years, and now you think I'm going to start a social media account?"

"Speaking of," said Kari, "let's go get my old phone activated for you."

They drove across town to State Street and walked into a glass storefront with a sign with an apple cutout over it.

"That's a cute logo," said Ashley. "It looks like that Apple computers logo."

Kari stared at her, eyes wide open.

"You know the Apple logo isn't just for computers anymore, right? Everybody has got an Apple iPhone now. I know that Robert kept you isolated, but seriously, I didn't know you were Amish."

Ashley giggled. She thought of the Mennonite women she had seen around, with their bonnets and old-fashioned clothes. She remembered thinking that at least they had looked happy.

"I mean, Robert has a flip phone... I just never even thought... I guess I didn't realize how completely isolated I actually was."

The next quarter hour involved high levels of frustration for Ashley, trying to answer the salesperson's foreign questions, Kari helping out so that Ashley didn't seem crazy. Ashley wasn't looking forward to trying to make Kari's old rectangle of glass, metal, and plastic do her bidding. And again, Kari was spotting Ashley some money. Ashley needed to keep better track, but at this point she already owed her more than she had made in the past year. The salesperson was looking at Kari's phone, looking almost as confused as Ashley.

"Wait, I'm taking this to the back for a sec," he said.

"OK," said Ashley. "By the way," she hissed to Kari, "how much am I going to be making?"

She hadn't even asked. Beggars couldn't be choosers. Kari said a number that made her eyes widen.

"Oh, don't worry," said Kari, misunderstanding her surprise. That's weekly."

"Weekly?"

Ashley hadn't made that much in a month since the glory days of their horse business.

"Yeah. We get paid every week because some of the guys at the stables tend to gamble and so they can't be trusted with a bimonthly paycheck, which is good news for you. And by the way, you may think that's a lot, but for here, it's hardly a goldmine. So you're gonna have to be really careful," said Kari.

"So how am I supposed to get ahead?" asked Ashley, starting to panic again.

"Maybe you'll meet a nice rich man in Montecito. That's what most of the women here hope for," Kari said.

Ashley stared at her.

"Yeah, I could never marry for money. My grandma once said that. If you marry for money, you earn every penny of that for the rest of your life."

"Your grandma is a wise lady," said Kari. "But she's also an idealist."

Ashley thought of Momma, and how she'd often complained that Papa didn't have enough money, even though they'd always had enough. She'd given the girls dreams of knights in shining armor, but it was Papa who had instilled the manners and the work ethic that he'd probably inherited from Grandma and Grandpa.

The salesguy came back with a white box.

"Hey, so great news. Your phone is so old I couldn't even believe it. My boss hasn't seen one this old in years, so you're due for a free upgrade."

Upgrade? Was it going to be even more confusing? Ashley stood frozen as Kari and the salesperson negotiated. Finally, everything was decided, and Ashley was walking out of the store smiling, the phone a comforting weight in her handbag, her head full of new terms like *alerts, apps,* and *WiFi.* Ashley was getting thirsty, and maybe hungry again. Maybe the stress had been tearing a hole in her belly, and now she was finally feeling comfortable to eat again. Kari read her mind again.

"Hey, it's Taco Tuesday, but first, let's get you a few more outfits. Sound good?"

"Thank you so much."

"Again, it's just a loan, baby. I'm not being that generous. I'm not made of money." Kari smiled and winked.

They headed towards H&M, in an outdoor mall off State Street called Paseo Nuevo, which was the most beautiful shopping center Ashley had ever seen. She felt like she was in Europe somewhere, not that she had even been there. The mall had beautiful colorful tiles, swaying palm trees, lush vegetation, and blinding white plaster. The whole place seemed like a dream.

Inside H&M, Ashley considered things carefully while Kari picked up items for her with abandon. As Ashley picked up another button-down shirt, she saw Kari shaking her head.

"You've been shaking your head ever since we got in here! What's wrong?"

"You've got such a cute figure, and you're just covering it up," said Kari.

"I have a cute figure?" asked Ashley, genuinely shocked.

"Stop fishing for compliments," said Kari.

But Ashley was baffled. She hadn't really considered what her figure was like in a long time. It was just her body, and it did what it needed to do. It got her through the chores, and then once in a while, it got black and blue, and once in a while, Robert wanted to have sex with it. But really, she didn't think he was truly looking at her whenever that happened. When was the last time she had thought about how she looked? Back when she was in high school, maybe? She used to try to dress up cute and try to make the nicest outfits she could out of her small budget. Babysitting money only went so far, but everybody had thought she was pretty elegant. Her grandma had been proud and had said that she looked like some French lady called Coco Chanel, but Momma had told her she was putting on airs.

"Here, try some cuter stuff on," said Kari.

"Look, what about this dress?"

"A dress? Where am I gonna wear a dress?"

"Well, at tonight's cocktail party, for example."

"Is it formal?"

"Well, it's at the Polo Club bar, so let's call it rich-people-festive-casual. Still, you'll want to wear something cute to compete with all the Montecito ladies who come and try to pick up the cute guys."

"OK," said Ashley, unsure.

"Here, what about this?"

Kari held up a caramel-colored silk slip dress.

"Isn't that a negligee?"

"It's a dress."

"I would feel naked. And I mean, isn't winter coming?" asked Ashley.

"Hello? This is the land of endless summer. You throw a denim jacket or a leather jacket over it and you're good. Or even a cashmere sweater. That's the look here. And look. This white dress is perfect, too."

"White after Labor Day?" Ashley looked at Kari, horrified.

"Girl, of course. Beige sweater, beige mules, white dress. Coastal grandma chic," said Kari.

"Wait- you said I need to look cute. Now you're telling me I should look like a grandma?" laughed Ashley.

"No, coastal grandma is just this funny trend. All the ladies here are dressed that way. It's just linen, cashmere.... You know, that sort of thing. It's elegant, and you can do it for cheap."

Ashley looked at Kari, a doubting expression on her face.

"I don't see you doing this coast granny thing," she said.

"Not my ethnic group," laughed Kari.

"You better not be teasing me," said Ashley.

"Trust me," said Kari. "Get those dresses, and we'll get you some work stuff now- but show off that little body of yours, OK?"

"Well, it's true we aren't getting any younger," Ashley sighed.

"Wait a second- you're a baby. Sissy and I are 35- what are you? 32?"

"Yeah, 32," said Ashley. She felt ancient.

"Oh stop it," said Kari. "You've still got your whole life in front of you. You still have time to meet some hot guy, get married, and have kids. Hell, I'm hoping to have kids one of these days, too, if Steve ever gives me the green light."

Ashley's heart leapt into her throat a little bit at that. She dreamed of having kids, had always thought that she and Robert would have them, and that their kids would be best friends with the kids that Sissy and Craig would have. But Sissy and Craig took their time enjoying each other, and right when they started trying, Sissy had had her accident.

Ashley had gone off of birth control, too, at Robert's request, despite knowing it was a bad idea. Every month, she would anxiously wait for her period, not knowing whether she wanted it to show up or not. After a while, she'd started wondering whether something was wrong with her. Maybe it was because she didn't truly want kids. Then, as more time went on, she'd realized that maybe Robert had hurt her too much, had damaged something inside.

Kari misread her expression.

"Well, you don't need to have kids if you don't want kids. But anyway, you can get some hot guy. You still have time for some exciting relationships. So I can live vicariously as I sit there with my old man."

"Sounds like you guys are happy, though," said Ashley.

"Yeah, we're good…now," said Kari, enigmatically.

They headed to the fitting rooms.

"I'll weigh in," said Kari, "'cause I don't think you know what's fashionable and what's not," she laughed.

Ashley tried on outfit after outfit, Kari approving or declining, and Ashley not even worrying about what she herself thought, because she knew she had no idea. She finally tried on the caramel dress.

"No, it doesn't work," she said, blushing at her reflection in the mirror. The outline of her breasts and hips was clearly visible. As she turned, she caught the curve of her buttock.

"What are you talking about?" said Kari. "That looks amazing on you. You have to get that dress. You'll wear it all the time. It'll be your signature."

Kari selected a few other items including the white dress, for tonight, and a few pairs of impractical shoes, and within 15 minutes, they were out of the store with three huge shopping bags.

"OK, let's get back home," said Kari. "Forget the Taco Tuesday. Let's just get to the cocktail party- they'll have some drinks and food."

Ashley's stomach growled, but she acquiesced. They got back into the car and headed back towards Montecito.

Chapter 15

Ashley stepped into the bar of the Polo Club, self-consciously. Smoothing down the front of her white dress and tugging at her denim jacket to make it cover more of her chest. She'd hurriedly shaved her legs for the first time in a long time and had slipped on the new sandals that Kari had made her buy. She noticed a few heads swiveling in her direction.

"They're staring at me like I have two heads," she whispered to Kari.

"No, they're staring at you 'cause you're gorgeous, girl, just own it," said Kari.

Ashley rolled her eyes. But she was glad to have someone so supportive by her side, someone who said nice things, because it had been so long since Robert had done that. It felt good.

"Here, let's get ourselves a drink and see who's here. I'll see if I can introduce you to people," said Kari.

They headed to the bar. The bartender also gave her an appreciative look.

"Hands off, Juan, Ashley is going to be working here," said Kari, once she had introduced them.

Ashley ordered a local rosé. Eventually she would branch out, but she considered this baby steps. They left the bar and went to circulate around the room.

"Oh look, there's Felix over there. I'll introduce you to him. He's a player."

Ashley looked over. Felix was a dapper, older, overly tanned gentleman with a lionlike mane of white hair.

"Wow, he still plays polo, at his age?" Ashley whispered to Kari. Kari laughed.

"Oh no- not that kind of player. He's a pick-up artist. But he's good for a laugh. Everybody knows him."

They made a beeline for Felix, who introduced himself in a strong English accent that sounded as fake as his teeth looked.

"Where are you from, Ashley?" asked Felix.

Ashley froze.

"Oh, middle of nowhere. Definitely nowhere you would know."

"Try me," said Felix.

Dammit. Ashley realized that she would need to have an answer prepared. More people would be likely to ask her the same thing. She didn't want to say the truth, didn't want to say Montana and have people play the game where they search for someone they have in common. Not like Ashley knew many people at all anymore, but it was a small world after all, like that stupid song said. Kari jumped in.

"She's from Dakota."

Felix smiled benignly.

"Wow. That's the one state I don't know anyone from."

"Well, there you go," said Kari. "Listen, we're going to go introduce Ashley to a few more people. See you around, Felix."

As they walked away, Ashley elbowed Kari.

"Dakota? Isn't there a South Dakota and in North Dakota?"

"Yeah, but does Felix know that?" asked Kari.

"Seriously, though, where do I say I'm from?"

"Just say you're from the Inland Empire," said Kari.

"That sounds like something out of an epic fairytale."

"Hardly. It's some armpit between LA and Palm Springs. Nobody here would want to admit being from there, so they'll leave you alone."

"Good plan," said Ashley. Which city am I from?"

"Near Ontario. I'm telling you, nobody knows it. You're fine."

"OK, thanks," said Ashley, still worried that she might, with her luck, run into somebody who was from there.

Then, she forgot all about the Inland Empire because something caught her eye. A man. A handsome one. All dark eyes and tousled brown hair, with an animal magnetism to him that she had never experienced before.

"Wow, who's that?" she asked Kari.

"Oh, him," said Kari. "That's Diego. A player in both senses of the word."

"With those looks, I guess I'm not surprised," said Ashley. "Does he have a girlfriend?"

"Girlfriends, plural, from what I've heard. Don't waste your time. He'll never be serious with anyone. But he is nice to look at, I'll give you that."

"Sure is," said Ashley. She couldn't take her eyes off him and started to worry that he would notice.

"Here, I'll introduce you," said Kari. "But seriously, steer clear."

"I promise," said Ashley.

They walked towards Diego, and as the distance between them shrank, they locked eyes. After that, Ashley felt like she was being teleported towards him, her feet barely touching the floor. She started to feel tightness in her throat, and tingling in her lips, and a crazy desire to have him kiss her there and then. Now, Kari was introducing them, but Ashley could barely hear her. Diego's eyes were still locked on hers.

"Hi, Ashley," was all he had to say.

His voice was a warm baritone with a very slight accent. Ashley wondered if he was from Argentina. That's where Kari had said all the players were from. She must have explained to Diego that she would be helping around the stables, and he must have told her about how he was going to be spending more time than usual there that winter, as opposed to his usual travel, because she seemed to remember that later, but in the moment, all she could experience was her full body buzzing.

"How's your knee?" Kari asked.

Diego briefly looked to Kari to answer the question, breaking the connection, making Ashley feel like she had just been dropped from being suspended three inches above the ground.

"It's better," Diego said.

"I saw that accident happen," Kari continued. "It was terrifying. I couldn't believe that that rider bumped you so hard and they barely called a foul."

"Ridiculous," said Diego. Anger briefly flashed in his eyes. "But anyway. These things happen," he said.

"Is it a very dangerous game? asked Ashley.

"Obviously," he responded. "Why do you think I play it?" He gave her a smile that hit her straight in the solar plexus and slowly made its way down her body, giving her chills. As she met his eyes, shocked, he gave her a discreet wink. Oh. He *was* a player. He knew exactly what kind of effect he was having on her. And why *did* he have such an effect on her? Yes, he was devastatingly good looking. But there were a lot of good-looking guys on this earth. She was being ridiculous. This was one of the first guys she'd laid eyes on since Robert. She couldn't go falling for the first guy she saw, could she?

"Listen, it was lovely meeting you, Ashley. I have to go. There is some business I need to attend to," Diego said. "I'll see you around."

He leaned in to brush her cheek with his lips and she felt an electric jolt course through her body, and wetness start between her legs. She watched him leave, feeling more and more chilled the further he got.

"I'm warning you," said Kari.

But it was much too late for warnings.

Chapter 16

I had to go on an emergency errand, said the note taped to the medicine cabinet.

Ashley wondered where Kari was off to. She knew that this meant she was expected to take over, to prove herself. In fact, maybe Kari had made up this excuse just to see how Ashley would do if thrown into the deep end. Ashley felt like, after a few days, she already had a good handle on how the barn worked. It wasn't rocket science. But she was a little mortified at the possibility of running into Diego without Kari for backup after their first run-in at the cocktail party a few nights prior. She hadn't seen him since, which was probably a good thing, but she couldn't stop thinking about him. Those green eyes of his. The perfect chestnut brown of his tousled hair, and the way he ran his hands through it. For a second, she imagined those hands on her body, and shuddered.

God. She needed to stop working herself up like this. She quickly stepped in the shower and rinsed off, knowing that she would need a more thorough cleaning later, and also not trusting what she would do if she spent more time under the steamy water thinking of Diego.

After the shower, she found herself choosing her clothes a little bit more carefully than usual. *Stop it*, she thought. She made herself breakfast, including a big cup of coffee. She was still little bleary eyed from drinks the night before. People in Santa Barbara sure did have a big drinking habit. It was something that she had not been used to, living in Montana, despite the fact that Robert drank a 6-pack of beer at least every night.

Still daydreaming about her new Latin dream man, Ashley walked over to the stables and got to work. She was pretty much on autopilot. Even though they were in one of the most expensive ZIP codes in the country, shoveling shit was shoveling shit. She patted the horses on the nose, already developing her favorites, and enjoyed the smells of the barn, which reminded her of the good parts of home. Again, she worried about her horses, and wondered about her mom. She hadn't heard back from Craig and Sissy yet, but hopefully today would be the day when Craig would have time to go and check.

She wondered what Robert was doing right now. Was he still looking for her? Was there anyone else he'd tried to harass into telling him where she was? There was no way he could have guessed that she'd hitched a ride, but then again, how else would she have done it? Well, even if he figured out a piece of it, there was no way he could figure out what she had done next. Even if he tracked her to the bus station, he wouldn't know exactly which buses she had taken, unless he had found Kim and had tortured her. He wasn't that bad, though, was he? *Was he?* He would have no idea which direction she had even taken. There was no way… unless she'd mentioned Montecito and Santa Barbara to him before, or unless Sissy had.

Ashley was picking up some hay with a pitchfork when she heard someone clearing their throat behind her. Her heart leapt into her throat. Was it Diego? She spun around, a half-smile already playing on her lips, but some embarrassment coming back to her as she remembered how her body had responded to him.

But it wasn't Diego. It was a stranger, or at least someone she hadn't met yet. Red hair. A strong jaw. Reasonably good looking, not exactly her type, but there was something about him- something confident.

"Hi," she said. "I'm so sorry if I seemed shocked- I wasn't expecting anyone. Are you looking for Kari?"

The stranger smiled at her, blue eyes twinkling. He did have very nice eyes, Ashley noticed.

"Uh, no, I actually was waiting for one of my friends to show me a horse."

Oh. Was the friend Diego? Never mind, she was being ridiculous. *Be professional, Ashley.*

"Maybe I can direct you to the right place- who is your friend?"

"Alan Greenwood?"

"Oh yeah, Alan," said Ashley. She could see Alan in her mind's eye. She had met him at the cocktail party. Tall guy, a little heavyset. Dark hair. Popular with the ladies, but he was no Diego.

"I haven't seen Alan yet today. Maybe check in with Alex in the office?"

She hoped she wouldn't have to lead this stranger to the office. She had a feeling Alex was a little annoyed with her after she had asked him a million questions as she signed the NDA a couple days prior. It seemed like a document that could put her at risk, but she'd ended up signing it, under duress.

"Thank you," said the stranger, still standing there, smiling expectantly, like he was waiting for Ashley to say something else.

"I'm Ashley, by the way."

"Nice to meet you, Ashley."

There was something about the way he spoke. It wasn't quite What Ashley was used to. An accent, maybe? She couldn't exactly tell. She wasn't really exposed to very many regional accents in Montana.

"And you are?" Ashley asked.

The man's eyebrows raised briefly. And a half smile played on his lips.

"You don't know my name?" he asked.

Ashley laughed. He was so awkward. Was this his attempt at conversation?

"Maybe you think I'm somebody else. We've never met."

Again, the man looked at her in surprise.

"You seriously don't know who I am?"

Ugh. Now he was getting weird. Ashley didn't have time for this.

"Listen. I promise we have never met. I would have remembered. I'm not from around here, and I just got here."

"Where are you from?" asked the stranger.

He still hadn't told her his name. No matter. She was going to need to get rid of him so she could get some work done.

"Middle of nowhere in Montana," she said.

Shit. She had forgotten to say Inland Empire. Her heart started hammering in her chest. What if this was someone that Robert had sent? Was that why he thought she should know who he was?

"Did Robert send you?" she asked panicked.

"No, he smiled. I'm waiting for Alan, not Robert."

If this stranger knew Alan, and he was talking about horses, he hadn't been sent by Robert. She was being crazy now.

"Sorry, I just was confused for a minute," she said. "So you said your name was…?"

The man hesitated for a second. Then two.

"What, you're not going to tell me your name? I told you mine!"

Finally, he smiled.

"Ah, it's …Henry," he said.

"Henry, there you go. See, that was easy," said Ashley. "Nice to meet you, Henry."

The man's smile grew broader. He actually was handsome. Not her type, exactly, but possibly a good rebound, potentially. He didn't come off as potentially devastating as Diego.

"Well, Henry," she continued, "I'm pleased to make your acquaintance, and feel free to keep me company while you wait for Alan, but otherwise you can go have a seat in the office or something while I shovel all this wonderful stuff."

"I would love to stay here with you," said Henry. "You're better company than Alex."

"I won't contradict you there," Ashley smiled.

"So, you say you're new here?" Henry asked.

"Brand new," said Ashley. "And really thankful to have this job."

"You've been around horses your whole life?"

"Yes," said Ashley.

She hoped that wasn't too much information, but plenty of people had been around horses their whole life.

"I've been around horses my whole life too," said Henry.

Ashley appreciated that he was trying to make conversation, but she felt a little awkward, and something about Henry's smile and demeanor made her feel a little uncomfortable. What was it about guys around here? They certainly seemed to pay a lot of attention to her. Or maybe she just wasn't used to being around men anymore.

"Do you play polo professionally?" Ashley asked.

Again, Henry looked a little surprised.

"Yeah, sometimes… I play on a polo team here," he said.

"I've only met a few polo players so far," said Ashley. "You weren't at the cocktail party the other day, were you?" she asked.

"No, I wasn't," said Henry. "I…uh…had other engagements."

"Next time. Anyway, it seemed like it was a casual thing, but I met some people you might know. Do you know Diego?"

Even saying the name made her mouth water and her knees buckle. *Pathetic.*

Henry eyebrows slanted down.

"Who doesn't know him? Number one local player and all."

Yes. Ashley kept hearing that. Well, it didn't matter. She shouldn't be looking for a serious relationship anyway.

"You know," said Henry, as if he was suddenly getting the best idea ever, "I would love to take you out sometime. You know, maybe a picnic or something?"

Ashley's heart beat double time for a moment. Well, he wasn't her type, but he was charming. And what was the harm in something like that? Maybe playing it safe with someone like Henry was the key to getting over her ridiculous feelings for Diego.

"Well, sure, that would be lovely. But yes, let's definitely make it something simple."

She didn't want to owe Henry anything, as she might after some fancy date. Did the three-date rule apply in Montecito? She hadn't gone on any kind of date in years.

"We could go to the beach," Henry said.

"That sounds dreamy."

"Great. I'll come up with a plan. Do you work every day?"

"I do, said Ashley, "Except for weekends. But Alex says I can take off for lunch anytime."

"Great. I'll consult my calendar and..."

Just then, Alan stepped into the stall.

"Oh, your..." Alan began, looking flustered.

Henry interrupted him, looking a bit panicked. *How strange.*

"Hi Alan. I was just chatting with Ashley. She's charming. Anyway, let's go talk about that horse."

He started to hustle Alan out of the stall.

"See you later," said Ashley.

"Absolutely," said Henry.

He left, leaving Ashley feeling somewhat confused, like something had happened that she didn't quite understand.

Late that afternoon, when Kari came back to the apartment, she asked Ashley how her morning had gone.

"Oh, it went fine. I met this guy. You know, a redheaded dude? Kinda awkward?"

Kari's eyes grew large.

"Wait- you mean the prince?"

Ashley laughed. When she thought about it, Henry *was* kind of fancy. She wouldn't go so far as to call him a prince, but it was as good a nickname as any. She was about to share this excellent idea with Kari when the phone in Kari's hand rang. Kari gave the phone a quick glance.

"Oh- it's your sister."

Ashley took the phone and swiped the answer button, fully expecting to hear her sister's voice, but instead, it was Craig, breathing hard.

"Craig, is everything OK?" she asked, panicked.

"No, no, it's not," said Craig.

"What? What do you mean?" Ashley's throat constricted.

"Is Sissy OK? Is Momma OK?"

"I went to try to check on your mother. Robert intercepted me. He was waiting in front of her place in his truck, and when I got there, he hopped out and it started to get physical. I ran back to my car. I'm sorry, but I couldn't afford getting beaten up and not being able to care for Sissy. I don't know about your mom- I don't know if he's done anything to her, but I couldn't get to her place. Do you think we should call the police?"

Ashley's throat constricted. This, too, was all her fault, wasn't it? Robert would never have gone to bother Momma or do anything like that if she hadn't run away. And as the daughter, she should be the one calling the police, but she just couldn't bring herself to do it.

"Craig, I'm so sorry that I put you in that position. Are you guys OK? He hasn't come to your house, has he?"

"No, not yet," said Craig.

"Craig, please call the police. And please don't tell them where I am."

Craig was silent. She could imagine him pinching his thin lips.

"I'm so sorry. I didn't want to bring you guys into this. I didn't know."

"It's OK. I'm going to call the police now. I'll keep you posted."

"Craig, I think it's time for you to erase Kari's number from Sissy's phone."

"OK. Done. I'm even wiping the call log... Will you..."

Just then, Ashley heard a crash on the other end of the line. "Wait, Craig, what's happening?" Ashley screamed, eyes wide. "Is that Robert? Is he there?"

Kari snatched the phone from Ashley and hung up.

"Wha...Why did you do that? Something is going on over there!"

"Craig's gonna be fine. He's gonna stand up for himself. You can't let Robert know where you are."

Suddenly, the phone started ringing again. Ashley looked at the screen.

"It's Craig. Pick up!"

Kari shook her head.

"If it's Craig, he'll leave a message. If it's not Craig, well then, who knows?"

Ashley stared at the phone as it rang and rang, its ringtone falsely joyous- some song that she'd never heard, but that she knew was probably something that had been popular at some point recently. Every musical note jangled her nerves a little bit more.

"Ashley, I need you to calm down. I need you to breathe. There's nothing you can do from here."

"What if he's hurting them?"

"You can't do anything about it."

"We need to call the police," said Ashley.

"Yeah, well, we're not calling them from my phone, or yours," said Kari. "Wait, I'll be right back."

Kari ran out the door and came back with one of the stable hands, a kind man from El Salvador that Ashley had met and chatted with a few times.

"Antonio, you have a flip phone with a card, right?"

"Yes, ma'am, said Antonio," his face worried, evidently wondering if he was in trouble for something.

"Can I borrow it?"

"But ma'am, I'm not doing anything wrong with the phone," said Antonio.

"I know- I need to make an important phone call. I'll buy your next card for you."

Apparently, according to Kari, using one of the old phones with a phone card made it harder to trace the number and the location. A *burner phone*, she'd called it.

Kari used her phone to look up the police station number near Sissy's house while Ashley texted her Sissy's address with trembling hands. Kari made the call.

"Yes, hi…Is this the police? I'm calling to report some kind of domestic disturbance at 321 Orchard Lane. I don't know what's happening, but I've heard all sorts of yelling and crashing… No, I'm sorry, I would like to refrain from giving my name. Please come quick. Thank you."

As Kari hung up the phone, Antonio gave her a disbelieving look.

"You called the police from my phone?"

"Don't worry, I called the police halfway across the country. Nothing is gonna happen to you. I'll get you a new card and you'll be fine. And stop dealing drugs, dude," said Kari.

Antonio scowled and Ashley opened her eyes wide. Antonio dealt drugs? She hadn't known that she was hanging out with criminals in the barn.

"Oh Ashley, you've got a lot to learn," said Kari. "Most drugs are legal here anyway, but Antonio needs to stop trying to supplement his income that way. He gets paid enough at the polo fields."

"Speak for yourself," said Antonio. "Do you know how hard it is to provide for your family here? This whole place is full of stinking rich people who don't even know how it is."

"Well, he does have a point," said Kari. "Thank you, Antonio. And I'm so sorry, but we needed to do this. I'll drop off your card later. Promise."

As Antonio skulked away, Ashley's heart was still beating out of control. Had Robert done something to her mother? Had he hurt Craig now too, and her sister? It was horrifying. Not being able to know, not being able to reach them. She thought about the old times, when people would have to write letters to find out what had happened to loved ones. She supposed that this was a little bit better, but it was still complicated and horrible. What would she do if something had happened to Momma? She just couldn't forgive herself. It was all her fault. She driven Robert to this. But she had to survive. And to survive, she had to leave.

She noticed that her head was now thumping, flashing lights in front of her eyes.

"Are you OK?" Kari asked.

"I think I'm getting a migraine," she said.

It happened when she was stressed, which lately, was a lot of the time. She just needed to lie down in the dark for a bit.

Kari told her she would deal with the chores.

"You go lie down. If you're feeling up to it later, we'll go out. If not, I'll cook for you."

"You're my guardian angel," said Ashley.

She got to the apartment, wet a washcloth, and took it with her to the room, where she lay down and closed her eyes, putting the washcloth over them. Before she knew it, she was fast asleep.

Chapter 17

Ashley never did wake up for dinner. The next day, she got up and found Kari already at the breakfast table. There were two plates with eggs on them, and two coffee cups.

"You made me breakfast, said Ashley. "To what do I owe the honor?"

"I discussed it with Alex- this is my official last day," said Kari.

"Wait- already? I thought you had a week to go?"

Ashley was anxious to do the work on her own and sad to see her friend leave, but also, she was worried about what would happen to her living situation.

"You've done such a great job- how lucky for me that I was able to bring them somebody like you to replace me. Alex thinks you have it under control. And, well, I'm kind of nervous about starting in the new place, but excited too. I think there's a lot of potential for me. And they're thrilled I can start earlier than planned. We're going to celebrate tonight, that's for sure, and have a good time working together on our last day, right?"

"Right." said Ashley.

Her head was spinning, and she wasn't sure if it was the remnants of the migraine, or panic.

As they were working in the stables, they'd been silent for a moment, when Kari cleared her throat.

"I just need to talk to you about the guy you were telling me about yesterday," she said.

Ashley rolled her eyes.

"Honestly, it was nothing. It was just some guy coming in looking to talk to someone about a horse. No big deal. He flirted with me a little bit and I seriously do not think he will be back."

"He flirted with you? Really?" asked Kari, a look of surprise and doubt on her face.

"Wow. Thanks for the surprised expression. I'm not a supermodel like you, but I'm not that disgusting," laughed Ashley.

"No it's not that. Stop it, you're gorgeous. But you're sure he was flirting? Not just being friendly?"

"Listen, I know I'm naïve and everything, and yeah, he was flirting. Damn, I must really be a bridge troll. He even invited me for a picnic on the beach," said Ashley.

Kari's expression changed from disbelief to delight.

"Wow. And you don't know who he is?"

Ashley sighed.

"Kari- how the hell am I supposed to know who he is? I just moved here."

Ashley could see that Kari was trying to contain hysterical laughter. She didn't know what was so damn funny.

"Well, I want all the gossip if anything happens between you and Harry."

"Henry," Ashley corrected. "And you told me no one gossips in Montecito, remember? Besides, I signed a NDA," said Ashley.

"I don't count," said Kari. "I'm your family friend. You're allowed to gossip with me."

"Got it," Ashley laughed. "Anyway, I don't think anything will happen. He'll probably ghost me, and anyway, I'm not that attracted to gingers."

By now, Kari was giggling uncontrollably. Ashley wondered if she'd bought something from Antonio the stable hand. Since she was in such a good mood, it was probably the best time to broach the subject of her living arrangements.

"So Kari… how much time do I have left in your place? I'm gonna need to find a place to stay, and I haven't made enough money yet."

"Oh- as a favor to me, they're letting you stay there for another two weeks," said Kari.

"Two weeks? That's amazing!"

"That's not a lot of time, I'm telling you. Don't underestimate how hard it is to find a place to stay here. You can always stay with me on the sofa or something in my new place, but I don't have that much space, and if Steve is home, it's gonna get too cozy real fast," said Kari.

"You've done so much for me already," said Ashley. "I would never…"

"Never say never. I'll keep asking around for you, and you ask around, too."

"Will do," said Ashley.

After yesterday, the panic of worrying whether Robert was going to show up at any moment had just begun to subside. But she still needed to call Craig and Sissy and her mother somehow. That burner phone thing was probably the solution, but she needed another paycheck before she could afford one. And Kari was right, the issue of where to live was still a problem, just barely deferred. Worst case scenario, maybe she would move into student housing in Goleta. Ashley smiled to herself, imagining herself pretending to be a college coed. She felt like such an old lady. She let out a giggle.

"What are you laughing about," Kari asked.

"I was thinking about pretending to be a college student and moving to Isla Vista, but then I thought how old I am."

"Well, you don't look like an old lady," said Kari. "I see how all the guys around here look at you. They all seem to think that you look like the tastiest donut they've ever seen."

"A donut?" Ashley laughed.

"I don't know. I couldn't think of anything else, off the cuff. But donuts are delicious. Especially the glazed ones," said Kari.

"I used to lick all the glaze off of Krispy Kreme donuts," Ashley laughed.

"I rest my case," said Kari, poking Ashley in the ribs with her elbow.

"I'm gonna miss you," Ashley said, growing serious.

"I'll be seeing you all the time. We'll be going out at night picking up dudes at local bars."

"Picking up dudes. You're hilarious. You're married."

"Barely," Kari said.

"Oh shut up, Steve's away on a business trip. He's coming right back."

"Oh shoot. You're right. I keep forgetting," said Kari with a wicked grin on her face, her dark brown eyes sparkling. Steve was a lucky man.

"I'll have to settle on living vicariously through my single friend, then, so don't forget to gimme any salacious details as they develop," said Kari.

Kari noticed that Ashley's expression had darkened.

"What?"

"Nothing, just wondering why Craig didn't leave a message yesterday. And whether we can call the police back and ask what's going on."

"For now, I just want you to assume that everything is fine," said Kari.

"And my mom?"

"Your mom is just not picking up the phone for some perfectly good reason."

"And the fact that Robert was in front of my mom's house?"

"Granted, that not awesome at all, but not conclusive. Maybe she wanted him to come to help her with something."

Ashley considered that. Yes, Robert had mentioned her mother harassing him to fix the hot water heater. Her mother was in enough denial to think Robert was just fine, after all.

"Here's the thing," said Kari. "It's not gonna help anyone to have you worried like this. You're gonna make yourself sick, like yesterday. You didn't go to all the effort of getting away only to ruin it because you gave yourself away by being reactive and impatient."

Kari had a point.

They walked into the beautiful stables, Ashley taking everything in with renewed appreciation. Soon, this was going to be her exclusive domain. She would almost be the boss of this place. Well, Alex was going to be the real boss, but he was barely ever there. Ashley and Kari had pretty much been calling the shots as to how the horses got treated and how they were taken care of, how things were organized. Ashley wondered if, now that the polo season was going to be over, maybe she could institute some kids' programs or something. Maybe it would be something that would bring in more money. She had heard rumors that the Polo Club needed more cash and had thought she had gleaned that there was someone trying to raise money to make the club have a higher level, trying to bring in some VIPs to raise awareness about polo and to make the club more exclusive. But she hadn't really been able to get any more information. Every time someone said VIP, other people would raise their eyebrows disapprovingly. And she recognized it for what it was, their damn reluctance to gossip, or the NDA everyone had signed. She wondered who this special VIP was who was supposed to raise up this Polo Club. She certainly hadn't seen anyone like that around.

Speaking of people who were never around, she wondered about Henry- whether he would come back to set their picnic date, or whether he'd just been talking a big game. She wouldn't mind going for a picnic. Especially as she knew that, once Kari was gone, even if it was just a few minutes away, things were going to get a little bit lonelier around there, at least during the daytime.

Kari had lent her a bicycle. It would be a nice way to see more parts of town. But she would soon need a car, and more people to do things with. For a split second, she allowed herself to think of Diego- she would love for him to show her around- but considering his bad reputation, maybe it was better for her to steer clear.

Kari had run off on a last-minute errand, and Ashley was coming down the aisle carrying a saddle she needed to put away, when she saw two silhouettes outside. The bright light behind them made it so that she couldn't quite see who it was, but it looked like two men, both of them long limbed and well built. She wanted to mind her business, but she also was very curious. Maybe she would see this mysterious VIP person at last. Maybe one of the people was Diego. She put away the saddle and started to make her way over to see if she could offer to help whoever it was. *It's not just curiosity*, she reasoned with herself. After all, she was meant to be responsible for this place, and maybe these people wanted something.

As she came closer, she recognized Henry and Diego. Her heart did a flip.

"Oh, hi," she said. "Nice to see both of you."

Diego looked at her strangely.

"You've met...?"

"Yes, said Henry quickly. We have met. She's so wonderful. She seems to be very good at her job." He turned to Ashley. "And you've met Diego, I see. Well, I suppose that you'd better be going, Diego. Just remember what I told you."

Diego gave Henry a look, his eyes tight. It didn't look like they had been talking about something very pleasant before she came up.

"I'll just stay here and have a chat with Ashley," said Henry. "Actually," said Diego, "This whole thing was your idea, so why don't you go talk to Alex, and I'll chat with Ashley."

Ashley had pivoted, looking at one and then the other. This was bizarre. And acutely uncomfortable.

"Actually, I have some work to do," she said. "I'll see you both at some point later, I guess."

Ashley backed away and retreated around the corner, breathing hard. *What the hell?* This was very weird. What were they fighting about? It had nothing to do with her- so why did it feel guilty? After a few moments, she had composed herself, and now heard a shuffling step coming towards her. Who could it be? She didn't even know who she hoped it would be. The best option, she decided, would be Kari coming to rescue her. But no, it was Henry. She saw his thatch of red hair right away.

"Hi, sorry about that unpleasantness earlier," he said.

Again, she was struck by how strange his way of speaking was. She'd never heard anyone talking that way. Diego also had some kind of accent. Maybe this was just a thing about California.

"You know Diego, he's very difficult to get along with," Henry was saying. "I'm trying to tell him things for his own good and he just won't listen, you know?"

Ashley flinched when Henry mentioned people who wouldn't listen, because that was one of the accusations that Robert threw in her face all the time, that she just didn't listen, and then he would shake her or grab her wrists. But then, just as she started to panic, Henry smiled. It was a smile so disarming, with his short but straight teeth and jovial expression and sparkling eyes, that it brought her back from the edge.

"I wanted to talk to you about that picnic you mentioned. I think it's a great idea," he said.

"Well, that's funny, you trying to make me think that it was my idea. Next thing I know, you're going to try to say that I asked you out," said Ashley.

"You certainly did ask me out," said Henry. "I thought it was quite bold, in fact."

"Absolutely not," said Ashley. "You said you wanted to take me out, and I maybe said that a picnic could be nice. Completely different."

"OK, so it was mutual," said Henry.

Ashley smiled. This banter was fun. She hadn't experienced anything like this in a very, very long time.

"So, when you were thinking about taking me out for a picnic, where did you think you would take me?" asked Ashley.

"Well," said Henry. "Though it was originally your idea, I guess I ran with it. I was thinking I could take you to a beach I know. There's a quiet part of the beach off of Padaro Lane where we would be on our own, with only the pelicans and the sea lions for company."

"How about dolphins?"

"And dolphins," Henry agreed.

"Sounds heavenly," said Ashley.

She could see it already in her mind.

"So, what are you packing in the picnic for me?" she asked.

"Huh," said Henry. "Since you invited me, I thought you were going to do that."

"Oops that's awkward. I thought you were. I really do like gourmet food," she joked.

"You deserve nothing but the best," said Henry, growing more serious. "I shall prepare you a princely buffet. Leave it to me. I'll make sure I have some Champagne and some delicious finger sandwiches. How does that sound?"

"Well, certainly not with real fingers in them, but otherwise it sounds great," said Ashley.

She giggled at how old-fashioned he was sounding. He was playing a role like someone from one of those Shakespeare plays she had seen sometimes on TV or during a class trip, and it was fun to joke around like this. She would be happy with peanut butter and jelly sandwiches, and she was pretty sure that this was what this Henry character would come up with, but it didn't matter.

"So, when are you taking me for the picnic?" she asked.

"How's tomorrow?" he responded.

So soon. She was surprised.

"Sure! That sounds great. I'll make sure that I've finished all my chores in the morning."

"See you here at noon?" asked Henry.

Ashley thought for a moment- Alex usually was gone around that time, but there were plenty of other stable hands who could deal with any emergencies. Alex had never mentioned anything about being gone at the same time as him.

"I'll see you tomorrow," said Henry.

"Wait, maybe I should have your number in case something comes up and I need to cancel on you or something," said Ashley.

"No, I'll just come back. If you're not there, I'll figure it out," said Henry.

"OK," said Ashley.

It was a little funny that, now that she had a phone, the first guy who wanted to take her out wasn't going to give her his number. Maybe she'd been a little forward asking for his number like that. But he was the one taking her out after all, and she didn't feel comfortable giving anyone her number except for Kari and Alex, so it was probably for the best.

Chapter 18

That night, Ashley found herself alone for the first time since she'd arrived. Kari had gone to the airport to pick up her husband and take him on a date, and Ashley acutely felt the solitude. It was funny, because she had been alone a lot in her marriage, but in Montana, it didn't feel like she was missing out on anything particularly exciting when she sat there at home. Here, it was different. She wondered what Diego was doing. Maybe he was at the Polo Club bar, having a drink? Alex had mentioned that there was a happy hour on Thursdays. Going to check it out wouldn't hurt. It couldn't be any closer to her temporary home. But a girl heading to a bar alone, was that scandalous? In California, it was probably OK, Ashley reasoned with herself. Finally, feeling very much not like herself, she ran a hand through her hair to fluff it, checked herself in the mirror, deciding to slick on some of the lipstick Kari had given her, and left the apartment, striking out towards the Polo Club bar.

She couldn't tell right away if there was anyone in there who looked familiar. Maybe that weird Englishman, Lionel, or whatever his name was, was there. It would at least be someone to talk to. Lionel seemed like he had no problem talking to anyone. Ashley found herself hoping that Henry wasn't there- first of all, the awkwardness of his exchange with Diego was still fresh in her mind, and secondly, she was going to see him the next day, and he might think she was stalking him.

She noticed two blonde women in a corner high top table near the window, chit chatting over glasses of Champagne, still illuminated by the pre-sunset light. A man and a woman who seemed to be married were at another table. And that was it. Oh well, it had been worth a try. Maybe if she stood at the bar for long enough, the bartender would feel bad for her and would strike up a conversation, even though he looked not much more than high school aged. She would just have a quick drink and then go about her boring evening in front of Kari's TV. It was funny how she hadn't had anything to drink in ten years, and now, it was becoming a daily habit that she should probably keep an eye on. She cast a discreet glance at the two women. They looked a lot fancier than she did, so chances were that they didn't think she was their kind. She stood at the bar waiting for the bartender to stop wiping down the counter.

"Hey, Ashley, right?" he said.

"How did you know it was me?"

"Well, I've heard descriptions." said the bartender.

"Really? Average height, average build, dirty blonde hair?" asked Ashley. "Who knew that was so rare in Montecito?"

"Yeah, that's not it," said the bartender, winking at her. "My name's Pete, by the way."

"Pleased to meet you, Pete," said Ashley. "I'll have a glass of rosé, if you have any."

"Sure thing. Margerum OK?"

Ashley nodded and watched as Pete filled her glass- a generous pour, she noticed. She took a grateful sip, risking a look back at the women. Someone had joined their party, or at least was standing by their high-top table. It took her eyes a while to adjust to the glare from the window. And then she recognized the figure. Diego. Of course, he would be flirting with the blonde women. All of a sudden, Diego noticed her. He locked eyes with her, said a few more words to the women, and then headed straight across the room. Ashley struggled to keep her breathing under control.

"Ashley, you're here. I would have called you to show you around, but now I'm seeing that maybe you're occupied with a certain royal pain in my ass."

"Are you referring to …"

"Obviously," said Diego, without letting her finish.

"Yeah, he's been trying to talk to me. He does seem like a safer option than you."

"What?" Diego spat.

Ashley peered at him. Why did it feel like they were having two different conversations? She would have given anything for the light banter she had with Henry…but of course, to have that banter with Diego.

"Well, you have a reputation, apparently," said Ashley.

"Interesting. Who told you that? asked Diego.

"Honestly? Pretty much everyone."

Diego seemed to simmer down at this.

"All right, well, in that case, would you be willing to have a glass with a man with a bad reputation? If he asked you nicely?"

He smiled at her, eyes sparkling. He really was so handsome.

"Sure, I guess I'll condescend to it."

"Thank you, my lady, so generous of you," he smiled.

Diego gestured to the bartender.

"Gin and tonic, please, with Hendricks, Pete."

"As if you need to specify," said the bartender, smiling.

"I just wanted Ashley here to know my usual in case she ever decides she wants to buy me a drink," Diego said.

"Really? You're a one-drink man?" said Ashley. "That's funny. That sounds like it's not part of your character."

"Hilarious," said Diego. "So, tell me, how's it been at work now that Kari is at her new job?"

"I don't know- it's only been a day, but I can already tell that, with her husband back in town, I'm gonna need to find some new friends."

"You could find a boyfriend, said Diego. Unless you've already found one."

"I've not already found one- why do you say that?" asked Ashley, indignant. "Anyway, I don't know if I'm ready for a relationship."

"Is that so?" asked Diego.

Well, she was probably lying to herself. If Diego asked her out, she'd have to use every shred to resolve to refuse him. But refuse him, she must. A guy with a bad reputation was not what she needed for her first relationship after Robert.

"I'll stop trying to flirt with you then," said Diego. "Tell me more about where you're from."

"You know, just a small town in the middle of nowhere," said Ashley. Nowhere exciting. There's not much to tell."

"I'm sure there's more to it than that," said Diego.

What was that supposed to mean? Ashley started to panic.

"I'm sorry, I hope you don't think I'm prying," said Diego. "I just think you're so amazing with the horses. Surely there's some story about how you got so good with them."

"Oh, that," said Ashley. "Yes, I've always been with horses. I had my own business, and I was almost thinking that maybe I could start a program here with the kids and teaching them horseback riding skills of some kind."

"That sounds like an amazing idea, something to consider. There are two different schools of thought on how this club should be run, though," said Diego.

"Yeah, I hear that you guys have some VIP that you want to have help raise this club's reputation and everything, but I also see that none of you want to say who it is, so…"

"Come on," said Diego. "It's beyond obvious that you know who it is."

Ashley was going to respond, but clamped her lips shut. No, it wasn't obvious to her. Diego might have been ridiculously hot, but he also infuriated her. Why couldn't he just speak simply?

"Forget it," she said. "Tell me more about you, and how you started playing polo. It just seems like a unique thing to get into," said Ashley. "Is it a family thing for you?"

"As a matter of fact, it is," said Diego. "My whole family plays—my uncles, my grandfather, my father, my brothers. It is a family affair, that's for sure. We started playing in Argentina and then, I had a little bit of a disagreement with some of them and, well, I came here to make my own way."

"Wow. And what brought you here?"

"I thought I saw an opportunity. It's not always easy, but I think I've made the right decision. Normally I'd be back in Argentina and Miami right now. But with my injury, and everything else going on, I think I'm just going to stay put and train those horses. So, if you decide to talk to Alex and he is OK with that program, I could help you with it."

Ashley smiled a broad smile. Now he was being the way she had hoped he would be.

"I would love that. How can you help? You seem like you would be good with kids," she ventured.

Diego smiled, but strangely, Ashley saw sadness behind it.

"You're saying that because I'm like a big kid myself, right? Immature?"

Ashley didn't think he seemed immature at all. There was something about him. She looked down at his hands, so capable, imagined them holding the reins as a little kid rode a pony, but then soon, she moved on to imagining those hands all over her body. God, she had to stop thinking like that. She was really desperate. She *would* have to find somebody. Someone to just have a quick fling with, to get these thoughts out of her mind. It would be awkward working with someone and having these dirty thoughts about them constantly. It was distracting- granted, in a delicious way, but she couldn't afford to do this.

"So, do you have someone in your life? Or at least someone you date kind of regularly? Or are you truly just playing the field like they say?" asked Ashley.

"I had someone. Back home. It's over, but it's complicated," said Diego.

"All right, say no more," said Ashley. "You keep some secrets from me, and that way, I can keep my own secrets too."

"Sounds fair enough," said Diego, smiling. "But listen." He turned more serious. "I just want you to know that if you need anything, I'm here for you."

Ashley gulped. She did need something. She needed something that was between his legs. She caught herself glancing down at Diego's jeans, focusing in on the bulge there. She snapped her eyes back up, but it was too late. Diego looked her right in the eye, grinning. It was like he was reading her mind. Her filthy, filthy mind.

"Well, I did say if you needed *anything*," he smiled.

"I don't know what you're talking about," Ashley said.

But she knew that he knew that she knew.

She'd been so faithful to Robert for all these years, first out of love, then out of fear, and now it was like her body was waiting for just one thing, especially when she found herself around Diego. Maybe somebody like Henry, someone who she liked well enough and thought was reasonably attractive but wasn't so crazy about, might be a good way of getting everything out of her system so she could actually work with people like a normal human being. She couldn't afford to lose this job, and if Diego was around the Polo

Club all the time, there was no way she could allow herself to do what she wanted to do.

"Well, I think I better go turn in," said Ashley a bit brusquely. "I have an early morning."

"All right," said Diego. "Do you want me to walk you back to your apartment?"

"It's only a few steps away," said Ashley.

"Still, I'm a gentleman. I'd like to walk you there."

"All right, be my guest," Ashley said. "But I'm not letting you in."

She was dying to let him in.

"Understood," said Diego.

He walked her out, putting his hand on the small of her back. Oh, how she wanted that hand to move down further to cover her ass through her jeans. Or under her jeans. To go between her legs. She felt herself starting to arch her back a little bit as she walked. *God, I'm worse than a cat in heat,* she thought. She wondered what it would be like- what Diego would do if she suddenly turned towards him and faced him. What would it be like to have him kissing her neck, her lips? To have him grabbing her hair in his fist, just like she'd imagined his hand holding the bridle just a few moments ago.

Calm down, Ashley, she thought. And anyway, tomorrow, she had that picnic with Henry, and she needed to just get her chores done, and have a nice, civilized picnic and stop thinking about her co-workers that way.

"Well, good night," she said, much more lightly than she felt. What wouldn't she have given for a goodnight kiss, knowing that it might turn into something much, much more? It was good that Kari and her husband were coming back to the apartment for one last night. At least it kept her safe from giving in to her impulses for one more day. She would just have to prevent herself from being close to Diego in the future.

"Goodnight, Ashley," he said.

There was something in his voice that made her want him right then right there, but she managed to take a step inside the apartment. Once she closed the door, she stood there for a moment, trying to make her breathing go back to normal. *What in the world?* She hadn't been like this, ever. This was ridiculous.

Kari's voice called out to her from the bedroom, a little breathless.

"Ash? Is that you?"

"Yeah, it's me," said Ashley. "You're back already? I just went for a drink at the club."

"Oh, was there anyone there?"

"Just two blonde women having Champagne, and Diego."

"Oh," said Kari. "Ok."

Usually, Kari would have asked her a million questions, but tonight, Ashley was starting to understand that she had probably interrupted something with her early return.

"Don't mind me," she said. "You guys sleep well."

"Thanks," said Kari. "Goodnight."

Sleep well, my ass, thought Ashley. She wished she had somebody to not sleep with. No surprise, that night, it was almost impossible to go to sleep.

Ashley kept experiencing vivid fantasies. Her body and Diego's, entwined. Them riding together, Diego behind her, cupping her breasts. Diego cornering her in the hay loft, and tipping her over a hay bale, taking her…

Finally, instead of letting herself think about sex, Ashley started counting sheep. She eventually fell asleep.

Chapter 19

Ashley's alarm went off much too early. It was still dark, as far as she could tell, but she needed to be up and out. She carefully selected an outfit. Maybe Diego would stop by and would see her. She wanted to be able to work comfortably, but also look cute, and transition to the beach and picnic with Henry. No bathing suit. It was October, after all. She wondered what Diego would think if he knew she was going to the beach with Henry, but then again, it really was none of his business. They didn't have a relationship, did they? They were nothing to each other, no matter what her body seemed to think. Henry seemed like a simple, nice, single guy. No harm, no foul.

She should bring a sun hat to protect her face, she decided. She looked outside. It was still dark, and a little hazy. Hopefully, things would clear up by the time they got to the beach. Finally satisfied with her simple outfit of denim shirt, jeans, and boots, she threw a sweater over her shoulders and left the apartment.

She'd almost finished her chores when that familiar voice rang out.

"Hello? Ashley?"

"In here," said Ashley.

She was bent over and picking out a horse's hoof, and suddenly became acutely aware of her ass facing the entrance of the stall. She hoped that Henry wouldn't come around the corner and have his first view of her be her rear end. But right then, there was no putting down this horse's hoof, because she would never get it up again. Thistledown was one of her big challenges. Kari had warned her about his stubborn pony, who tended to pick up any rock that happened to be in his vicinity, but made it impossible to pick his hooves.

"I'll be there in a second," Ashley huffed. "I'm just finishing this last hoof."

Then, she heard Henry's voice- much closer. *Damn it*. Now she knew that he was literally looking directly at her ass and nothing else.

"You're looking particularly ravishing today," said Harry, his voice mocking.

"Yeah, thanks," said Ashley. "I know exactly what you're looking at right now, and I am not pleased."

"I'm a practical man," said Henry. "I tend to just appreciate what's there in front of me."

"Very funny. I'll be done in a second. Did you pack a nice picnic lunch for me? I hope it's of the quality to which I'm accustomed," said Ashley, putting on a hoity toity voice, something she would have heard from a TV show in her youth.

"I think it should suit," said Henry.

Finally, Ashley finished picking the hoof and set it down. Thistledown thanked her by shoving her with his nose, throwing her off balance. *Jerk*. Ashley turned around, smoothing her hair and her shirt back down.

"Sorry, I must look a mess."

"You looked pretty good from where I was standing," said Henry.

"Well, I'm ready to go," Ashley said. "I'm looking forward to it. I could do with a little bit of beach time before getting back to work."

"Glad to hear it. I've got my car up front, so let's go," said Henry.

Ashley took one last look around the stables. Everything seemed to be in order. She stepped out into the bright sunshine.

"Oh wait, let me get my hat," she said. She rushed back into the office to grab her hat and noticed that Alex was sitting in the next office over.

"Oh- you're back," she said. "I'm just going for a quick lunch, Alex. I've done most of my chores. I'll be back soon."

"Oh yeah? Who you going with?" asked Alex.

"That's a funny question," said Ashley. "I signed an NDA, remember?"

"Touché" said Alex. "Have fun while I sit here waiting for our VIP. I thought he'd be here by now, but his schedule is his own, I guess."

Ashley felt a pang of regret. She would miss seeing this mysterious VIP yet again. Oh well. She walked back outside, to where Henry was standing, waiting for her.

"My lady," he said, and walked her towards an SUV with tinted windows. It was all blacked out, Ashley noticed. Nobody drove anything like that in Montana, except for maybe drug dealers. And this was fancier than even that.

"Wow, I've never seen a car like this," said Ashley.

"You haven't?" Henry asked, looking confused.

"No, I'm used to pickup trucks and in terms of SUV's, old beat-up Dodges and Chevys. What is this thing? It looks very fancy. Like a limo SUV, I guess."

"You've truly never seen a Range Rover?" asked Henry.

Ashley rolled her eyes.

"Honestly, I lived in the middle of nowhere, in the country. I didn't have TV or magazines or even a phone. And I don't really know cars that well, so no, I don't think I know them."

"You really were that isolated- you weren't joking," mused Henry, a smile playing on his lips.

"I'm not as dumb as you think I am," Ashley protested. "Or as ignorant. I just was in an odd situation."

"No, you're absolutely not stupid, Ashley," said Henry. "Let's go- get ready for a treat. The beach where I'm taking you is stunning. One of my favorites. I can come there, and no one bothers me."

"Well, I should hope nobody would bother you- especially at the beach," said Ashley. "Where I'm from, people value each other's privacy."

"Right," said Henry, his smile getting wider.

"Why are you smiling so big?" asked Ashley.

"I'm just really looking forward to our picnic," said Henry. They rode along, making fun chit chat. Ashley looked in the shiny sideview mirror, enjoying the look of the clouds and palm trees moving by. And then she flinched.

"I don't want to be paranoid, but it looks like there's another dark car like yours that has been following us since we left."

Henry checked the rearview mirror.

"Must be your imagination. Don't worry about it."

"OK, it's just…I watched a bunch of police shows when I was younger, with people tailing people and that's what this looks like. Are you sure you aren't a drug dealer?"

Henry burst into hysterical laughter.

"Drug dealer? You're funny! Pay attention to what's in front of you- it's much more beautiful. Look, we're about to get there. This is it, the Padaro beach parking."

"It's by the train tracks," said Ashley, wrinkling her nose.

"Well, yes, that is one disadvantage of the beaches here, the other disadvantage being the tar, but really, it's not too shabby."

"That remains to be seen," said Ashley.

She almost laughed at herself, pretending that she was used to going to beaches all the time, as if this wasn't literally the second time she'd ever been to a beach in her life. They got out of the car and walked down a path under the railroad tracks. And finally, the vista opened up to the most beautiful sight Ashley had ever seen.

"Wow, you were right. This is stunning," she said.

"Which beach do you like to go to generally?" asked Henry.

"To tell you the truth, this is the second time in my life I've ever been to a beach."

Henry looked at her, shocked.

"But where do you vacation? You don't go to the islands?"

"The islands?"

"You know- the Maldives, the Caribbean, Hawaii…"

"Never. I mean, don't get me wrong- I've heard of those places. I'm not completely uneducated. But I've not been. My parents really didn't have extra money to travel. Until today, I only stuck my toes in the sand once. Today will probably be my first time with my ass touching the sand, which will be perfect logic considering how you found me when you came into the stables."

"You're trying to make me think about your ass now," said Henry. "Wow, I see how you did that. Very crafty."

"Don't mock me," said Ashley. "I absolutely did nothing of the sort. I don't like to be the butt of anyone's jokes, by the way."

Henry cackled delightedly.

"Oh my God, where did that laugh come from? That is frightening," said Ashley. "You know how they say some people have really bizarre laughs? Yours qualifies."

Henry was grinning at her, looking absolutely delighted. Finally, he broke his gaze.

"Let's set up this picnic, shall we? I brought a blanket for that ass of yours. So it doesn't need to touch the sand if it doesn't want to."

"I'll ask it what it wants later," said Ashley, smiling.

She helped Henry to set up the blanket. It was a beautiful blanket, softer than anything that Ashley had ever touched. If she hadn't known any better, she would have said that it was cashmere. She only knew what cashmere was from Grandmama's old sweaters- Grandmama had allegedly been some kind of old money back in the day but had run away- for love. But who would bring a cashmere blanket to the beach? The blanket had the letter H all over it.

"Wow, H for Henry? I've never known guys to monogram their blankets," Ashley remarked.

"No," Henry smiled. "It just worked out that way."

"If you say so, but I'm starting to wonder what kind of guy has monogrammed cashmere beach blankets."

"The kind of guy that I am, I suppose," said Henry.

Ashley helped him to bring various items out of a picnic basket, as well as a bottle of Champagne and two flutes.

"Wow, I literally thought you were joking about the Champagne."

"Why would I joke about the Champagne?" asked Henry. "I wouldn't promise Champagne and then not bring it."

"Well, that's very noble of you," said Ashley. "Thank you."

Henry gave her an odd look, which she ignored. She looked at the food he'd set out. Little tea sandwiches- egg salad, salmon, and cucumber and cream cheese, perhaps.

"Wow, this looks very fancy," Ashley remarked.

"Oh, it's nothing," Henry shrugged. "I just had the chef prepare it."

"You're funny. Is the chef's name Henry?"

"No, it's..." Henry hesitated. "Oh, you got me, yes... it is Henry. You're a wise one."

They sat on the blanket, Ashley happily munching at the sandwiches. It was fun and easy to hang out with Henry. He didn't have too terribly much of substance to say, but he was good at banter, and it just felt comfortable sitting there with a man who was elegant, and handsome enough, and gentle.

"So, tell me, Henry, what do you do?"

"You mean for a living?" asked Henry, looking at her strangely again. *What's wrong with him?* Then she realized.

"I'm sorry. My grandmama would have said that's a rude question," said Ashley. "I'm not trying to find out anything crazy about you. I just was wondering, like… what you're interested in, if you don't want to tell me what your job is…*Are* you one of those people who thinks it's rude to ask people what they do?" Ashley asked. "I can tell you what I do. I work in the barn, and it's fun. I like working with horses… so you can answer that way too, you know."

Henry smiled.

"It's just that no one has ever asked me what I do."

"What? That's crazy."

"Well… I guess you could say that I'm a consultant right now. I'm kind of… in between jobs, I guess you would say. But I've got a few prospects…"

"Well, that was suitably vague," said Ashley. "I guess I set myself up for it. But tell me- what do you *like* to do? You mentioned that you've spent time around horses."

"Yes, I love that," said Henry. "And, well I used to be in the military."

"Oh, wow. Afghanistan?"

"Yes, that's right," said Henry. "How did you know?"

"Well, I know a bunch of people who were deployed to Afghanistan, so it was just a lucky guess."

"Oh. And, well, I like dogs. And kids."

"Are you planning on having any kids?" Ashley asked. "I mean, I'm not asking about me or anything, I'm just asking about kids."

"Yes, I wouldn't mind having kids. Maybe two kids, a boy and a girl."

"Yeah, that sounds pretty ideal," said Ashley, trying not to think about whether she would ever be able to have kids of her own. "And do you live near the Polo Club?"

"Well," said Henry, "it's a little complicated... I live.. kind of close to the Polo Club... or I'm supposed to, and then I'm moving. Or maybe I moved..."

"Seriously, you're a hard man to pin down," said Ashley.

"My situation is in flux," said Henry.

"OK, you clearly don't want to talk about it," said Ashley. "And that's fine. I'm not trying to pry at all, Mr. sometime consultant in between jobs, maybe living nearby. You're lucky that I don't know how to use Google, because I'd be able to know everything about you if I wanted to."

"Lots of people don't really use Google," said Henry, looking troubled.

"I pretty much think I'm the only one on Earth. But I was in a situation and, well, I didn't have a phone and, well, I don't really want to talk about it," said Ashley. "So now we're even."

"Let's just enjoy ourselves, shall we?" said Henry.

He lay back on the cashmere blanket, but Ashley started focusing on two suspicious men in dark clothes who seemed to have followed them, from the car that had been tailing them.

"Henry, I swear. Those guys followed us. I know you think I'm being paranoid but believe me."

"I would never say you're being paranoid- I get it," said Henry. He looked over at the men. "But I'm telling you, from my military experience, I can tell you, this is nothing."

He pointed, and sure enough, one of the guys was disrobing, getting ready to swim. Just an innocent person enjoying the beach, after all.

Ashley breathed a sigh of relief and went back to enjoying the company and this gorgeous autumn day.

"So this is what they're talking about when they say endless summer," said Ashley. "Back where I'm from, it's freezing cold already."

"You said you were from the Dakotas or something like that, right?"

"Yes, that's right," Ashley lied, feeling guilty, but also feeling that it was justified. She couldn't trust every stranger she came across, even if this one looked innocent. Even with the slight amount of reddish scruff on his face, he looked clean cut, like he'd been raised by the right kind of people, at least. But he also had a little cheekiness to him, which didn't displease her. Henry poured her a glass.

"I can't believe you actually brought Champagne to the beach," Ashley laughed. "I mean, I've literally never been to the beach, and also, I've literally never had Champagne, I think."

"You've never had Champagne?" asked Henry.

"I've always imagined it. How it would taste. The color. The bubbles. When I first got to Santa Barbara, I decided the light was made of Champagne."

"I like that," said Henry. "The bubbles are the best part. If you've never had Champagne, I guess you've never tried kissing someone while drinking Champagne?" he asked, looking her straight in the eye.

Ashley blushed. Yeah, she could see that Henry was attractive. Having fallen as hard for Diego as she had, it was hard to look at anyone else. But she needed to snap herself out of that. Diego was an obvious ladies' man, whereas nobody had said anything bad about Henry… yet.

"I've never done that," Ashley smiled. "I'm sure my ex-husband tried to do that with beer, but I'll bet it's not the same."

"You were married?" asked Henry.

"Yes," said Ashley, not mentioning that she was still very much married, and wondering how she was going to manage to remediate that situation.

"So… what ended the relationship?" asked Henry. "Or is that an indiscreet question?"

"He didn't treat me right," she said. "So… I literally ran away."

In her mind's eye, she saw Robert's hands squeezing her arm. She saw the bruises, felt the pain constricting her throat when he wrapped his hands around it. Saw his hand raised, the horse rearing up, and Sissy falling...

"I'm so sorry. I really don't want to talk about it. We're having such a nice time," she said. "How about you?"

Again, Henry gave her that funny look. Then he seemed to reconsider.

"What about me? You mean relationships? Suffice it to say that it's complicated. I …uh, my family is pretty controlling and, well, I did meet someone, and they didn't like her, and they thought that she was wrong for me …I begged to differ at the time, and let's just say that they probably had a point."

"Oh," said Ashley. "I'm sorry to hear that. Why didn't they approve of her?"

"My family is really… traditional. They just like things done a certain way. And I met her, and I thought that she was my way out. I thought it was my opportunity to finally be independent and be an adult. But then, I realized she was just trying to isolate me from everyone."

"Wow, that sounds intense," said Ashley. "How did you end it?" she asked.

Henry squeezed his eyes shut.

"As you said, we're having such a nice time. Let's not talk about the past. Here, do you want to try some foie gras?"

"Foie gras?" Ashley tested the foreign word on her tongue. "What in the world is that?"

"It's fatty goose liver… i No, I swear it doesn't taste as disgusting as it sounds. It actually is quite delicious."

"I'll taste a little bit, but I can't promise you I'll like it," said Ashley. Henry spread a little bit of the foie gras onto a French toast crisp and handed it to her. She popped it in her mouth. It was like butter.

"Oh man, this is delicious. Tell me it's got no calories."

"I can't tell you that," laughed Henry.

"I might wanna eat this every day," said Ashley.

"Except, it's illegal in California."

"Well, then, how'd you get your hands on it?" asked Ashley.

"I have my ways," said Henry. "I know, I feel terrible. I'm supposed to be such an environmentalist. That's what everybody wants for me, and I just can't help myself."

"Well, for an environmentalist, you sure have a big car," said Ashley.

"Yeah, that I do," said Henry. "And you don't know the half of it. I was trying to be more environmentally conscious and, well, my wife, she always wanted us to go on the private jet, things like that."

Ashley almost spit out her mouthful of Champagne.

"Private jet? You've been on a private jet before?"

Henry gave her a strange look.

"I mean, just once. Just once. Not many times. Maybe a couple. But it's nothing special, you know. Once you've been on one, you've been on them all."

Ashley laughed.

"Well, I've not been on a single one, so I guess I'll take your word for it."

Ashley would have pressed him further, but the Champagne was doing its job, and she felt giddy. Giddy and bubbly. The golden sunlight felt like Champagne bubbles again, doing that gentle popping on her arms thing again, the image even more apt now that she knew what it actually tasted like and felt like on her tongue. It was getting warm out.

"Are you getting warm?" she asked Henry.

"I am," he smiled. "Why? Do you fancy a swim?"

"I didn't bring a bathing suit," she said, dejected.

"I won't tell if you don't tell," Henry said, smiling.

He was more charming than she'd given him credit for at first.

"I mean, there's no one on the beach, right?" she asked. "Those guys over there, they're probably together or something. They don't seem to be paying much attention to us."

"That's right," Henry said.

"My bra and panties are black anyway. It kind of looks like a bathing suit, right?" Ashley asked.

"Black? That sounds a little naughty," Henry responded.

"Not really," Ashley laughed. "It's just what I could find at Target."

"Last one in is a rotten egg," said Ashley.

Henry laughed, starting to peel off his shirt. Ashley did the same. As Henry kicked off his trousers, Ashley noticed that his boxer shorts were had a Union Jack design.

"You've got the British flag on your boxers? That's hilarious. Is that where your accent is from?"

Henry nodded, focusing on getting his jeans past his ankles. "Well, those boxers aren't the most discreet thing if you don't want people to know that you're wearing underwear when you're swimming."

"There's no one here," Henry smiled.

He was right. They got up and ran to the water. The sea was calm, less choppy than it had been the previous time Ashley had been. It was a deliriously beautiful day. She noticed pelicans, or at least, she thought, that's what they were, bobbing on the surface. And then noticed a glossy little head, just fifty or so yards away from them.

"Oh look, do you see that? Is that a seal?" Ashley asked.

"Looks like it."

"So cute. They don't bite, do they?" Ashley asked.

"I hope not. We'll keep to ourselves, and it'll keep to itself."

Ashley laughed, dipping one toe into the water. It was cool, but not uncomfortably cold. It would feel good after sitting in the sun and that heavy lunch. It would also clear her head from the bubbles of the Champagne. She did need to go back to work, after all. She hoped her underwear would have time to dry. Or maybe she'd have to go commando. She blushed as she thought of it. Henry dove and swam underwater for a few seconds, and then bobbed up. He turned around, shaking the water out of his russet hair. Ashley noticed a spray of freckles on his shoulders. Not her type, but he did have some kind of charm she couldn't quite put her finger on.

"Are you coming in, rotten egg?" he asked.

She waded in further. She hadn't grown up by the ocean, but she had swum in her share of swimming holes and had taken swim lessons at the Y as a child. It still felt foreign, but the ocean water was buoyant. The bottom was a bit rocky. She wondered if there were lobsters in here, or crabs. What kind of fish were here? She looked around, suddenly not sure that there weren't any sharks.

"Come over here, said Henry.

"I found a flat rock to stand on. If you're tired, I can hold you up."

"All right, Ashley said, taking a deep breath and swimming over. Henry grabbed her arm as she came closer. At first, she had a moment of panic as she remembered Robert squeezing her arms like that, but then she relaxed. Henry wasn't the same, he was just grabbing her to keep her from having to swim. He pulled her closer. His skin felt warm despite the iciness of the water.

"Hey," she said, surprised, as her body came to drift against his.

"Hey," he responded, his voice gruff.

Unexpectedly, Ashley felt a throbbing between her legs. Henry wasn't her type, but there was something about him, and something kind of sexy about being in that sea water together, their two slick bodies against each other. Henry pulled her in closer to him. Now their bodies were glued together. Instinctively, she wrapped her legs around him, and then blushed.

"Sorry," she said, and disentangled her legs.

"Don't be sorry. I like it."

Henry put his hands on her bottom, positioning her so that she could feel the hard lump in his boxers between her legs, rubbing her. It felt pretty good, she had to admit. She suddenly saw Diego's face in her mind and froze for a second. *No.* She was stupid. Henry would be a perfect antidote to Diego. They couldn't be more different. Henry stroked Ashley's back and she arched it, sending her breasts closer to his face. He dipped his head down and kissed one of her breasts, moving the fabric of her bra aside to suck on one of her nipples. She felt her insides clench, heat between her legs. She started to rub herself against his hard length, and he groaned.

"We shouldn't do this," Ashley finally said, with difficulty.

"Why not? No one's around," moaned Henry, his hands cupping her ass, positioning her so that the thin fabric of her underwear and of his boxers was the only thing between them. A flash of Diego's hands came into her mind, imaging them on her. It excited her. She started to writhe, and then caught a glimpse of Henry's face. *Shit.* Not Diego.

Snapping out of her trance, Ashley noticed the two men, still on the beach.

"Those two guys are still there," she said. "I don't like it."

"They're fine. They're not going to do anything," Henry responded, sounding a little frustrated.

"Oh yeah. How do you know? Are they friends of yours or something? I feel like they followed us here."

Panic was creeping back into Ashley, supplanting the lust that had almost taken her over, almost driven her to do something she might regret.

"But we're having such a good time," said Henry.

It almost came out as a whine.

"I know we were," Ashley responded, all business now. "Can I take a rain check? We were having a good time, but I need to get back to work, and I'm not the kind of girl who does this on the first date."

"Oh, so you're calling it a date?" said Henry.

"I don't know," said Ashley. "I mean, we've got this picnic basket and Champagne and foie gras. How could it not be a date?"

"You're right. So, in this country, after how many dates does a man get lucky?" Henry asked.

"Well, that's a bit formulaic," said Ashley. "But in the US, technically, it's usually the third date."

"Well, I've seen you in the stables twice before," said Henry, winking, trying to pull her close again, but the moment had passed.

"Very funny," she responded. "Those aren't dates. This was a date…maybe."

Would she really? Would she so quickly find somebody else to be with after Robert? She wondered if that was the kind of person she was, now. And how could she do this while still thinking about Diego? But Diego didn't think anything about her, did he? In fact, right now he was probably off romping with some other woman or doing something that certainly didn't involve thinking about her in any way.

"We'd better go back," said Ashley. "I'm freezing." Now that she didn't have Henry's throbbing manhood pressing between her legs, she didn't have anything to keep her warm. To make matters worse, the sun had gone behind a cloud.

"All right," said Henry, regretfully. "But I'll make sure that next time, there aren't any meddlers to make you feel that we're being watched," he smiled.

"Sure. I don't know how you could possibly ensure that," Ashley laughed.

They waded back to shore. They didn't have any towels. Ashley stood there, shivering a bit, hoping to dry off somewhat.

"Here, you can wipe off on my blanket," said Henry.

"Are you kidding me? I'm sure it's a gazillion dollars," she said.

"I can buy another," said Henry.

"What did you say you did again?" Ashley laughed, wrapping herself in the deliciously soft blanket. "Are you sure you aren't some kind of celebrity or something?"

'Well, I do have a book coming out," Henry said.

"Wow. I never knew anyone who wrote a book," said Ashley. "I wanted to at some point, but then, you know, life took over and I didn't. And then some of my friends talked about writing books, but then I thought that's something that you get to do when you're retired or something."

They got dressed. Ashley decided to keep her underwear on, even though it was still damp.

"Alex is gonna kill me," she said. "I told him I was going to lunch, but I didn't tell him for how long."

"He'll be fine," said Henry. "In fact, I'm late for a meeting with him, too."

"Don't tell him you were with me," Ashley said.

"As long as you don't tell him I was with you," Henry responded.

She laughed at first, but then realized, was Henry embarrassed to be seen with her? The stable girl? Was that what it was? He was probably wealthy or something, granted, but did that make him so much better?

"Yeah, don't worry, your secret's safe with me," she said. "You can drop me off at the entrance to the Polo Club and no one will be the wiser, how's that?"

"Great," said Henry.

By this point, the mood had been completely killed. Ashley pulled her damp hair into a bun and turned away from Henry. They walked back to the car in silence. The two men on the beach had disappeared just before them, but she wondered if they were looking lurking somewhere nearby. She and Henry didn't speak as they rode the short distance back to the Polo Club.

"Just drop me off here," said Ashley. "Thanks for the picnic."

"You're welcome," said Henry.

Ashley hopped out of Henry's car and headed into the stables. She grabbed herself a big glass of water. She was so thirsty, and still a little bit buzzed. Even though her last exchange with Henry had knocked out a lot of the drunkenness. As she walked past Alex's office, he called her in. She hoped Henry wasn't already in there.

"Hey Ashley. Wow, that was a long lunch break. Did you literally just come back?"

"I did. I hope that's OK. I decided to go for a swim," she said. "It's such a beautiful day."

"Yeah, totally fine," he said. "You should ask me next time- I'd love to go skinny dipping with you."

"Ha, ha," said Ashley. "That's inappropriate."

For a second, she imagined what Alex would be like in the water. Would he press her to him? *Gross.* Alex wasn't unattractive, but he was older and he definitely one hundred percent wasn't her type. And of course, here came the unbidden image of Diego, doing to her the things that Henry had. She shuddered.

"Sorry. You're right, I'm an old dog," said Alex.

"Apology accepted. I'm gonna get all my chores done, even if I have to stay late," said Ashley.

"Oh, I totally wasn't worried about that," said Alex. "You've been doing a great job. You're a joy to work with. I was just going to ask you- I'm sorry that you have to be out of that place in two weeks. Have you found another place to stay?"

Ashley sighed. It had just been a couple days of looking, but so far, everything was so expensive. She just didn't know how she could possibly find anything, especially not knowing many people in town.

"It's hard," Ashley said.

"Well, I was gonna tell you- I have a place," said Alex.

Ashley narrowed her eyes.

"Seriously? This isn't going to lead to one of your gross dad jokes, is it?"

"I'm serious. I have a garage apartment that has just come up. You can rent it."

"Thanks. I'll think about it," said Ashley. She wasn't sure if this was a great idea. She'd have to ask Kari what she thought about it.

"Well, don't think too long," said Alex. "Things in this price range don't come up every day."

"Can you tell me more about it?"

"Yeah, it's the guest apartment over my garage. It's super independent, it has its own kitchenette and bathroom, and it wouldn't be that expensive. Just 1500 a month."

Ashley shuddered. $1500 a month? That was more than a luxury house rental where she'd grown up. And this was for a studio? But at least she was making OK money now, and she could afford it. She wouldn't have much left over, but that was probably the cheapest place she'd heard of so far. She just wondered if it was a good idea to live so close to Alex, with his reputation and the warnings Kari had given her.

"Well, I'd love to come and take a look at it," she said, cautiously.

"Sure thing," said Alex, "why don't you come over tonight after work? I'll wait for you, and you can follow me."

"I still don't have a car," Ashley said.

"All right. You drive a hard bargain. I'll drive you and I'll take you back. How's that?"

"Alright, I really appreciate it," Ashley responded.

Later that afternoon, as she was working on mucking out one of the stalls, her phone rang. *Sissy*, she thought for a moment. But of course, it wasn't. Sissy and Craig didn't have her number, and she was going to try to call them tonight. It was Kari.

Kari told her about the new job, and that she was going to pick up the last of her stuff from the apartment.

"How about you?" asked Kari. "How are you doing? Is Alex being OK with you?"

"Yeah, he is. In fact, he offered for me to rent his garage apartment," said Ashley. "Do you think that's gonna be iffy?"

"He has a garage apartment? Why did he never offer it to me?" Kari snapped. Ashley was taken aback. Was she jealous?

"Then again, I guess I had the stable apartments," Kari allowed. But he could have offered it rather than let me leave."

"He said it just became free," said Ashley. "He said he'll drive me over there and back."

"Do you want me to come with you, so you have a chaperone?" asked Kari.

"I would love that," said Ashley. "It would make me feel a lot better, I think."

They solidified their plan and wrapped up the call. Not for the first time, Ashley was overcome by how kind people had been to her here. Yes, some people had been a bit weird, but most had been willing to give their time, energy, and care to her. It was helping to renew her faith in humanity. One day, when she'd earned enough money, she would pay for Momma, Sissy, and Craig to come stay with her here in California. Her mom always hated winters, and she'd be so happy to be where the skies were always blue and sunny. But that dream would have to wait. For now, she didn't even have a car. Who was she trying to kid? It was going to take a long time to build the kind of capital she needed to be truly independent.

She hung up with Kari and went back to work. At one point, she heard a crack behind her. A step, or something hitting against the wall. She jumped. Back when she'd been living with Robert, every little sound was cause for alarm. Every time he would come home, she would listen intently for the tell-tale signs that he was approaching to complain about the quality of the work she'd done, or coming to yell at her about something, or threaten her, or worse. She whipped around, and her face fell into a huge smile. It was Diego, standing there against the stable door. His white jeans looked like they were custom made for him. He wore a light blue polo shirt that set off the dark gold of his arms. His eyes flashed green. Damn, he was handsome. Her swim with Henry had been thrilling, but it was nothing compared to this. *Stop it*, she told herself. Diego was a ladies' man. And a crucial part of her new life was not falling in love with some guy who would hurt her.

"Hey, Diego," she said, trying to clear the tremble from her voice.

"Hello beautiful," he said back. "I came looking for you around lunchtime. I wanted to take you out, but Alex told me you'd gone."

Ashley blushed.

"Ah yeah, what else did he say?"

"He just told me you were out. Is there something I should know?"

Ashley was glad she hadn't told Alex who she was out with. Henry was probably right. It seemed like these people, even though they pretended that they didn't like to gossip, in reality really did.

"I just went for a swim," she said. "It was a beautiful day."

"I could have given you a ride," Diego said.

"It was fine- It's such a gorgeous day."

She felt bad lying to Diego. But then again, she didn't owe him anything.

"Where would you have taken me if you'd taken me out for lunch?" she asked, to make conversation.

"Anywhere you wanted," he said. "Or I could have taken you to one of my favorite little places that serves delicious empanadas, and we could have gone on a bluff I know, where we could have looked down at the ocean."

It sounded dreamy. Ashley didn't even need any Champagne if she was going to be sitting next to Diego. She remembered the way he'd smelled last time he'd come close to her. He was delicious.

"Would you be OK if I asked you out one day?" he asked. "I mean, I don't know if you have someone or if you're pining away for someone back home, or if you're just not into dating right now, but I would love to take you out… it doesn't even have to be a date. We could be friends," he said with a devastating smile that told her that no, no they could not be friends.

She couldn't trust herself to be alone anywhere with him. She'd never felt this before in her life.

"Yeah, why don't you come up with a fun plan and you can ask me, and I'll see if I say yes," she said coyly.

She didn't want to shut him down completely, but she knew she should be careful to protect her fragile heart. She heard another step.

"Oh, there you are."

It was Alex.

"Is Diego bothering you, Ashley?" he asked. "I swear, this guy is always after the ladies, aren't you, Diego?"

Diego scowled.

"Here I am, you found me, Alex. OK, let's go talk about that horse," he said. "Ashley, I'll see you soon."

Diego winked at her, and she gulped. She went back to work, her head spinning. She'd been married to Robert for so many years, had been with no one else, and then, all of a sudden, she had these two, maybe even three men circling around her. Alex wasn't even in the running, but he seemed to be at least jogging after her, that was for sure. Would she say yes if Diego asked her out? What would it be like? Where would they go and how would she keep her hands off him? She didn't want to get hurt. She'd gotten hurt so many times before, when it wasn't her fault, and now, knowing that he was a womanizer, she was going to throw herself into his arms? It was idiotic.

She stabbed the ground with a pitchfork, trying to clear her head by exhausting herself physically. When she had a wheelbarrow full of dirty hay, she wheeled it outside to dump it on the manure pile. Such a glamorous job she had, though the pretty horses and the eye candy certainly were worth it. She checked her watch. It was almost quitting time. She hadn't told Alex that Kari was going to accompany them, and now she found herself reassured that she was. Sure enough, she heard a car door slam, and saw Kari coming towards the stables, looking even more like a supermodel than ever. Kari was the whole package. Stunning, kind, and knowledgeable with horses. Kari had explained to her how her ancestors were the original Buffalo Soldiers- cavalry in the Civil War who impressed the local Native Americans with their riding prowess and bravery and with the unique texture of their hair- like buffalo pelts. After the Civil War, her forefathers had stayed out west and had become cowboys.

Ashley watched as Alex came out and said a few words to Kari. Kari's whole body seemed to stiffen, and then she veered off towards Ashley.

"Hey," said Ashley when she was within earshot. "How are you doing? You look stressed out."

"Oh, it's nothing. It's just fucking Alex. He can't help himself," she said. "Let's go see this place. If the price is right, I guess you'll take it, but make sure there's a lock on the door."

Ashley nodded. She didn't just want a lock on the door for Alex, she wanted it in case Robert showed up. Not that a lock would help. Robert would have a lock shot out in seconds.

"Is Alex ready to show us his place?"

"He said in a couple minutes."

"Perfect," said Ashley. "I have to put away these last things and then I'm set."

Kari followed her into the stables, looking around appreciatively.

"Man, you're making me look bad. This place looks spotless." Ashley smiled, pleased.

"You know, if you're going to do it, you might as well do it right."

"Still, I don't know how you managed to do all of this. You're like a machine."

"Believe it or not, I even took a lunch break," said Ashley proudly.

"You did?" asked Kari.

"I went to the beach, and I went for a swim."

She was going to say, *with Henry*, but she froze. Kari was looking at her with her eyes narrowed.

"Oh, did you go by yourself?"

"I… yeah, I did," said Ashley.

"Oh, OK," said Kari.

"Yeah, it was great swimming. I saw a seal and some pelicans, I think, and I got some tar on my feet. So, I guess I'm a local now, right?"

"Yeah," said Kari, smiling. More relaxed now.

"So, have you been getting hit on by any more of the guys around here?" she asked.

"No, not really," said Ashley. "I mean, I saw Diego. And that's it. He didn't say much to me," she lied.

"OK, good," said Kari. "Just make sure to separate your work and your personal life- that's the best policy, you know what I mean?"

"Yeah, absolutely," said Ashley, wondering how the hell she could separate her life and her work life, considering that she didn't have a life, and that she lived right where she worked. She didn't have much of a choice there. Kari went back outside while she wrapped up. Once everything was put away, Ashley closed the stable doors behind her. Alex was coming out of his office at the same time.

"OK, you ready to come look at it?" Alex looked around, making sure they were alone. "I wish you hadn't told Kari about it," he said.

Alarm bells started to go off in Ashley's head.

"Why not?"

"Well, because I never offered it to her," said Alex. "So she might have an issue with it. Especially since maybe she wouldn't have gone off and gotten that other job if I had offered this to her when the stable apartments stopped being available."

"Oh," said Ashley. She was relieved. This seemed to be aligned with what Kari had said. "Well, why didn't you?"

"Maybe it's just a personality thing," said Alex. "Kari and I have a weird history. Don't read anything sinister into it."

Ashley's head swiveled around. She was worried Kari might come any minute. But she needed to say this.

"You know it's not OK if you try to pick me up, right?" she asked Alex.

"I would never," said Alex. "I've got a dirty mouth and a dirty imagination, and I've made mistakes, but I've learned my lesson. I know the limits now. Some people, however, don't. You should be very careful."

"I am being careful," said Ashley.

"Yeah, right," said Alex.

"What is that supposed to mean?"

"You've been hanging around with the…"

Just then, Kari strode into the stables.

"What's going on? What are you guys talking about?" She asked, brusquely. "You both look guilty as hell."

"Nothing," said Alex. "Just telling her off because she didn't put away the hoof pick."

"Bullshit. Seems like everything is perfect around here," said Kari. "You're being a hard ass."

As they headed outside, Alex gave Ashley a look and held his finger to his lips. She looked away. Ashley and Kari got into Kari's car and followed Alex's pickup as he took a left out of the polo fields and took another left up what quickly turned into a country lane.

"I'm gonna need to get a car," said Ashley. "Do you know anyone who's selling a cheap car that I can get?"

"Yeah, all those spoiled students over at UCSB can probably sell you a car," said. Kari, "I'll ask around. But usually, if you go around Goleta, those kids are trading up from the already fancy car mommy and daddy gave them, to a brand-new BMW or something."

Ashley laughed. She'd read somewhere long ago that BMWs were fancy yuppie cars with asshole drivers, but the whole idea of having luxury cars was so far removed from her experience to date.

"Say, Kari, have you heard of a Range Rover? Is that an expensive car?" she asked.

"Only one of the most expensive ones," said Kari. "Why do you ask?"

"Oh, nothing," said Ashley. "I thought I saw one and I was just wondering. I mean, it looked pretty nice."

"Yeah, even used, you won't be getting one of those, honey. But let me get you set up with the student listings and we'll find you something that runs, at least."

"Thank you. Your help means so much to me," said Ashley. "Now what are we going to do about Sissy? I can't go back there to check, but I can't just let it lie. I haven't heard from my mother at all for almost 2 weeks. And Sissy, now, for a couple of days. Can I call back, do you think?"

"I don't want you calling them too much from your number, and I can't very well call them from my number. You know what? We'll ask Alex if he can call Sissy's number once we're at his place. How's that?" said Kari.

Chapter 20

They pulled off the main road and onto a narrower country lane with stone walls on either side. There were giant wrought iron gates for some of the properties, and Ashley gaped at them.

"Can you imagine what it would be like being so rich that you lived behind those gates? What do these people do all day?" she asked Kari.

"They hide," said Kari. "They do everything behind those gates, and then once in a while, they emerge and go to a benefit or something. All I know is, other than polo and a few charity benefits, you almost never see those people. I think they have homes all over the place."

"Imagine…" said Ashley. "I can't even imagine having one home at this point. I really hope that this place works out for me."

"I hope so too," said Kari. "I'm still a little bit shocked that he never offered it to me."

Was Kari jealous? Ashley wasn't sure. She'd been so helpful to her; she didn't want to think badly of her. But she would have to be careful just in case. They finally took another right turn and headed down a driveway. Alex got out of his car to unlatch a more modest gate, but it was still impressive to Ashley's eyes. He hopped back in his truck, and they proceeded down the drive. They pulled over at a garage that was two stories tall. It looked kind of like one of the outbuildings back at the farm, Ashley thought. In Montana, you could build anything you wanted, pretty much, as long as nobody could see it from the road. She had a feeling that wasn't the case here in Montecito.

"OK, it's now or never," said Kari. "I hope it looks good."

"Me too," said Ashley.

"I'm surprised, places like these usually run more around $4000," said Kari, the bitterness sneaking into her voice again.

They emerged from the car and followed Alex towards the building and up the stairs.

"OK, so it's not much to look at," said Alex. "But it is what it is."

He opened the door into a space that looked like a rec room from the 1970's. There was orange velour everywhere, and brown furniture, and reading lamps with fringed shades flanking the bed. Ashley laughed out loud.

"Yeah, I know it's pretty bad," said Alex.

But Ashley wasn't laughing because it was amusing, though it was, but also because she was relieved. There was no way he could charge a lot of money for this. He wasn't being slimy or doing her some huge favor, for which she would owe him forever. She looked again, taking in more of the details. There was plush brown carpeting, and orange velvet cushions on a little avocado loveseat in the corner.

"Wow, Alex. You could make money renting this place out for movies, if anyone's making a movie set in the seventies featuring people with the worst taste ever," Kari sneered.

But Ashley didn't care. There was enough light, and enough space for Ashley to do whatever she wanted, enough space for her to start a new life. Hope started to swell in her heart. Would this actually work out?

"So, there's a little kitchenette," said Alex. "Not a full kitchen, and I really don't want anyone cooking up here too much. But you can make salads and coffee and such, and then there's a little bathroom."

Ashley popped her head into the bathroom, took in the molded fiberglass shower and the vinyl tile. She'd seen a few of these bathrooms as a kid, at her friends' houses. But still, none in the past two decades.

"How much did you say it was again?" she asked. She had done the math, and $1500 would truly leave her with almost nothing.

"Yeah, I've been thinking about what I told you- it's my fault that you're paid what you are- so what do you say to $1000, but you need to keep it clean and maybe do a little yard work around to compensate?"

Ashley made a quick calculation in her head.

"That'll work as long as you take it off my paycheck before you pay me, that way I'm not paying after taxes," she said.

Alex's eyes grew large.

"Wow, somebody is business savvy," he said.

"No way. I skipped home economics and didn't finish college," said Ashley.

"Oh, I bet you met somebody, and got your MRS degree instead of your bachelors' degree," said Alex leering. "Well, where is he now?"

"He died," said Kari. "It's a sensitive subject. Stop asking."

Ashley gave her a look. Kari shot her a look back. But Kari had a point. This way, she didn't have to speak about Robert at all. Nobody would dare ask about him again if she said he was dead. She caught herself almost wishing he was. She looked around the apartment again.

"I'll take it," she said.

The first thing she imagined as she said the words and thought about moving in was bringing Diego here. Rolling around with him on that hideous orange coverlet. Diego would make even this place sexy. Then she thought of Henry. Henry would clash with the orange, she decided. She repressed a giggle.

"What's so funny?" asked Kari.

"Nothing, nothing. So it's a deal?" she asked Alex. "Do I need to sign something, another NDA or something, or do we shake on it?"

"This is strictly a friendly contract. This isn't something that I would advertise. After you leave me, I'm going to charge a fortune for this place. I mean, as Kari said, it's authentic 70's details- that must count for something."

"Agreed," said Ashley.

Alex wasn't as bad as she'd initially thought, she decided.

"Hey Alex, can I ask you for another favor? I mean, this is already huge. And by the way, when can I move in, move in?"

"Whenever, girl."

"Well, OK, as soon as I find a car," she said.

"Go check out those rich kids over in Isla Vista. They're always trading up," said Alex.

"That's what I told Ashley, and she just couldn't believe it," said Kari.

"Yeah, welcome to rich people land," said Alex. "So what's the favor, if it's not a free car?"

"Well, do you have a free car?" asked Ashley, smiling.

"Don't push your luck," said Alex.

"OK, can I borrow your phone? I need to call my sister."

"Oh, she's mad at you, and you think she's not picking up because she knows your number? You chicks are all crazy."

"Yeah, something like that," said Kari. "Can you just let her call her sister?"

Alex handed over his phone and Ashley dialed her sister's familiar number. The phone rang and rang and rang. Dread settled in her heart. What the hell was going on? She couldn't keep going this long without news. Sissy had never gone so long without telling her how she was, or keeping in touch. Why weren't they picking up? She checked her watch. 5:45 Pacific time. It was one hour ahead in Montana. Craig should have been home by now. They should have been almost done with dinner, maybe already watching TV. She cursed the fact that she didn't have Craig's cell phone number memorized. She envisioned it in her little red address book, back in the kitchen drawer by the now non-working phone at the farm. Voicemail picked up, and she clicked the phone off.

"You're not going to leave a message?" asked Alex.

"No," said Ashley.

"Wow, she must be really pissed at you," Alex whistled.

"Can I try one more number?"

"Sure," he said.

Ashley dialed her mother's number. Same result. No answer. She hung up.

"I better go," said Ashley. "Thank you for the place. I can't wait to move in."

"I'll see you tomorrow at work- I'll give you the keys then," said Alex. "You girls can let yourselves out. By the way, just pull the gate closed- it's never locked- just wind that chain around to keep out idiot trespassers."

They said their goodbyes, and Ashley got back into the car with Kari. Kari's normally full lips were drawn in a thin line.

"Kari, I hope you're not mad that he offered me his place and that..."

"It's fine," said Kari. "It's not your fault. Maybe it's just a timing thing. Anyway, my situation right now is pretty sweet. I don't have anything to complain about."

"Thank you," said Ashley. "Really, you've done so much for me, and I've done nothing in return, and I promise I'm going to start paying you back soon."

"It's my pleasure," said Kari.

But Ashley thought she detected a little chill in her voice. She hoped that she was imagining it. Kari was her only friend here. She should really start settling in, she thought. Maybe meeting a few other people so that she wasn't so dependent on her. It was probably a burden for Kari.

"Well, do you want to grab a bite before you go back home?" she asked Kari.

"I think I'm going to go do some errands," said Kari. "I hope you don't mind. I can drop you off at the Honor Bar if you don't want to go back to the stables right away. You can Uber home, or I can always swing back by and pick you up if you're done early."

"OK," said Ashley, hesitating.

She didn't have anything to eat at home. And she didn't want to be alone. Sitting there at the Honor Bar and people watching would be a great distraction. And also, she wanted to celebrate having found a place, ugly as it might be, with a glass of local rosé. Kari stopped at the stop sign and Ashley hopped out of her truck, heading towards the now familiar yellow parasols.

She briefly considered sitting outside by the fireplace, but the marine layer had come in, and it was a little misty. *Whatever happened to endless summer?* she thought. Ashley walked into the dim space of the Honor Bar. Inside was dark and welcoming, and in the dim light, everyone looked impossibly glamorous, despite the fact that this was supposedly a casual spot. The bartender gave her a broad smile as she sat down at an empty seat at the bar.

"What'll you have?"

"I'll have a glass of your local rosé," said Ashley.

"Sure thing."

The bartender opened the bottle, poured her a generous glass, and pushed it towards her, along the glossy wood bar.

"Do you want a food menu?"

"I'll just have some French fries," said Ashley.

She was craving comfort food, and this seemed like the best, cheapest bet. She sat there happily, taking a sip of her drink, and as the fries arrived, she tucked in, discreetly looking around, trying to determine the stories of the people around her. There were two beautiful blonde women at the bar, a little older than she, giving her nasty looks. Were they the two from the other night at the Polo Club? Hard to tell some of these women apart. She didn't know why they whispered to each other, and she noted how their clothes fit, how they were different from what she had on. Ashley noted that maybe she should improve the way she dressed to fit in a little bit better. Maybe that's why they were looking at her- she still had on her barn clothes. Maybe that was not appropriate in this spot. She looked over at a couple. The woman was throwing her head back and laughing, putting her arm on the man's arm. He was much older than she was, and Ashley saw the tight lines around the woman eyes, the determination in her expression. This woman, Ashley decided, was desperate to find a wealthy boyfriend, and she was trying much too hard with the man in question. Ashley felt that maybe this man maybe wasn't as rich as the woman believed, either. People were funny. Ashley hadn't seen very much in Montana, but maybe she'd learned a lot about human nature from watching the animals, and also from being treated so badly by Robert. All that time of self-reflection, and all that solitude had probably made her more sensitive than most. There was a man sitting alone at the bar, a few seats from her. A bit rotund, with a slightly receding hairline. A little ruddy in the face, he was hunched over and nursing a drink that looked like a Coca-Cola. As if he felt Ashley looking at him, he turned to face her. She gave him a quick smile and went to look away, but he gave her a broad grin.

"Are you alone?" he asked. "Mind if I come sit with you? It's nice to have company while one is having one drink."

"Sure," said Ashley after the briefest of hesitations. The man seemed harmless, and she couldn't afford to be rude to people in her new hometown, could she? They were in a public bar with the bartender right there. It should be fine.

"Have a seat," she said, patting the empty stool next to hers.

"I'm Jim," said the man.

"Ashley," said Ashley.

"You're not a local, are you?" asked Jim.

"It's that obvious, huh?"

"Not really," said Jim. "I just thought I knew everyone in town."

Ashley smiled a big smile.

"Everyone? What are you, the mayor?"

Jim smiled.

"Something like that. Where are you from, by the way?"

"Middle of nowhere," said Ashley. "Where are you from?"

"Here. But originally? I'll be a tick less vague than you- Eastern seaboard."

"It doesn't seem like anyone is from here," Ashley remarked.

"You're right- they always say back east and down South, but why back East?"

Ashley considered this.

"I mean, everything is pretty much east from here, so I guess it makes sense."

Jim looked at her.

"Well shit. that actually does make sense. So what brings you here, Ashley? I mean, I know it's a rude question to ask up front, but what do you do? I ask because you seem like you have an interesting life story, certainly atypical."

"You're very perspicacious," said Ashley, tempted to look towards the exit, contemplating escape. She was silly. It couldn't hurt to tell this harmless man where she worked.

"I work at the polo fields," she said.

"Oh wow, very cool job," said Jim. "What do you do, train horses or something?"

"Ah, I basically just, you know, do what needs to be done. I'm mucking around, not very glamorous," said Ashley. "But I like it. It's familiar to me. I'm good with horses."

"I guess one of the perks is those hot polo players, isn't it?" said Jim.

Ashley started to blush.

"What do you mean?"

"Oh, surely you've noticed all the girls throw themselves at them. They can't stop talking about them," said Jim. "I mean, I would view them as competition, but I guess we're not really in the same league."

"Noted," said Ashley. But now, of course, she was thinking of Diego again, and blushed. All of a sudden, there was a tap on her shoulder.

"May I cut in?"

Ashley's ear tingled as she recognized Diego's voice.

"Speaking of," said Jim, "it looks like one of those hot polo players is hitting on you. Do you want me to protect your chastity and your innocence? I can ward him off if you like."

Diego smiled.

"Jim. I see you found my beautiful Ashley."

"Damn, Diego, is she yours already? You do move fast."

Ashley would have expected a reaction from Diego, but he smiled.

"Ashley, this is my old friend Jim. He and I go way back, don't we, Jim?"

"Yes," said Jim. "Are you going to tell her, or am I?"

"Fine," said Diego. "Jim's the local police chief. He pulls me over all the time for rolling through that stop sign over on Jameson Rd. But I just can't seem to stop there, Chief. It makes no sense. Over time, we've become friends."

Ashley sputtered.

"You're the police chief?" she asked Jim.

"Yeah, I know. I'm too handsome to be police chief, right?"

Ashley smiled. She liked this Jim. She thought he was quite amusing. And he might come in useful, if Robert ever got the terrible idea to come find her.

"Diego, I didn't know you were such a troublemaker," said Ashley.

"Yes, he's very dangerous," said Jim. "But basically, we've become friends because, I mean, how can you be enemies with this guy, am I right?"

He pointed at Diego, which gave Ashley an excuse to look Diego up and down. She suddenly felt hungry. Or thirsty. Or maybe both.

"Yeah, I guess," she said.

"Well, do you mind if I sit down?" asked Diego.

"No, go right ahead," said Ashley.

Diego sat on the other side of her, his knee pushing against her thigh. Accidentally, maybe- or maybe not. Ashley started to sweat. Started to imagine the things that she'd thought about when she'd been visiting the apartment.

"So how was your day? Did you do anything good?" Diego asked. "I think Alex said he was going to show you his place."

"Yeah, he showed it to me. I mean, it's hideous, but the price is right," said Ashley. "So I think I'm going to be moving in there."

"That's great news," said Diego.

"Oh, Alex over at the Polo Field?" asked Jim.

"The very same," said Diego.

"I could tell you some stories about him, too," said Jim. "But I wouldn't want to be indiscreet."

"That's mighty big of you," said Diego.

"Well, I've got to be going," said Jim. "My wife is going to kill me if I don't get home soon."

"It was really nice meeting you," said Ashley.

She had the distinct feeling that she'd met someone who could be a friend to her, someone who would make her feel less lonely in this new place. She couldn't count Diego, who didn't make her feel comfortable, but rather acutely uncomfortable. That knee of his was still against her thigh, but now it was brushing against it, and she couldn't tell him to stop because she didn't want him to.

"It was really nice meeting you," Jim said. "I'm relieved that I once again know everyone in town. Do you hang out here all the time? Will I get to see you again?"

"Of course, you'll get to see me again," Ashley said. "You won't be able to avoid me."

"Hey, let me give you my phone number, in case you need a supercop. Also, I think you'd really like my little lady. Actually, she's not a little lady. She's a little bit of a hard ass. She's an executive at one of those big tech companies over in Goleta. So she's my sugar momma, I guess you would say. But I think you would like her."

Ashley smiled but wondered in what world a big female executive would be friends with her. She hadn't yet achieved very much in her life.

"Anyway, I'm off," said Jim. "Why don't I just call your phone, that way, I'll have your number and you'll have mine, too."

"Sure," said Ashley. She noticed Jim glancing at her phone.

"Wow, you don't have lots of messages, do you?" said Jim, giving her a probing look.

"It's a new phone," said Ashley. "I'm a new convert to the iPhone, never had one before. I'm a country girl, I told you."

"Well, I find that refreshing," said Jim. "I have something like 23,000 messages left unread."

When Jim had gone, the atmosphere became instantly more charged. Ashley was afraid to look at Diego, because how the hell could she look at him without feeling that weird feeling down in her gut, a feeling that would quickly make its way to between her legs, she knew from experience. What the hell was wrong with her? Leaving one bad relationship and throwing herself immediately at the bad boy with a bad reputation? But somehow, she found herself making conversation with Diego. She answered his questions about her mother, and told him how she was worried about her, without explaining exactly why she was worried. And he told her about growing up in Argentina, riding across the pampas, the feeling of freedom that being on a horse gave him. He told her how his dad was tough on him, and how he came from one of the famous families in polo but had to go to the US to make his own way. She found out how he'd been picked up by an American fashion designer who wanted to put him in his campaigns, but he'd refused, because he'd really wanted to just play. He described to her how he came to the country to go to college, and how he'd ended up dropping out after he found someone who trusted him enough to build his first polo team. And then, apparently, everything had gone sideways.

"What happened?" asked Ashley. Maybe this was where the bad boy stuff would come out.

"Well, the guy's wife accused me of hitting on her."

"Oh, so there it is. That's the bad boy coming out. You can tell me the truth now. Did you hit on her?"

Diego looked frustrated.

"Ashley, I know you're not going to believe me when I tell you this, but she hit on me. I just was a young guy trying to do my work."

Ashley must have gotten a funny look on her face, because, well, who could blame anyone for hitting on Diego, but he must have misinterpreted her look for doubt.

"Are you kidding me? I wouldn't have been stupid enough to ruin the good thing I had going on. I was building a polo team at the age of 21. I was wine-ing and dining a bunch of potential sponsors. I was living my dream. I never would have jeopardized that. But she kept coming on to me and…" at this point, he lowered his head. "Maybe a couple times, I was inappropriate, if you want me to be completely honest with you. But come on, I was 21, and as I'm saying, she was really forceful, and eventually, when I wouldn't give in to her, she started spewing out lies. And then, who would they believe? The hot to trot South American guy, or the rich, respectable business owner's wife? I was out on my ass after that and had a few horrible years."

Ashley tried to keep her eyes from welling up as she listened to what had happened next. The brief return to Argentina. Being rejected by his family. The years of hardship, of working at menial jobs, kind of like the one she was working. But for Diego, this somehow sounded worse, because he'd had a bigger dream. In Ashley's case, she was living her dream already. She'd gotten out. She hadn't even had the opportunity yet to think about what would come next. After all, she knew that the Polo Club wouldn't be forever for her, but Diego had a passion. He had something that drove him in his every day. Diego stopped talking and gave her a look.

"Stop looking at me like that," she pleaded.

"Like what?"

Granted, he probably wasn't looking at her in any specific way. But if he didn't stop, she might do something unbecoming of a lady in public.

"I don't know. You're giving me a weird look."

"No, I'm just looking at you, thinking that there's something else to your story, Ashley, and I wish you would let me in. I mean, I know you don't know me enough, but I think that you can tell that you can trust me, can't you?"

"Oh, that's very funny," said Ashley. "I've been told I absolutely cannot trust you."

Diego sighed.

"Listen, you have to know that..."

"No, don't even try to explain yourself. You don't owe me anything," said Ashley.

"But…" said Diego.

Ashley noticed a hand clamping down on Diego's shoulder. It made her jump. It would take a while until she didn't have that kind of reaction.

"Oh, hey, Ross," said Diego. "Ashley, this is Ross. He plays on one of the other teams sometimes. He's not that good, though," he cracked.

Ross scoffed.

"Yeah, neither are you, man. How's it going? Another girlfriend? This one is really pretty."

Ashley felt a clenching in her jaw. This was ridiculous.

"This is my friend Ashley," said Diego. "She works at the Polo fields and she's off limits, just so you know."

"We'll be the judge of that, won't we?" said Ross.

Ashley had the distinct impression that she did not like this Ross character. He had a smug, self-satisfied pink face, and was sweaty, even in the cool atmosphere of the Honor Bar.

"Well, it was nice seeing you, Ross," said Diego. "I'm going to take Ashley back home. She's got an early morning, and so do I."

"Yeah, sure," said Ross, walking away.

"Wow, do you guys have some kind of history?" asked Ashley, as they left the bar.

"I guess you could say that" said Diego.

"Another woman story?" asked Ashley.

"I'm telling you…" said Diego.

She cut him off.

"It's fine. I really don't need to know."

Mostly, she admitted to herself, because even hearing about his transgressions with other women would have her thinking about him in that way, and she was thinking about it enough as was.

"Wait- I forgot to pay for my drinks," said Ashley.

"The bartender put it on my tab," said Diego.

"You shouldn't have."

"I wanted to."

They walked in silence down the sidewalk for a moment, Ashley acutely aware of the warm scent Diego's cologne.

"Hey, by the way," said Diego. "I've noticed that maybe you've met a certain ginger haired denizen of our barn."

"There's nothing to talk about," said Ashley.

"Fair enough," said Diego, his mouth set in a straight line. God, even with his lips stretched thin, he was gorgeous.

"Just take me home," said Ashley. "I do have an early morning, and I'd better check on the horses before I go to bed."

"You're a treasure for the Polo Club," said Diego. "My car is over there."

They walked up the street a bit further. Night had just fallen, and the air temperature had dropped by quite a few degrees. The marine layer was in, and little pinpricks of fog tickled Ashley's neck and the exposed parts of her arms.

"It gets cold here," she marveled.

"Yeah, they always say endless summer, but people say you never get so cold as you get in Santa Barbara sometimes. Here, here's my car," said Diego.

Diego's car was similar to the one that Henry had driven, but more angular, and a matte green color.

"Is this… is this a Range Rover?" asked Ashley, testing out the car name in her mouth.

"It is, but it's an old one," said Diego. "My family always had these cars, and, well, they're ridiculous and they break down all the time, but once you've driven one, they're just so damn comfortable that you can't drive anything else. I know it makes me look like a snob," he said.

"Don't worry, I don't even really know what a snob is," said Ashley. "And I've never seen these cars until I got here, honestly."

"You've never seen a Range Rover before?" Diego marveled.

"I told you- Montecito is like a foreign planet for me."

"Well, you seem to be taking to it like a fish to water," said Diego.

They drove to the polo grounds. Ashley found herself missing Diego's knee on her thigh. She still felt the ghost of the warmth and the pressure from where it had been and had to resist the urge to put her hands on his leg. She'd noticed his legs. He looked like he had strong, well-muscled thighs from gripping a horse's flanks. She wondered how those thighs might look without those jeans on. God, she had to stop thinking that way. She was turning into a lecherous monster. Yes, she'd had a few fantasies about Robert early on in their relationship, but then, she had completely shut that part of herself down, except for when she'd had to fantasize about things to try to disassociate from the times when Robert was being rough with her. What would it be like, to be with someone kind and gentle? Well, maybe not too gentle. *Stop.* As Robert had repeatedly told her, she just didn't know what was good for her, did she?

"Well, here we are," Diego said as they pulled up to the Polo Club apartments. "Let me know if you ever need a ride again. I know you don't have a car right now. Alex told me to look out for good deals for you."

Ashley felt a pinching in her heart. Everyone was so kind.

"Thank you so much. I don't know how to repay everyone for their kindness," she said.

"It's my pleasure," said Diego.

Damn her, she'd had to go and look at his lips right when he said the word *pleasure*. And again, a chill went through her body. Diego leaned forward and put his hand behind her neck gently, raising goose bumps and her nipples, as well. He kissed her gently on both cheeks. She'd seen this before on TV. It was some kind of European thing. Feeling his lips on her cheeks, she was dying to feel them all over her body. She liked this European kiss concept, but she didn't want to stop there.

"Well, good night," she said, looking at him, her whole body yearning. "I guess I'll see you soon."

"Yes, soon," said Diego, giving her a faux-innocent smile.

That bastard. He knew how badly he turned her on, didn't he? He could probably smell it by now, for heaven's sake. She would have to work harder to hide her attraction.

Chapter 21

She stumbled out of the car, got into the apartment, closed the door, double checked the lock, and took a few deep breaths to try to cleanse all thoughts of Diego from her mind.

But what she also really needed to do was find out what had happened to her mother. She knew that her phone had some kind of searching service on it called Google, but she'd never used it, or anything like it before. She'd been to the library and done some searches when she was younger. It couldn't be that different. She checked the phone and saw a little rainbow-like icon on it that seemed to mean it was connected to the Internet. She started hitting the various buttons on the screen, trying to remember what the guy in the Apple store had explained to her. Different things popped up, but nothing that looked promising- then finally, she saw *Google* in multi-colored letters. There was a rectangle with a button saying *Search* and underneath something saying *I'm feeling lucky. I am feeling lucky*, thought Ashley. Maybe this was exactly what she needed. She typed in "Cascade County Montana Police Department" and hit search. A bunch of text popped up with blue lines under some of it. There were different words that described things in Montana and police-oriented things. She tapped on one of the blue-lettered phrases and a whole page popped up. A website. She knew what this was. OK. She decided to go back. There was a back arrow- maybe that took her back to the previous search. She hoped so. After a few frustrating minutes, she finally ended up on the actual web page of the Cascade County Police Department. From here, maybe she could see if there were incident reports, anything she could see pertaining to her mother. But she didn't have much luck. There were entries about traffic incidents and domestic violence. She shuddered, thinking that if she'd had access to a phone, she might have been one of those entries. So many times, she had been left lying on the floor, broken, crying, wishing someone would come help her, but knowing that no one in the world knew what was happening, because she was so far removed from it all, in the middle of nowhere.

Maybe she should search up news stories. She tried to remember what the news channel was that she used to see her mom watching. She entered that in but didn't have much luck, just a lot of different listings that seemed to be not very useful. Finally, she decided that maybe she would search for Robert's name. She entered in his name and saw some listings, but it seemed that most, if not all of them, were for people that were probably different Roberts. She knew she should look up her mother's name or her sister's name along with Robert's name, just in case. But she was afraid. It was like she was trying to hold back, and not have to know if something horrible had happened.

She remembered when Papa died, and how she had found herself wishing that she'd had just a couple more minutes to live thinking that he was still alive. Because, at the moment you knew, your whole life changed and was never the same again.

She was about to type in her mother's name when a number popped up on her screen. At first, she panicked. It wasn't Kari's. And it wasn't Jim's. But it had the same 805 prefix. She picked up the phone.

"Hey Ashley, this is Alex. Sorry to disturb you so late in the evening," he said. "But I think you need to know. I got a really weird phone call. Some guy called Robert, looking for you. It came from one of the numbers you dialed from my phone today."

"Which one? The first one or the second one?" asked Ashley, about to throw up.

"The second one."

Momma. He was calling from Momma's house. Had he done something to her? Ashley's head started spinning.

"Listen," said Alex, "I got a really bad feeling from him, so I told him he had the wrong number, and hung up as fast as I could. But I just thought you should know. Ashley, is there anything you need to tell me? Are you in trouble or something?"

Ashley was trembling, sweating, clenching her phone in trembling fingers. It felt like Robert had come a step closer to what she'd hoped would be her paradise. It would be turned to hell by him if he ever found her.

"Alex, please, I don't want to…"

"Just tell me. I'm not gonna tell anyone else. I just need to know because this guy sounded really deranged. I don't even want to tell you the things he said."

"I think maybe you need to tell me," said Ashley.

"He just sounded violent. Threatened me, and I guess he has your sister's phone, so..."

"My mother's phone," Ashley squeaked.

"Say," said Alex. "Your husband's not really dead, is he?"

Ashley gulped back tears.

"Yeah. Sorry I lied. Robert's my ex-husband," she lied again.

Ashley didn't bother saying that she hadn't left him legally, just via Greyhound bus.

"He was very abusive, and I swear he has no way of knowing where I am. You just need to block that number."

"Consider it blocked," said Alex. "Listen, we'll talk in the morning. I just want you to know that you can trust me."

Ashley thought about this. Funny how Kari had told her not to trust Alex. Several people here had told her to trust them, and not to trust some other people, or to trust no one, and if she was to listen to them all, who *did* she have to trust?

"OK, we'll talk in the morning," she said. "Again, Alex, thank you so much for giving me the apartment. Even though it's really, really ugly."

She laughed weakly, trying to distract herself from the terror that was gripping her very bones. It didn't work.

"You need to figure out what to do about this guy. Be careful and call me if you need anything," said Alex.

Ashley went to bed, but she couldn't sleep. She just lay there, trembling, terrified. What was she going to do? What if Robert found her? Would he put two and two together, the 805 area code, and the fact that Sissy had a friend in Montecito? Could he do a reverse lookup on Alex's number and see that he worked with horses? What if Robert hurt the people she newly cared about? What if he had hurt her sister, again, and Craig, and her mother? He must have hurt Momma, at the very least. But that crash she had heard while on the phone with Craig- it had been ominous, and she had tried to lie to herself to make herself believe everything was OK, cavorting on the beach while her family suffered. She thought about calling Diego, but she didn't have his number. She had Jim's number in her phone. He was a policeman, maybe he could help. But that was ridiculous. What was she going to do? Call the police chief and say, *hey, my crazy ex-husband has a one in one million chance of finding me, but he's scaring me*? No, she needed to just sit tight and think of what to do.

Chapter 22

The next morning, Ashley woke up, determined to figure out a solution to her problem. She'd managed to get a couple hours of sleep. It wasn't much, but it was something. She dressed in her usual jeans and boots, and a thin T-shirt that Kari had given her. It was a little lower cut than what she usually wore, but it already seemed like the day was shaping up to be a hot one.

She was picking up bales of hay when she heard a step behind her. As always, she reacted on instinct, straightening up, panic skating across her nerves, hackles raising in the back of her neck.

"Relax, Ashley, it's just me," said Alex.

"Oh, thank God," said Ashley.

"You're really terrified of this guy, aren't you? You know, you should report him to the police."

"It's too late," said Ashley. "In any case, my injuries have all healed, and I don't know if there's any proof of anything he did. Kari and I called the cops once already, and I'm afraid that if I reach out again, they'll track me down and he'll somehow find me. It was hard enough to get away."

"So wait, did you just leave this guy? Did you just run away?" asked Alex.

Ashley looked at him. What should she say? Maybe he wouldn't want to have a liability like her around.

"Can I not talk about it?" she pleaded.

"It's a little too late for that," said Alex. "Listen, I really don't want any trouble here, but I also don't want to throw you out on your ass, and you're the best worker I've ever had. So figure it out, is all I can say, I guess."

"Yeah, said Ashley. I will."

"Good, because I am a pussy-ass chicken shit and this guy has me believing he's gonna come by and beat my ass, and I am absolutely not into getting my ass beat," said Alex.

"I know," said Ashley. "Same."

"OK, I'll see you later," said Alex. "I think the prince is on his way to see me."

"The prince?" asked Ashley, puzzled.

"Oh, you know," said Alex. "The pain in my ass. See you later."

As Alex left the stall, Ashley puzzled over what he'd said in her mind. It was a welcome distraction from worrying about Robert. Who was Alex referring to as the prince? Was is Diego? Diego sometimes seemed to want to act like something of a boss. Or was it a client who was a little too demanding and exacting? So far, everyone she'd met was rather kind. In fact, it was just a few of the women who had been a little bit catty, but most of the guys had been nice to her, even if they'd been a bit flirtatious. Well, she didn't have to worry about this character, it had nothing to do with her.

She went back to work and was working up a good sweat, when she noticed a shadow falling across the ground in front of her. *Here we go again,* she thought, as she braced for the panic she could not control.

"Ashley," said a familiar voice. She smiled. Oh, good. It was just Henry.

"Hey Henry, I needed to thank you again for that picnic," she said. "That was fun."

"Yeah, we must do it again, date two," said Henry, smiling at her in his flirtatious way.

She could find him a little bit attractive if she concentrated on it, she thought. There was something about the way he grinned like a child. It was cute. Not devastatingly sexy like Diego, but really, she needed to learn to go with what was safe and easy, not with the complicated stuff.

"Well, we could make another plan," said Henry.

"I would love that," said Ashley. "What are you thinking? How about dinner out? There's this place called the Honor Bar?"

Henry's eyes opened wide. He cleared his throat.

"Oh. I was thinking someplace less… public."

Ashley squinted at him. Was he one of these guys who was ashamed to be seen with a girl, and only wanted to see her alone to maybe take advantage? It had happened to some of her high school friends.

"So you're saying I'm not fit for being seen in public with, is that it?" asked Ashley.

"Absolutely not." Henry smiled. "I just… I just want you all to myself. It's just a lot more fun to get to know each other, you know?"

"Ah."

"Listen, said Henry. I have a great idea. There's a garden that I know nearby that's extraordinary. We can have a happy hour there. I'll bring some Champagne, a picnic blanket…"

"Oh, another cashmere blanket? Ashley laughed.

"I'll bring two, if you want, if you say yes. You'll see- this place is magical," he said.

"OK, sounds good to me," said Ashley. "When do you want to do it? It's not like I'm the busiest person on Earth, but I just need to find a car, and after that, move into my new digs."

"Oh, you're moving?" asked Henry.

"Alex offered me the apartment over his garage. It's hideous, but it'll do."

"That'll be great to have your own space," said Henry, "somewhere far from the public eye."

"I mean, it's not a really a public eye to me," said Ashley. "I don't know anyone in town, so I guess I'm pretty anonymous, but yeah, having my own place is going to be a nice change."

"Excellent," said Henry. "Well, let me check with the garden to see when we can go and… by the way, I don't have your phone number," he said.

"I think that's something I only give out after the third date," Ashley joked.

"No, you told me what the third date thing is," said Henry, laughing and waggling his eyebrows at her.

Ashley felt a twinge. She'd been too forward when talking to Henry last time, maybe.

"Well, that's actually negotiable," she said. "But sure, here's my phone number. Don't give it to anyone," she said.

"I'll keep it as my most treasured possession," said Henry. "Listen, I'll text you when I hear about the garden."

"I'll see you later," said Ashley.

She turned back away and looked at the stall she'd been working in. There were a few chips in the wood on a side wall, and she figured that she'd go sand them down just to make everything perfect. Apparently, a very valuable horse was going to come into this stall, and she didn't want it to have any rough surfaces to hurt itself against. Not on her watch. She went to grab a piece of sandpaper in the workroom, and almost ran headlong into Diego.

"Oh, hey," said Diego.

"Why do you look so surprised to see me?" asked Ashley. "I'm the one who works here, remember? What are *you* doing here?"

"Well, I had to deal with the prince," said Diego, a smirk playing on his lips.

"God, you and Alex with your prince and your other code words-ponies and chukkers and stuff… you're hilarious. Well, anyway, I better go," said Ashley.

She was starting to feel the tingles again and needed them to go away so she could think straight.

"Thanks for the ride yesterday, by the way."

"You're welcome," said Diego. "It was my pleasure."

That word again, on his lips. Ashley shuddered, the tingles running across her neck and down to her breasts, and around to the small of her back.

"Well, I've got a lot to do," she said, brusquely. "Maybe I'll see you around."

"Yeah, let me know if you ever want to grab a drink or something."

She smiled to herself. *Sure. A drink couldn't hurt, could it? Stop it. You know damn well what it could lead to.* She'd have to see when Henry wanted to go to the garden. And then she could figure out when to have a drink with Diego. She'd gone from being married to one very abusive man to having two charming men flitting around her. So many options for evening plans that it felt positively complicated to juggle.

She took a brief break for lunch, observing the guys exercising the horses, four abreast. She watched the polo ponies, as she'd learned to call them, galloping across the fields. It was amazing how just a little square of green like that, smaller than any of the fields that they had back in Montana, could be so valuable. She'd heard people talking about how much land cost per square foot in

Montecito, and it was simply mind boggling. She watched as a stable hand exercised another group of four horses. There, on the right, she noticed a glossy black horse with a broken gait. That could turn into a problem if they hadn't noticed it. She waved the stable hand down as he came by.

"Hey, hi, I'm Ashley," she said.

"Andreas," said the man.

He was more of a boy, actually. Maybe 18 or 19 years old, handsome, with tawny skin and white teeth. A little skinny, but strong looking.

"Hey, I noticed that that horse on the right, it looks like it's in danger of going lame. I think it has a problem, maybe something in its shoe?"

Andreas looked at her, surprised.

"I would have noticed if there was anything," he said, defensively.

"Well, it's subtle, but I'm telling you, it could turn into more if you don't watch it," said Ashley.

"What's going on?" said a voice behind her.

She stiffened for a moment, then relaxed. It was Alex.

"I was just telling Andreas. There's a problem with that horse's gait. I think it's got something going on."

"OK, Andreas, here- leave the rest of the horses with Ashley, and let me see you run that one," said Alex.

Andreas obediently handed the leads to Ashley and started running along with the black horse.

"Damn, Ashley, you're good," said Alex. "Yeah, there's something going on. OK, Andreas, take that one back. Ashley is gonna put these away and I'm gonna come check. I might call the vet. Fuck. These horses are worth a fortune, and they're more delicate than a damn teacup chihuahua."

The horses were definitely more expensive than anything Ashley had back home, but a horse was a horse. She worked on putting the ponies away, marveling at this whole other stable complex, one she had seen in passing but had never been in or worked in yet. This one was more populated than the one that she worked in every day. There were more people helping here, too, and she smiled at them and introduced herself. Some of them gave her lecherous looks, but some of them seemed open and friendly, others minding their own business.

After a while, she wandered back to her own stables, and found Alex in his office.

"Thanks Ashley, that's amazing what you did, he said. It was so subtle, but there was a little infection in that horse's foot and if we hadn't caught it, it could have progressed overnight, and it might have been devastating. You saved me a ton of money."

"Good," said Ashley. "What do I get in return?" she teased.

"How about a new bed cover for that damn orange room?"

"You're an angel," said Ashley. "Thank you. I hope I find a lot of other horses with problems, or maybe I don't. I hope I prevent the horses having problems, but I guess I'll have to let you know, so that you know to be thankful," she teased.

"I am thankful," said Alex. "Speaking of which, I'm sorry about being a little hard on you about your ex, yesterday. I just want you to know that I'm here for you, and as long as you're not playing any games and not trying to let him know where you are, OK?"

"I don't play games like that," said Ashley. "That would be crazy."

"OK," said Alex. "I've just been burned before. I've had some crazy chicks in my life."

"Well, I've had some crazy guys in my life," said Ashley. "So I guess that makes us even."

"Speaking of…" said Alex. "I don't want to speak out of school, but I thought I noticed something between you and..."

Ashley gave him a look and cut him off.

"I don't need to talk about this, Alex."

"Just be careful," said Alex.

Ashley left the office in a bit of a huff. When she had gone a few steps, she realized that she didn't know who Alex was actually talking about. Was it Diego, or Henry? Silly. Alex was doubtless referring to Diego. She was surprised that he'd even noticed, but if he had noticed, she needed to be more careful, or people could start talking, not that she would care that much. *What would they care if yet another girl succumbed to their attraction to Diego?* she wondered. Well, she supposed that being with Henry would be the safe alternative. People would probably have nothing bad to say about that, she thought.

Her phone pinged. She jumped. What in the world was that? Then she realized. It must be a text message. Her first. She peered at her phone's screen and noticed a little red mark by a green bubble icon. She clicked on it and a message from Henry popped up. *Meet me in front of the stables at 5:30 PM?* he had written. That was right before sunset, thought Ashley. She would have to hurry take a quick shower as soon as she was done with work.

"Is that message anything I should be worried about?" asked Alex, coming out of the office and noticing Ashley's pensive face.

"Oh no, nothing, just a friend," she said.

"Oh good, you've made friends already," said Alex. "Well, that's great. Let me know if you need anything, but I'm glad."

Ashley felt somewhat bad for lying to Alex again, but then again, Henry *was* a friend. Still, they'd had that one date. Maybe this did count as number 2. She shuddered. Next came #3. Well, she would deal with that as it came.

"OK, well I better get back to work 'cause I'm going to meet my friend at 5:30."

"OK," said Alex. "By the way, I saw what you did in the stall to smooth those walls. That horse I told you about that's coming in, it's worth a fortune. Your attention to detail will really come in handy."

Ashley wondered whether the horse belonged to this guy they were calling the prince. It probably did.

"OK, well, you know, it's my job," she said, and went back to work.

Chapter 23

At 5:30 on the dot, Henry's car, which she now recognized as a Range Rover, pulled up to the apartment.

"I want to get to the garden before night falls," said Henry by means of hello.

"That's happening earlier and earlier. I'm not looking forward to shorter days," said Ashley.

"That was one of the things I hated most from growing up," said Henry.

"In England, right?"

"Yes, in England." Henry looked at Ashley strangely. "Did I tell you that?"

"Of course, you told me that. How else would I know, other than your accent, which I barely even identified? God, you must think I'm so badly traveled."

"Never," said Henry happily.

As they drove along, she caught him up on her day.

"I feel like I'm making things work better, you know what I mean? They say there's this guy- kind of a difficult customer- who's going to be boarding one of his horses there, so I made this stall perfect for him. Apparently, it's a very valuable horse."

"Oh?" said Henry. "Interesting, I wonder who that would be?"

"Yikes," she said. "I hope I didn't just violate the NDA I signed. Anyway…So what's this place called that we're going to?"

"It's called Lotusland. It belonged to a Polish opera singer. It's one of the top botanical gardens in the world."

"Wow, I feel so lucky," said Ashley. "I mean, I've noticed all the beautiful plants around here. I can't imagine anything prettier. Where I grew up, we basically had grass and a few trees and some people had flowers here and there, but they didn't last very long, that's for sure."

"How big is this garden?"

"Not sure. Big for being right in Montecito, that's for sure," Henry said.

"I'm so sorry- I forgot. You live in Montecito, don't you? I could have taken an Uber or something, so you didn't have to go out of your way."

"No, of course not. That's silly. And then it wouldn't count as a date, then, would it?" said Henry.

Ashley smiled. Dammit, he was really counting these dates, wasn't he? As cute as she felt he was, she wasn't that attracted to him. She did feel a spark once in a while, but she didn't really know what she wanted. It would probably take her more than a few dates to determine if there was anything there at all.

They arrived at some wrought iron gates with a sign that read *Staff Entrance*. Henry dialed a number on the intercom.

"Private visit," he said.

"Of course, Sir," was the response.

There was a buzzing sound, and the gate started to swing open.

"That's funny," said Ashley, "Seems like anybody could say private visit and they would let them in, right?"

"They knew to expect me," said Henry.

"So- what's your relationship to this place?"

"I've given donations, because my family was very into gardening, so basically, I'm a member, and I'm allowed to come when I want."

"Oh, so there may be other members there while we're here?"

Ashley was a bit relieved. It meant no funny business.

"No, they closed the place down for us."

"Wait, that sounds pretty fancy, especially for a second date," said Ashley.

"Nothing's too fancy for our second date," said Henry, smiling at her wolfishly.

Darn. She should have kept her mouth closed. They stepped out of the car and into a wonderland. They headed down a stone path, and were immediately surrounded by lush leaves, bigger than any she'd ever seen in her life. There were gigantic ferns, and flowers she thought she recognized as begonias, but their leaves were so huge and glossy. She hadn't seen anything like it, except maybe in picture books.

"This is amazing," she gasped.

"I know, right?" Henry smiled. "There's more. This is just the beginning. Let's do a quick walkthrough before our picnic. I've set up a spot, but I'll show you around first."

After the shade garden full of ferns, they entered a garden full of trees with spiky leaves.

"That," said Henry, gesturing to the reddish sap on some of the fallen fronds, "is dragon's blood."

Ashley was only half listening. She was casting her eyes around, staring at the incredible vegetation. The main house on the property, which they now came up to, was pink, very beautiful and strange, with cacti in front of it, and a fountain across from it burbling happily.

Ashley's heart was burbling happily too. This was just magical. She had never imagined that she would have the opportunity to see something like this in her lifetime. She felt so special. It had been a long time since Robert had brought her to see anything special or had done anything just for her. Having Henry close the whole garden for her, well, that felt really magical. She didn't know how to thank him. She knew how he *thought* she would thank him, but that wasn't happening today.

After seeing the house, they walked into something that Henry called a Palmetum.

"They have about 150 varieties of palm," he said. Everything but coconut palms. They don't grow here."

"Oh," said Ashley. "That's a disappointment. I mean, if you don't have coconuts, is it even a palmetum?"

Next came the water garden.

"There are lotuses here up until mid-September," said Henry. With or without lotuses, it was still beautiful.

"This pond used to be the pool of the property," said Henry. "What do you think of skinny dipping in here?"

"I don't know," Ashley laughed. "It looks a little bit messy."

She remembered their lunchtime swim. *Messy in more ways than one,* she thought, and she was not planning on that happening today.

Next came a garden full of aloes, and then a Japanese garden that was so beautiful that Ashley could scarcely believe it.

"This is where I've set up for a picnic," said Henry. "There are some more plants, but I hope to be able to take you back- maybe for the next date."

"Maybe," said Ashley, smiling back at him.

He was being naughty. They got to an exotic wooden pavilion in the Japanese garden. There were candles set up throughout the pavilion, which was like a vision glowing in the gathering dusk. There was a picnic set out already on the benches.

"Wow, you set all of this up before picking me up?" asked Ashley.

"I called in a few favors," Henry smiled.

"Well, it's beautiful," Ashley said. "Hey…Did you bring some more of that goose fat?"

"No, not this time. I've got some different things. Some oysters and some shrimp. Does that sound good?"

"Honestly, I've never eaten an oyster. But I'm willing to try."

Just like the time before, there was a picnic blanket covered in the letter H on it, spread out on the floor of the pavilion. This time, there were also fresh flowers and a Champagne bucket with a bottle of Champagne already chilling in it.

"You really pulled out all the stops," said Ashley. "I'm impressed. What a Prince Charming."

"Yes, well…" Henry blushed.

"I bet you're a mama's boy, aren't you?" asked Ashley, ribbing him.

Henry's face grew serious.

"My mother passed away," he said. "And yes, she was very special to me."

"Oh my God, I'm so sorry, I wouldn't have said it so lightly if I'd known," said Ashley.

"Right. You didn't know, did you? About my mother?"

Ashley was taken aback. What was that supposed to mean?

"Of course not. How would I know about your mother? Henry, I've just met you. Anyway, we can stop talking about our mothers, because I'm worried that something bad has happened to my mine."

"What do you mean?" asked Henry.

"I haven't heard from her since I got here," Ashley admitted. "Can't you call someone? A friend or a neighbor to check on her?"

"Not really," said Ashley. "It's complicated. My ex-husband isn't a good man, which makes it even more complicated," she said.

"That's devastating," said Henry. "I know something about that, too."

"Oh, that's right- your ex. Were you married?"

"Something like that," said Henry.

"Alright, sounds like it's a sensitive subject for you, too. Let's stop talking and start eating."

There were pillows set up on the blanket, so Ashley plopped herself down next to Henry, and there they sat, as the frogs started singing and the moon rose over the pond. Ashley felt like she was in a movie set, it felt that surreal.

Henry spread some cheese on a cracker and added what looked like strawberry jam to it.

"Jam with cheese?" smiled Ashley. "That looks a little crazy."

"Try it, you won't believe it."

She tried it. He was right. It was possibly the best thing she'd ever tasted.

"Delicious," she moaned.

"You're delicious," Henry said. He leaned in and kissed her neck, as her head was thrown back in ecstasy from the cheese.

"Oh, you caught me by surprise," she said.

"I'd like to catch you any way I can," said Henry.

Ashley smiled, a little embarrassed. She wasn't used to this kind of banter. Robert had never gotten her used to that sort of thing, at least not recently. Maybe at the beginning, they'd enjoyed teasing each other, she now remembered. She had to admit, she was very attracted to Robert when she'd first met him. Nothing compared to Diego, but that was a different story altogether. But Henry was sweet, and gentlemanly, and safe. She had to admit that the kiss felt good. It felt good to be desired by someone gentle. Henry ran a finger along her throat and down her back. She shivered.

"Are you cold?"

"No, that felt good," she admitted. "But I just want to take it slow, you know what I mean?"

"Of course," he said. "I was just thinking about, you know, when we were in the water the other day. I don't know if you felt it, but I like you a lot, Ashley. You know that, right?"

"I do," she said. "And yes, I felt it, but maybe I'm not completely ready. I'd like to get to know you better before anything happens, you know?"

"Of course," Henry said. "But can I still be close to you? Are you OK with a kiss here and there?"

"You can always try," she said.

Henry leaned in and kissed her on the chin, oh so gently. It did feel lovely, like a butterfly landing, but there were none of the chills she'd gotten when Diego had simply kissed her on both cheeks, which had been meant as a much more innocent gesture. She wasn't sure whether Diego knew what kind of an effect he had on her, but it was profound.

"Here, let me give you a grape. These taste like cotton candy," said Henry.

He put a grape between her lips.

"Oh, they're delicious," said Ashley. "Back where I'm from, there's nothing fresh in the supermarket. When it's not summer anymore, and you can't get things from the farmstand, everything just tastes stale."

"I know," said Henry. "Even where I'm from, wintertime is a bit bleak. We do lots of roasts on Sundays and things like that."

"Is your family from the countryside? Or are you city people? You seem sophisticated, but I can't really tell. It's, you know, maybe culture shock," she admitted.

Henry smiled.

"Well, a little bit of both. We have country homes and city homes, I guess you could say…"

"Homes, plural? Wow. Sounds like your family is a bit wealthy. I didn't know you were a rich boy. You seemed a little bit fancy, but I had no idea."

"Well, I've kind of gone away from my family," said Henry.

"We do have that in common," said Ashley.

"See, there's a reason we belong together, isn't there?"

Henry stroked her arm, his fingers running up it, dangerously close to her breast. He looked her in the eye. She could tell that he wanted more.

"I find it very hard to remain gentlemanly with you," he said.

"Well, try hard," she said. "Because that's what it's going to take."

Did she feel guilty that she was using Henry as a way of forgetting Diego? A little bit, maybe, but wasn't love a game? Clearly you didn't end up marrying everybody you ever met. People could date casually, couldn't they? Sure, she'd only seen that on television, but it seemed to be a thing. Robert had been her first boyfriend. She'd had some crushes before him, but he had really turned her world upside down- at first for the better, making her feel grown up, and like she had something else to look forward to other than times with her friends, who were a little simple, and her mother, who kept her contained. But then, of course, her world had started to turn upside down in all the wrong ways.

"Here, try this," said Henry. "It's Spanish ham."

"Well, we have ham where I'm from, too. That's not that fancy," Ashley laughed.

"This is from Spanish pigs that only eat acorns. This stuff costs a fortune."

Ashley laughed. Was he making fun of her? How could a ham possibly be that expensive? Pigs were a dime a dozen.

"Are you teasing me just 'cause I'm naïve?"

"I would never do that, Ashley. No. This ham is very fancy."

"Well, it's probably wasted on me," said Ashley, picking up a piece of ham and popping it in her mouth. "Oh my God, never mind. This is the most delicious thing I've ever put in my mouth."

"Is it?" said Henry, giving her a look and a wink.

"Oh, come on, don't try to make it like everything I say is so suggestive," said Ashley. "This is just really delicious. I let my guard down, and you took advantage."

"I would like to take advantage of you much more than that," Henry said.

Now, he put his hand on her leg, and she shivered a little. He was attractive. He was confident. But … He tried to kiss her again, this time planting his lips closer to hers. Well, she might as well give it a chance, she thought. She turned her head slightly, and now he really kissed her. Nibbling at her lips, starting to explore her mouth with his tongue. She could taste the ham on his tongue, which wasn't a bad thing. And Champagne too. That damn Champagne. Making her lose her resolve to resist him. His hands moved onto her breasts now, and she lay back onto the cushions. He moved on top her, holding her tight and kissing her harder. She felt her body responding, her back arching, her nipples starting to tingle, wetness and heat between her legs…but of course, that was because at that point, she had started thinking of Diego, imagining his dark curls instead of Henry's ginger hair… Going down, down, kissing her between her breasts and going further down still. She shuddered, caught in the moment.

But no. She really needed to stop this. Here she was being kissed by a perfectly charming man, and she couldn't bear to stop thinking about the bad boy, the one she shouldn't have.

"Henry, this feels really good, but you need to stop."

"Oh, come on," said Henry, running his hands down her back and cupping her buttocks, pulling her closer until she could feel his erection between her legs.

"Come on, it feels good, doesn't it?"

"It does," she mumbled into his mouth. "It does, but I just need to take it slow, please."

Henry pulled away, pouting.

"Oh, really? You're going to pout?" she smiled.

She thought he was teasing, but no, the pout didn't evaporate.

"You're not mad at me, are you? I really appreciate this picnic you put out for us- it's magical. No one's ever done anything like this for me, and you're wonderful. But isn't it my prerogative to want to take things slowly? I mean, it's like no one's ever said no to you before or something."

"No one has ever said no to me before," Henry snapped.

Ashley's eyes widened. *What the hell?* Panic started to course through her veins. But then, Henry's demeanor changed, and he smiled again.

"I'm just teasing you, Ashley. I just really want you so badly, and I'm sorry if I was a little forceful. I promise to be a perfect gentleman in the future. I won't even hold you to the third date thing, but I do want to see you again. You will see me again, won't you?"

"Yes," said Ashley. "Of course, I will."

She felt guilty, though. Henry was showing her places she'd never been. Introducing her to a beautiful life she'd never even imagined. Was she using him for wonderful picnics on cashmere blankets? Was this what gold diggers were about? She didn't care about Henry's money, even though she was starting to realize that he must have a lot of it. But it was just so dreamy to go to these magical places that normal people didn't get to go to. It was making her want things that she'd never wanted in her life. She'd always been simple, and now she felt conflicted.

"Here. I've got one more delicious thing for us to try," said Henry.

He held up a square of chocolate.

"This isn't one of those edibles, is it?" laughed Ashley.

"You got me," said Henry. "It is. Will you try it with me?"

"Sure, why not? Do we split it? How much are we supposed to eat?"

Sissy used to bring some of this stuff to the stables, back in the day. Ashley remembered that she could only have a tiny bit before it started making her feel like she was losing her mind, but tonight, with the food, the singing frogs, the starry sky, and the water gently lapping at the edges of the pond, she thought it would be incredible. She felt high already, watching the little sparkles as the moon shone off the ripples on the pond. Could there be anything more trippy than sitting in this amazing garden that she couldn't even imagine existed?

Henry broke the chocolate square into pieces and gave Ashley a small one. He kissed her again, more lightly this time. She sat back and relaxed, listening to the sounds of the night.

"How long do you think they'll let us stay here?"

"As long as we want," he said.

They sat there, until the night started to grow wavy. The stars assembled themselves into confusing patterns, and the branches of the trees were as if she Ashley was seeing them through a kaleidoscope. Her mouth grew dry. She took another sip of Champagne.

"Whoa, this is some trippy stuff that you gave me," Henry, she said.

His only response was to kiss her, harder than before, straddling her now. Or was he? She wasn't sure.

"Are you feeling what I'm feeling?" she asked.

"I am. It feels good," he said. She could feel his fingers trying to undo her jeans. Or was that her imagination, too? His fingers wiggled town, trying to reach her clitoris, but they were rough. It didn't feel good.

"Stop," she said. But maybe she hadn't actually said it out loud, because he didn't stop.

Now, she wasn't feeling so well. The pavilion was spinning. She started feeling a little paranoid, worrying at every rustle, every sound.

"Henry, I don't feel so good. I think we need to go find a bathroom or something. I'm sorry."

"Seriously? Oh, all right," he said. "Here, let's go."

Ashley didn't know if she could make it. She tripped over her feet. She felt so tired, so dizzy. Not very well at all.

"This was a bad idea, Henry. Could you just remind me- Never again?"

Henry seemed to be doing just fine. He tried to hold her up, but she knew she was dead weight. At some point, she lost the ability to speak. She noticed cacti looming over her, in nightmarish forms. This had started off so fun, and now it was not fun at all. She was scared. She crumpled to the ground, and the earth started spinning faster. She thought she heard Henry's voice, far away. Then, she felt a set of strong arms pick her up under her armpits. Something had her ankles too. She would have panicked, but she had no strength to panic anymore. She heard a brouhaha; voices mixed all together. Was there more than one person there? Maybe it was someone who worked at the garden, helping her? She didn't know and didn't care. She just wanted to get home, get back to her cozy bed. Why had she done that? She'd thought she was going to be worldly and cool in front of Henry and well, it had been a really bad idea. She was lifted down and then placed on a surface. *Watch her head*, she heard. She vaguely lifted up her head and then let it drop again. She started moving, which made her feel even more sick. And then, before she knew it, she was in her bed. At least it felt like her bed. She hoped it was her bed. Someone was shushing her and putting a damp washcloth on her forehead.

"Henry, is that you?" she mumbled. "You need to take me to the hospital. I feel like, so sick… you don't even understand."

"No, it happened to me like that the first time, too," he said. "I was taking the stuff to calm my nerves after everything that happened to me and…"

She vaguely heard him speaking, and she vaguely wondered what had happened to him that he needed to take this stuff, but everything was muffled. And then she closed her eyes.

Chapter 24

When Ashley opened her eyes, it was morning, the light already brighter than it should be. She panicked. She was late for work. What had happened? She saw a note on the nightstand, with formal handwriting on it. She picked it up and squinted. She still felt a little dizzy and very thirsty, but she felt infinitely better. Almost back to normal, thank God.

Dear Ashley, she read. *Don't worry, I didn't take advantage of you in your weakened state, though I would have loved to. I promise not to try to give you any more chocolate on our third date. I'll come up with something fun. Love, Henry.*

She smiled. At least he had been a gentleman. A flash of the previous evening came back to her. *Wait a second, not that much of a gentleman,* she now remembered. She was embarrassed, and angry. Not so much at Henry, but at herself. She had been such a naïve idiot that she had taken too much of this edible thing and had thrown caution to the wind, when she had no idea what was in it, when it was. She was on her own, now. She couldn't afford to do anything that could put her in jeopardy.

And then, of course, the thought came barging in again: Diego. What if Diego found out that she'd been out with Henry? In the dark, in the park. She was being ridiculous, she thought. Why would Diego care? He probably had oodles of girlfriends. It's not like they had anything between them. He wouldn't care at all. He might even be happy that his slightly pathetic friend the stable hand had a boyfriend, if that's what Henry was. She didn't know if she really wanted Henry to be her boyfriend, but she had almost no experience in that domain, so what did she know?

She made herself a cup of coffee and scrambled herself an egg. She needed something in her stomach. She was starving. She made another egg. She was ravenous, in fact. But now she was definitely late to work. *Shit.* Well, at least work couldn't be closer. She would miss the convenience when she moved to Alex's guest apartment. And she urgently needed a car.

At the stables, she stopped by the office to check in with Alex.

"You look like shit. Rough night?" he said.

"Just had a little bit too much."

"Well, you better learn how to check yourself before you wreck yourself," said Alex. "People around here are pretty heavy drinkers. Guzzle some water or something, because we've got a lot to do before the prince's horse arrives."

Alex enumerated a few tasks, including polishing up a plaque with what was supposedly the horse's name on it.

"HRH's Marwan al Nasser the 4th? Is that some kind of an Arabic name?" Ashley asked Alex.

"Yeah, it's an Egyptian Arab horse. They're super valuable. Super flighty too. Stupid to use it as a polo pony. We're going to have to be ultra-careful with this one."

"How much do these things cost?" asked Ashley.

"Oh, this one is probably $3,000,000. Which is cheap for a racehorse or dressage horse. Insane for a polo pony."

Ashley almost choked on the water she was obediently drinking.

The most expensive horse she had at home had cost a tiny fraction of that. She couldn't imagine the degree of wealth that it would take to afford an animal that valuable. They would have to be extremely careful with it, indeed. She would treat the horse like her mother's fancy china that she was always afraid to wash when her mom used to have dinner parties, back when Papa was still alive. After Papa passed, Momma had stopped bothering, she realized.

"OK, what else can I do?" Ashley asked, still wondering to herself, *How the hell do you pronounce HRH's? What a crazy word.*

"Let's just set up a whole corner of the tack room with the prince's stuff so that he doesn't have to mix his things in with those of common folk," Alex said, rolling his eyes.

Wow, thought Ashley. *They're taking this prince thing really far.* She wondered what kind of a pain in the ass client this was, and why it was worth it to work with him.

She took the briefest of lunch breaks in the empty grandstands, eating a sandwich she cobbled together in the apartment. She was disappointed that Diego was nowhere to be seen. She was also almost disappointed not to have Henry showing up and whisking her away to a beach picnic, not that she had time. She got back to work, trying to keep her mind blissfully clear.

At 4:00 o'clock, Alex came and found her.

"Hey Ashley, you know what? The prince is coming with the horse in just a few."

"OK great, we're ready, I think. What else do I need to do?"

"No, I think that, you know, he's super private, and I think his wife is coming too, and they never like to see very many people around, so I think you might as well just take off early. Go back to the apartment, relax, or go out and have a good time. You deserve it. You've been working your butt off."

"OK," said Ashley, a little disappointed not to be able to see this difficult client that she'd been doing all this work for.

Perhaps he would come back, and then she would finally find out who they were really talking about.

She walked back to the apartment. It had been an exhausting day, after a difficult night. She closed her eyes for a moment, wondering if maybe she should take a nap, but she felt restless. It was still damn early. Funny, she hadn't heard from Henry, other than the note she'd found on her nightstand that morning. But she didn't know what she'd been expecting. They weren't in that kind of relationship, were they? Once again, she thought of Diego. Where was he tonight? What was he doing? She wondered if her new friend Jim was at the Honor Bar. It would be fun to go and check it out, maybe. Why not? Wasn't the Honor Bar her local now? Anyway, she didn't have any compelling food here in the apartment. She texted Kari to see if she was free, but didn't hear anything back and decided that, too bad, she would get as dolled up as possible, and go check it out. Start building some friendships. She knew that it wasn't ideal to meet all her friends in a bar, but she really didn't have a million options at that point.

She took a shower, enjoying the feeling of the water on her body, trying not to think of Diego as she rubbed the soap into her skin.

What would she wear? She looked through her H&M stash and through the things that Kari had given her and settled on a pair of form fitting black trousers and a sheer white button-down shirt, which she decided to pair with her black bra. It would be a little bit edgy, she thought, if someone got a peek of the bra. She almost laughed out loud at herself. She'd lived for years just thinking about practicality when it came to clothes, and here she was trying to look cute. She wasn't quite back to her Coco Chanel years, stylistically, but that might have been on the horizon.

Once she was ready, she ordered an Uber on her phone, like Kari had shown her, and shuddered when she saw the estimate of how much it would cost. But she couldn't very well stay home alone all the time. Alex had given her a little advance and, well, she needed to get out, didn't she? She would have just one drink and then go home. She checked her phone to see where the car was. It was getting closer and closer. She hadn't seen too much action around the stables, but it was around the time when the prince was supposed to arrive. She had to admit, she was curious. *What kind of a man inspired so much respect and fear in people that they referred to him that way?* she wondered. Was he a wealthy businessman, or was he a Hollywood star? Or maybe he was one of those trust fund babies? Damn NDA… She had heard people talking about trust fund babies, and she knew it wasn't a good thing- to have inherited money and to do nothing with it, but maybe that's what it was.

Her phone pinged. *Your driver is approaching,* she read.

She stepped out of the apartment. Two cars were coming down the driveway. A Prius, which she guessed was her Uber. And then, a dark car that looked just like Henry's behind it. She opened her eyes wide for a second, but then relaxed. *Silly.* After all, she had seen many of those cars by now. It seemed like everyone in town had one. The prince probably had a Range Rover, too. It sounded like something very prince-like to have. Hell, even Diego had a Range Rover. Even though his was old, and green instead of black. She wondered if she would be so forward as to text Diego and ask him out for a friendly drink. As if it wasn't obvious that it was more than friendly. Could he tell that she had the hots for him?

She got into her Uber, and as they drove past, she watched the Range Rover stopping in front of the stables. Was that Henry getting out of the car? It was! She almost asked the Uber to stop so she could ask him what he was up to, and if he wanted to come for a drink with her. But then she remembered how the night before had gone and thought the better of it. She watched Henry walk around the car and go to open the passenger side door for whoever else was in the front seat. *Interesting.* She swiveled her head, very curious indeed. *Did Henry know the prince?* And then the Uber turned out of the driveway, and she lost sight of everything.

Chapter 25

The Uber dropped her off in front of the Honor Bar. Just seeing the yellow umbrellas in front of the door and the fire roaring on the patio and the kind waitresses with their starched aprons made her feel like she was coming home. She smiled to herself. She had almost already found her Cheers bar, the place where everybody knew your name. *Wouldn't that be nice?* She thought. Having friends and places that she was used to going to. She really hoped that Jim would be there, and -dare she dream? Diego. She walked in and was pleased when the hostess recognized her.

"Hi, nice to see you again," said the hostess.

"Nice to see you. I'm Ashley. By the way."

"That's funny. My name is Ashley, too," said the hostess. "Welcome back. Will you be wanting a booth or are you at the bar?"

"Oh, I think I'll go to the bar," said Ashley.

"Have fun," said the other Ashley.

Ashley walked towards the bar, scanning it to see if Jim was there, or Diego, or even those two bitchy Montecito ladies she kept seeing around. There were a few other ladies who looked similar to the ones she'd seen, before, and she thought to herself that maybe if there was someone close to her age, she could sit next to them and strike up a conversation. It would be good to have a girlfriend other than Kari. Kari had been a little standoffish since Alex had offered her the apartment, but otherwise had been so kind to her. She should really make sure that Kari wasn't upset at her for any real reason. Maybe she would text her again later when she was sitting at the bar. *Yes*, she decided. That's what she would do. She found a spot with a seat open on either side, so that it didn't look like she was crowding anyone who was already there. Also, it could be an invitation to anyone who wanted to sit next to her and strike up a conversation. *A girl could dream.* While she waited for the bartender to come take her order, she quickly sent off a text to Kari.

Hey, you. I hope all is well. At Honor Bar if you want to meet me for a drink. And a bite. I'm starving. I've had a long day. I hope you're doing well. I hope the new job is treating you well.

She hit send. *That was kind of a long text,* she thought. She wasn't sure what texting etiquette was, exactly, but to her, it was kind of like leaving a voicemail message, which was something she used to do on Momma's machine. Or on her sister's machine. She missed being able to leave them messages, and worried about them again, but Robert calling Alex's phone had put her on high alert.

Pretty soon, the bartender came up.

"Hi. Ashley, right?"

"And you're Andrew, right?"

"That's me. Nice to see you. Are you waiting for either one of your friends?"

"I don't know. I don't think they're coming," she said. She was pleased to hear Andrew refer to them as her friends. "I think I'll have a glass of something different than that rosé. I'm going to branch out," she said.

"Sure thing," said the bartender.

They spent a moment discussing the merits of Chardonnay versus Sauvignon Blanc, with the bartender deciding that if she was just starting to branch out, maybe she would like the Chardonnay best.

"Great. I'm actually starving, too," Ashley admitted.

"Actually? Damn." Andrew winked at her. "I'll get you the menu."

The bartender returned with a chilled glass of yellow wine and a menu. Ashley perused it for a minute. There were a lot of choices, and all of them looked good.

"What do you recommend?" she asked.

"The ladies like the kale salad because they feel like they're eating something healthy and good for them and maybe low calorie. But what they don't know is that our kale salad has more calories than even the Ding's crispy chicken."

"Yeah, I heard that."

"My girlfriend and I usually split the Ding's and the kale salad 'cause she's skinny and she doesn't care anyway."

"If I had someone to split it with. I would do that in a heartbeat," Ashley laughed.

"Ask and ye shall receive," said a voice to her right.

She spun around, and there was Diego, like the answer to her prayers, or at least the star of her dirty dreams. She blushed furiously. Andrew noticed and winked at her. She knew what his look was saying: *somebody's got a crush on somebody.* And oh boy, did she.

"I was hoping I would find you here," said Diego. "I didn't see you at the stables- the prince was there."

"Oh yeah, I didn't get to see the prince," said Ashley. "Alex told me to take the afternoon off. He said that the prince likes being all private and everything. I'm surprised he let you stay."

"Well, the prince knows me, so I was kind of required to be there to hand-hold for a moment, I guess you would say," said Diego.

"So what's this guys's name, really?" Ashley asked.

Diego gave her a funny look.

"Oh, never mind. You guys are just also mysterious about this guy. I mean, it can't be that major. Or is that why I signed the NDA?...Anyway, forget it. So, you were saying you're gonna split the Ding's crispy chicken and the kale salad with me?"

"Not only will I share it with you," said Diego, "but it's on me."

"No way," Ashley laughed, "first of all, I noticed you picked up the tab last time, and secondly, if you pay this time, maybe you're going to think it's a date or something."

"I wish it was a date," said Diego. "But don't worry, you won't need to put out after dinner, if that's what you're worried about." he winked.

An image of Diego kissing her naked body, those hands of his cupping her breasts, flashed into her mind. *Hell, I would put out for free for you,* Ashley thought.

She quickly changed the subject so that Diego couldn't tell that she was fantasizing about him so vividly, but it was probably too late.

"My new friend Andrew got me a Chardonnay. What are you drinking?"

"I'll have a Negroni."

"What's that?"

"I'll give you a sip of mine," said Diego.

He looked at her, while she thought of her lips on a glass where his lips had touched She broke eye contact. Her damn heart was beating faster than it had any right to. This was ridiculous. What if, she thought… what if she decided to just succumb to her desire for Diego, and that way she would just be over it? That could be the best way to deal with it, to make it a non-issue, because it didn't seem like going after Henry was solving anything at all. But no, that was a dangerous idea. What if she just ended up wanting more? She'd been warned about Diego. She didn't want to find herself in a situation where she was taken for a ride and then unceremoniously dumped.

The Negroni arrived. Ashley took a sip and convinced herself that she didn't like it. Too bitter. *So there.*

While they waited for their food, Diego told her a bit about how they'd been hoping to make the Polo Club world class, and finally opened up enough to tell her that the prince was the one who was supposed to raise the international standing of the club, but he was not really holding up his end of the bargain. Before Ashley could ask again who exactly this character was, Diego started explaining how he would maybe like to move someplace a little bit less expensive than Santa Barbara one day. Ashley looked at him, nodding. But she didn't want him to go anywhere.

"I love Santa Barbara so much," she said, "but maybe one day, I would love to have my own dressage stables or my own boarding stables somewhere pretty, and warm. Somewhere where I could really put down roots and have a nice life. I'm guessing you don't want a family, do you, Diego?"

"Why would you say that?" Asked Diego.

"You love playing the field, don't you?"

"Family is very important to me."

You're just not gonna be ready for one for about a million years, thought Ashley. Ashley thought again about how, when she and Robert had first gotten married, she'd quit the pill after a year- she'd assumed that they would have kids pretty soon. And it hadn't happened. And then, everything had gone south, and she had started doing everything in her power to not get pregnant. Robert didn't let her go to the doctor to get a new prescription for the pill or anything, but she'd always made sure to ensure he went to sleep before she went to bed when she knew she was at a particularly fertile part of her cycle. She needed a doctor here. She would probably have to think about what kind of protection she would be using, when the time came.

"So do you want a boy or a girl?" she found herself asking Diego.

"A couple of each, he said. I want a whole polo team, boys and girls."

She smiled at him.

"Well, you're going to have to find someone patient enough to put up with you and all of them, apparently," she smiled.

"I definitely want to be a partner to whoever I end up with," he said. "I want to have a foundation of honesty, and to be equals in life. That's really important to me."

Ashley gulped. He was saying all the right things, but she knew that that's what players did, after all. Robert had said all the right things when she'd met him, too. It wasn't until later that he started acting out. If she was honest with herself, there had been some signs. Even when they've just been dating, he'd been a bit rough with her a couple times, said some things, grabbed her wrist. But how was she to know? She'd been young, she'd never experienced anything else. She just thought that she was driving him crazy, and Momma had agreed with that hypothesis.

But so far, Henry and Diego had been nothing but gentle with her, well, maybe Henry maybe less so. He'd been a bit insistent when they were making out, but that was in the heat of the moment, she decided.

"What else do you like to do when you're not playing polo and doing business and running after the ladies?" Ashley asked.

Diego looked at her.

"Ashley, honestly, you're always making these comments about me and the ladies, and I don't want you to get the wrong idea. My reputation is…well, maybe it was earned long ago, but I'm not that person anymore."

"Let's change the subject," Ashley said. It wasn't worth discussing. People didn't change that much, did they? And anyway, it was none of her business.

"I think we started off on the wrong foot this evening," she said. "I'm looking forward to the kale salad and the Ding's crispy chicken. And I'm looking forward to you paying for it."

"I would love to take you somewhere, else, too," said Diego. "You know, take you somewhere nice. You've not really explored Santa Barbara, have you? Has Kari shown you around?"

"She showed me around a little bit," said Ashley. "But not since Steve came back. I need my own car so I can explore things as well and go places, but yeah, I would love for you to take me around," she admitted.

Diego started to enumerate the places he would take her. When he mentioned the courthouse, Ashley laughed.

"Oh, the courthouse. Maybe you've seen the inside of that more than once, with Jim?"

"Only a few times," Diego smiled. "In fact, I thought Jim was coming today, but maybe he got called away for something."

"I like him," said Ashley. "Is he as nice a guy as he seems?"

"I would say so," said Diego. "And I hope that the fact that I'm best friends with him says something good about me,"

"It just might," Ashley allowed.

They passed the rest of the evening with easy banter, moving closer together as more people crowded around the bar. Finally, Diego's knee rubbed up against her leg, like it had the time before, which was something that she realized she'd been craving. She allowed herself to look into his eyes. They were green, with specks of gold she hadn't noticed before. His chestnut hair was perfectly tousled as always. He really was so ridiculously handsome. He probably knew it, too.

He was telling her a story about riding his horse in Argentina, and she couldn't stop looking at his lips, at his warm smile, with just one slightly twisted eye tooth providing a reprieve from too much perfection. She wondered again how those lips would feel on hers. Would Diego be better as a friend? No good would come of being so impossibly into somebody. Or maybe... did she dare explore her theory of succumbing to him just to get him out of her system? She would play it by ear, she decided. She wouldn't be so calculating as to plan something like that. If it happened, it happened. Oh God, how she wanted it to happen. Would once be enough to get him out of her system? *No way.* But she really liked him as a person, too, she really did. And it would be sad to get him out of her system and then not talk to him anymore, because then it would be awkward, wouldn't it?

"I'm sorry, what did you say?" she said, after he'd paused and looked at her in a funny way.

"You weren't even listening to what I said," he smiled. "Am I boring you?"

"No, not at all. On the contrary," she said. "I'm so sorry, I had something else on my mind," she lied. She had him on her mind, one hundred percent,

"You're worried about your sister and your mom, aren't you? I heard about that. If I can help in any way, please let me know."

Could he be any sweeter?

"I'll let you know," she said.

She'd barely paid attention to her chicken and to her kale salad, beyond noticing that it was true- they *were* absolutely delicious. She would have to investigate these dishes further at a later date, with less distraction.

"Do you need a ride home?" asked Diego when they were done with their food.

"That would be great, if you don't mind," she said. "I still don't have a car. I don't know where you live, but I hope it's not completely out of your way."

"Don't worry- it's a privilege to drive you back," he said. Ashley allowed herself to think about whether he would try for a good night kiss.

But then, as they were emerging from the restaurant, the young stable hand Ashley had seen exercising the horses earlier came hurrying up to Diego.

"Diego, we've been trying to reach you for the past hour," he puffed. "The prince is pissed. He's wondering why the hell you left early."

"That's ridiculous. The meeting was over. He'll get over it," said Diego.

"I don't think so. He said he's back in his home office, and you'd better go over there right now."

Andreas added something in Spanish that Ashley didn't understand, and Diego responded, angry now. Ashley was working hard to pretend she wasn't listening in, not that she could understand their rapid-fire Spanish.

"I'm so sorry," said Diego, finally. "I have to go. Andreas will take you back to the stables."

"All right," said Ashley, disappointed. Not even an opportunity to feel that kiss on both cheeks that she'd been secretly looking forward to. "I'll see you around, Diego."

"I'll more than see you around, Ashley. I'll make sure to come find you."

"Is that a promise?" she asked.

She gave herself a mental slap on the wrist. *Stop flirting with him. He knows you have the hots for him. It's ridiculous.*

She walked back down the sidewalk with Andreas.

"Thanks again for telling me that that horse was having a problem with its leg," said Andreas. "You really saved my ass. I would have been in huge trouble if you hadn't noticed that, and the horse had gone lame. That horse belongs to an uber wealthy client, and they are not forgiving.

"Wealthy, like the prince?" asked Ashley.

Andreas gave her a strange look.

"Oh, so you're panicked about the prince too?" said Ashley. "It's ridiculous. He's just another client. You don't need to bow and scrape to him."

"OK," said Andreas. "If you say so."

Did she imagine it, or did he roll his eyes at her? The ride with Diego would have been so much better. When they pulled into the Polo fields, Alex was just pulling out. Andreas slowed his truck and opened his window.

"Hey there, Alex. I found Diego. I sent him over."

"Good. I hope he smooths it over. Hey- is that Ashley in your truck?"

"Just driving her home," said Andreas.

"Oh," said Alex.

Shit. Now Alex thought she was getting in on with a much younger man. *Whatever.* She had other things to worry about. Andreas dropped Ashley off in front of the apartment and she went in, feeling very alone indeed. She checked her phone, hoping for a message from Kari or even from Henry, but there was nothing. *Damn it.* How disappointing. She picked up one of the books that Kari had lent her and tried to read it until she fell asleep.

Chapter 26

When she woke up that morning, she had a text from Kari. *Hey girl, all is OK just really busy here. I hope to see you soon. I'll ping you. I may have found a car for you. I let Alex know about it, so why don't you ask him in case he has time to take you to see it? xoxo.*

Ashley thought of what to respond to this. It was hard to tell via text, but she felt like Kari was holding her at arm's length. Then again, she understood that Kari had just changed jobs, and she did have a husband, and her own friends.

After a coffee and her usual getting ready. Ashley stepped out of the apartment. The sky was still pink, the light magical that morning, and it already felt like it might be a warm day. She would go to the beach at lunch, she decided. That would be a perfect plan. She might as well take advantage of living here. Kari's bicycle was still here. She'd be able to make it to the beach on that, wouldn't she? She would also ask Alex about the car situation. She walked into the office. Alex looked like he hadn't slept at all.

"Are you OK?" Ashley asked.

"Rough night. I swear to God. That fucking guy. I just can't deal with his demands anymore. It's like he's a teenager or something. He thinks that we all need to bow to him."

"The prince?" asked Ashley.

"Who else?"

"Man, I hope I don't ever have to cross him. I'm glad you spared me by letting me leave early," Ashley said.

"Yeah, you're welcome," Alex responded. "And if you think he's bad, his wife is a terror."

"I take it that Diego went and smoothed things over?"

"Yeah, hopefully. We were texting into the night, but who knows? I don't even know that it's worth it. Diego assures me that it is. I'd rather find somebody else to be our royal poster child."

"Oh. Right. You're using the prince to increase the reputation of the Polo Club so that it becomes a world class club…wait a second… are you actually saying that there's a *real* prince?"

"Hello? Earth to Ashley, have you not heard? I mean, you've been in Montecito now for how long? Never mind Montecito. It was all over the news. The prince left England and came to Montecito…"

He was an English prince? Ashley wondered if he knew Henry. Henry was kind of a fancy guy. Maybe if Henry was friends with him, he could help to smooth things over.

"Does he know Henry?" she asked.

"Henry?" Alex gave her a blank stare.

"You know him… Henry. You know…"

She paused and thought about how best to describe Henry, without mentioning the ginger hair and crooked smile, which kind of made him sound like a clown.

Just then, a horse started neighing loudly in one of the far stalls. It sounded panicked.

"What the hell?" said Alex. "Can you go check on that? I need to go deal with paperwork and… no, never mind, I'm coming with you."

"No, I'll go," Ashley said. "Don't worry. I think it's just stuck."

The whinnying was getting louder. Ashley worried a bit, but she was used to dealing with all kinds of equine emergencies. She hurried over in the direction of the noises. Just as she had thought, a horse had its neck stuck between the bars of its stall.

"You silly Willy," she whispered to the horse. "Come on."

As the horse continued to thrash around, she tried to gently navigate his head around without hurting it and without hurting herself. She wished she had some help, but of course, she had reverted to her comfort zone of dealing with shit alone, and now she didn't want to disturb Alex, who had seemed absolutely haunted that morning. *This prince fellow was an actual prince,* she thought to herself. *Only in Montecito*, she decided.

Finally, she got the horse disentangled. She tried to calm it down, but it was tossing its head nervously. *I'll go exercise it*, she thought. It would be good for the horse, to work out its stress. And it would be good for her. She clipped the halter on it and started leading it out and toward the paddock. As she was walking around the paddock, she noticed Henry coming up. He sure was around the stables a lot. She wondered if this guy had a day job. She'd never thought to ask.

Well, he'd said something about consulting and entertainment, so he must be some kind of Hollywood type. Nothing much to discuss there. What would she know about that, anyway? She waved to him, and he waved back at her slightly, distracted, she thought. Well, so much for him being the easy alternative to Diego. Maybe he could take her to the beach for lunch, so she didn't have to ride the bike. She hadn't given him time to pack one of his fancy picnics, but they could go pick up a sandwich or something and go sit on the sand. That would be fun.

But Henry headed straight for the offices and ducked in, and she didn't see him again. It was disappointing. She kept walking around with the horse, wondering if he would reemerge. And then, she saw his car leave. *How rude*, she thought. She felt her phone ping. A text message. *Diego?*

But no, it was Henry.

I'm so sorry. Lots of drama going on. Don't worry, I'm trying to come up with a great plan for our next date. Our third date. No pressure. He'd added a smiley face and a kissy face emoji to this. *Haha*, Ashley responded. *No interest in going to the beach with me at lunch?*

Sorry, not today, I'm stuck. I'll let you know as soon as I can get away, he responded.

No worries, she wrote back.

But that sounded like a great plan, she thought. Sandwiches and the beach.

Another message came in from Henry.

This Thursday, I think I can meet you for lunch if you can get away. Why don't I take you to the Buddhist Temple?

Buddhist Temple, was he for real?

Sure. I can pack us a picnic, she responded. *See? You don't have the monopoly on them.*

Ah, but I have the monopoly on cashmere blankets, came the response.

If it's easier, we can just go out to lunch somewhere local, Ashley wrote.

No, this place is magical. You've got to see it.

Ashley put away her phone. He really didn't want to be seen in public with her, did he? Was he embarrassed because she was so simple and unstudied, not one of the fancy Montecito women? She didn't want to think that of him, but it felt like maybe that was the case. She would confront him later, she decided, and got back to work.

When lunchtime rolled around, she popped her head into the office.

"Hey, Alex, need anything? I was thinking of borrowing Kari's bike and going to pick up a sandwich and going to the beach."

"Girl," said Alex. "That's a long bike ride. Why don't you borrow my truck? It's so much easier. There's a great supermarket over at the Montecito Country Mart. You can grab a sandwich there, and then you can go to Butterfly Beach. You'll love it. I'll explain to you how to get there."

"You would lend me your truck?" Ashley asked.

She hadn't driven in a long time, she hoped she still remembered how. But she didn't want to say that to Alex. It sounded great to get a wonderful sandwich at a Country Mart and drive to a beach with butterflies on it.

Alex gave her the keys and the directions.

"Take your time," he said. "The prince finally settled down and is being reasonable with us. We're not as panicked as we were. But I'm going to need some help later this week- we're going to start some happy hours for some of the ladies. They love being able to hit on hot polo players."

"Sounds like that's right up Diego's alley," said Ashley.

"Well, I may be a little bit tough on our friend Diego," Alex said. "Anyway, here, take the car. Don't come back too soon."

Ashley got in the truck and made sure to adjust the seats and mirrors as well as she could. She was nervous as she pulled away, but soon got the hang of it, and then her thoughts went back to what Alex had said about being hard on Diego. She pulled into the parking lot for the Country Mart. It looked pretty much like an ordinary strip mall from the outside, but she was sure the shops inside were expensive. As she walked in from the parking lot, she noticed the fancy looking coffee shop to her right, the one where

Kari had taken her when she had first arrived. She saw those delicious ham sandwiches stocked in a vitrine inside, and was tempted, but then reasoned with herself that the supermarket would have lower prices. Also, she thought of something else. Back when she and Sissy were teens, they used to love reading the gossip magazines. Momma thought that was incredibly lame and tacky. That was years ago. She hadn't read one in forever. Missing her sister as she did, she thought that it would be fun to just get one frivolous gossip magazine. They were cheap, weren't they? She could read up on all the Hollywood stars she knew nothing about anymore, and see what was happening in the world, in a way that wouldn't make her sad or upset, just happy. Silly news. That was a great idea, she decided. She would also get a Coca-Cola and a ham and cheese sandwich. Her heart leapt. For once, she was doing things on her own terms. This was going to be so fun. She would read the gossip magazine on the butterfly beach, in her new hometown.

Finally, things were looking up. She wasn't as worried about Robert showing up any minute. She hadn't even worried about Momma today, and nope, she wasn't going to think about that. She nearly strutted into the Vons supermarket, a smile playing on her lips. An older gentleman, elegantly dressed, looked at her, caught her eye, and smiled. She smiled back.

"Well, you're a sight for sore eyes," he said. "I love seeing somebody with such a beautiful smile. Keep on smiling, girl."

"Thank you," she said.

If that was a pickup line, it was the nicest one she'd ever heard. She marched straight back to the deli and ordered her sandwich, went to the refrigerated case of drinks and fished out the coldest Coca-Cola she could find from the back, and then she proceeded towards the cash registers. There! There were her gossip magazines.

She approached to see which one she would decide to read. The trashier the better, of course.

And then she froze. *What the…?*

She didn't know what she saw first. Was it the familiar ginger shade of hair? Was it the crooked smile? Was it the squinty, friendly blue eyes? *Could it be?* There was Henry. *Henry* …on the cover of a gossip magazine? With a woman, a beautiful dark-haired woman, standing slightly in front of him. Her mouth grew dry. *What in the world was this?* What was she seeing?

Insulting the Queen, she read. Insult the queen? *What?* Her heart started beating so fast, she couldn't trust herself to read this magazine without fainting, or without starting to scream in the middle of this damn store.

So she quickly slammed the magazine down on the conveyor belt, trying not to look at it, and paid cash for that, the soda, and the sandwich she was suddenly not hungry for at all. She clutched the brown paper bag to her chest as she hustled back to the truck. She couldn't bring herself to drive- her hands were shaking too hard, anyway.

What the hell? What the hell? She looked at the magazine cover again. Yes, it was Henry, but here it was saying that his name was Harry. Duke of Sussex, *Prince* Harry. *Henry* was Harry...the prince they were talking about? How had she been so stupid? Why hadn't anyone told her? Everything started to make sense now, except... Henry...Harry was married? She studied the photo of the woman. An ex-actress, she learned from one of the numerous articles about the pair in the magazine. Well, yes, she was very beautiful. She had a brilliant smile. Great skin with pretty freckles. She looked so happy standing there in front of Harry. In fact, they looked very much in love in some of the other pictures of them walking together to various elegant events. But Henry had put his arm around Ashley like that- he had smiled that way at her, as well, hadn't he? She noticed now that she was not heartbroken. She was disgusted. How had she been so stupid? How had she not realized she was a terrible judge of character? Of course, she had a quick thought for Diego then, as she often did. If she'd been starting to think that Diego was maybe boyfriend material after all, that probably meant he was a serial killer.

Ashley read every single article and blurb, holding the magazine with trembling hands. Henry...Harry... had left England, had left the royal family because he and his wife had been pursued by something called paparazzi, which she came to decide meant the press, or photographers. They wanted their privacy, and now they were in Montecito making a TV special and having interviews with Oprah, who even Ashley remembered from back when she'd had a TV? It didn't make any sense.

And now, here were pictures of their children. Adorable little tykes toddling on the perfectly green lawn of what was apparently their mansion in Montecito.

How had Ashley been so stupid? Everyone talking about the prince this and the prince that, and she had thought they were being cute. And they'd been telling the absolute truth. It boggled the mind.

She wasn't at fault, was she? Henry…Harry had been the instigator all along. He had lied to her, or at least had omitted literally all the important details. Then again, when she had told him about her past, she had glossed over a lot of the details, too hadn't she? Why was it fine for her to do this and not for him?

But no, that was different, and this was massive. He was a public figure. All of this about wanting to treat her to private experiences and passing it off as more romantic. When really, he'd just been sneaking around.

Ashley's throat was parched, but her appetite was dead, and so was the desire to go to the beach and enjoy herself. In fact, she didn't know how she'd ever enjoy herself again. Would she be forced to quit her job? Henry would want to keep this secret, she reasoned with herself, but she needed to talk to him, to know his intentions.

Ridiculous to think that she had thought that Diego was such bad news this whole time, and instead, she'd gone running into the arms of someone possibly even worse for her. Certainly something much, much messier. What if someone found out that she and Henry had been together and posted pictures in a magazine like this one? What if Robert happened to be flipping through one of those magazines at the 7/11 where he got a daily coffee and cookies, and there was a picture of her? *Royal Homewrecker* is probably what it would say.

When the cab of the truck had turned into a sauna and she could take it no longer, she got out of the truck on shaking legs and tottered back into the supermarket, where she grabbed each magazine that had anything about Henry-Harry on the cover, and paid for them all, even though she knew that her budget was so tight that she needed to watch every penny. This meant she wouldn't be able to pay for that delicious fried chicken sandwich tonight. But it was worth it. After this, all she needed was a drink. She smiled grimly, thinking how she'd gone from healthy farm girl to desperate single woman who looked forward to hanging out in bars. And a homewrecker, to boot. She took herself to a bench in a shaded corner of the shopping center. Happy families walked by, with their adorable toddlers and perfect hair and expensive looking outfits in tones of caramel and white. She read every word in detail, even re-read some of the articles.

Henry had lost his mother when he was young, so that much was true. He had decided to leave his country and come to California with his wife. It seemed like no one liked the wife much. Ashley wasn't sure why. She certainly looked beautiful and sophisticated, certainly the kind of girl Ashley could imagine a prince falling for. Infinitely more understandable than what Henry could possibly see in a farm girl like Ashley.

She read more stories, her nausea growing as she did so. This wasn't helping. What she needed to do, she decided, was contact Henry. She would talk to him. Maybe there was something that she wasn't understanding about this whole situation. Maybe it wasn't the way it looked. But there definitely needed to be some truth between them. She hadn't been exactly falling for him. Not quite, but she had thought they were building something that might end up growing into something real. And now, she felt completely untethered. She picked up her phone. Should she text him, or call him? Would he pick up if she called? She debated for a moment more. They had always texted, and he had always been the initiator. What if she called, and he was in the room with his wife?

How naïve was she to think that a handsome, wealthy guy like Henry didn't have a significant other? Despite the fact that he wasn't exactly her type, she could tell that he was the type that women would throw themselves at.

She would text, she decided. That way, she would at least know that he got the message, and it wouldn't give him the opportunity to not pick up. He'd have to see it. She composed a text, after deleting 10 different versions of it. Hard to figure out what exactly to say. After all, how often did one find out that one's paramour was a prince, one who was married, to boot? She was pretty sure that this was a situation that not too many people had been in.

She finally settled on:

Henry, we need to talk. You may find this unbelievable, but I just found out who you are. I don't want to jump to conclusions or assume that you were just taking advantage of me, but you should reach out to me to explain.

She saw the three dots appear almost instantly. Henry was typing.

It's not the way it looks, said the message. *I can explain. I'll pick you up after work.*

Fine. When she responded, she made sure to include a period after the single word. She was new to texting etiquette, but she was relatively sure that this communicated that she was not delighted.

She went back to the stables and evaded Alex's questions about the beach, throwing herself into her work. Still, towards the end of the day, she found herself rushing back to the apartment, fluffing her hair, and tucking in her shirt in the front just so, the way she'd seen some of the women in Montecito do it. Why did she care how she looked for him? She hated to admit it. She still wanted to look good, especially compared to that stylish wife of his. The situation certainly didn't look promising, but maybe he could explain it all away. Maybe he did have a good excuse. After all, what did she know? Maybe these celebrity types had fake relationships for show, for their image or for their reputation. She wouldn't assume anything more until she spoke to him. She could at least give him that. She was changing her shoes and still fidgeting with the hem of her shirt when she heard wheels crunching on gravel. Henry. His Shiny Range Rover freshly washed as usual.

Henry got out of the car and opened the passenger side door for her. She remembered how she had seen him coming around the Range Rover to open the door for someone the other day, when she had gone by in her Uber. She had just missed seeing a glimpse of the wife in person, she realized. Henry-Harry tried to give her a hug, but she evaded his grasp.

"Not until you explain to me what's going on," she said.

"Please get into the car," he responded, his lips drawn in a thin, straight line.

Ashley missed seeing the sparkle in his eye and the open smile that she found so endearing. But this was no time to be thinking about that.

"Where are we going?" she asked, once he was back behind the steering wheel.

"I'm going to take you to one of my favorite places," he said.

This shit again. She would have found it charming just yesterday, or even this morning, this propensity to take her to special places that made her feel like she and he were alone in the world. But now she found it disingenuous. He was just trying to hide away. They drove up the mountain.

"What is this favorite place? A cave or something? I've figured out what you're trying to do, Henry. You're trying to hide because you have something to hide. Why weren't you honest with me?"

Henry stared at the road, still driving, clenching his jaw.

"I can explain," he said. "You didn't tell me everything about your life, and I just liked the freedom of not having to tell you about mine. I swear to you, this marriage I'm in- it's a sham now. I started off thinking I was in love. And then, I saw the truth, and it was too late. I get the feeling you might know what that's like."

Ashley gulped. Of all the things he could have said, this one did affect her the most, because yes. She knew exactly what that was like.

"Listen- at this point, I've made such a huge mistake," Henry said. "I've turned my whole family against me. A whole nation pretty much hates me and hates her... and she just scares me all the time. She threatens me. I've got two children to think of, and I've basically lost everything... and without her... without us being a happy loving couple, our whole brand is gone."

"Your brand?" asked Ashley.

That didn't sound right. She'd been following, until he mentioned a brand. What did he think he was, a business? Was that what was important to him? She was silent. The Range Rover stopped in a small dirt parking area on the side of the road.

"Here, let me show you my special place."

"Yet another special place," said Ashley.

"Yes," he pleaded. "Let's walk for a moment, and I promise I'll make you understand. At least I'll try. I know that I was unfair with you, but I really care about you, Ashley. I really do. There's just something about you."

He was blabbering now. He sounded desperate, Ashley decided. Did he think she was going to give in this easily? Swallow his outlandish tale, just because he made pathetic excuses and took her to another special place?

They walked a bit and arrived at a Buddhist temple. Ashley only knew it was Buddhist because Henry had told her what it was, but it was certainly beautiful. She'd never seen anything like it. None of the churches back home were this breathtakingly simple, with a natural air of the divine. This. This was what religious buildings should be like. Anyway, Ashley had started to lose her faith when Robert started hitting her and had completely abandoned it when Sissy had her accident and none of Ashley's prayers did Jack shit for her.

Ashley took in the distant view on the ocean beyond. Everything was bathed in pastel tones in the dying light.

"I didn't have any Champagne ready, but I did bring this," said Henry, and he passed her a beautifully polished flask.

"What's this?" she asked.

"I pre-mixed us my favorite cocktail. "It's called a Negroni."

Ashley shook her head and handed him the flask back without drinking. That was Diego's favorite cocktail, and she already knew how it would taste- bitter, but a bit sweet, strangely delicious. Kind of like her life in Montecito to date. God, she'd been so stupid.

Henry put his hand on her back, and she shivered, but not in delight this time.

"I'm telling you, Ashley. When we came to the states, my wife told me that we had to be a united front. We had to be a brand. That was the only way we were going to make money and afford our life here."

"Afford your life?" Ashley laughed. "Looks to me like you're doing a lot better than just affording a life. You're living high on the hog. Ridiculously expensive polo ponies. A massive oligarch's mansion in Montecito. Two kids in private school. I mean, you really could leave her and live with less, you know."

Henry glanced at her, and at that moment she knew. It would never work out.

"I can't do that. I grew up with everything, Ashley. I can't give up my lifestyle." Henry seemed panicked at the very thought. It was laughable.

"I read in all the magazines about how you're such an environmentalist, but you drive a gas guzzler, and you fly private jets. I think you're a hypocrite, Henry."

"I'm a good person," he whined.

Disgusting.

"I'm sorry, but you were trying to push me to do more than I even wanted to do with you, and I let it slide because I thought you were really into me, and that maybe we could build something. But come to find out that you're just a liar."

"Not true," said Henry. "I was well brought up. I know how to behave."

"Oh, you certainly know how to behave," hissed Ashley. "You know how to behave all suave and smooth to trick girls like me. But I don't think you know how to behave in a real sense, because if you really are this miserable with your wife, you would man up and get away from her."

"I swear to you," he said. "I'm trying. I'm planning on it. It's a lot of legal stuff ... All our companies are linked. I'll lose everything if I make the wrong move."

"Seems to me like you already lost what mattered," said Ashley coldly.

Here was a man with all the resources in the world, and he couldn't man up and leave his wife? She, Ashley, a small-town girl with nothing, had managed to find a way. Maybe she wasn't as helpless as she'd thought.

"She's very suspicious... she watches everything I do," Henry was saying.

Ashley trembled for a moment.

"If she watches everything you do, then why are yo
risk to come see me like this? Wait… those guys on th
when we went to the beach- were they bodyguards or s

Henry nodded sadly.

"She says we need security all the time. She gets suspicious when
I go anywhere without them."

"You've been planning dates for when she was away, haven't
you?"

"Yes," he admitted. "She had a photo shoot the other day. And an
interview the last time we saw each other."

The nausea that had gripped Ashley earlier in the day came back
with a vengeance.

"Everything we did that was fun, everything magical…it was a
lie," she gasped. "I might as well have…"

She was thinking she might as well have just jumped on Diego
like she'd wanted to, but then she decided that she'd better keep that
thought to herself.

"You might as well have what? Asked Henry. "I'm telling you. I
adore you. I might even love you."

"No, Henry, there's no way. It's much too fast to fall in love with
somebody you don't even know."

But that wasn't true, was it? She lusted after Diego so much that
it was the closest thing to love she'd felt in a long while, even
though she barely knew him.

"Please. Just a little kiss. A little hug. To make me feel better.
That's all I ask," Henry pleaded.

Ashley felt sick. He was like a little kid. One who took no
responsibility.

"I'm sorry, but I just can't," said Ashley. "Please take me home.
We're done here."

"I promise I'm going to prove to you that my marriage isn't real.
I'm going to prove to you that what you and I have *is* real."

"Oh yeah, how are you going to do that, pray tell?"

"I'm going to start taking the steps to get away from her. In fact,
I'm planning on moving away from the house."

"Oh yeah?"

Ashley looked at him closely, analyzing his expression. His eyes looked shifty. There was something both true and untrue in what he was saying, she decided. It was like that game she used to play with Sissy. Two truths and a lie. She decided to play along for a second. She lied to herself, now, telling herself she was doing it out of courtesy, but really, she had a sick desire to get more ammunition to verbally best this man who had done her wrong.

"Oh, really, so where are you going?" she asked.

"I'm leaving her the house in Montecito and moving to Hope Ranch, to a house with a polo field."

"Sounds tough. A private polo field must take a shit ton of water. The guilt must be staggering. Why do you need this lifestyle? How are you paying for that, when you just said that you couldn't disengage from her for business reasons?"

"It's all true," he said. "Do you want me to show you the house?"

"Why would I want to see the house, Henry? You think that's enough of a sign that you're being honest? In fact, I would love to speak to your wife, if you're being so open with her about things ending."

"No," he gulped.

"See, I rest my case," said Ashley. "I think that we're better off not speaking to each other anymore. Anything further would probably violate the terms of that NDA that I'm just now figuring out I had to sign because of you."

She would miss her times having fun with Henry, maybe. It had been an exciting interlude. But it was time for her to wise up. She realized that she couldn't possibly maintain a relationship that was based on lies. She would have to find a way to be completely honest, too, with whomever she ended up with. She wondered whether Diego was a liar as well. Was it all men who were like this? Was it all men who showed one face and then hid another, only to reveal it later, when it was too late?

Henry grasped both of her hands in his.

"Please just stay here with me for a moment," he begged.

His grip grew stronger.

"Henry. Please let go of my hands."

"No, just stay with me a little bit. Please?"

He sounded like a child. A scary one.

"I said let go. You're hurting me!"

A spark of fear started to make its way into the back of her throat and the forefront of her mind. This was disturbingly familiar.

"Henry, I'm serious. Please. You need to let go."

"I can't, I need you."

Now he was yanking her hands up and down. She started to see black creeping around the edges of her vision. She couldn't go through this again. Were all men like this?

"LET GO OF ME," she shrieked at the top of her lungs, wresting her hands away from him.

Henry's mouth fell open.

"I'm… I'm so sorry. I don't know what came into me," he said.

"Take me home. I've asked you one too many times."

"Yes, of course," he stammered, jumping to attention.

They walked back to the car in silence. He opened the passenger side door for her, back to being the perfect gentleman.

"Are you not going to speak to me the whole way back?" he asked, clenching his jaw as they drove down the hill.

She just looked at him. There was nothing left to say. She owed him nothing.

Chapter 27

When Ashley got back to the apartment, she fell onto the bed. All the emotion of the past hour, all of the strain, all of the fear, it all came to the surface, and she started to sob. Why had she thought that this would be an OK thing for her to do? Why had she thought that she, stupid Ashley from Montana, would be capable of moving to one of most glamorous places in the country and starting a new life there? How could she possibly think she could get away from her husband and live happily ever after? Instead, she'd left her family behind to fend for themselves against a monster, and she'd ended up in a den of wolves and had gotten entangled in the worst possible relationships. She had lied to herself, telling herself she was being brave, but it had been an easy decision to leave, when there was nothing much to give up. Except for her mother, and her sister, and her horses. She'd put them in danger by leaving selfishly. They probably were in danger, or worse, at this very moment, and she'd barely given them a second thought as she ran off to what she naively assumed would be paradise. She should have just let Robert finish her off. That would have been easier. Instead, she'd pursued this empty California dream. It was irresponsible. And what would come of it anyway? She was barely getting paid enough to pay for her rent. She was going to be living in a horrible 1970s orange velour mess of an apartment above somebody's garage, not even knowing very much about the person renting the apartment to her, either. Who knew? Alex might decide to put the moves on her, as well. And to cap it all off, here she was pining after somebody that everyone said was the most terrible ladies' man on Earth. She was 32 years old, and she had learned absolutely nothing in life. She was a sorry excuse for a human being.

Eventually, her sobs slowed and turned into hiccups. She wiped her eyes. She needed to figure out something. She needed to do something. To move forward with her life. Leave behind all this stupid behavior. And she needed to grow up. She needed to file for divorce from Robert and do things properly. She needed to find out once and for all what had happened to her mom and her sister. But the solution to how to do all of that wasn't immediately apparent. She was at a dead end. Maybe with more options than she'd had a month earlier, she allowed. But still very much backed against the wall.

After a while, her eyes stopped tearing, and she fell asleep.

The next morning, she woke up to glorious sunshine. It was a new day, she decided. No more moping around. She was going to move forward. She would absolutely ignore anything that Henry had to say to her. The good news was, he wouldn't dare communicate with her out in the open at the stables. Would she see Diego today? She needed to stop thinking about that. There were other men in this world. Ones who were available and who weren't saddled with a bad reputation. She headed to the barn after a small breakfast, ready to start fresh. She stopped in the office.

"You look tired," said Alex.

"I'm fine. I'm just looking forward to moving. The coyotes were out around the stables and kept me up all night," she lied.

"It's Montecito. Coyotes are everywhere. Hey, speaking of ruckus, one of the prince's horses has been making a bunch of noise this morning, kicking around in the stall. I was going to go check on it, but I'm waiting on an important phone call. Do you want to go down and check?"

Ashley noticed the casual way in which Alex said *the prince's horse*. She'd been so blind, and this whole time, they'd been telling her exactly who he was. How many other important things had she missed as well?

She hurried down the aisle to the stall where the prince's prize horse, the super expensive one, HRH's Marwan something or other, was being boarded. *Hey dumbass, HRH is short for His Royal Highness*, she realized as she rushed over. As she approached, the banging sounds got louder. The horse was kicking its hooves against the wooden wall of the stall. *Not a good sign*, thought Ashley. But maybe he simply needed some exercise. She wasn't as familiar with high-strung horses like this one. Except for Midnight, back home. And look what Midnight had done to Sissy. She decided she would try to get the horse under control. Halter him and lunge him in the paddock.

As she peeked into the stall, she saw that the horse was bleeding from a fetlock. He'd hurt himself and was still thrashing around. She'd never really seen this type of behavior. Some horses got neurotic when locked up, sure, but this horse had been exercised the day before. Had he eaten something bad? She started to panic a bit.

She managed to calm the horse down by putting her hand on its muzzle and slipped the halter on it. She trotted it outside as quickly as possible before it had a chance to wheel around and kick the wall again. Its eyes were wide, the whites showing, rolling around in its head. It bared its teeth.

There was something very wrong. And then Ashley noticed. The horse was limping. That fetlock injury was worse than she'd thought. She was going to need to call Henry- Harry-the prince- and alert him. That was the last thing she wanted to do. But she couldn't avoid it, and Alex was busy. She picked up her phone and sent off a text message.

Your horse hurt itself. You need to come down here ASAP, she typed. *I'm in the field by the stables with it.*

Within a few seconds, a pair of exclamation points appeared on the message.

His only response. He must have still been angry with her for putting her foot down the night before. *Tough shit.*

Ashley would have busied herself with other tasks as she waited for Henry to arrive, but she couldn't trust his horse to not hurt itself worse, so she kept pacing with it, walking it around as it spun, panicked. She was hoping Alex would come out of his office and take a look, but he never did. It would have been nice to have some backup, but she had this. She was an experienced horse woman after all. The funny thing was, she'd never seen this specific issue before. It was like the horse had been drugged or something.

Finally, she saw Henry's Range Rover speeding down the road towards the club. Her heart started hammering in her chest. It was weird, having gone in a single day from excited to see someone you were having what she'd heard a young girl at Honor Bar describe as a *situationship* with, to dreading it. From flirtation to anger. That's where they were.

Henry got out of the Range Rover and ran towards her.

"How is he? What's going on?"

The horse tossed its head in the air as if in response.

"He's limping, but that's because he hurt his leg kicking at his stall wall like crazy for no reason. It's like he ate something or was drugged."

"What did you give him?" Henry demanded.

Ashley raised her eyebrows.

"I'm sorry. Are you saying you think that I gave him something to make this happen? What is wrong with you?"

Henry grabbed her shoulders. Ashley stiffened.

"Tell me!"

"Let go of me," Ashley said, struggling to keep her breathing under control. *What the hell?* Henry, or Harry, was much more violent than she'd thought, and his actions in the past few days told her that, prince Charming or not, this was not the kind of person she would ever want to be with.

"I'm so sorry. I'm so sorry- I'm just panicked," Henry said, pulling her into a hug, which she started to struggle out of.

He was trying to nuzzle her neck, while she fought to disengage, when she noticed a flash out of the corner of her eye. *What the*? She turned her head and noticed a few men with cameras with long appendages on them. Telephoto lenses maybe? Her uncle had one for bird watching photos.

"Henry… Henry! There are people taking pictures!" she hissed.

Henry let go of her, and violently shoved her away from him. His normally ruddy face had turned white.

"Fuckers!" he yelled.

He ran towards the men, waving his arms around like a child having a tantrum.

Stupid, thought Ashley. She saw the men firing off a few more photos. This would be in every newspaper, every magazine, she realized. Too bad for him.

Then her blood ran cold. Her photo would be in there too, wouldn't it?

Now, she started rooting for Henry. She wanted him to get to the photographers and rip the film out of their cameras. But that's not how it worked anymore, was it? They probably had digital cameras. He wouldn't very well throw them to the ground and destroy them. This was a nightmare. Her dream life in the golden California sun was turning into a nightmare. There was no way Robert would miss this. Sure, he didn't care about gossip magazines, hadn't in the past. But this was front cover stuff. It would catch his eye at the 7/11, or somebody else would see it and tell him.

Ashley saw the men jump into their cars and speed off.

"Well, they won't come back," said Henry.

How the hell did he know?

"But are they going to publish the pictures?"

"I don't know," said Henry. "I don't know if they got a good shot. This is my life. Anytime I go anywhere, this is what happens."

"Well, I'm sorry for you," said Ashley, "but this is also terrible news for me."

Henry hung his head, dejected.

"Forget it," said Ashley. "Nothing we can do about that now. Let's focus on the horse. Do I call the vet? What do we do?"

"The vet's already on her way. You can talk with her and decide on next steps."

"Me?"

Ashley stared at him. His prize horse had a serious issue, and he was going to leave the stable hand to deal with it?

"I need to go. We have a meeting with a TV network."

"Oh, now you have a meeting with your wife? What about that independent home that you're moving to? Does she know about that yet?"

"I've got to go. Can you just keep me posted about whatever the vet says?"

"Sure," said Ashley, "I'll do that. Why not? It's my job."

She watched Henry walk away, dread in her heart. Not at seeing him leave. No. That part was completely dead to her now. But dread at what her brief indiscretion might bring in terms of dangers to her. What would Robert do if he saw her? Would he come out here and try to hurt her, or worse, try to bring her back to Montana?

The vet arrived and got the horse calmed down with an injection and did some blood work. They moved it to a larger stall and Ashley worked on repairing the damage it had done.

Mid-morning, she texted Kari. It was the only thing she could think to do. *Help. I totally fucked up,* she wrote.

Kari didn't respond right away. A bit later, Ashley's phone rang. It was not Kari. It was the veterinarian.

"I detected some concerning drugs in Marwan's blood work," she said, concern in her voice. "The effects should dissipate, but that's why the horse was freaking out. Now it's important for you guys to find out how this happened."

"Thank you. I'll let the owner know."

"I'll text you a full tox report so you guys know what I found."

Once she'd gone over the report, Ashley texted Henry. *Just heard back from vet. Horse was given Epinephrine, Tylenol, and some other things. Thinking it's crucial to find out how this happened.*

She tucked her phone into her back pocket to finish her chores. The phone pinged again. Surely it was Henry, so she picked her phone back up. But it was Kari. *Sorry, had a crazy day,* the message read. *Do you want me to pick you up and take you to Honor Bar? We can talk about how you fucked up. I can't imagine it's that bad. Also, we can figure out when I'll take you to see the car I found.*

Ashley sent off an enthusiastic response, relief making a smile play on her lips. Talking it all through with Kari would be so much better than moping by herself in the apartment.

The phone pinged again. Henry. *Who is this?* said the message. Ashley squinted at the words. What did he mean? He had her number in his phone. And he was expecting a text from her.

Duh, it's Ashley. I'm just trying to let you know about your horse. Don't be weird. We can still talk about professional things, can't we?

She saw the three dots appear and disappear. Then, a message came through. She looked at it, her eyes bugging out.

How'd you like the photographers?

Ashley gulped. What in the world?

H, this isn't funny, she wrote back.

This isn't H, said the return message. *This is his wife. You're about to be in a world of pain.*

Ashley's heart started to hammer in her chest. *Oh no.* She wondered if Henry's wife had found all the flirtatious messages between Henry and herself. Of course, she had found those messages- unless he had deleted them.

Not knowing what to do, Ashley deleted the message and threw her phone down. What was she going to do? What would she do if Henry's wife came to find her? Ashley was a farm girl. She could probably take a fancy duchess on in a fight. But why should she even have to? None of this was her fault. She hadn't been the one to go after Henry…Harry in the first place. It was him. Maybe she could explain it to his wife, woman to woman. But then, she heard tires in the drive on the gravel. Was it Henry?

No. It was Kari.

"Kari! You're early," she exclaimed.

"I know, I hope that's OK," said Kari. "I just finished work, and I don't know, but I've got a really bad feeling about what you're about to tell me, so I thought I'd better come quickly."

"I'm almost done," said Ashley. Let me just put this away and take a quick rinse and we'll be on our way."

Ashley put away the saddle pads she'd just washed, and they went back to the apartment.

"It feels funny to be back in here," said Kari. "I spent a happy couple of years here. And it feels funny to think that you're here for a few more days, and then you're going to go to your new place."

"About that…"

"No. I owe you an apology. I'm sorry I totally freaked out when Alex offered the place to you. It has nothing to do with you. It's me, and it's just different circumstances. I'm sorry, I did something I regretted with Alex a while back that could have totally fucked up my life with Steve, and Steve and have I worked it through, but … I couldn't get past it. I should have seen that you're smarter than I am in that respect. I just want you to know that I'm here for you."

Ashley was a little bit shocked to hear that Kari had had an indiscretion with Alex, but it all made sense now.

"Thank you, Kari. Your support means so much to me. And I'm glad you told me about Alex, but I am no smarter than you."

Kari's mouth dropped open.

"What? You and Alex? Is that…?"

"Oh no, not Alex. Much, much worse."

"Then…who?"

"We're both going to need a drink for this," said Ashley.

"All right," said Kari.

They headed out to her car.

"By the way," said Kari, "I've been trying to call your sister's number whenever I meet someone with an out-of-state phone. So far no luck."

"I didn't tell you," said Ashley. "Robert called Alex from my mom's phone."

"Oh shit."

"Yeah, Alex hung up and blocked the number, but that is too close a call for comfort. But that's the least of it."

As they pulled out of the Polo Club, a Range Rover passed by them in the opposite lane. Ashley thought she saw an elegant brunette behind the wheel, looking not unlike the pictures she had seen in the magazines of Henry's wife. *Shit*. She was probably coming over to open up a can of whoop-ass. Ashley's insides started to liquefy. In any case, the duchess couldn't afford to come make a scene at Honor Bar, so it was probably the safest place to be. She decided against saying anything to Kari.

They arrived at Honor Bar and got rock star parking.

"Let's sit outside while you tell me about your fuck-up. I'm guessing it's boy trouble of some kind, and people here pretend they're not gossips, but I don't want anyone listening in."

They sat in two of the Adirondack chairs by the fire and ordered two glasses of wine. Once they had their wine, Kari looked Ashley in the eye.

"Please tell me that you didn't mess around with Diego and get your heart broken."

"No, and I almost wish I had," said Ashley. Strike that, she absolutely wished she had. It would have been more fun, and she wouldn't be in this mess.

"What's that supposed to mean? If it's not Alex, and not Diego…holy shit, you didn't go for that baby stable hand-Andreas?"

Ashley wrinkled her nose.

"Oh my God, Kari! No!"

Kari rolled her eyes, as if to say, *stop wasting my time, then.*

Ashley cleared her throat and took a swig of liquid courage, otherwise known as Chardonnay. Not super badass, but what could you do?

"Well, you're not going to believe this, but… I didn't realize there was a prince at the polo field…"

"I don't like where this is going, but how the hell did you not know that? Everyone in the world knows that. It's been in every single newspaper and magazine, in fact I thought that's why you wanted to come in the first place- we'd been getting slammed with offers from young women to come work for us. I figured that you were a safer bet than most of them 'cause I at least knew your sister. And of course, we made you sign that NDA."

"No. I literally had no idea. Kari, you don't understand how isolated I've been these past few years," Ashley admitted.

"Oh God, and to think I was joking with you about it when you first started out, but I thought you were in on the joke…I'm afraid to ask…what happened?" asked Kari, wincing pre-emptively.

"Well, this red-headed guy who seemed nice enough started to come on to me, and I wanted to distract myself from Diego, who I guess you can guess I absolutely have the hots for, and, well, he asked me out on a couple of dates."

Kari's eyes widened.

"You didn't go, did you?"

"How was I supposed to know not to? Of course, I said yes. I mean, a gentlemanly guy asks little old me on a date, with Champagne and a beach picnic on a cashmere blanket, and then a private visit of Lotusland? Who would say no?"

"He took you to Lotusland? Lucky," said Kari. "But seriously, how far did you get on these dates?"

"We made out a lot. And there was a lot of genitals rubbing. Fully clothed, well almost. Second base. Eek. Maybe third base. I wasn't that attracted to him, but he's not bad, you know?"

"Not bad, she says," Kari laughed. "Most people would agree that he's kind of a catch, except he is VERY married. What were you thinking, girl?"

"I told you- distraction!" Ashley was blushing furiously by now. "I had no idea who he was, or that he was married at all, until I went to the supermarket, and I saw pictures of him and his wife on every magazine in the newsstand. And I almost had a heart attack."

"Oh my God," said Kari, "You're telling the truth, aren't you? I can't even imagine."

"No shit. And then he wanted to talk to me, and he tried to tell me that he and his wife weren't getting along and that they're just together for their business contracts, and I don't know what to believe."

"Well…OK. That's fucked up, but no harm, no foul. Just stay away from him from now on. You're not that into him, so just cease and desist."

"But wait. It gets worse," said Ashley, her voice weak.

"No way. There's no way it gets worse, "said Kari.

"Oh, believe me it does. So this morning, his horse was acting all crazy. Kicking the stable wall. And I knew there was something wrong with it, and it hurt its fetlock, so I called the vet, and called Henry…sorry, Harry over, to come figure out what was going on, cause it's his stupid expensive horse. But he starts trying to talk about our relationship again, and kind of pulls me into this awkward hug and is nuzzling my neck, and these guys were taking pictures with telephoto lenses..."

"Oh no." Kari groaned, "That really is bad."

"Yeah, I know. But even worse, when I wrote him to tell him that the vet said somebody probably injected his horse with drugs, his wife had his phone."

"Fuck. I mean, if you're to believe the news stories, his wife is a raging bitch," said Kari.

"Honestly, Kari, she seems like one…I think I just saw her driving in the other lane as we were pulling out of the polo club. She told me to get ready for a world of pain, and I don't know how much my sister told you about my husband, Robert? But he's way scary."

Kari looked down.

"Yeah. She finally told me. She blames him for…well… you know."

"She should blame me. I never should have married the guy. But what if these photographers- paparazzi I guess you would call them- what if these guys got a good shot of me and Henry? And what if it goes into the newspaper or magazine? And what if Robert sees it? He's going to fucking kill me."

"I don't think you need to worry about that," said Kari.

Ashley stared at her.

"Why not?

"Why would there be paparazzi at the polo club in the off season? Sounds more like the duchess is trying to get ammo against her Prince Charming in case of divorce. It's not in her business interests to have that come out."

Ashley sighed, briefly relieved.

"Except," said Kari, "Those shots, if they're clear, could fetch a fortune, so she'll have to pay a lot to silence them."

When she saw Ashley's stricken face, Kari quickly said, "seriously, the Duchess does not want this out. She'll pay anything."

"So what do I do?"

"Steer clear of the wife, avoid Prince Charming like the plague, and wait for things to simmer down," said Kari.

They had both finished their glasses by now. Ashley's stomach was growling, after skipping lunch yet again.

"Let's go inside," said Kari.

They wandered into the Honor Bar. Ashley's breathing calmed as soon as she was enveloped in the now-familiar dark atmosphere. There, across the bar, was a pair of men that she would have been very happy to see had she not been with Kari. Jim and Diego. Obviously telling each other some kind of funny story. And there were two empty seats next to them. Diego looked up and locked eyes with her. She started heading towards him, as if attracted by a magnet, Kari be damned. What was wrong with her? What kind of power did he have over her?

"Look," she managed to say to Kari. "Two seats. Right there."

"Oh! Diego, what a coincidence," said Ashley as she slid into the seat right next to him.

"Hi Jim!"

"Nice to see you, my old friend," he said.

As Ashley introduced Kari to Jim, who of course announced her knew her already, she couldn't stop herself from turning to Diego, whose eyes burned deep into her soul. God, if he made her feel this way with just his eyes, what would it be like if he actually put his hands on her, or… something else? *Stop thinking that way*, she chastised herself. *Your life is falling apart.* But then, Diego put his hand on her shoulder. She shuddered. Even that felt delicious.

"It's good to see you," he said. "You know you never did give me your phone number?"

"Well, you didn't give me yours either," she shrugged, faux casual.

"That's right," he said. "I think we need to remedy that right now."

Ashley glanced at Kari, who gave her a disapproving look.

"Come on," said Diego, "Don't believe Kari if she tells you that I'm a bad influence or some kind of bad guy. She doesn't know anything about me."

"Oh, I've heard stories," said Kari.

"Well, everybody's got stories. Doesn't mean they're true," said Diego. "Are all the ones about you true, Kari?"

Ouch, thought Ashley. Now, she knew exactly what Diego was referring to. Kari did not answer.

"Do you want to split a chicken sandwich?" Kari asked.

"Perfect. I kind of blew my food allowance on gossip magazines," Ashley said wryly.

"I didn't know you read that trash," Diego smiled.

"Well, I don't, usually," said Ashley, "But something caught my eye."

"Your drinks and your chicken sandwich are on me," said Jim, "so go crazy. Order the kale, too. I know you want to."

"That's very kind," said Ashley. "But I actually owe you dinner-I need to ask you a few questions a little bit later, if you don't mind. I just need to pick your brain about something."

Screw being discreet. Everyone had a story. She needed to be proactive from now on.

"All right, said Jim. You have my number."

"Yeah."

Diego looked curious, as did Kari, but Jim changed the subject, ever the consummate professional.

Now, Diego's knee was against her thigh again. Was this the only type of action she would ever get from him? No matter- just his knee on her thigh made her feel all trembly inside. They finished their sandwiches and Kari checked her phone.

"Babe, I'm so sorry, my husband's whining about being hungry. I need to head home. Do you want me to drive you back?"

"I'll drive her back," said Jim. "Don't worry, I'll make sure she gets back safe and sound." Ashley grinned. She'd been lucky to find Jim. She secretly wished that Diego would drive her home instead, but she didn't need Kari to know that.

Everyone bid their goodbyes to Kari, after which Diego ordered Ashley another drink when she sat back down. She took a sip of the delicious white wine. She had branched out from rosé and Chardonnay, onto Sancerre, and she felt a lot more sophisticated for it.

"I have to go make a phone call," said Diego, "I know you guys have something to talk about, so why don't I make my call and come back? It's only going to take a few minutes." "Sounds good," said Jim.

Ashley nodded. Was he calling one of his girlfriends? Probably. Why was she thinking like a jealous wife? Diego didn't owe her anything at all, and here she was worrying about other girls when they hadn't even had anything happen between them. Once Diego had left the restaurant, Jim's expression turned more serious.

"OK Ashley, I don't know you well, but I can tell there's something big going on."

"Well," said Ashley. "It's really, really bad."

Jim just looked at her.

"OK, I think that I can preface this with, I didn't know there was a prince living in Montecito."

"Oh, boy," said Jim. "I probably don't want to hear what's coming next, do I?"

"Probably not," Ashley admitted. "I'll keep it short and surface level. It wasn't me. He came on to me and he took me on a couple dates."

"He took you on dates?" Jim's eyes narrowed. "Where was his wife?"

"I don't know," said Ashley. "Photo shoots, a trip to LA, something like that. I didn't know, Jim, I swear, but here's the problem. As soon as I found out, I obviously cut it off, but then some guys with cameras started taking pictures of us while he was hugging me on the polo fields."

"Please tell me he was just hugging you and not ramming his tongue down your throat, Ashley."

"Yes, he was still just hugging me. Not to say that he hasn't rammed his tongue down in my throat, but that'll never happen again," Ashley said. "And besides…I…"

She blushed and was silent.

"Besides what?" Jim laughed. "Oh, come on. It's kind of obvious. I don't know why you two crazy kids aren't together already. What are you waiting for?"

Ashley stared at him.

"Are you talking about…"

"Oh, we all know who I'm talking about, Ashley. He's not in the room right now. I see the looks between you guys. I mean it's ridiculous. Your chemistry is off the charts."

"Well, everybody keeps telling me he's a horrible womanizer. I thought…"

"Oh, Ashley…it's kind of a joke," said Jim. "I mean yes, maybe he was a womanizer in the past, and he's just so damn good looking that all of us are jealous, but I mean he's no better or no worse than anybody else. If you like him, I don't understand why that would hold you back."

"OK. Well, good to know. But before I unwrap that, there's another huge issue," said Ashley. "My story gets worse."

"It gets even worse?" asked Jim.

She couldn't tell if he was serious or if he was mimicking her, but it didn't really matter at this point. She needed to get this off her chest.

She told him about how she had left Montana to run away from her husband. How he had hurt her, and how she was worried about her mother and her sister, and how Henry's wife intercepting their texts might mean that she might track down Robert and have him come hurt her.

Jim listened; his expression serious.

"OK, you got me," he said. "This is a lot more serious than anything I thought you would tell me. I'm going to take this seriously, Ashley. You know that you can call me 24/7. And I'm going to make sure that I have patrol cars going by the polo fields."

"I move from the polo fields to the garage apartment at Alex's place later this week," Ashley said.

"Well, that's bad news," said Jim.

Ashley sat bolt upright. She'd thought it was too good to be true. Had she made a mistake, accepting Alex's offer?

"Oh, don't worry- it's not anything to do with Alex. Yeah, he's got a reputation too, but he's a fine guy. No, I'm just worried because that place is a little bit more isolated. It's harder for us to do drive-by's. He's got that gate and everything, but maybe I'll talk to him."

"No!" pleaded Ashley. "Please don't talk to him. I don't want him to think that I'm more trouble than I'm worth."

"Come on, I know how much you're worth to him," said Jim. "He thinks you're the best employee he's ever had. He wouldn't want to lose you for anything."

"I don't know," said Ashley. "If I'm bad publicity, I can imagine that it would not be worth it after a while."

"Don't worry," said Jim, "We're going to work this out. And I know that you've got a lot on your plate but let me just say this. I would tell you if there was any reason not to go for Diego."

"Yeah, but as you said, I've got a lot on my plate."

"Speaking of, where is that boy? I think it's time to take you home."

Diego was still gone.

"By the way," said Jim, "I'm going to try to track your mother down. Can you give me all the details? Her name, address, all that stuff?"

Ashley told him and he jotted it down. Jim looked towards the entrance of the Honor Bar.

"Well. Time to drive you home. Too bad for Diego."

Jim paid up and they left the bar, stepping onto the sidewalk. There was Diego. He seemed to be just wrapping up his conversation.

"Sorry," said Diego. "Where are you going?"

"I guess I'm taking Ashley back. I think it's time to call it a night," said Jim.

"I'll take her back," said Diego. "I'm going in that direction."

Jim looked to Ashley.

"Well?"

She shrugged.

"Doesn't make a difference to me."

Except of course it made a difference to her. Her heart had started beating double time already.

"OK," said Jim, "let me know if you need anything and I'll be in touch."

Ashley thanked him again, and she and Diego walked down the street. The night air felt cool on her face. She'd grown to love that marine layer that snuck around like a gray cat, cooling things down in the evenings, making everything a little bit moody.

Diego took her arm.

"You're cold," he said.

"I'm not too bad,"

Not taking no for an answer, he draped his jacket over her shoulders. It felt deliciously warm and smelled musky and spicy, just like him. She breathed in hard, hoping he wouldn't notice that she was just like a lovesick teenager.

He opened the passenger side door of the old green Range Rover for her, and she got in. *The prince is not the only gentleman around here,* she thought.

"Sorry I was on the phone," Diego said, once he was seated at the steering wheel. "It couldn't be helped."

"Talking to some beautiful young woman no doubt?" Ashley teased.

"In fact, yes. I was."

Ashley stiffened and sat bolt upright. Dammit. She'd known he was too good to be true. At least he was brutally honest.

"My daughter," Diego said.

"You have a daughter?" Ashley asked, stunned. As long as he didn't have a wife, she could work with this.

"Yes," he smiled. "She's five years old. And she's the apple of my eye. She lives in Argentina with her mother. I wish I could be with her more often, but her mom and I aren't on good terms."

"Oh, so you're separated?" Ashley asked, a little bit too fast.

"Yes, divorced. It's not something I ever would have wanted, but unfortunately sometimes things just don't work out, you know? No one here knows anything about it. Except for you, now."

"Your secret is safe with me," Ashley said. Now that he had been honest and raw with her, she had to ask: "So are you dating anyone right now?"

Diego smiled.

"Why do you want to know?"

"Just answer my question," she said.

"I'm not dating anyone right now," he said, giving her that look that made her melt.

And then, it was as if someone had flipped a switch. Ashley was out of her seat belt, and straddling Diego in the driver's seat of the car, devouring his soft lips, running her hands through that thick hair that she dreamed about so many times. He threw his head back and let her kiss his neck. His Adam's apple. The sharp line of his jaw. She didn't know what had come over her. Well, of course she knew what had come over her. She'd had he absolute hots for him for a month, now. Had never felt this way before. Never felt so hungry for someone. He ran his hand down her back, grabbed a buttock in each hand, and squeezed. She felt a twinge between her legs, and sudden wetness. Her breasts grew engorged and tingly as she rubbed them against his chest. He unbuttoned her shirt and took a nipple between his teeth. When she gasped, he started to gently suck on it, and then started on the other side. She ran her hands. down Diego's back, feeling his hot skin under his shirt, feeling the hard muscles underneath. His tongue explored her mouth, and he tugged at her lips with his teeth. She moaned. The windows of the car were fogging up, and she started worrying that a cop, probably not one as sympathetic as Jim, was going to catch them.

"We're gonna get caught," she whispered, as he sucked on an earlobe.

"You want me to stop?" he whispered.

"No. But I think you should."

He gave her one last lingering kiss, running his hands down the sides of her face, looking into her eyes. She felt devastated to be stopping at all, but she needed to make things right before going all in.

"Let me take you home," said Diego. "You've had a hard day, I can tell, and I'm a gentleman. I've not taken you on an official date yet. I wouldn't dare take advantage of you in a car for our first time."

Oh, but how she wanted him to take advantage of her, right there and then. Just the tiny taste she'd gotten of him so far was not enough to satisfy her hunger. But he was right. She wanted to take this slow. Hearing from Jim that he wasn't the lady killer everybody made him out to be had changed things in her mind, but nothing could change what had happened with Henry. She needed to fix that before she could jump into this.

"Thank you for being a gentleman," she said, against her wishes. "I'm expecting a date sometime soon."

"If you would give me your phone number," he smiled. He ran his fingers gently down her throat, making her shiver.

"You win, I'll give you my number," she responded.

He handed her his phone, and she entered the digits into it, just realizing then how that simple act of him handing her his phone had demonstrated more trust and more openness than anything she'd experienced in a long time.

"Feel free to call me or text me anytime," she said.

"Oh, I will," he responded, smiling too. "Ever since you arrived, I could think of nothing else. You wouldn't believe what I've done to you in my thoughts."

"What? Tell me," she groaned, about to throw herself at him again.

"Well, maybe I'll just have to show you, but not before we've gone on a few proper dates. I told you- I'm a gentleman, and you deserve that."

"I can tell," said Ashley. "I can see your little gentleman is paying attention, too," she said, gesturing to the bulge in his pants.

"Touché," said Diego. "He's not well trained yet. Maybe you can help. But don't call him little."

Ashley laughed. No, it was absolutely not little.

"You're getting silly. Drive me home."

They drove towards the polo club, Diego telling her a bit more about his daughter. From what Diego said, Ashley could sense the love he had for his daughter, despite the difficulties in seeing her.

"You're a good dad," Ashley said.

Diego grew serious.

"Not as good as I want to be. A good dad would be present, and unfortunately, I'm not really in a position to do that, and now, there are other obstacles. But maybe one day."

Ashley thought about Henry, about how he'd said he needed to stay with his wife for his family, and she realized that maybe it was more complicated than she'd allowed. Maybe Henry was right. He couldn't get out of this. Not easily, not without losing his kids. She didn't have any children, so she didn't know what it was like.

But thinking back to just a few moments earlier, in the parked car, made her quite sure of what she wanted, and that was Diego. They pulled up to the apartment at the club.

"Do you want me to walk you in?" Diego asked as he opened the passenger side door.

"If you walk me in, I might not let you leave," said Ashley. "I might not want to leave either," said Diego, smiling, "But I will walk you to the door."

He walked her to the door and gave her another delicious, deep, sexy kiss, one that left Ashley's knees weak. She unlocked the door, turned on the lights, and turned to watch him walk back to the car. That perfect body of his. His ease of movement. The way his ass looked in those jeans, which would look ordinary on any other man.

He was delicious in every way. She could still smell his scent from where he'd put his coat on her shoulders, and where he'd kissed her neck. She couldn't bring herself to shower it off that evening. After he drove away, she closed the door, and spent some time looking up police reports and news stories from her hometown, but there was nothing she could find. She wished she had just remained with her pleasant thoughts of Diego, but unfortunately, the minute he'd left her, the negativity and the fear of her situation kept rushing back in. Tomorrow, she would have to see if any stories had come out in the gossip magazines. She was going to need a car. She couldn't just keep borrowing Alex's truck or depending on rides, though getting a ride from Diego had been exactly what the doctor ordered.

She got ready for bed, went to sleep, and had a dream.

She was in the stables, currying one of the horses. The prince's horse, back to its healthy glossy self. As she curried the horse, she noticed that she was naked. Henry was watching her from the corner of the stall, also naked, looking unmistakably aroused. He came towards her, and she kept brushing the horse, ignoring him. He put his hands on her breasts and leaned her against the warm withers of the animal. She could feel the warmth of the horse's sides on her back, and then Henry's hands on her breasts, then running down her body, and making their way between her legs. Stop, she said in her dream. And then, Henry transformed into Diego, and it was Diego standing there, no shirt on, his white jeans open to reveal a splendid erection that made her feel weak. He came to her, and touched her the same way Henry had, but now, it was magical. Every touch felt delicious. Diego's hands moved down, and his fingers found the wetness between her legs. He put a finger inside of her, then two, biting her neck as he did so. She bucked against his hand, wanting more. She arched her back, and begged him, and he pulled her closer to him, and shoved her against the wall of the stall, entering her, filling her with his length, sending waves of pleasure between her legs and throughout her body.

And then, almost immediately, she came.

She came in her sleep, waves of pleasure pulsating through her, and woke up, gasping, the throbbing between her legs still giving her pleasant jolts. Slowly, as Ashley took stock of where she was, she realized that it had all been just a dream. But a delicious dream, a dream she wanted to reenact in real life, the presence of the animals adding a primal dimension, the danger of getting caught in the stables adding to the naughtiness of the whole situation. Ashley finally got her breathing under control and fell back into a deep sleep.

Chapter 28

She was jolted awake at 8:00 o'clock in the morning, by her phone buzzing.

Crap. how had she slept so late, again? And who was calling her?

She noticed Kari's number on her phone's display.

"Kari," she gasped into the phone. "Everything OK?"

"Oh girl, everything is not OK," said Kari.

"What do you mean?"

"Well, I would say that you don't want to see all the gossip websites this morning, but then again, you probably do, and it's all over the internet. Just go check out the Daily Mail online. You're not going to like what you see."

Ashley screwed her eyes shut.

"How bad is it?"

"Well, the good news is that you can't really recognize you in the pictures, but it's still not great. Who knows if another photographer didn't get a better picture in? Later, there might be a bidding war of some kind or something. You said there were several photographers there. Who knows?"

Ashley gulped. Funny, Kari had been the one insisting that the pictures would probably never come out.

"OK, I've got to check on this," said Ashley. "Thanks for letting me know."

Her heart was beating. She was definitely going to be late to work, but this was crucial. She typed in the web address of the Daily Mail and the first article that popped up was titled, *Royal Homewrecker?* If she wasn't so panicked, she would almost have found it funny. That was the title she'd imagined in the first place.

She peered at the photos. She saw Henry holding her wrists, and remembered how it had felt at the time, how he'd been hurting her, and how she'd been scared, but the photos made it look passionate. If you didn't know who you were looking at, Ashley wasn't recognizable, but this was still not good at all. The gossip magazines, knowing that Henry had someone he was having some kind of an illicit relationship with at the polo fields, were going to bring all kinds of unwanted attention to their operation. And it would probably bring Henry's crazy wife even further out of the woodwork, too. Unless she had been the one to orchestrate it, int the first place. Ashley jumped into her clothes, not having had time to shower after all. She brushed her teeth as quickly as possible, guzzled a black coffee, and hurried over to the stables. First stop, the office.

Alex's face was grim.

"Ashley, this isn't good," he said.

"Who told you?"

She'd been hoping to break the news herself.

"Nobody needed to tell me. It's all over every single website. And on top of it, people called me 'cause it's the polo fields. How could you do this?"

"Alex, I swear, look at the pictures. Look at the pictures. Just look at them. And you tell me. Does it look like I'm initiating anything? I swear to God I didn't do anything that would bring trouble here. I didn't know who he was!"

Alex opened up his phone and stared at some pictures. He was shaking his head. Ashley's heart beat double time. She was telling the truth, standing up for herself. Would it be enough?

Alex rubbed his eyes with a fist.

"OK, I'm giving you the benefit of the doubt, Ashley, but I don't want any trouble. I can't have this. Diego and I have been working so hard on making this a world class facility, and now you come along and…"

"I come along and what? You guys brought in a wild card with this prince of yours. He's the one who did this. Not me. Blame him."

"I'm sorry, Ashley. You have a point. I shouldn't have spoken to you to like that. But can you please just keep away from him. Can you do that?"

"I absolutely promise," said Ashley, "I have no intention of getting anywhere near him. Just… if you can help to make that happen too, that would be great."

"OK, I'll do that," said Alex. "Since there's nothing we can do about this right now, let's focus on work- I've got a bunch of things for you to do. There's that damn event that we're going to be putting on to raise more funds. That Meet the Players thing. Seeing all those hot Argentines always brings out the Montecito ladies with their checkbooks."

"Oh," said Ashley.

She had an unwelcome vision of a bunch of Montecito ladies with their perfect blonde ponytails and tennis skirts flocking around Diego. She bet they threw themselves at him all the time. I mean, who wouldn't?

"OK, so what do you need me to do?"

Alex gave her a laundry list of tasks, and she set about achieving as much of the list as possible. It gave her a reason not to dwell on what was going on. The event was to take place in just a couple days, now. As couple days in the course of which there was every chance that there would be more newspaper and magazine articles coming out.

And even worse than this leading to Robert finding her, what would Diego think?

Chapter 29

Ashley was eating a sandwich that she had made out of the paltry groceries she still had in the fridge in the apartment, regretting the good old days when Henry used to invite her out for a glamorous beach picnic with foie gras and Champagne. She hadn't been back to the Honor Bar, either, and hadn't heard from Diego. She was terrified to reach out lest it confirm that he was livid at her.

The good news was, she was saving money. The terrible news was, she was terrified of stepping foot outside. Her phone pinged. It was Kari.

Hey, should we go see your car? The message read. Ashley's heart leapt. She was desperately needed a car. She was officially moving the next day.

How much? She responded.

Dirt cheap, came the response.

Apparently, the car was ugly but dependable. How bad could it be? The car belonged to a colleague of Kari's who lived in Carp, and they planned to meet up after work to go check it out. Ashley put her phone away. Having a car would be amazing. It would be another piece of freedom in her new, newly shitty but still better than before life.

She smiled, but then her smile faded. Would she be able to step out in public ever again? When would this whole story with Henry-Harry blow over? She still couldn't believe she'd let herself fall into this situation. It was the last thing she wanted to do.

She finished her uninspiring sandwich and went back to work, picking up the pace. She was excited about the funds that this event might possibly raise, and curious to see what would happen with the Montecito ladies, though preemptively jealous lest they lust over Diego the way she did. Maybe this would be the opportunity though to see if he had a secret affair going on, too. She wanted to trust him implicitly, but she'd been burned now, and she couldn't afford to believe just anyone. Then again, as far as she knew, Diego might be thinking she was a liar right about now, too. She went and checked on Henry's horse. She experienced a little shiver, as she recalled the dream from the night before. This was the location of that wild romp. Just thinking about it made her blush. She checked that everything was in order, popped into the office to make sure that Alex didn't want anything more from her, and quickly changed into a casual outfit appropriate for going to look at a car.

Kari came to pick her up just on time.

"OK, so I'm warning you," Kari said, "it's nothing to look at, but it runs."

"I have absolutely no problems with an ugly car," said Ashley. "How bad can it be?"

"Oh, you have no idea," said Kari.

They drove towards Carpinteria. Ashley had not had the chance to explore there yet. It was much more working class than Montecito but felt colorful and fun. She noticed quite a few restaurants that looked like something she might want to try out if she could ever afford it. They drove down a narrow street and stopped in front of a light blue painted beach bungalow.

"We're here," said Kari.

"This is one of your co-workers' places?"

"Yeah, he inherited it from his parents, and lives there with his family. And they have a renter in the garage. That's the only way they can afford it."

Ashley noticed a lot of deferred maintenance on the property. It was cool, though, and close to the beach. Maybe one day she could afford a place like this. But for now, she was already better off than she'd expected. Kari and Ashley made their way to the front door, which was painted a bright pink. Ashley wondered whether the car would have the same aesthetic. *No matter- as long as it runs*, she thought.

A rotund man with a sweet face opened the door.

"Hey Pablo," said Kari cheerfully.

She leaned in to give the man a hug.

"Hey, hot stuff," said Pablo.

"Pablo, this is my friend Ashley I was telling you about. She desperately needs a car. She doesn't care how ugly yours is."

"Are you saying my car is ugly?" Pablo laughed. "It's not ugly, it's hideous. Here, let me show it to you."

They made their way around the house. The side yard was littered with children's toys and colorful decorations for the Dia de Los Muertos. Ashley liked the personality they had put into the place. She looked forward to decorating the ugly Orange Palace above Alex's garage, too.

"So here she is," said Pablo, gesturing at something that Ashley could barely comprehend by simply looking at it. She squinted and shook her head, and the details started to grow clear. It was a light blue Datsun, she realized, with pink and orange hibiscus flower stickers all over it, and a graffiti painted surfboard on the roof. The seats looked like they had been reupholstered in some kind of faux shearling.

"It's not so bad," said Ashley, hopefully. "I mean, once you take off the surfboard..."

"Well, that's the thing," said Pablo. "You can't take the surfboard off. It's glued on."

Ashley blinked.

"It's glued on," she repeated.

"Maybe screwed on, too. Don't ask."

"OK," said Ashley. "Well, can I give it a test drive?"

"Be my guest," said Pablo. "I don't think I'd be able to tell if you damage it along the way, so go for it."

Ashley looked at the car. Other than having a surfboard on its roof, it also had a series of mysterious dents, several per panel, but none of them seemed that severe. The good news was, the hibiscus stickers were probably holding it all together.

"Was this an old bumper car or something?" she laughed. "Or a clown car?"

"Maybe," said Pablo. "It belonged to my brother."

"Oh, so did he trade up to a BMW or something?" Ashley laughed.

"He's in jail," said Pablo.

"I won't ask," said Ashley. "Well, Kari, do you want to come with me for the test drive?"

"Are you kidding me? said Kari, "I wouldn't be caught dead in that thing."

"Suit yourself," said Ashley, "I'll be back in a minute."

She got behind the wheel. It felt great to be behind the wheel of a car, even one as ugly as this one.

She turned the key in the ignition. The key was painted to look like a spider or a scorpion or something, she couldn't quite tell. The paint was all chipped off. But the key worked. The engine turned over and sprang to life. She took herself around the block, then found a straightaway, to gun it a little bit. The car wasn't going to win any prizes in the speed department, in the power department, or in the style department, but it did run, and there didn't seem to be any disturbing rattles or squeaks or smells. She made her way back to Pablo's house, which was not hard to find, with its crazy paint job. She suspected that bad taste ran in the family.

"Can I have a look under the hood?" she asked Pablo.

He smiled at her.

"Wow, I didn't know any ladies who know what's going on under the hood of a car."

"Now you do," said Ashley.

She was proud of her farm background. Proud of how capable she was with machinery and horses and things like that, despite how Momma had mocked her for it. She might have sucked at the financial, paperwork stuff, and she would never be one of those Montecito ladies, but she was proud to be herself, and she certainly wasn't embarrassed to be driving this clown car if it meant that she had a car. She checked everything, and it seemed to look OK. In fact, better than expected.

"How much?" she asked, a pit in her stomach.

She was still terrified that it would be much more than she could afford.

"This piece of shit? Is $600.00 too much?" asked Pablo.

$600. She couldn't believe it. She had been expecting so much worse. She didn't quite have $600.00. Not exactly, but…

"Can I pay you in installments?" she asked.

"How many installments?"

"Two? Maybe three?"

She would have to limit the delicious Ding's crispy chicken sandwiches she enjoyed, but she could do it in two, and then the car would be all hers.

"No problem," said Pablo. "Just give me 300 now."

"I don't have the cash on me."

"You can Venmo him, silly," said Kari.

"What's that?"

"Sorry," Kari explained to Pablo. "She literally grew up in a barn. She has no idea. Listen, I'll Venmo you, and I'll make her pay me back."

"OK," said Pablo.

Kari took her phone and made a few jabs with her finger, and Pablo's phone pinged.

"Done. OK, it's all yours," said Pablo.

"Really? That was easy," Ashley laughed.

Pablo tossed her the keys, and gave her the second set, as well.

"Good luck with it. Don't forget to register it."

Register it? She wouldn't tell Pablo, but how did she do that without having to show her driver's license and maybe be trackable? The blood rushed in her ears. As if in the distance, she thought she heard Kari's phone ping. Kari excused herself and took herself around the corner while Pablo explained a few more of the car's features until Kari came back.

"Come on," Kari said, her teeth clenched. "Time to go. I'm starving. I know a place that we can go to for seafood."

Ashley nodded, her mind racing. Why was she suddenly acting weird? Was she what Ashley 2 the hostess at Honor Bar referred to as *hangry*? Usually Ashley was the one starving, Begging Kari to go somewhere to eat. She got in her new car and followed her friend to a parking lot.

They got to the restaurant and sat in a booth.

"Listen," Kari whispered. "I just heard from your sister. Well, I heard from Craig."

"What did he say?"

"After Craig went to try to check on your mom, Robert followed him back home and beat the crap out of Craig, almost killed him."

"What?" Ashley gasped, tears springing to her eyes. "I need to…"

"You need to nothing. Listen, Sissy is fine, and in a safe place. Craig is still in the hospital, but out of the woods. He wanted you to know that they're both OK."

"But Momma?"

"We're still not a hundred percent sure. She's not at her house. But here's the good thing- there's a warrant out for Robert's arrest, now, for attempted murder. And, well, this is not good, but depending on what happened to your mom, maybe actual murder..."

Ashley's eyes flooded with tears. Momma hadn't been the best mother. But she hadn't been the best daughter. Sure, Momma had been frustrating at times, when she didn't want to address the reality of Ashley's life, but she had raised her well, and didn't deserve anything bad to happen to her.

"Don't jump to conclusions," said Kari. "There's a chance your mom is hiding, too. Did she have anywhere she might go? Any friends or..."

"Maybe," Ashley allowed. "And she's smart enough that she wouldn't try to reach out to Sissy, if she thought it would put her in danger." She didn't mention that Sissy spoke to Momma as seldom as possible. Sissy called her a narcissist.

"So, focus on the positive. Your sister and brother-in-law are OK, and Robert will soon be arrested."

But Ashley thought that, on the contrary, this was very bad news. Robert was obviously not at home anymore, or he would have been found. What did that mean for the horses, and where would he go? He might not have been motivated to go looking for Ashley before, but now, he didn't have anywhere else to be. Had Craig truly not told him anything at all, even while fearing for his life and for Sissy's?

"Oh, one piece of good news," said Kari. "I guarantee this one will make you smile."

"What?' Ashley didn't think that anything could make her feel better.

"Your horses are all doing great."

"How?"

Ashley really started blubbering now, tears and snot running down her face. Through this whole ordeal, as much as she was scared for her family, she had been experiencing crushing guilt for her animals. She had reasoned with herself that even Robert wouldn't let innocent animals suffer, while knowing in her heart of hearts that he didn't care. It had been a matter of survival for her, but she felt wretched that she'd put her own needs first.

"Craig told me how, before any of this even happened, probably before you had even left the state of Montana, a mailman said he was concerned about something weird happening at your farm. I don't know how that…"

"I spoke to the mailman the day before I escaped! He must have thought I was crazy- I was so panicked, asking to use his phone…"

"Well, apparently, he didn't work the next day, the day you must have escaped, but the day after that, he decided to go down the driveway to make sure you were OK."

Kari explained what Craig had related to her. How the mailman had found the house a mess- front door open, holes punched in walls, Ashley's meager belongings strewn on the floor. She explained how, when the mailman had checked on the horses, he'd noticed they had not been fed, stalls not cleaned in at least a couple days, so he called a relative of his that had a horse rescue, and they had stepped in. Sissy's information had still been on the LLC documents for the horse business, so they had tracked her down.

Ashley was hiccupping now. She was still worried about her mom, of course, but so relieved about Sissy and Craig, and the horses. She was so thankful to Kari for relaying the message that she didn't want to saddle her with her fears regarding where Robert might be at this very moment.

Once Ashley had calmed down somewhat and gotten some food in her- she was actually ravenous, she found- Kari explained to her how to sign up for Venmo and how to register the car. Kari even walked her through logging into her old email address, which Sissy had thankfully been using up until just under a year ago to deal with horse business, to find the scan of the birth certificate she had sent herself years ago. Along with her social security number, which she had memorized, her old Montana license, her credit cards, and the electricity bill she had just signed up for over at Alex's place, it would be enough for a new license and registration.

"Thank you so much. Dinner should be on me," she told Kari.

"Except I saw how much you have in your bank account after all of this," teased Kari. "So I guess it better me on me."

"This is the last time," said Ashley.

"You bet your ass it is," laughed Kari. "At least this time, I don't have to drive your sorry ass home."

"I can pay you back with a fun invitation to a cocktail party, though," said Ashley.

"Oh?" Look at you, miss local, letting me know about things going on in this town that I don't know about."

"Maybe it's not that exciting," Ashley allowed. "But it's all Alex can talk about. They're trying to do some outreach with the Montecito ladies, and they have a bunch of polo players coming."

"Oh," said Kari. That sounds like a potential train wreck."

"So, you don't want to come?" Ashley was sad not to have her wing woman.

"Oh no, I love train wrecks. I just need to ask Steve. He's understandably a little weird when it comes to stuff at the polo club."

"Oh. Yeah." Ashley peered at Kari. "You don't need to answer this, but why did you even tell him about you and Alex?"

"Because full honesty is the best policy, even if it makes things messy."

Ashley thought guiltily about how Diego had opened up about his daughter, but she hadn't told him that she was married, or about Henry-Harry. She needed to fix that.

"Well, let me know if you can come," said Ashley.

It would be good to have someone at her side, someone she could chat with while the Montecito ladies threw themselves at the players. She didn't dare hope that Diego would pay any attention to her at this event. That's not what it was for. She was also starting to see the economic divisions in this community. Diego seemed reasonably wealthy to her, by her standards, and so did Alex, but with their old trucks and casual airs, compared to someone like Henry and his wife, they were not in the same ballpark.

The friends said goodbye, and as she drove back to the polo club apartment, Ashley realized that she now had her own car, and

243

tomorrow evening, she would move into what would hopefully be a long-term home. Things were looking up. The prince thing had just been a blip. She was going to get over this. The newspapers and magazines were going to get sick of this whole mystery woman thing, and then the whole episode would just be something far, far in her rear-view mirror. Speaking of rear-view mirror, she looked behind her and saw a set of high beams. *What a jerk,* she thought. The high beams came closer. God, this person was certainly in a hurry. Just in case it was a cop who was not Jim, Ashley stayed exactly at the speed limit, but the headlights stayed close, blinding her until she finally turned off at the Polo Club, heart beating. She was terrified that the car would follow her, but as she looked behind her, she saw the dark, sleek car accelerate, blasting past the entrance and continuing on down the road.

She drove up to the apartment, carefully parked her new car in a parking spot, and went inside. She would probably have to do something about the design of the car. It really did call too much attention to itself. Having a surfboard on the roof wasn't too much of an incongruous detail in this town, but the color had to be changed. She went to sleep, fantasizing about pretty color combinations for her new ride.

Chapter 30

The next day, Ashley barely got to take a breath. Preparations for the next evening's cocktail party were in full swing. After she finished her usual stable chores, Ashley helped set up tables in the bar.

"Tomorrow afternoon, make double sure the horses all look gorgeous," said Alex, as he hurried past, attending to some other detail.

Ashley hadn't realized how many moving parts there were to this simple cocktail party, but seeing how Alex was acting, she could tell it was more important than he was letting on.

"I've got the caterers coming," said Alex. "You need to make sure that they have a space to work in."

"On it," said Ashley.

The whole day flew by. Mercifully, Ashley had been so busy that she hadn't had any time to worry about Henry, Robert, and Diego. Around 5:00, she headed to the office.

"Thank you for your help today, you must be exhausted," said Alex. "Are you really going to move into the house this evening?"

"I wish I wasn't, because I'm so tired, but I have to get out of the Polo Club apartment sometime, and, well, I'm excited for the new chapter," she said.

"Do you need any help?" asked Alex.

"I'll be fine. I don't have much stuff," said Ashley.

She heard a cough in the doorway. Diego.

"I'm here to help," he said.

Alex gave him a look.

"How generous of you. Well, I don't think Ashley needs any help, she just said no to me," said Alex.

Ashley looked at Diego.

"I mean...actually, I may have a few things to lift, if you don't mind."

"I don't mind at all," said Diego.

"Ooooh," said Alex, as if realizing something for the first time. "Well, all right. Don't do anything I wouldn't do."

"I'll keep that in mind," said Diego. But he wasn't laughing.

They went to the Polo Club apartment, and Diego helped Ashley to load some things into her car, and some into his. It was a good thing he was there. She hadn't realized how much stuff she'd really amassed.

"See? You needed me," he said.

If he only knew how much she needed him. How much she wanted him. Thankfully, he hadn't given her so much as a peck on the cheek today, because she wouldn't have been able to concentrate on the move if he had.

"OK, so now you follow me, and we'll get to Alex's guest apartment."

She would have expected Diego to make some joke about following her anywhere, but he was oddly silent. Had he seen the pictures? Who was she kidding? Who in the world hadn't?

It was dark by the time the cars were packed, and she drove through the night, Diego's headlights shining reassuringly behind her. What a contrast from the day before, when those headlights behind her had been so menacing and scary.

They got to the gates, and Diego hopped out and passed in front of her car to open them for her. *What a gentleman.* She proceeded through, and he followed her, stopping his car to close the gates behind them. "We don't want to have any surprise visitors," said Diego.

She caught a look on his face. It was strange. Something had definitely changed in his demeanor. Had Jim told him anything that she had told him? She hoped not, even though, after what Kari had said about honesty being the best policy, she owed Diego a full explanation of her situation, including Robert and what had transpired with Henry. But not today. They stopped in front of the garage.

"Home sweet home," she said.

They made their way up the stairs, loaded down with a load of Ashley's belongings.

"Wow, it's even uglier than I remembered," Diego said drily. "I once helped Alex get this thing ready to Airbnb, and well, that was a flop. It was just too ugly. Though that was a few years ago. I suspect that these days, he'd be able to Airbnb it no problem."

"Why? What changed?"

"All the hotel prices have gone sky high, especially since the prince moved here," Diego scoffed. "Every woman in the country seems to want to get a chance with him."

And then he looked at Ashley. It was not a look that made her knees weak. It was a look that made her stomach sink.

'What's that look for?" she asked.

"That's what brought you to Montecito, isn't it?"

Ashley's heart dropped. So that's what he thought of her. He thought she was just a prince chasing bimbo.

"Absolutely not. I didn't even know there was a prince here, until..."

"Until you did. Forget it, Ashley. I know everything."

Shit. So he had seen the pictures.

"I can explain. It's not like that. I spent the past five years of my life…"

"Drop it, Ashley. I know. You're married, too."

"It's not like that..I…"

Wait. How did he know she was married? Had Jim broken her trust and spoken to him about it? Even after understanding her intentions? Of anything, that almost hurt the most.

Diego interrupted her. The look in his eyes was devastating.

"I find it rich that you were so concerned about my so-called lady killer reputation, and then I let my guard down, tell you things that I never told anyone else, I fall for you, and then I realize that you're the actual player. And say what you will, but I don't mess with married women."

"Please!" said Ashley, tears in her eyes.

"Have a good time moving in. I'll see you around," said Diego.

He ran down the stairs and got into his car. Ashley watched him go, tears in her eyes. She hadn't even had the opportunity to explain the truth to him, and he'd been so categorical. The most devastating part was that this proved what a man of principle he was. But now, it was too late. She picked up her phone, wanting to text him. She typed out a message, and then deleted it. No, he had a point. She was technically a married woman. A married woman who had messed around with a married man. She'd lied to Diego by omission. If only she could have told him the whole story, then maybe he would understand.

She took a deep breath. Their relationship wouldn't have worked out anyway. He would have realized that she wasn't good enough for him. Better to end it before it even began. She would just have to build her professional life first, get on her feet, and then maybe she would find somebody, once she was legally out of this mess with Robert. She wondered how one filed for divorce from someone who was on the run, or in jail. No matter. She would figure it out, and then could hope to build a new relationship on a healthier foundation with somebody new. But that thought really destroyed her. She didn't want anybody else. She wanted Diego. She would have to make him understand one day. Maybe one day he would be ready to listen to her.

She finished putting everything away in the new apartment and looked at the place with fresh eyes. Yes, it was very hideous, but for now it was home. She had a hideous home, a hideous car, and it probably matched what was inside of her, because she had just managed to mess things up with the most beautiful man she'd ever met.

But in her misery, a tiny spark of joy. She was standing on her own two feet for the first time in years, maybe the first time ever. And maybe she was going to make it after all.

She got into the bed and fell into a deep sleep.

Chapter 31

She woke up the next morning to birdsong. Alex hadn't been kidding. His place was in the wilderness of Montecito. It felt lovely, like being in an enchanted forest. She jumped in the shower and was pleased to realize that there was strong water pressure. She was out in no time, with no fantasies of Diego to keep her in there any longer. Today was going to be a long day. She didn't know whether she was in any mood to go to that evening's cocktail party. She would decide later. She decided to pack a change of clothes, just in case. She had few options for what to wear, so she was forced to settle on that caramel silk slip dress Kari had forced her to buy, and a pair of high heeled sandals. She hadn't heard back from Kari, so maybe Kari wasn't coming, either. Ashley should take that as a sign to sit this one out, even though she felt intense curiosity about the event. Strike that- she felt ownership for it. She was entitled to go, especially since she'd worked so hard for it.

She got to work and went about her usual tasks. She'd almost forgotten she had to head to the DMV. She popped her head into the office.

"Alex, I'm running to the DMV. Let me know when I get back what I urgently need to get done."

"You did such a good job yesterday, said Alex. "There's not too much. How was your first night in the Orange Palace?"

"It was great," Ashley said. "Other than my eyes burning and having PTSD from all the orange, I'm really doing well. Seriously, it's a beautiful piece of land you have."

"Thank you," Alex said. He seemed pleased. "Did everything go OK with Diego?"

"Oh, yeah. He left after a second. He just ran everything up and then left."

"Really." said Alex.

"Really." said Ashley. "None of your business, though, right?"

"Nope. None of my business, I suppose," said Alex, "I'm just curious. You're coming tonight, right? Diego is going to be there. Can I trust you to behave?"

"Of course, you can trust me to behave."

Little did he know that there would be no more fireworks between her and Diego. It made her sad. Jim had mentioned that the tension between them was palpable…she had almost forgotten she was livid at Jim for spilling the beans to Diego, but even madder at herself for withholding the truth.

Ashley almost asked Alex if the prince was going to be at the party, but then decided that Henry wouldn't condescend to attend such an event, and she also didn't want to remind Alex about her indiscretion. That whole thing seemed to have blown over, as far as Alex was concerned, at least for now.

"OK, I'm just going to go check on the horses, then I'll go to the DMV and I can pick up some ice on my way back so we can start to pre-chill the bottles of wine and Champagne."

"What would I do without you?" Alex smiled.

Ashley drove into Santa Barbara and went to the DMV. She shuddered when she saw the length of the line. She worried whether they would accept the paperwork she had. Hopefully, this would help her to start a whole new life.

It was stressful navigating administrative stuff without Kari to help her, but Ashley had managed to get her new driver's license and registration, all on her own. The picture wasn't as good as she would have liked, but she was feeling pretty good about herself. She decided to text Kari.

I did it. Officially a California resident.

Kari pinged her back right away.

Congrats! We need to celebrate. I can come to that cocktail thing for a little bit. Should be good fun. I need a break.

Yay. Can't wait to see you, Ashley wrote back.

Yesterday, she'd been praying that Kari would want to join, to be her wing woman, to be with her while they sipped Champagne and ate hors d'oeuvres and watched Montecito ladies making fools of themselves, but today, everything had changed. Now, she was only going out of a sense of obligation. Well, the least she could do was show Kari a good time. This evening was going to be a chore.Having to rub shoulders with the impossibly graceful Montecito ladies, with their perfect hair, fancy cars and glossy nails.

What are you going to wear? Kari texted.

The slutty dress you convinced me to buy, and now I'm not so sure that's a great idea, Ashley responded.

Oh shit. Alex will probably be mad at you cause you're going to take all the attention away from the Montecito bitches, was Kari's response.

Ashley smiled. Kari was too kind. But then, she started thinking about the event through a different lens. It felt like these poor polo players were being objectified for the benefit of the club. Never mind that some of the younger players would be all too happy to have a cougar sink her claws into them. But some of the other guys were happily partnered up or married. And then there was Diego.

Ashley got back to the barn just in time to see a stable hand, Andreas, she realized as she got closer, bringing out a string of polo ponies. Too many for a single person to handle, surely. She could tell he was going to try to exercise all of them at once, riding in the middle. That was what Robert had made Sissy do- what had led to the accident.

"Hey- need some help with those?" she called out to Andreas.

"Well, they need to be exercised before the ladies come to visit them, and right now they're all pretty feisty."

"Yeah, there are too many for one person. That's crazy."

"Fine," said Andreas. How many can you handle?"

"Five. Let me just get on my riding helmet."

"Riding helmet? Oh really, you're a wimp, huh?"

"Yep, I'm a wimp," said Ashley.

She didn't want to have to explain what had happened to her sister to Andreas, knew it wouldn't sway him either way. But riding helmets could save your life, or at least your lifestyle. She closed her eyes as she re-played the accident in her head. Sissy, riding around the ring, four horses abreast, Robert yelling at her. *They need to gallop. They'll never get their exercise at a trot.* Sissy had just shaken her head at him. Robert didn't know anything about horses. Ashley could still see Sissy's beautiful blonde hair as she shook her head. Sissy hadn't thought she needed a helmet, because she'd known herself, and her horses, and what she was going to do with them. Ashley not wanted to give up the exercising duties to Sissy that day, because Midnight had been acting up, and Ashley had a better handle on him, and besides, she would have preferred for Sissy to do the paperwork. But Robert had seen an opportunity to fuck with her, and had run after the horses, giving Midnight's hindquarters a giant smack. In her mind's eye, Ashley saw Midnight rearing up and spinning around, the other horses starting to panic, wrenching their leads out of Sissy's hands. Sissy, still trying to hold on, and a horse bumping into Midnight as he balanced there on two rear legs. And then, in slow motion, Sissy falling off, and the horses' hoof striking her head, and a cracking sound Ashley would never forget. It had happened in an instant, and it had ruined Sissy's life forever. The doctors had said that maybe there was hope of her walking again, but it had been almost a year, and there had been little progress, especially as Sissy's depression had deepened.

Ashley shook the dark thoughts from her mind. If she was to continue doing what she did, she needed to put them out of her head.

"I'll be fine, I'll be right back," she told Andreas.

She hurried into the stables, and almost bumped into Alex.

"You doing OK?" he looked concerned.

Honestly, Alex probably looked more stressed out than she did.

"I'm fine. I'm going to go help exercise those ponies, unless you need me for something else."

"Thanks, you do that and then come back. I'll have a few extra last-minute things for you, but I'm glad you're helping with those ponies. Andreas is still pretty green."

"Thanks for the vote of confidence," Ashley said as she put her helmet on her head and headed out to where the young stable hand waited with the ponies. He now had two of them saddled up. She grabbed the leads for all the horses under her care and got on her pony, tightening the leads in her hands to keep the other ponies under control. Just from the energy emanating from them, she was sure they probably all wanted to run. She saw Andreas taking his ponies towards the field.

"Bad idea," she yelled at him.

As her grandmother used to say, *I was born in the morning, but she wasn't born this morning.* These horses were dying to run out of control. She was going to stick to the paddock, and start off walking, to work off some energy. The horses tossed their heads. Yep.

Clearly, they were itching for a faster pace, and she could tell that Andreas had managed to give her all the orneriest ones. *Good.* She squeezed her horse's flanks, and it broke into a trot, as did all the others. They seemed to be OK, she decided.

After a few minutes, she decided she would start cantering them. What could possibly go wrong? She urged them into a canter, fighting her ride a little bit to prevent him from breaking into a gallop, but doing OK at it. Until suddenly, she saw a blur of movement off to the side. A sleek brunette head emerging from a car, and then, something flashing in her direction, blinding her, and scaring the horses. One of the horses tossed its head, and started to rear up, surprised. Ashley tried to yank its lead, but that was it. All the horses started running in a chaotic mass, with she stuck in the middle, dangerously close to losing her balance. What was she going to do? If she was unseated, she would fall under their feet. She imagined herself falling like her sister had done and getting kicked in the head. At least she had her helmet on, but that didn't mean it would save her. In a split second, she decided. She was going to have to jump clear. It was idiotic and dangerous, but so were all the other alternatives. The brunette woman was still flashing whatever it was. It looked like a mirror from a compact or something, but Ashley couldn't be sure. Now she realized, she was doing it on purpose, wasn't she? Ashley didn't have time to worry about this. She let go of the other horse's leads, waited for them to run clear, and focused on trying to slow down her mount. But with this infernal flashing now seemingly focused on her pony's eyes, the horse was simply growing more and more panicked. Ashley put all her weight in her left stirrup and somehow managed to launch herself off the horse. She hit the ground hard and focused on getting out of the way, adrenaline powering her as she rolled back to her feet and managed to gather all the running ponies.

Soon, she had them all under her control again. By the time she had a chance to look back up to where the woman had been, the car and the woman were both gone, as if they'd been a figment of her imagination. When she replayed the scene in her mind, Ashley decided that yes, it had been a mirror compact that she'd been using to blind the horses. But more disturbing, the woman had been a dead ringer for Henry's wife.

Ashley shuddered. She heard Alex's voice behind her.

"Oh my God, Ashley, I saw what happened. You're a rock star. What happened to get them out of control?"

"No idea," said Ashley, "Maybe a leaf or something," she lied.

"Yeah, well, you certainly had me scared," said Alex.

"Listen, you get yourself dusted off. You're a mess. I'll put these guys away."

"Thanks," said Ashley.

Once her shaking subsided, she took the time to give herself a pat on the back. She was proud of the job she was doing. Even if she'd been terrified, she'd done the right thing. She went to dust herself off and freshen up. She downed a glass of water to calm her nerves. As she walked down the aisle of the stables, she noticed a thatch of red head peeking over the top of one of the stables.

Shit. It was Henry. She didn't want to have to confront him or talk to him, so she ducked, and left in the other direction. She certainly hoped he was not coming to that evening's event, but she couldn't very well avoid him for the rest of her life. She wished that Diego was around, and then she remembered that Diego didn't want to talk to her anymore. That was devastating, more devastating than having to deal with the awkwardness around Henry.

She would have thought that Diego would be more upset with Henry than mad at her, if Jim had told him the whole story the way she had related it. She still needed to tell Jim off for that. Or maybe Diego just thought she was a hot mess in general, and not worth fighting for.

She headed back to the office, where Alex had just returned.

"OK. Last minute details. Did you get the ice?" he asked.

"Oh crap. I forgot."

"No worries, why don't you go get it now, and then it'll be pretty much time for us to get presentable for all the high society people. This event is really important," Alex admitted. "I need the community to be invested in this place. We're counting on them to support us as we try to level up."

"Hasn't the prince helped to do that?" asked Ashley.

"He's not exactly pulling his weight," admitted Alex. "He shows up the strict minimum, and the drama his wife created with all the extra security and NDA's and basically ruining Diego's reputation and threatening me…"

'Wait- she did that?"

"She's a monster," Alex said. "Best to steer clear of her. Don't be on her bad side."

Ashley left the office, her blood running cold. She was very, very much too late for that, and firmly on the duchess' bad side. The duchess had told her herself that she would ruin her life. Had she managed to find Robert yet?

Ashley hopped in her car, marveling at how ugly it was. She drove it to the gas station in Summerland. All these landmarks were becoming familiar to her. She was starting to learn her way around, and it felt good. She walked into the gas station and requested ten bags of ice.

"I can help you load them in your car," said the man behind the register.

As they were putting the bags in her trunk, she thought she saw Diego's car go by, and her heart jumped into her throat. It hurt to have this chasm between them. She wondered if it would ever stop hurting. She was being stupid, though. It wasn't like they had even had a relationship. All they'd had was off the charts chemistry and a few empty promises.

She got back into her car and headed back to the polo fields, feeling like she was heading onto the battlefield. Time for her to put on her war paint. Alex had told her she could use the old apartment to get dressed. She quickly rinsed off in the shower but, as there was no towel, she ended up having to blot herself dry with some of the paper towels she had left behind. *Classy.* She took the dress out of her bag and slipped it over her head. The fabric was so thin. After wearing old jeans and chambray shirts and flannels all these years, the thin, silky fabric felt indecent. It tickled her flesh in a suggestive way. She caught a glimpse of herself in the mirror. Damn. Her underwear and bra were showing. No choice, she had to take them off. She stuffed the undergarments in her bag, looked at herself in the mirror again, and blushed. *Shit.* She might as well be naked. The caramel silk of the dress skimmed over her, highlighting her ever curve. *Oh well*. She fluffed her hair and put on the pair of dangly earrings Kari had given her and dabbed on some lip gloss. She looked at herself in the mirror one more time. Well, it would have to do.

Chapter 32

Ashley stepped into the bar at the Polo Club. Alex did a double take. Ashley laughed it off.

"Well, here goes nothing," he said to her. "Let's have a glass of Champagne while we wait for everyone to get here."

Thankfully, the first person to arrive was Kari, looking like a glamorous Amazon, in a silver and gold metallic knitted dress with a zig-zag pattern that set off her dark skin, her hair newly arranged in two long braids. Kari hugged Ashley and greeted Alex cautiously. The three of them stood there and laughed when they realized they had all taken a deep shaky breath in unison.

"Pretty nervous, aren't we?" Alex said.

"I may not work here anymore, but I know how much is resting on this," said Kari. "Here they come."

As if flood gates had suddenly been opened, a parade of Range Rovers, Audis, BMWs, and even a Rolls Royce SUV made their way down the drive. Ashley shuddered every time she saw a black Range Rover, even though she had heard Alex angrily saying on the phone that the prince couldn't be bothered to show up. Diego had given him a talking to, apparently, but Alex didn't think that it had had any effect.

Ashley felt bad for being relieved. Now she just had to worry about Diego. She thought she saw his Green Range Rover coming down the drive, and her heart pinched again. She was going to have to learn how to be around him without being so weird. He obviously didn't want her, and didn't want to hear her explanations, so she was just going to have to deal with it.

Anyway, tonight was not about that. Tonight was about helping out the Polo Club, and she would do her job.

A few ladies made their way into the clubroom, laughing

"Where's the Champagne?" said a gorgeous redhead.

"Right this way," said Alex, a wolfish grin on his lips.

"He's certainly in his element," Kari muttered.

Two pretty brunettes flanking a blonde wandered in. All three wore casual, summery dresses that nevertheless managed to look incredibly elegant, as if they had just thrown on something from their closet, and it happened to be the perfect thing. Ashley smoothed down her own dress self-consciously.

"Girl, stop stressing. You look hot, maybe too hot," said Kari. Next, some of the polo players started trickling in, all of them wearing the tight white jeans that made Ashley decide that the polo uniform was the best uniform. Button down shirts, deep tans, and colorful belts rounded out the look. They were all damn sexy, but none of them compared to Diego. And right on cue, there he was.

Diego stepped into the room and scanned it, as if trying to ascertain the situation. His eyes fell on Ashley. As ever, she found herself drawn towards him, but this time, she fought the urge to go to him. Finally, he tore his eyes away from hers, and his glance lingered on her body before he looked away. *Good.* She hoped that maybe he wanted her just a little bit too, despite not wanting to talk to her. She hoped he was suffering as much as she was, but he was the one who had made the decision to cut things off, so that was unlikely. The minute Diego approached the bar, all the ladies there were on him like flies on a ham steak. Touching his arm flirtatiously. Cocking their heads to one side, batting their eyelashes, and biting their lips. It made Ashley sick.

"Come on," Kari said, "don't be so transparent. You've got to learn how to act when you live in Montecito. You've got to be a little bit more ruthless than that, or you'll get eaten alive."

"If I had known it would be like this, I wouldn't have moved here," said Ashley. But she loved it here. She probably still would have.

More women and more polo players trickled in. A few husbands were thrown into the mix, looking lost and sullen. Their bored, pissed off expressions almost made Ashley laugh out loud.

"OK so should we flirt with the husbands do you think?"

"Why not," said Kari. "That should be good for a laugh. Here, let's refill our glasses first."

They bellied up to the bar, which, Ashley noticed only too late, put her right next to Diego. She could feel the heat coming off him. His fresh-musky smell, the one that drove her wild, tickled her nose. His eyes were trained straight in front of him. Definitely trying to ignore her. But she couldn't be satisfied about that for long because she didn't want him to ignore her at all. She wanted his hands on her. That wasn't appropriate for this event anyway. Another woman came up to Diego and put her hand on his arm.

"Looking hot, Diego," she purred.

Gross. Her voice was already annoying the crap out of Ashley. As soon as their glasses were filled, she and Kari repaired to a corner of the room, where some of the husbands had congregated, downing tumblers of whiskey.

Ashley introduced herself to a few of them, feeling awkward. She realized she was not in the mood for flirting, not at all. *Just make them feel welcome*, she reminded herself. *Tell them about how cool the polo club is.* They probably felt as awkward as she did, she reasoned. She tried to be her most charming self and went from one to the other, chit-chatting, until it started to feel more natural. Kari was doing the same. Soon, Ashley felt comfortable to throw in a little flirtation, and she noticed then men warming up to her even more, and some of the women taking notice and wandering over to keep tabs. She toned it down a little, so Alex wouldn't get mad, and focused on chatting about how fabulous it would be for the club to become a major player on the international polo circuit.

During a break in a conversation, she let her eyes wander over to Diego. She froze. He was talking with a glamorous brunette. A glamorous brunette she recognized as the woman who had been blinding the horses with her compact mirror. And now that she was closer, she could also confirm that she was the same brunette from the pictures on the magazines. It was Henry-Harry's wife. And she and Diego seemed to be having a very tense conversation. Ashley's hands and feet turned to ice. She gulped.

"I'm sorry. What were you saying?" she asked the man with whom she was chatting, some dude named Paul who was a fund manager or something, whatever that was.

"Oh, I was asking where you lived before you got to Montecito," he asked. "You're very different from most of my wife's friends."

"Oh yes, Midwest," she said vaguely. "You?"

"Connecticut," said the man.

Well, that was another thing they didn't have in common. She struggled to make the conversation revive.

"Well, if I may say so, you're gorgeous," said Paul the fund manager.

You may not say so, Ashley thought to herself, but she just smiled.

"Excuse me, I need to go refresh my drink."

She headed back to the bar, despite knowing that it would take her dangerously close to Diego and the duchess.

"Another glass, please," she told the bartender.

"You sure?"

She appreciated that he was looking out for her, but dammit, she was an adult.

As she tried to discreetly walk past Diego and the duchess, the duchess hissed something in Ashley's direction.

"Sorry?" Ashley pivoted her head. "Were you speaking to me?"

"Oh, I was speaking to you, bitch," said the duchess.

Ashley blinked. She looked for Diego to defend her, but he had walked away.

"You and I need to talk," said the duchess. "Remember how I told you I was going to make your life hell? How do you like it so far? It's a shame you never told our little friend Diego about how you're married, and how you have a husband who lives in Montana, while you're fucking around with my husband. Isn't that interesting?"

Ashley felt a cold sense of dread, but she also felt relief. It wasn't Jim who had given away her secret, after all.

"I'm sorry, do I know you?" Ashley asked.

Back when she was growing up and wondering whether her mother had indeed been a textbook narcissist, as Sissy had charged, she had read that the best way to torture one was to challenge their sense of self-importance.

"Oh, I bet you don't want to know me, bitch, but you know who I am. Everybody knows who I am," the duchess seethed.

"Well, I didn't," said Ashley. "I just recently saw some embarrassing pictures of you playing all lovey-dovey with that philandering husband of yours, and I read that you were some D-list actress, but I hope there's more to you than that."

"Oh, there is," said the duchess. "Here's all you need to know: when I set my mind to something, I always, *always* succeed. So you and I are going to have a little chit chat after this event. And if you don't do what I want you to do, I think good old Robert Miller is going to be making a trip to beautiful Santa Barbara, California to collect his wayward wife."

Tears sprang to Ashley's eyes. She looked desperately for Diego, but he was on the other side of the room, not meeting her gaze. She couldn't count on him to help her in this situation. If only he understood. But then, she understood: had the duchess threatened Diego in some way, too? Too bad, she was not going to give in, not going to play her games. The duchess walked away, waggling her fingers at Ashley.

Once Henry-Harry's wife was occupied speaking to a polo player Ashley recognized from a magazine ad Ashley had seen somewhere, Ashley looked desperately for Kari, who was nowhere to be seen, and made a beeline for the bar.

"You've definitely had too much," said the bartender.

"I'll be the judge of that. Make it a double," said Ashley, even though the room was already starting to spin a bit. She noticed the woman from before, the one with the annoying voice, talking to Diego again, her hand on his arm. He was certainly paying attention to her. He, who supposedly had all of these principles that prevented him from associating with a married woman. This annoying woman had a giant diamond wedding band on her ring finger. The stones flashed in the light of the dying sun. It was quite obvious that not only was she married, but she was very married, unlike Ashley whose crazy husband was someone she hoped never to see again. *That's it.* She was going to say something. She started making her way towards Diego and the woman when somebody grabbed her arm. Kari.

"Ashley, I think it's time we get out of here."

"No, I was just going to speak to someone," said Ashley.

"No girl, you weren't. You're coming with me," said Kari.

She not so gently guided Ashley towards the exit door. They were almost out when a hand grabbed her other arm. Henry's stupid wife.

"What do you want?" asked Ashley.

She would never have spoken to her that way before, but now the alcohol was making her bold.

"I told you, you and I need to talk," said the duchess. "You think I didn't tell your husband that you're in Southern California, and that, unless you do what I say, I won't tell him exactly where to find you?"

Ashley's head started reeling. She was going to be sick.

Kari said, "sorry, duchess, but you'll have to make an appointment at a later time."

Ashley just had time to see the duchess' stunned expression,

Before Kari yanked her outside just in time for Ashley to duck behind a Range Rover and puke all over the grass of the parking area. Once she'd thrown up everything in her stomach, she felt a little bit better physically, and a lot worse mentally.

She'd made an absolute fool of herself, hadn't she? She hoped Alex hadn't noticed. He would be pissed.

Chapter 33

Ashley woke the next morning to another beautiful day, in fact, a hot day. Indian summer seemed to be in full swing, but oddly, the birds were not singing. There was a strange pall over the whole place. At least it matched her mood, and her hangover. She tried to shake it off. Was the duchess really going to track down Robert? Who would be crazy enough to do that?

She got ready quickly and was driving to the barn when her phone pinged. With everything that was going on, she was tempted to check it as she drove, but she reminded herself not to. That would be irresponsible, and she'd been irresponsible enough for a whole lifetime, just in the past month. Only when she arrived at the stables did she pick it up and check the message. It was from Kari. As soon as she read the words, her blood ran cold.

I think Robert tried to call my phone, Kari had written.

How do you know? Did he leave a message? Ashley typed.

No. But I did a reverse look up and the number is under your business LLC.

Ashley started sweating. What to do? Had Henry's wife actually contacted him, or had he seen the news? He never looked at the news. Her story hadn't made it to the front of the gossip magazines, in fact it had been squashed, and she probably had Henry or his wife to thank for that. Or had Sissy said something? There was no way of knowing, of course, unless she called him back, and Kari probably wouldn't let her do something that stupid.

What do you want me to do? Kari wrote.

Kari could very well be justified in calling him. She could say that she recognized the Montana number and was worried about Sissy.

Call him and ask him if he knows Sissy. I'll be standing by, Ashley typed.

Ashley sat in her car, waiting, holding her breath, feeling nauseous. She glanced out the window and saw Alex looking towards the vehicle, gesturing for her to come in. She held up a finger. Alex waved his arms around.

She texted him. *Sorry, but I'm on a really important phone call. It's a family emergency.*

Diego and the prince have put me in a world of pain right now. I need your help, Alex typed back. His hands were on his hips, broadcasting his impatience. It would have been almost comical if Ashley hadn't been so stressed out.

I'll be right there. She didn't want to risk Alex's wrath, but this was life and death. Her phone rang, making her jump. Kari.

"He didn't pick up. Don't freak out. It doesn't mean anything. I'll let you know if I hear anything else, and I'll try again later."

Ashley left the car and strode up to Alex.

"What do you mean, Diego and the prince…What does Diego have to do with anything?" asked Ashley.

"Are you kidding me? You mean, other than the fact that I put on this whole event for him, that thanks to you, a bunch of the husbands decided to invest in the club…"

'Wait- what? They did?" Ashley's mouth fell open.

"Yeah, well good thing they didn't see you barfing in the parking area like I did," said Alex. "But anyway, we put on this successful event, and the prince is whining about his wife wanting them to move the whole operation to Hope Ranch, and Diego is forcing me to jump through hoops to retain the majority of the games here."

"I don't get it. Why does Diego get to order you around?"

Alex looked at Ashley incredulously.

"Ashley, hello? He's the majority owner of this club. He's the one who had the bright idea of bringing in the fucking prince, and I made the mistake of investing in this pipe dream, and now, somehow, the prince seems to have him by the balls, and I don't know why. The prince was supposed to be our show pony."

Wow. Talk about lying by omission. Not that she'd ever asked. Not that she hadn't signed an NDA. Not that it was any of her business, except that, if she had been let in on any of this crap, she wouldn't be in the messy situation in which he now found herself.

Also, she had the feeling that it wasn't poor stupid Henry who had Diego by the balls. It was his wife.

"Let's figure this out," said Ashley, trying to calm herself down by helping Alex. They headed to Alex's office. His face looked grim.

He was clearly worried about what was going to happen to the stables and to the Polo Club if everything blew up in his face.

She hoped he wasn't blaming her for any of it, but it would be fair if he was.

"Listen, I'm sorry," Ashley said. "I hope you don't think that this all my fault."

Alex waved her off.

"No, don't worry, you're not making it easier, but this seems to be all the prince's fault. He's acting like a spoiled brat. As far as I can tell, Diego is just trying to manage him. He needs him for the club's reputation, and he needs to keep him happy. And apparently Henry is being delusional about security risks and things like that."

What a crock of bullshit, thought Ashley. But they might as well deliver what he wanted. She launched into problem-solving mode. Having pulled off the impossible in her stables back in Montana day after day, she had developed a strategic mind.

"OK, let's just go through every single one of their requests, and give them a plan for how we can address them. How much money was pledged yesterday after the event? Let's show them how much we have, how much their bullshit will cost, and make them make the decisions. That money was pledged to you, Alex. So if they run to Hope Ranch, we'll have something to start over with. It'll be a shame to lose Diego, but my guess is that the local community will stand behind you, rather than behind a royal pain in the ass."

"Damn," said Alex. "I like this version of Ashley."

Alex explained how the prince had demanded anti-theft devices for the stalls, added security for the games in strategic locations, and dedicated golf carts for his bodyguards. Ashley laughed.

"Gimme a break- that's easy. Let's just give them everything they want."

She outlined how they could rig the stalls with the same cheap alarms that Robert had installed for his gun safe, available at Home Depot or Amazon. She asked Alex if he had a blueprint of the Polo Club dating from its last renovation and a schematic of the grounds. He did.

"This is all about ego," Ashley said. "So, we feed his ego. In addition to the security stuff, why don't we give him special golden plaques for all of his horses, a royal box with a gold sign and fancier seats, and magnets to put on whichever golf cart he wants to ride around in, with whatever he thinks his title and his bitch wife's title is, on them? It's beyond pretentious but seems to be the type of thing that would placate them. Also, we super-inflate the cost, because he has no idea of reality."

Alex laughed.

"I think you may be a genius."

"No, I'm pretty sure I'm a dumbass. Speaking of bitch wife, she's out to get me, and I just hope I don't bring anything bad on into these stables, but my ex-husband may actually be on his way."

"I'll keep an eye open," said Alex. "What does he look like?"

"Tall, dark, handsome, and psychotic. About 6 foot 2. Maybe 6 foot 3. Short black hair. Super light eyes. Probably carrying a gun."

"Sounds terrifying," said Alex. "And I didn't wanna tell you this, but ever since I woke up, I've had a bad feeling about today."

Ashley didn't think it would help to tell him that she'd had the same feeling. She really hoped today wasn't the day her crazy ex was going to show up.

She didn't have time to dwell on it, though. Better to address the prince's demands. She set off towards Home Depot in Goleta, thinking about how much her life had changed in a short time. She never wanted to go back to how things had been, but walking into the home improvement store, she reflected on how there was something about the familiarity of a Home Depot that soothed her. Maybe it was the smell of sawdust and chemicals, or the presence of all those brand-new tools that made one believe in the possibility of making something better with one's own two hands. She used to go with Robert, back when they were fixing up Papa's property, back when Robert was still kind. Ashley would always look at the tile, and look at the flooring, and dream about making things prettier and fresher at the farm. At the beginning of their marriage, Robert had been happy to let her pick some finishes- it was, after all, her father's place. But towards the end, he'd been impatient with her, not even letting her dream anymore.

It would be nice to have a place of her own one day, a place where she'd be able to call the shots. For a second, she allowed herself to visualize Diego in that place, but then shook away the wistful feelings and gathered the materials she needed for the stall security systems. After Home Depot, she headed to a trophy and plaque store she had located online. She flirted enough with the bored guy behind the counter to have everything made on the spot: gold-toned plaques engraved with the full names of each of the prince's horses, and one made for the so-called Royal Box. She also ordered large car door-style magnets printed with *Santa Barbara Polo Club Special Security* for all six golf carts they had managed to round up that morning. The employee's surprised expression as he carefully noted the words was priceless.

"Wow. Usually, I'm making Little League participation trophies and Employee of the Month plaques. Come back anytime," he said.

He even gave her a discount.

Next stop: the office supply store, where Ashley had large copies of the stable and polo ground diagrams printed out. She also bought poster board, glue, highlighters, and colored pens.

She got back to the Polo Club and got to work making a security plan that they could show Henry and Diego, complete with special access and strategic postings for any security forces and bodyguards the prince wanted to hire. After all, no polo club should be expected to hire security. Just facilitate. Alex was laughing his head off, torn between relief and hilarity.

"This is ridiculous," he kept repeating, "but it just might work."

Soon, Ashley was done. She was sure that at least Diego would be impressed. If not by her, at least by her ideas.

The day had gotten hotter. The atmosphere was heavy. At Alex's request, Ashley had gone to grab them some sandwiches at the French deli, which was thankfully air conditioned. The other clients there were restless. *Fire weather*, she thought she heard one mutter.

When Ashley stepped outside, sandwiches in hand, she thought she detected the smell of smoke. The last time she'd smelled something like that, there had been a prairie fire, caused by Robert setting a big pile of trash on fire in the middle of their pasture at an unsanctioned time. They'd almost gotten fined, but thankfully, there had been no loss of life or destruction of property beyond acres of grass burned, and when the authorities had investigated, Ashley had pleaded innocence and had pretended that she'd accidentally set the fire with a power tool. And so, they'd gotten off. Rather than thanking her, Robert had acted as if it was indeed all her fault, and her mother had asked her if she was absolutely sure it hadn't been her, after all. She squeezed her eyes shut to banish useless thoughts of the past.

There was something wrong here and now. She felt a sense of alarm, something primal. She scanned the horizon in all directions. Nothing.

Then, as she looked towards the mountains, she saw it: smoke. There *was* something on fire. The source of the smoke was in the direction of the mountains behind Montecito. Her heart started to beat harder.

She got into her car and got on the highway, a feeling of dread in the pit of her stomach. As she drove towards the Polo Club, she felt that the smoke was getting thicker. There was no mistaking it now. It was definitely a fire. And then, looking at the hills, she saw a ring of flame lapping at the peaks. *Oh no.* She had read somewhere that fire could advance as fast as a galloping horse once it got started. But of course, it would take wind for it to do that, and today, thankfully, had been an exceptionally still day so far. But then, she noticed the palm trees swaying. The wind had picked up. Gripped by panic, she hit the accelerator. There were ten horses currently in the stables under her care, thankfully less than during the official season, and at least thirty more in the back stable complex. She knew there was a crew guys to deal with those, but the front stable complex was currently under her and Alex's unique domain. She tried to dial Alex, but there was no response. And now, the traffic was slowing down. Drivers who were just passing through were rubbernecking, looking at the flames, others were struggling to get home and grab loved ones and belongings. There would be evacuation orders, she imagined.

Up ahead, the highway was getting completely blocked. And Ashley had just passed the San Ysidro exit. She checked behind her and made a split-second decision, putting on her emergency blinkers and executing a three-point turn, driving up the shoulder in the wrong direction, and skidding onto the exit, right in front of a truck.

She heard screeching tires and an accusatory long burst of the horn, but too bad. She could see the flames starting to make their way down the mountain, towards the luxury mansions of Montecito. Towards the Polo Club. The people living in those mansions had the means to start over. The polo fields that were Alex and Diego's whole livelihoods, and her literal survival at this point, were another story. But most of all, she didn't want the horses in danger. When she hadn't had anyone else, these innocent animals had been the ones to make her feel better just by their very presence, just by their calming energy. Horses had, in many ways, taught her everything she knew, made her everything she was. She needed to get to the stables and take them all someplace safe. *To the beach,* she decided. That was the safest place for them.

She tried Alex again. This time he answered the phone, his voice panicked.

"Where are you?"

"Close," Ashley responded.

"The fire is coming fast," said Alex. "I'm grabbing important documents, and I need to load the horses into the trailer. I wish I had your help."

"I'll be there in two minutes. Are we taking them to the beach?"

"Good idea," said Alex. "I hadn't even thought that far. Just get here as fast as you can."

"Pulling in now," Ashley said.

She had a brief thought for her orange velour palace. She imagined it being lapped up by flames that matched its decor. It was hideous, but it was her only home for now. She hoped it would be OK, but those horses were more important.

Where was Diego? Knowing Alex, he had been overwhelmed with what needed to be done and hadn't called him. If Diego was busy in Hope Ranch, there was a possibility he had no idea what was going on. She needed to give up her pride. She dialed his number. Diego didn't pick up, so she left him a message.

"Diego, I don't know where you are right now, but there's a fire coming. We're trying to get the horses to safety on the beach. If you're nearby, any help is appreciated."

She tried to sound calm, but she was far from it. She leapt out of the car and sprang into action, gathering halters for all the horses and hooking them over her arms. One by one, she went to the stalls and slipped the halters on. She would clip on the leads later. Of course, the prince's expensive horse was the most problematic, but he would calm down if he knew what was good for him. Some horses were nervous, knowing something was wrong. Others had defaulted to docile mode, deciding that their human knew what she was doing. Ashley took no chances. She was going to lead them to the trailer one by one and secure them. She couldn't have them seeing the flames and freaking out and trying to make a run for it.

Alex had already parked the trailer as close as possible to the stables and was loading papers and document boxes into the passenger side. Ashley broke into a run, jogging the horses one by one into the trailer. Their ears were spinning around, their eyes opened wide, showing the whites.

What would happen if they got the horses to safety and then didn't have a place to take them back to? Well, they would have to figure it out. This was part of the responsibility of having animals. She would never let her animals down again. She got the last horse. The smoke had grown so dense that she couldn't see where the flames were. She started coughing. She dragged a few buckets of water into the trailer, and then a few buckets of feed. Not enough, but the best she could do under the circumstances. She rushed to the office.

"We need to get out of here," she told Alex.

He nodded and handed her his laptop.

"Here, give me your keys," he said. "You take the trailer. Keys are in it. I'll take your car. You head down to the beach, I'm just gonna try to get to my place to turn on the sprinklers."

"What about your car, Alex?" Ashley asked. She knew how proud Alex was of his brand spanking new Audi station wagon.

"I can find another one like mine, but you'll never find another one like yours." He gave a dry laugh that turned into a cough. "Go."

Ashley threw him her keys.

"Go," he said again.

"Don't do anything stupid," she responded.

Ashley got behind the wheel of the trailer. It had been a while since she'd driven one of these, but it was like riding a bike. You never quite forgot how, but it was scary and awkward when you did it again. She eased out of the Polo Club drive, nosing into the frontage road. There were cars everywhere, probably people evacuating. She hadn't thought to listen to the radio, but she might do it once she got to the beach, via her phone. How convenient this little piece of technology had become in such a short time. Again, she wondered if Diego had gotten her message, and how Officer Jim was doing. He was probably helping people evacuate right now. She hoped he was safe.

Ashley pulled up to the parking for Padaro Beach, the same place she and Henry had parked on that first beach day that felt like it had happened a lifetime ago. The smoke was now so thick. She could barely see in front of her. She debated on whether she should stay on the parking, to evacuate more easily if things got really bad, but then decided that having the horses on the beach was the safest thing to do. The highway had been completely backed up, anyway. The air was smoky and might be cleaner on the waterfront. And what if the flames came this far? They would be burned as they tried to escape.

She texted Alex and Diego, *I'm at Padaro Beach.*

There was no immediate response, but hopefully they were going to see the message when they needed to.

She secured the doors of the truck, knowing that all of Alex's important documents were inside and that she couldn't very well carry them all, clambered into the back of the trailer, and as she ran each one out one by one and clipped them to a loop on the trailer, she tried to work out how she would control all ten horses on her own. She finally decided to link the more docile ones up so that they would follow each other in a long line. It would look ridiculous, and one of them might rebel, breaking the lead, but she had no other choice. She held the four most valuable ponies up front, with her. The prince's expensive Marwan. Hermanito, the one that she knew to be Diego's favorite, Maldon, Alex's old white horse from back when he used to still play, and her personal favorite, Carioca. Carioca was sweet, and besides, had seen some pretty spicy action in Ashley's dream. The others trailed behind. It was lucky that Ashley had thought to grab a long length of rope. As she got to the beach, she looked back, and saw that she hadn't been the only one with this idea. Other people with horses, donkeys, goats, sheep, a woman with a pair of zebras, and even a guy dressed like a butler with a pair of Cheetahs filed down the path to the beach. *Those can't be legal.* Despite the trauma, Ashley almost smiled. Through the smoke, through the tears in stinging eyes, the numerous animals milling around were a mirage of bizarreness. The horses were growing nervous, tossing their heads. Ashley prayed that the fire would retreat. That somebody would stop it. That something good would happen. Finally, Alex materialized, coming through the smoke towards her. He handed her a cold can of Coca-Cola. She almost cried with gratitude as the sticky liquid soothed her burnt throat.

"How close is the fire?" she asked.

"It's come down in spots. A few upper houses impacted so far. You never know. With these things, it could go either way."

They were silent after that. Time ticked by. Ashley didn't know what time it was, but the light started to wane. Phones were not working properly anymore. Either the network was overtaxed, or a cell phone tower had burned.

Then, Ashley saw Diego coming through the smoke. As always, her eyes were drawn magnetically to his, even though hers were tearing and so were his. Despite the drama of the day, she got the same old feeling in her heart. She really couldn't get over him, could she? He came closer. She could only stare. He took her hand. The feel of his touch almost made her cry.

"Ashley, thank you for everything you did."

"I didn't do anything," said Ashley. "I just did my job."

She was kicking herself for not responding to his peace offering. Her inner voice was saying, *smile at him, say something nice.* But she stayed silent. She'd had too much worrying. Too much danger, between Robert and the fire. And Diego had not been willing to give her the benefit of the doubt. She needed someone who would treat her right, always. Diego dropped her hand, and the empty feeling left behind almost made her throw herself at him. But she resisted.

"I brought some food and water for the horses," Diego said.

"Thank you," said Alex. "But so did Ashley. Why don't we bring it down to the beach? Safer than being up there."

"I'll wait here with the horses," said Ashley.

After a while. Alex and Diego were back, lugging some feed and buckets of fresh water. It wasn't enough for a full meal, but it was enough to make the horses more comfortable for now.

It had become almost completely dark, and now they could see the glow of the ring of fire on the mountain. It had come down lower than earlier in the day, for sure, but not as low as Ashley had feared. And then, a flash.

"What was that?" Ashley asked.

"Looks like lightning," said Alex.

"That's great news," said Ashley.

"Don't be so sure," said Alex, it could just mean lightning strikes and more fire, in more spots. This could be really bad news. Another flash. Ashley's heart was in her throat now.

"Look over there," Diego cried.

Up on the hill, lower down, there was an isolated spot of flame.

"You think that's from the lightning?" Ashley asked.

"Could be from embers. Could be from lightning."

Another flash. Ashley couldn't take any more of this. She squeezed her eyes shut, the tears running down her face. Diego rubbed her back. She let him. She just dropped her head and sobbed. She felt a tear fall on her hand, and another. And then a tear on top of her head.

What?

Suddenly, it was as if the sky was a dam that had burst. Lashings of water started pouring out from the clouds that had gathered and been camouflaged as smoke.

Ashley lifted her face to the sky and let the rain wash the smoke and soot from it. All around them, people held their hands out to the raindrops. Even though it had grown cold, they were laughing, drenched. Ashley hadn't realized how cold she was. Diego put his jacket over her shoulders. She shivered, enveloped by his delicious scent. She was going to make him listen to her, dammit.

The smell of the smoke changed. It became more acrid, colder. And as they looked, they could no longer see any flames on the mountain.

"Do you think do you think it's safe to go back?" Ashley asked.

"Not sure," said Alex.

After a while, people started answering their phones, getting news of loved ones, and confirmation that it was OK to go back to their homes.

"Well, let's go," said Ashley. They led the horses back to the trailer. It was much easier with two other people to help her. Alex handed Ashley her car keys.

"I still can't believe you were willing to give up your baby Audi to let me keep this hideous beast," she laughed.

"I wasn't thinking straight," he said, winking at her.

"Where's Diego?" she asked, noticing that he was gone. She still has his coat on her shoulders.

"The prince summoned him, apparently."

When they returned to the stables, it was such a relief to see them all in one piece, that a laugh escaped Ashley's throat. She realized she hadn't thought about Robert in hours. Is that what it would take to stop worrying about Robert finding her? Non-stop life and death situations? She was going to need to address this head on. She couldn't let the duchess make her into a victim. And she knew how to deal with her. She'd grown up with Momma.

She checked her phone. There was a text from Kari, checking on her.

Just brought the horses back from Padaro Beach, Ashley wrote.

Lol. I was at Butterfly Beach, Kari responded.

Fancy bitch, Ashley wrote.

Once the horses were back in the stables and fed and watered, she and Alex bid each other a good night and she headed out. Her phone pinged. Diego? But no, it was Jim.

Honor Bar? I'm driving by the stables, can pick you up.

She looked like hell. Probably smelled like hell. Had been through hell. But hell if she didn't deserve a Ding's crispy chicken sandwich and a glass of wine. She was sure that there would be lots of stories from locals, and she was looking forward to just absorbing the atmosphere and seeing her friend Jim. Jim pulled up before she could wonder at the happy coincidence of him being in the neighborhood.

During the short drive to Montecito, Jim caught her up on everything. There had been just one fatality, somebody who thought he could shelter in place on his property on the mountain top. Other than that, everything was remarkably good. Fires were a fact of life around there, and now they got to worry about mud slides.

They pulled up to the Honor Bar and walked in. She joined Jim at the bar.

"We need to talk," said Jim. "Let's have a drink."

"We do need to talk," said Ashley. "Did you tell Diego anything about what I told you about the prince, and about my ex-husband?"

"I would never," said Jim. He didn't even bother to be indignant. It was so completely not something he would do.

"I didn't think so. So, I think the prince's wife did."

"Wouldn't put it past her."

"Wait- you know how she is?"

Jim shook his head.

"Who doesn't? Common knowledge around here, I'm afraid. And let me tell you something. If certain people aren't acting towards you the way you would like, consider that maybe she's got them by the balls somehow."

"Wait- Diego?"

Jim just shrugged.

So that was what had happened. What had she threatened Diego with?

"Well, I think she is trying to get my husband to come here and find me."

"Ashley, that's what I brought you here to tell you. Your husband was taken into custody this morning."

Ashley's heart leapt.

"He was? How?"

"Stopped for speeding in Idaho. Maybe on his way to find you. But now, he's waiting to stand trial for the attempted murder of your brother-in-law."

Ashley breathed a sigh of relief.

"Thank God. And what about my mother?"

"Apparently, he doesn't know where she is," Jim responded. "That is a work in progress. But at least you don't need to worry about Robert anymore."

Ashley couldn't help it- she gave Jim a huge hug.

Things were looking up. Knowing that she was safe gave her an appetite, and she devoured everything on her plate.

When they were done eating, Jim drove her back to the Polo Club to get her car.

"You gonna be OK?" he asked.

"Perfect, don't worry about me," said Ashley.

It was only when Jim pulled had away and driven off that a glossy black Range Rover nosed around the corner of the stable complex. For the time being, Ashley didn't notice it, much too preoccupied by the odor wafting over from the direction of her car.

Chapter 34

The chemical, pungent smell hit her nose and eyes water. Fresh paint was her best guess. Ashley pulled out her phone to illuminate the car. Sure enough, in the beam of the light, she made out the word *SLUT* spray painted in red on the car's formerly cheerful exterior. By the time Ashley noticed the Range Rover, she didn't have to wait for the car door to open to know who was driving. She knew Henry-Harry's wife was an actress, and she'd certainly nailed the drama, but Ashley hoped the duchess didn't decide to start writing her own scripts, because this was so over the top that she almost felt like laughing.

Granted, her relief at knowing that Robert was safely behind bars probably had something to do with that. The duchess didn't know that was the case, which meant that Ashley had the upper hand. She leaned casually against her car, waiting for the duchess to emerge from her vehicle.

The duchess did not disappoint. Out came one long leg, then another, until the elegant brunette was posing by the Range Rover, glossy hair parted down the middle, eyes perfectly made-up, freckles standing out against the smooth tawny skin of her cheeks. She wore an impeccable cashmere outfit. Gold jewelry glinted at her ears and wrist in the stable's harsh exterior lights. Must have been nice to spend the day primping in some spa instead of worrying about losing everything in a fire. *What a beautiful woman on the outside*, thought Ashley. *And what a thoroughly rotten ugly bitch on the inside.* Ashley could tell from the strange blank expression on the woman's face, which soon morphed into a sneer, that the duchess didn't quite know how to play this. She had probably hoped that Ashley would be terrified.

"Can I help you?" Ashley asked politely.

"No, you can help yourself," said the duchess. "You need to stay away from my husband. Don't you realize that he and I are ridiculously happy and that people like you are so jealous of our relationship?"

"Could've fooled me," said Ashley.

"What do you mean? We share an office. We have two palm trees in our yard that are joined at the root- we are like that. No one tears us apart."

"Well, *almost* no one."

"…Or at least no one tears us apart and lives to tell about it," said the duchess.

A laugh escaped Ashley lips.

"Are you absolutely bonkers?" she asked. "I'm sorry, your ex royal highness. Do you think anybody really believes that shit? Do *you* actually believe that stuff?"

"Listen, slut…"

"Oh honey, about that…I much prefer the C-word. It feels so much more shocking, more raw, don't you think?"

"Your husband is on his way here, he'll put you in your place," the duchess cackled.

Ashley wasn't about to tell her the truth. Yet.

"Listen, sweetheart, you need to hear this. I know you're delusional and will probably not listen but know that I never pursued your husband. Usually, I would be on the woman's side, but in this case, I'll make an exception. You've threatened me and destroyed my property, so now it's my turn. And by the way, what exactly did you think you would achieve with your paparazzi trick? You know what you did, right?"

The duchess stared at her, confused.

"I think that the press would be awfully interested in the threats that you made towards me," said Ashley.

"Oh, they're not threats, honey, they're promises," said the duchess. "And you're forgetting that you signed an NDA. You can't say shit."

"Such an inelegant way to speak, for ex royalty," Ashley cooed. "Before you thought of sending photographers to get me and your husband in a compromising position, I was taking my own video," she bluffed. "Think orange pubic hair and compromising positions galore. I made sure to get all the best angles."

The duchess blanched.

"NDA. You can't release that."

"Actually, I've been doing some research about NDA's. First of all, I signed it under duress, and without understanding what it meant. I'm a dumb, simple country girl. Secondly, from the moment those photos of me and Henry were released, his so-called affair became common knowledge. So whatever I release simply corroborates that. Thirdly, I recorded this conversation and...boop!" Ashley took her phone out of her pocket and tapped it.

"What was that? What did you just do?" the duchess snarled.

"Oh, I just texted our chat to the police chief of Montecito. Call it insurance."

"You'll see- your husband will be here any minute, and he'll take care of you!"

"Yeah, I wouldn't bet on that," said Ashley. "Why don't you go home to your husband- a real prince, that one, and maybe call your lawyers, and ask them what they think of this deal: you leave me the fuck alone, and leave everyone I care for alone, and I don't release my home videos and tonight's recording? And tell ginger boy to stop harassing me, and to stop thinking he's the boss of the polo club?"

The duchess took a few steps towards her, and for a moment, Ashley thought she was going to have to bring out her farm girl fighting skills, but then, Henry's wife just stared at her, jaw clenched, got into her car, and drove away.

Ashley stood there, heart beating, watching her leave. Had it worked? She looked at her phone. She did have a recording, but the text to Jim had never even gone through. Only when she turned back to her car did she realize that the duchess had slashed all her tires. *Damn.* She stood there, and almost laughed when the skies opened up again and cold rain started dumping on her head.

Just then, her phone pinged. Alex.

Well, we're not out of the woods yet. Possible mudslide danger. My neighborhood is being evacuated. Let me know if you need to find a place to stay.

Fuck, it had been a long day. And she still needed to return Diego's coat to him.

Chapter 35

Ashley sat in her car until she saw Diego's headlights coming down the drive.

"Are you OK?" he asked, jumping out of the car, and rushing towards her.

She simply gestured to her car. Even in the pouring rain, the spray paint and the slashed tires were apparent in Diego's headlights.

"The duchess?" Diego asked.

"The very same," she said. "But it's over."

"What do you mean?"

"I'm guessing she threatened you, too? Lied to you about me?" Ashley asked. God, she hoped she was right.

"She became friends with my ex in Argentina. Said she was going to make sure I never saw my daughter again if I didn't do exactly as she and the prince said. I don't scare easily, but this is my daughter…She had me by the balls."

"Suffice it to say that I have her by the balls, now," said Ashley.

"I don't want to know, do I?" asked Diego?

"You don't," she said.

"Come on," said Diego. "Get into my car. We're going to catch pneumonia."

Once they were sitting in the Range Rover, Diego blasted the heater.

"Here's your coat," Ashley said, peeling the soaking wet garment off her.

"Gee, thanks," Diego laughed, tossing it in the back seat. He turned serious. "I owe you an apology."

"You do," said Ashley. "And I know you hate me, but you also owe me a favor. There are evacuation orders. I need a place to stay tonight."

Diego took her hands and looked into her eyes. Ashley tried not to melt.

"I am so, so sorry. I promise to do everything in my power to make up my behavior to you. And don't hate you at all. I'm so completely taken with you that I don't know what to do."

"Apology accepted," said Ashley. "As long as you have a place for me to stay. It'd better be nice."

Diego smiled.

"That can be arranged."

Chapter 36

"Where are we going?" Ashley asked, as Diego navigated the car down the road, buckets of water hitting the windshield.

"Just a place I know," said Diego.

"Aren't we mysterious?"

Just being in the car with him made her feel like everything was right in the world. She didn't really care where he took her, as long as he stayed with her.

They drove to the harbor. Diego swiped a card and drove into a parking lot Ashley had never noticed before.

"Over here," said Diego.

He held his coat over Ashley to protect her from the spitting rain, not that she wasn't completely soaked already, and led her down a big dock. Diego punched a code into the keypad and opened a metal gate. Once they were through, he pulled it closed and it clicked shut behind them. They walked down a smaller dock, sailboats on either side of them. They arrived at the end, and there was a big, sleek, modern thing that Ashley thought was probably a yacht, not that she'd never seen a yacht in real life.

"This is the place you know?" she asked.

"Yes," shrugged, Diego.

He helped her onto the boat and entered a code on another keypad by a door.

"Dang, I forgot to spy on the code," said Ashley.

"I'll give it to you," said Diego.

The door hissed open, Diego hit a switch on the wall, bathing the space in warm light, and they found themselves in a small but modern and elegantly appointed living room. Everything seemed custom made, with gleaming woods and luxurious fabrics.

"Wow, some people really know how to live," said Ashley. "Who does this belong to?"

"I would tell you, but I'd have to make you sign an NDA," Diego smiled. "Come, your bedroom's over here."

She was expecting something cramped and dark. But this place was elegant, cozy, and lovely.

"Wow, what a dream," said Ashley.

"Yeah, it's not bad," said Diego. "You've got a charger for your phone here. An extra toothbrush here, and a bathrobe on the back of the bathroom door."

"You seem awfully familiar with this place," Ashley said. She looked around the room. "Wait- if this is my room, where are you going to sleep?" she asked, her eyes starting to twinkle mischievously. But then, she felt dread in the pit of her stomach. "Wait, you aren't going to leave me here alone, are you?"

"I would never," said Diego. "I can sleep up in the stateroom, if you want."

"What if I don't want? I had a scary, stressful day," she said. "I might have nightmares."

"Well, I suppose that if you are very scared, I should stay down here."

He came closer to her. Again, she could smell his masculine scent. Just being in close proximity to him made her wild.

"You know what I wish you had on this shithole of a boat?" she asked.

"Ding's crispy chicken sandwiches?" he asked.

"Damn. That would hit the spot, but I was going to say a bathtub. I could really have used a bath."

"What will you give me if I tell you that it does have a bath?" Diego smiled.

He led her to the bathroom, where, sure enough a huge, luxuriously deep tub stood in the corner.

"I would say that we're in a drought and that you should conserve water, but considering the rain we're having, and how dirty you are, I think that you deserve a little bath," Diego said, "and since I'm dirty too, I'm thinking that to save water, maybe the two of us should use it at the same time."

Ashley smiled. That was exactly what she'd been thinking. While the tub was filling, Diego retrieved a bottle of wine for them. He filled their glasses and clinked his glass against hers, looking her in the eye and winking.

"You know that if you don't look someone in the eye when you say cheers, that's seven years of bad sex, right?"

She doubted that would ever be an issue with Diego, but now Ashley did feel a little awkward. Attracted as she was to him, despite the heavy make-put session in the car and all the fantasies and dreams about him, how were they going to go from sipping wine together fully clothed to getting into the tub together? She took a sip of liquid courage.

"I think our tub is ready," said Diego. He stripped off his shirt and she gaped at him, taking it all in. His perfect chest. His gorgeous abs. The v shaped muscles below his navel pointing down to what was under his jeans. She suddenly felt shy.

"You get in first, I'm going to go make sure the boat is locked up tight," Diego said, as if sensing Ashley's embarrassment. As soon as he left the bathroom, she quickly stripped off her wet, filthy clothes and dumped them in a corner. She smelled like a barbecue grill. She put a toe into the water. It was deliciously warm, the perfect temperature, with citrus-scented bubbles. She gratefully sank into the tub and stretched out, feeling the bubbles tickling her limbs, enjoying the buoyancy. She ran her hands through the water and sighed. She'd never been in a bath this deep in her life, but she could get used to this.

"Ready?" Diego called.

Her cheeks flushed both from the heat of the water and from the fantasies that started running through her head at the sound of his voice. The door to the bathroom opened, and there he stood, a towel around his waist. *Damn.* She'd imagined his body so many times, but this was so much better than she had even dared to expect. He was slim, with well-defined muscles, the perfect olive skin tone, and just enough hair trailing down from his navel to what lay under the towel. She could see a growing bulge under the white terry cloth, in fact could barely tear her eyes away from it. But then, she squeezed her eyes shut and said, "go ahead, I won't watch."

Diego dropped the towel, revealing an erection even more spectacular than the one from her dream. Her eyes wandered down to his powerful thighs. Without preamble, he lowered himself into the bath, between her legs.

"That escalated quickly," she said.

"Well, so did something else," he responded, looking her in the eyes and eliciting a shocked gasp and a laugh from her.

"I noticed," she said.

She felt the throbbing tingle between her legs already. Just imagining him inside her had her growing more excited by the second. What it would be like, to finally have him inside of her?

"Before you talk dirty to me, you're going to need to clean me up," she said.

"Gladly," he responded. "I seem to have misplaced the washcloths. I'll have to improvise."

He scooped up some bubbles in his hands and ran them all over her body. He started in the usual places, like her shoulders, and under her arms, but when he cupped her breasts, she gasped.

"These look like they got really dirty today," he said, rubbing circles around her nipples and finally ducking down to suck on one. He was driving her crazy. She writhed in ecstasy. How could this get any better? *With him inside of me, that's how*, she thought, and just the idea of it nearly sent her over the edge.

"I need to wash your back."

Diego gently turned her around, so she was no longer facing him, but was now sitting between his legs. She could feel the length of him, hard and hot against her back. He whispered in her ear, telling her which body parts needed to be washed, making her squirm. Now, he had her breasts in his hands again, and was pinching her nipples, making her cry out. She arched her back, mewling, and reached behind her to stroke him, wrapping her hand around his shaft and squeezing. Now, he groaned, and ran his hands down her body under the water, and between her legs. She could feel a finger make its way inside of her while another one stroked her clitoris. She moaned, and bucked against him, as waves of pleasure came over her. Now, she felt his lips on her neck, and shuddered in pleasure. She needed more. She ground harder against his fingers. It felt good, but she knew it could feel better, and she told him as much. She stroked his manhood faster. He groaned.

"Better slow down," he gasped. "Do you know how long I've been thinking of this? Dreaming of it"

Diego put his hands on either side of Ashley's waist, and pushed her forward, onto her knees. She grabbed the edges of the tub, as he kneeled and entered her from behind. The shock of it was delicious. Finally feeling the whole length of him inside her was almost more than she could bear. He drew himself partially out, and then slid back into her, grinding against her at the end. He did it again, and again, holding onto her breasts now, pinching her nipples between his fingers as he did. He was thrusting into her faster, and faster.

"Slow down," she gasped. "I want to feel you. I want to feel all of you."

He did as he was told, slowing down so that she could feel every ridge of his shaft inside of her, touching every magic spot that had been craving him for so long. She could feel the tension mounting, and mounting as she backed up against him, wanting to take in even more of him. She thought she'd never felt so wet in her life, never felt so excited. She felt more tension, her insides quivering. She squeezed her muscles, wanting to hold him inside of her forever. Until finally, in a rush of ecstasy, she felt a throbbing release. She cried out, as she came, harder than she ever had, crying out his name.

"Don't stop," she gasped.

And he didn't. When her shaking had subsided, Ashley felt Diego's shaft grow even harder inside of her.

"Are you close?" she asked, turning around to kiss him and feel his tongue inside her mouth. He nodded.

"Are you using protection?" he asked.

Damn. In the heat of the moment, she hadn't even thought about that. She knew it was stupid, but...

He pulled himself out, then and came all over her back. She could feel it spraying onto her, hot and thick. She already missed having him inside of her.

"It made you all dirty, again," he said.

"You have- you are filthy," she laughed. "Sorry, I don't ever do this. We should have been more careful," she said.

"No matter what you might have heard, I'm not in the habit of doing this, either."

Ashley turned around to face him. Looked into those eyes of his. He gave her a gentle kiss.

"Hopefully we can go again soon," he said.

She was already ready. She hoped he would be soon. She'd never felt such pleasure in her life.

"Come on, darling," he said, after he'd washed her back off and gently cleaned between her legs. "Let's shower you off."

They stepped into the shower, and he started running his hands down her body again. She was already ready for him, and saw that he was ready for her, too.

"Already?" she asked.

He grabbed her hips and lifted her up, backing her against the shower wall, and sliding into her with a single thrust. She wrapped her legs around him as he ground into her. He nibbled at her neck, and she gasped. There was no way he could keep doing this. He was strong, she knew, but he needed to put her down, or they would both collapse.

"Is there any way we can adjourn to the bed?"

Diego regretfully withdrew his penis from her, and she had to quiet a disappointed sigh. He grabbed a plush bathrobe for her, wrapped her up in it, and gave himself a quick try with the towel. They burst out of the bathroom, onto the bed. He pushed her onto her back, onto the deliciously cool sheets. He kissed lips, then her neck, then each breast, and down her stomach, until his head between her legs. He used his hot tongue on her, teasing her clitoris, using his fingers, too, until she was gasping and writhing in pleasure.

"Come back up," she begged. "I need you inside me."

"Not yet. You're too sexy," he said. "I need a second."

He went back to licking her and reached up to pinch her nipples. She arched her back and cried out. Robert had never done these things to her. She'd thought things had been good enough in that department in the beginning, quite good in fact, but this was next level. Diego made her come again, and just as she thought she could take no more, he came back up, and thrust into her, making her come again almost instantly.

He slowed down a bit then, kissed her deeply while grinding against her in the most delicious way. She could taste herself in his mouth, knew how juicy she must feel to him, savored the feeling of his hot, hard cock inside of her.

He whispered into her ear.

"Have you had enough?"

"Never enough," she said. "But I suppose it's your turn."

He gave a few more delicious thrusts, squeezing her buttocks in his hands. She felt him tensing again. Just as she came one last time, her whole body shuddering, he pulled out, and this time, came all over her stomach and breasts. He dropped onto her, spent.

She laughed.

"You know we're going to have to shower again."

"Separately," he said. "Because otherwise, we're never going to manage to get to sleep."

"Separately," she finally agreed.

At last, they were both freshly showered, both in bed, lying in fresh sheets. Diego kissed her. A slow, delicious kiss goodnight, one that was full of promise. Ashley didn't know what exactly was waiting for her in the future, but for now, she wouldn't have wanted to be anywhere else.

Chapter 37

First thing the next morning, Ashley was holding her phone, calling the new number for her sister provided for her by Jim. She held her breath. She didn't know what to expect from this conversation. She just wanted to know that Sissy and Craig were ok, and that they weren't too angry with her for putting them in such a horrific situation.

The rain had stopped, revealing a golden morning and the news that all was well- there had been no mudslides, and the fire was completely out. Diego had woken Ashley up with a sweet kiss and a promise of coffee and pastries, followed by an actual date- to one of his favorite places in Santa Ynez, including an equestrian property he had been thinking of buying.

The call picked up and Ashley held her breath.

"Sissy?"

"Ashley?"

Hearing her beloved sister's voice made tears jump to Ashley's eyes.

"Sissy! Please tell me you and Craig are OK. Please tell me you forgive me."

There was a brief silence, during which Ashley squeezed her eyes shut and begged every possible higher power to let this work out.

"Ashley, I don't understand you."

Ashley's heart dropped. But still, after standing up for herself yesterday and doing battle with the duchess, she was prepared to fight for a relationship with her sister. She was about to speak when Sissy continued.

"You have been so brave. You left Montana with nothing but my blessing. You managed to survive and thrive against all odds..."

Ashley gasped. Sissy was too kind, too generous of spirit.

"But I ruined your life! If I hadn't been such an idiot and a pushover, I would never have let Robert run Papa's property into the ground...you never would have gotten hurt, and Craig wouldn't be fighting for his life."

"Darling, you fought so hard to make that business work. You were so brave. And it's my fault Robert was able to stick around long enough to abuse you. After the way Momma treated you all those years, how she gaslit you. Honey, she is a fucking narcissist. She made you doubt yourself, over and over again. It's a miracle you're as strong and competent as you are."

Ashley gasped. Sissy had spelled out what she'd finally started to understand about her mother. This was something she would have to figure out later.

"Speaking of Momma, have the police found anything out?"

Sissy laughed, a harsh sound that sounded more like a bark.

"You're not gonna believe this shit. That bitch is living it up in Palm Beach. Her hot water heater broke, and it was too much trouble to get it fixed, apparently, so she cleared out what Papa had earmarked for us from the family trust and skipped town. Didn't bother to tell any of us, obviously. And when I finally tracked her down thanks to your cop friend's efforts, she had the gall to berate me for not calling her sooner. You do what you want, but I'm done."

Ashley searched inside herself. Yes. She was done, too. No more.

"So Sissy, how are you, really, how's Craig?"

"Craig is hanging in there. I'm taking care of him. He deserves it, after everything he's done for me."

"You?" Ashley's voice raised in shock.

How was her poor incapacitated sister doing anything at all?

"We all have to face the truth sometimes. And mine was, I let the depression get the better of me after my accident. I was given a gift- the doctors said that there was a chance I would walk again, and what did I do? I chose helplessness, and drama. Now I'm not saying that I'm gonna be riding horses and skipping across fields anytime soon, but I've started physical therapy. You're not going to believe this, but I'm upright, right now. In my very own wheelchair that I'm able to control."

"You are? Oh my God!"

Tears of relief and thankfulness sprang to Ashley's eyes.

"And don't worry about Craig," said Sissy. "Robert beat him enough for it to count as attempted murder, but he's tough."

"Are you able to go back home, now that Robert's in jail?"

"Craig's still under medical care, and I'm doing my therapy, but I was gonna ask you- how would you feel if Craig and I moved to the farm? He needs a change of pace, and I thought I'd make a good office manager for a riding therapy program. I've checked- we're gonna be able to get the horses back from the rescue."

Ashley's heart leapt. It made her so happy to hear this.

"Will you come back and help us, little sis?"

Ashley hesitated.

"I'll come back and visit- all the time, I promise. But I've been building a life here, and I just got a huge promotion at the Polo Club as of this morning."

"This morning? Isn't it super early over there? And it's the weekend!"

Ashley smiled.

"Well, let's just say I'm very close with the boss."

As if on cue, Diego came through the door. Ashley pointed to the phone, and in response he held up a coffee tray and a bag of pastries in one hand, a box of condoms in the other.

"Gotta go. I'll call you tomorrow. I love you," she said to her sister.

Ashley realized she was starving. But the pastries could wait. She saw something much more delicious she just had to have, right there, right then.

The end.

When author Kiki Astor, known to many as Auntie Kiki, is not writing stories, she is living a rich life with her delightful husband and her very demanding lap dog. In her spare time, she tries to provide the best rich life advice she can to her TikTok followers at her account @kiki_astor .

Printed in Great Britain
by Amazon

16934982R00169